...JUST SOU

...JUST SOUTH OF HEAVEN/JIM ODY

Dedications

This book is for all of the sorry souls working their socks off in large corporations around the world. The unknown faces sat behind monitors counting down the hours until they can break free from their shackles and be themselves. The dreamers who fantasize about a better place, of vacations and lottery wins, whilst all the while wondering when they will be able to retire.

This escapism is for all of you, whether you're minimum wagers, no-star trainees, or anonymous middle-management. And for those of you, who've never experienced the inter-departmental politics of being another corporate cog in a huge machine, then please take this as a completely normal example, and why you might also end up going down a similar path as Caper…

For those about to walkout on their jobs – I salute you!

...JUST SOUTH OF HEAVEN/JIM ODY

...JUST SOUTH OF HEAVEN/JIM ODY

Chapter One

She looked up at me as I walked through the door to the bar. Surprise was soon replaced by a huge grin. She was cleaning glasses behind the bar. Stale alcohol and drunken lies hung in the air.

"Well, look what the cat dragged in!" She winked and placed the now gleaming glass down onto the top of the bar. She was a butch-middle-aged woman. She had a bob-haircut and a nose that looked like she'd fought more than fucked. She'd had four husbands, each in turn disappearing. I liked to imagine they were locked in the beer cellar. Each pleading more than the one before. All falling on deaf ears and double locked doors. I wasn't the only one to think this. Many a local, when plied with enough liquor, became loose-lipped, and one of the first theories in life to tumble from their mouth was talk of her husbands having never been seen again.

None of us were ever brave enough to ask her.

"Mo, how goes it?" I said as a salutation rather than as a question.

She nodded towards my suit. "You take a wrong turning at the photocopier, Mr Corporate?"

It was mid-afternoon. The lunchtime rush had come and gone. A guy was snoring in the corner, an empty pint glass sat in front of him for company. Neither looked like striking up a conversation anytime soon.

"I just got the sack," I stated with a shrug. The words felt good out loud. It was almost boastful and made me happy.

"You get caught fucking a temp again?" she enquired, pouring a cider for me without being asked. She knows what I like. Assumptions from women is one of them.

...JUST SOUTH OF HEAVEN/JIM ODY

"That was a one-time thing. It was at the Christmas party, which doesn't really count, and she was nearly thirty."

"Uh-ha. Her age means nothing," she said handing over the pint. "So, what did you do? Knowing you, there must be a story."

"It was a misunderstanding."

"It usually is."

And so my story began:

I've underachieved. All of those years through school and college I'd studied moderately hard. And for what? An average role at best. I was still at entry level. Perhaps my face didn't fit. Maybe I didn't sleep with enough of the board members. But I sat in a corporate sea of desks that all looked the same. I cared more about entertaining my colleagues than the job at hand. The writing had been scrawled on the walls for years. It was surprising how long it took for the penny to finally drop.

Earlier, and with the help from my work colleague Raj, I added what would be the final rubber-band to my quite impressive rubber-band ball. It was now as big as a size 5 football. That last band had been stretched almost to capacity, with both myself and my side-kick holding our nerves like Jeremy Renner in the movie *Hurt Locker*. We'd attracted quite a crowd and onlookers gasped at our brave-feat and total disregard for doing work.

You cannot underestimate the time and dedication focused on this one task over the many years that I had worked here. The powers that be failed to see the achievement of this.

My boss hates me. He's a year younger and completely intimidated by me. One birthday, I got a card from him that played loudly the Oris Redding song *Respect*. I think that he was trying to make a point, even if the tinny-robotic voice sounded nothing like Otis Redding or Aretha Franklin – unless of course

...JUST SOUTH OF HEAVEN/JIM ODY

the late Professor Stephen Hawking was doing a Karaoke version. I would think this to be incredibly unlikely. This was funny to him, and of course, on a quiet open-planned floor, to everyone else around. I guess for fifteen minutes he actually did gain some R-E-S-P-E-C-T. Although if I remember correctly, he lost it the next day when Tina saw him walking his cat proudly in the park.

Today I'd had enough. Everything had come down to this time. It was just after lunch and I was sat at my workstation clutching my paper cup of medium roast Columbian coffee, like it was a bottle that a genie might appear from at any moment. Fleetingly I jotted up the number of cups I went through in a week and pondered: if trees were planted by way of carbon-offsetting in the rainforest, then could I make a legal claim to an acre or so? By rights it was my insatiable need for caffeine that caused this incredibly long-winded evolutionary environmental cycle. A bit like sponsoring a monkey that I would never see, such grandiose claims that required a lot of trust between two people that had never met, and possibly a sea of deceit between them large enough to lose a nation.

As I savoured the bitter drink, I looked around this place with disdain. Ten years and I had amounted to a little more than nothing. No, scratch that. Nothing was the level above me. I longed to be at the vertigo-induced heights of nothingness.

I wanted to attack the designer of opened planned offices in a bad way. It was pitiful news to those of us who wanted to take life a little more gently than the other kiss-arses. Walls were for hiding behind and jumping out on people so they spilled their coffee – that was a fact. Sometimes you had to make your own fun. I'm not saying it's for everyone, but I'm a firm believer in trying to bring the successful school dynamics into the workplace. My wages certainly bear a resemblance to that of a school-leaver, so I guess they started and ended there. Small partitions were quite frankly useless, and were purely there so as the bosses could watch you daydream and surf-the-internet without leaving their fish-bowl glass offices. There was nowhere to hide anymore. It was an awful state of affairs and I for one had had enough. I'd run out of suspects to blame so I was ready to finally do something drastic.

I am of course a team-player. The other jokers around here may not wholeheartedly agree, but then most of them are arseholes. Not Raj. He thinks I'm cool. I like Raj.

I had taken it upon myself to write an email of a few things that I was unhappy with in the workplace, specifically regarding the employer to employee relationship. Historically this has always been a partnership of fire and ice, rough and smooth, David and Goliath, Beavis & Butthead. Okay, maybe not the last one.

I took another sip of my coffee and pecked out with my fingers the final touches to the email:

...And so to conclude, the whole of the management are about as much use as a one-handed man in a clapping contest.

Here's hoping that this company goes down the proverbial and you all receive an STD from the leprous whores bought with your overblown and completely undeserved pay rises.

Yours incredibly sincerely

Caper Juggins (Unknown hard grafter).

Raj had been reading over my shoulder and now grinned like he had wind. He was enjoying being part of this but without the risk of unemployment. I'm pleased for him. Maybe he'll find himself another hero. Or his balls.

To me this was a cooler way of handing in my notice, so I was happy to be the one to do that. No embarrassing presentations whereby you're forced to pretend that you will miss each and every one of the snitching-back-stabbers known as your fellow cohorts, and faking gratitude over the measly useless offering of some joke gift everyone but you finds amusing. *Billy Bass the Singing Fish?* Thanks a fuckin' bunch, it can go and sing *Don't Worry (Be Happy)* in the bin.

The email in question was addressed to everyone in the company, and with an innocent click of the left mouse button over the send icon, around a thousand employees would be enlightened by my caffeine induced meanderings, and what could be the thinnest of lines between a good and a bad idea.

...JUST SOUTH OF HEAVEN/JIM ODY

Chapter Two

Mo rolled her eyes at me. It was part of her job description to stand and listen to the lowlifes as they retold their story. I could tell in the laughter lines of her eyes that she didn't take many of them seriously. Most men fabricated their tales. Mine, however was completely kosher. The whole truth, and nothing but the truth.

She knew me well enough to believe every word.

"So, they'd fired you for that?"

I nodded. "Indeed. The truth isn't something that sits well with them."

"What happened? Your boss ask you to leave?"

"Now that would've been good to see. It would've given me a chance to tell him what I thought of him. Or better still I could've stapled my void contract to his forehead!"

I sipped my cider again and proceeded to tell the tale of what happened next:

After the email act, it took a long thirty-four minutes before upon the horizon the company's soldiers-of-fortune strode through the partitional jungle ready to arrest me on treasonable charges of contempt of the corporation. However, in reality the soldiers were in fact two bumbling security guards who would have a job putting the fear of God into a four-year-old with a nervous disposition.

The hairless figure of Bart, or Soldier One as he was also known, limped like one leg was a foot longer than the other. He shrugged his shoulders and shook his head, though it was not clear whether this was in sympathy for me or at the stupidity of my literary actions. "Caper," he started clearing his throat. "We have been asked to escort you away from the building, as your contract has officially been terminated by the powers that be."

...JUST SOUTH OF HEAVEN/JIM ODY

"Ah ha," I replied, unplugging my MP3 from my laptop and slipping it into my pocket – next to the three Biros I had stolen like a cat thief. It was interesting that my boss didn't have the balls to speak to me, but make the required phone calls and stay hidden in his office. His blinds had been pulled down, but like a peeping Tom I saw them twitch and bend a gap for him to peer through. What a pussy.

"No offence, gentlemen," I said to them, "but I'm not going to walk anywhere." I was polite even in times of stress.

"Uhh?" was all I got by way of a reply, though there was the added bonus of two puzzled looks on the faces of the corporation's first and last line of defence against evil.

"I said - I am not going to walk anywhere. If I am to leave the building then I shall have to be moved forcefully. It's nothing against you two, I'm sure you realise."

"Jesus Christ!" Blasphemed Roddy, the tubby security guard, who couldn't outrun a fish out of water and would never remember me as anything but That-Asshole-Who-Fucked-Up-My-Back.

They looked at each other. Looked at me and then bent to lift me.

"I'm joking," I grinned. "You don't have to carry me."

"Arsehole!" Roddy spat under his breath, not even trying to hide his disdain

"I thought your email was kinda funny," Bart, the bag of bones wheezed out as he tried to keep up with me.

"Thank you."

As we stopped for the lift, Roddy, the more short-sighted of the two, looked at me with eyes that showed no love and that were as big as tennis balls through his strong lenses, and grumbled, "I don't see why you can't just leave. Sending an email was stupid. Making me do this walking is bad for my health. I could have a heart attack! Do you want that on your conscience?"

"Chin up, old timer," I said flippantly. "You'll be retired soon."

"I'm forty-three!" he said shocked by my comment. Not as shocked as me though.

"Really? Life's been hard on you, mate."

"Don't I fucking know it," he said to his scuffed steel-toe capped boots.

It was a strange sight to see before me – my reflection either side of two old guys reminded me of a dream I once had, the only difference being that in my dream they were eighty-year-old prostitutes dressed as schoolgirls. That was reason enough to never touch blue-cheese before bedtime.

So, this was to be my last day at this marvellous corporation, though I had actually foreseen this little hitch in my stunted career, which had seen me change jobs as frequently as toothbrush brands, with a list of rcfcrccs made up of liars and slackers alike. Onwards and upwards.

"Cheers lads!" I said as the crinkly security guards gave up on me running back into the building as we got to the reception area. Clutching my box of desk-crap, I pretended to look cool much to the amusement of a couple of clients. They were sipping the cheap bitter excuse for coffee which was in my opinion one of the forerunners of the company's failings - that and the seventies décor that cried out for some TV makeover crew to get busy with MDF and paint.

I nodded to one of the hopefuls. He was smartly dressed in a suit that was so new it was all stiff lines of fabric. He'd probably be my replacement. Less hours and more money. HR moves quickly nowadays.

He shuffled and looked nervous. I whipped my finger over my neck making a cutthroat sign. He looked about ready to shit in his shorts.

So, after committing ungentlemanly conduct, I waltzed off of the pitch knowing a red card and rather longer than a three-match ban was coming my way, just as soon as HR caught up with me. I guess it would be unwise to use them as a reference for another job.

The MD's car was an Aston Martin as seen in one of the recent James Bond movies. The obvious difference was most likely the 'I suck cock' sticker that I had added to the back window.

...JUST SOUTH OF HEAVEN/JIM ODY

Chapter Three

"You're something, Caper!" she grinned nodding at my glass. "You want that filled up?"

"I'd love you to, but I have stuff to do."

"You still fucking that crazy bitch?" she enquired, changing the subject.

I shook my head. "Nope. We're through."

"It's about time you saw passed a nice pair of tits."

The door opened and a couple of lads walked in. Guilty faces weighed down their feet. Eyes darted about.

"Can I help ya?" Mo said as they walked up to the bar with swagger. They were trying to be the Gallagher brothers but falling short. They also looked about fourteen.

"I'll have a lager," black-hoodie said in a voice that sounded deeper than natural. It was like a choirboy impersonating Barry White.

"You eighteen?" He looked at his mate. His mate went red and looked like he might cry.

"He know better?" Mo pushed. This wasn't her first rodeo by a long shot. She enjoyed it. It broke up the monotony of the quiet times.

"Yes," he nodded.

"What, you're eighteen or he knows better?"

"Eighteen."

She nodded slowly and looked at them both in the eyes carefully. A bar owner can read a lie at three paces. They have to.

"I don't think so. I've knickers older than you. Got more hair in 'em too!"

The lads both looked at each other again glowing red.

...JUST SOUTH OF HEAVEN/JIM ODY

"Fine. We'll go somewhere else!" Embarrassed they turned and swaggered off again, but this time it was completely put on.

"Try going to school," she called after them.

"You believe that?" she said to me.

Then suddenly the sleeping guy bolted upright. "Kill 'em all!" he shouted.

"It's okay, Ken!" Mo shouted back. He looked over dazed and confused. He nodded his head, smoothed over a few long white strands of hair and closed his eyes again. He was back asleep before we had a chance to say another word.

"Poor old sod."

I glanced at my mobile and saw that I had a number of missed calls. This was of no surprise as I kept it muted. Of all the things a mobile phone could be used for, making and receiving phones calls was one of the least uses I had for it. Which is why there were missed calls and voicemails. Times had certainly changed.

The first was from an Asian guy who was checking on my well-being and informing me that I had recently been in a car accident. This was news to me; I was pretty sure something like that wouldn't have slipped my mind. He wanted me to ring him back urgently. He had an insurance payment waiting for me. Of course he did. Just like I had a big cock and a harem of women to share it with.

The next message was from my mother whom I hadn't spoken to in a couple of weeks, something that was on par with killing a priest or being cruel to animals.

The stern voice began, and I was almost cowering under the bar as I heard her cold words, "*Caperson!* I can only imagine that you must be dead on your lounge floor and rotting away to hell. If not, then you had better ring me straight away! I brought

...JUST SOUTH OF HEAVEN/JIM ODY

you into this world, my boy, and I'll sure as hell kick you out of this world too!

"Bessie Mcgaran's son rings her every other day, you know! I'm not asking for much here, just a son who cares about his mother once in a while, but no, what have I got? An ungrateful lazy lump!" And I would bet my last biscuit she had slammed the phone back down on its cradle too. Bless her and that special - *and slightly psychotic* -bond between a mother and her son.

The next message was timed at a knuckle full of minutes before I came in the bar. It simply went, *"Humph!"* Now, Sherlock Holmes I'm not, but my investigative senses told me that it was one of three people. It could well have been my mother again, but she would have left another long message emphasising the growing problem of parental abuse due to telephonic neglect that's suddenly (and somewhat unheard of) sweeping the country. The truth was she couldn't remain quiet and would have to leave me a message. The next suspect could've been Nancy, a girl who I had been out with the night before on a blind date. The problem had been that I wasn't blind, and even if I had been blind, I wasn't deaf and would still have had to endure her whining voice as she repeated, "Oh, Caper, that's *so funny*!" and "Oh, Caper, *that's great*!" She was harmless, and I'm sure by the time she gets around to leaving her third message without a reply, then she will realise that our first date was indeed our last. It was a shame as she was a girl that from a distance looked fine. As you got closer there was something about the way her mouth moved that was odd. I couldn't get over it. Then her voice completely blew out any chances of romance. If these things annoyed me now, then God knows how I'd feel after a few years.

...JUST SOUTH OF HEAVEN/JIM ODY

The last person that it could've been then decided to call me at that moment, and it was an extremely bleak time for me indeed. Lady luck was laughing her head off as she urinated down on my euphoric parade. Welcome to my world.

It was the girl who Mo had been referring too.

Two whole weeks had passed since I had split up with a girl-friend called Trixibelle – or Jezebel – as I'd nicknamed the cheating bitch.

I always thought that it was great that she got on well with my mates, truly I did. I just didn't realise that she had taken the liberty of getting to know them whilst they were naked and panting on top of her. Right after the '*I'm so sorry*' & '*One thing led to another*' lines had each penetrated my heart with different stabs of pain, and made me feel like a right tit, her female inbred back-up plan of tears kicked into action. She had cried and screamed, then screamed and cried, and this went on for such a period of time that I thought I'd been reincarnated as a fool.

I may've felt sorry for her to start off with, but after she had held me hostage in her flat for what felt like a week, I was contemplating leaving by the bathroom window, however being a true man, I stayed – well, the fact that her flat was four stories up and I have a severe case of vertigo did sort of seal the deal so to speak, but that's beside the point. I was also a little nervous, as she now resembled Alice Cooper, as her mascara had run down both of her cheeks and also above her eyebrows. Had she whipped out a boa constrictor and started singing, *I Love the Dead*, then four stories or not, I would have taken my chances.

So a girl-friend and a couple of mates down, I was left relieved that I wouldn't have to spend much on Christmas presents this year. So sometimes you had to take the good with the bad.

...JUST SOUTH OF HEAVEN/JIM ODY

I listened to the message.

Her voice as usual started softly then worked up into a dramatic sneer. "Pick up the phone, Boo-Boo. I know you're there!"

Trixibelle.

My name is Caper, or even Caperson - not Boo-Boo, but that was the endearing name she called me when she wanted sex. The longer our relationship had gone on, the less we had made love, and the more we had just had sex. I could have been anyone, and if I was to be completely honest, so could've she. Our relationship had run its course before she decided to run her tongue over the even courser hairs of my ex-friends.

It may have been over two weeks since we had indulged in the evil pleasures of the flesh, but even my usual overactive hormones were not reacting to her lustful games. Not since she had taken up a new past-time known in the legal profession as stalking – which she's very good at, by the way.

She had spent so much time sat outside my house, the neighbours thought I had a life-sized gnome dressed as a hooker. Maybe if I was lucky, on Guy Fawkes Night, some of the local hoodlums might mistake her for a Guy and set her on fire. But rarely do my dreams come true...

She was indeed Glenn Close to my Michael Douglas, and thankfully I had never bothered with getting a pet bunny rabbit although I did have a little wet friend known as Scaly Dave. He's a fish of some description. Please ignore my vagueness but I only know two types of fish, and they are battered and non-battered. Scaly Dave was of the non-battered variety, this I was sure.

"I've gotta go," I said to Mo as I clicked off my phone.

"Girl-troubles?"

"I've got ninety-nine problems..." I started but she was already filling up another pint for Ken. She held up her hand.

...JUST SOUTH OF HEAVEN/JIM ODY

"Look after yourself, Caper!" she called after me as I left and headed home.

At my house I stood and shook my head. The thing was I probably wouldn't be here for much longer. I had a new job and it would take me away from not only this house but from the whole area.

I looked over fondly at this house. I'd lived on my own for a few years now since splitting up with a girl way out of my league called Genevieve Deboise. We'd shared a high-end apartment for a few months, but she was too high maintenance. She could eat a man up in one bite and would most likely be the death of someone one day.

Then I saw my little buddy, Scaly Dave. I smiled as I saw the little fellow in his wet little world and said to him, "Dave, it's time to look over your little scaly shoulder a little more and remember not to go off with strangers!" He swam around and looked me straight in the eyes, then seemed to look up to heaven, shrug his scaly shoulders, and swim into his little plastic shipwreck. The shipwreck was Scaly Dave's *happy place*, though he's never told me this – I just know.

I have always flown fairly close to the sun, but it might surprise you to know I rang Trixibelle back.

This wasn't about getting one last parting sexual liaison in before we finally parted ways, or an opportunity to try a few things I'd been curious to try without fear of disgust and repercussions. No, I had purely sensible reasons in mind.

...JUST SOUTH OF HEAVEN/JIM ODY

Chapter Four

I parked my car behind a vehicle that was once a small basic Citroen hatchback. Someone had seen fit to lower the suspension, increase the wheel size and modify the body to such an extent that I had to wonder why they didn't just buy a new car. Essentially, they had spent money to make the car impractical, an eyesore, anti-social, less efficient, and increased or invalidated their insurance. It was about the worst things you could do with a car. It was another example of something I would never understand.

A couple of lads with baseball caps showed an interest in my car, more than likely already stripping it of its parts to sell second-hand the minute my back was turned. My tyres had tread on them for a start which was a novelty around this estate.

This wasn't the best area to live in unless of course you wanted to be near drug-dealers, gangs, and prostitution. I'm not sure many estate agents would be listing these in their brochure or mentioning it in a viewing. These details would be replaced with affordable, starter home, community, and near to amenities – if drugs, drink, prostitution, and gambling was your idea of amenities.

There was an air of familiarity about my tentative rapping on the white front door, and I was aware of how many times previously I'd been in this very position. She swung the door open and looked me up and down like we were still very much the lovers we'd once been.

"Hey Boo-Boo," my former girl-friend said sweetly, and it was very easy to get caught up into her false charms, however I was still bitter about her bedroom gymnastics with my ex-friends, so I wasn't going to unbuckle my belt with desire anytime soon.

"Hey," I replied, looking at her stood in a dressing gown, her flame coloured hair flowing over her shoulders.

She reached out and gently touched the wooden beads around my neck, and then smiled as she said softly, "Why won't you return my calls?" A line which really didn't want to be said softly or with a smile.

"I called you earlier," I pointed out.

"You did, but not before then. Why not?"

"Do you really need to ask?" I said trying not to snap.

"It was a moment of weakness, *you know*?" But I didn't. I sighed, knowing that this was how she would play it.

"No, I don't know. I know how you felt to me, and I know how much you hurt me, each and every time."

"We can try one more time. It won't happen again!" Her voice rose an octave in defeat, and maybe this was the first time that she truly realised that it was over for good.

I was shaking my head as she undid her dressing gown and exposed her breasts. "You don't like these?" she asked cupping them. Her hands barely covered them.

"I've always admired and enjoyed your breasts – it's just the person attached to them that I've grown tired of." She screwed her face up and swiftly pulled closed her dressing gown as if to make some sort of empty statement.

"Don't think you'll be getting you hands on them again!" she snapped. "You think I can't do no better than you?" Her double-negative annoyed me even more than usual.

"Look, I just came to say that it's over. It's not just about you fucking my friends. Well, it's a little to do with that, but we weren't going anywhere, were we?"

...JUST SOUTH OF HEAVEN/JIM ODY

She started to cry. I looked around and saw the baseball cap wearers stood watching the whole scene, probably hoping that she would flash her tits again. One of them was already shuffling his package around in his sweatpants, the dirty little fucker.

"You can't do this to me, Caper. We were going to get married and have kids!"

"Whoa, a little presumptuous. We weren't engaged or anything…"

"We were going to though, weren't we?"

I was lost. I didn't remember the conversation. "We were?"

"Remember when my cousin, Cathy came around and we got drunk that night?"

I nodded but the whole night was a blur. I remember drinking a lot of tequila and the three of us ending up naked. I wracked my brains over the details and couldn't remember a thing. I wondered whether I could relive it through hypnotherapy. In fact, I'd love to do that. But also figured it might end up being slightly embarrassing for me. I'd probably be brought out of my trance only to find myself with my trousers around my ankles and beating off like there was no tomorrow. No professional person needed to bear witness to that.

"I asked you whether we should get married just as my cousin went down on you, and you said sure!"

I frowned and pulled a face. "It's not legally binding though, *is it?*"

"You're a pig!" she shouted.

One of the baseballers then shouted. "Show us yer tits again!" to which she flipped them her middle finger and slammed the door.

"Hey, Romeo! How'd we get a bird to flash her tits at us like that?"

...JUST SOUTH OF HEAVEN/JIM ODY

I walked towards them shaking my head. "Forget about marriage when having a threesome with her cousin, ought ta do it," I said like it was a normal thing.

"What!" They high-fived. One of them held up his fist for me to bump. I probably shouldn't have bumped it, but I did. It's not every day your ex shows you her tits, slams the door in your face, and then you're seen as a hero by the future criminal generation. They then laughed together and pulled out some roll-up cigarettes.

I got back into my car. I felt like Scarface.

...JUST SOUTH OF HEAVEN/JIM ODY

Chapter Five

Dylan Ray Carlson, more commonly known as Dice, worked in antiques, which was really a posh way of saying that he was a wheeler-dealer. He made a bit of money here and there buying this and that and selling it on. It was all boringly legal and above board, which meant that he wasn't fulfilling his true sales and marketing skills, nor making the sort of money his dreams had projected each tax year in his annual personal budget.

He was based in Cornwall, but often ventured further inland to buy and sell. In Cornwall, he trawled around car-boot sales, junk shops, and flea markets picking up old furniture and ornaments for next to nothing. He would then peddle these goods along the A30, up the M5 then across the M4 all the way to London where folks would pay stupid prices for patina and nostalgia.

Dice also found himself with clients looking for more specific items and spent wasted days sitting in musty auctioneer houses, bidding in vain with ruthless retirees who had more money than hair and no intention of making a quick buck. They were buying back the things their late-wives had made them sell years ago.

This was the reason why he had put an advert in the paper for an antiques assistant. Really though he was looking for a partner. Just one that he didn't have to pay much.

Dice was looking for someone he could trust fully. Part of the reason was he had a multitude of bad habits that most would find odd. He needed someone with thick skin, a sense of humour, and with a misunderstanding of what might constitute a good wage.

...JUST SOUTH OF HEAVEN/JIM ODY

The person for the job was a guy that Dice knew from his college days when he was fooling his family into thinking he wanted to become an engineer. This guy had been slacking around with a group of dropouts, whilst being able to con his way, and fool the whole educational system into thinking that he was bright and gifted. He was always seen chatting to some of the most attractive ladies around and always told the funniest jokes before anyone else. Blessed with overwhelming charisma and charm that seemed too polished to be natural, he was well liked and a great person to be around. Not only was he the coolest guy in college, he was also a complete genius and drop-dead good looking - But then I would say these things, because that guy was me.

When I was young, I wanted to become the greatest basketball player in Britain, admittedly not the total height of ambition, but nevertheless that was my dream.

By the time I was twelve it became painfully obvious that I was somewhat vertically challenged, and by eighteen I realised that my impressive pornography collection had probably gone against me, as Mother-Nature was clearly unimpressed to the point that I would only ever be considered tall by midgets and small children.

A psychiatrist may feel as though I have issues, but I cannot afford to pay one to tell me how defective I am in life. It strikes me as a waste of time. I know what I am, and I'll deal with it my own way – thank you very much. That's how I feel about it.

My parents were relieved that another of my wild dreams would be unfulfilled and pushed me to become a doctor of medicine. It was wasted energy on their part. Most of the time I didn't know my arse from my elbow, or have the inclination to give a rat's backside on each of the one's whereabouts. Now my

...JUST SOUTH OF HEAVEN/JIM ODY

parents – still not giving up on the slim chance that Einstein might still be trying to fight his way out of my then chubby frame – sent me to college to try and learn some basic skills that might fool an employer into giving me a semblance of a job. No matter how boring and laborious it be.

I met Dice one day when he caught me climbing out of a classroom window with an arm full of other people's assignments and humming a tune by the glam rock band Poison.

"You lose the door, Bud?" he had asked. I looked over at this tall strange-looking lad with long black hair who was puffing on a funny-fag like there was no tomorrow. He looked a little like Marilyn Manson would if he dressed normally and forgot the make up.

"I prefer a challenge," I had replied searching for the sideshow he might have escaped from.

"You want a hit?" he had asked me holding out his large joint, which resembled an albino cigar.

"No, thanks. I have a habit of falling asleep when anyone smokes one of those near me."

He nodded a silent *fair enough*, took one last drag, and flipped the small torpedo into the neglected long grass. I almost expected a small explosion.

"What are you studying?" he asked, scratching his neck where a pewter cross hanged down over the top of his Skid Row t-shirt.

"Do I look like I study?" I grinned.

"You look like you've done *a lot* of studying," he grinned back and grabbed the assignments from my hands. "Or rather someone else has been doing a lot of studying." He flicked through and read out a couple of names. "Caroline Maston, Simon Leonard, Angela Guppy. You know these people?"

...JUST SOUTH OF HEAVEN/JIM ODY

I smiled and shook my head. "I've never met these people in my life, but these are the three highest scorers in last year's exams, and being as they did so well I thought it only right that I should pay my respects and let them give something back to the college, or rather through my excellent, albeit plagiaristic, exam papers. You know that phrase about the highest form of flattery?" Dice nodded, grinning like a beaver with plans for the new dam and a forest full of trees to build it with.

"Well, this is exactly what that phrase was coined for, don't you think?"

"I think it's probably still cheating, but I couldn't give a shit. We all like to be entertained."

"To a layman, it could still be deemed as such, but I came to college to get a certificate of a qualification, and that is exactly what I am doing. You think when I'm in a dead-end job, my employer is going to give a flying flapjack about whether I know what the fiscal policy is all about—"

"A flying what?"

"Exactly."

"Well, Einstein, let's make like a shepherd and get the flock outta here."

"Yep, *ewe* could be right." Immature, but we both laughed and went and got a couple of beers at the local student hang out. An hour later and we were chucked out for throwing vinegar drenched chips at each other – but it was a good time, and it makes me wonder how we lost touch. I remember it being something to do with a woman and him being shipped off to live with his Uncle Fresno. Wasn't it always the way.

The years had rolled by us. I'd aged and got less flexible, and middle-age was creeping up fast.

I had seen him a handful of times in the last few years when we would meet up to go to a rock gig someplace. I've

...JUST SOUTH OF HEAVEN/JIM ODY

always found it hard to keep in touch with people who I didn't see week in and week out. I guess it was something to do with my blinkered existence. Or just that I'm a product of a lazy generation.

Once again as the hand of Lady Luck was taking a large swing for my bare buttocks, I tripped and fell into the proverbial and got up clean and smelling of roses.

I'm at the top of the mountain and it all looks good.

...JUST SOUTH OF HEAVEN/JIM ODY

Chapter Six

When I got home from my meeting with Jezebel, I decided to crack on some Guns N' Roses at an unacceptably loud level. Life can do all it can to age me, but I'll be damned if I won't still unleash my snake-hips when trying to dance like Axl Rose in the *Sweet Child O'Mine* music video. I was then Slash air-guitaring blistering licks to all the ladies in the front row. It was a good time. Had there been a crowd, then they'd have loved it too.

When I was out of breath and feeling my age, I decided to run a few things by my little wet friend Scaly Dave. He's a good guy; he doesn't talk much, but he does sort of nod or shake his head if he doesn't agree with what I say. Which he doesn't - often.

"So Dave, d'you think that getting the sack today by using my literary skills to attack the '*Corporation,*' and cunningly weaving together silky euphemisms, amazing analogies, and mild references to the Third Reich, was pure genius or perhaps the stupidest thing I've done since farting at church when I was twelve?"

Dave swum up to the surface and sort of shrugged his gills. I couldn't blame him - it was a tough call. It's also incredibly hard for a fish to shrug so kudos for that, buddy.

"So how was your day, Dave?" I asked him, but once again he ignored me. Selfless to a fault. He's a great listener but not too hot when it comes to conversation.

I sat back down on the sofa seeing as Dave wasn't talkative tonight and thought about what I was going to do in the weeks to come.

...JUST SOUTH OF HEAVEN/JIM ODY

Antiques wasn't exactly what I had studied and slaved through years of education for, but then I realised, I didn't study and slave through education at all. I had copied work, drunk a lot, and slept with more women than I could remember. Some might say I had only myself to blame, but I've always been one for making memories. When I'm old that is all that I will have. I was too young for world wars.

I had always thought that I would get into a large corporation and work my way from the bottom up into a modest height, even though the multiple-choice careers test came back calculating my ideal job as being a roofer. An interesting conclusion what with the fact I get vertigo. I had preferred the idea of becoming a fireman, and even though my fear of heights may be considered a hindrance, I wondered whether I could specialise in bungalow and ground floor fires. I could have a separate number and a slightly smaller truck. I would be an expert at chip-pan fires. Let's not forget that more old people live on ground floors and bungalows than any other age group, and we all know what types of senile shenanigans they get up to. I'd probably get medals and be made a late addition to wills, or a special mention by the Queen in her Christmas speech. But anyway, it wasn't to be because apparently to them you have to be able to deal with all fires. This was a detail that they weren't budging on.

It would be good to have a goal in my life once again, though I wasn't entirely sure what was going to be in store for me, I was just happy not be part of the whole large corporation thing anymore. Sod them and the horse they rode in on.

A knock at the door pulled me from my reverie. I opened it to find a girl with a scowl standing threateningly in front of me.

...JUST SOUTH OF HEAVEN/JIM ODY

"I'm selling cookies for the Girl Guides," she said. Her smile must've been left with a previous neighbour. Perhaps she had sold it. She didn't look like a Girl Guide.

"Really?" I said, a surprised tone creeping in.

"You want one or not?"

I looked at the closed box unsure what I was being asked to buy. "Can I see them, before I commit, or is it potluck?"

She huffed like this was too much and flipped open the lid. Inside was a number of bakery rejects. They were deformed and barely able to be labelled as cookies. I couldn't tell whether they were double-chocolate or just burnt.

"And you're a Girl Guide?"

She nodded.

"Only, the reason I ask is you have tattoos, which would make you over eighteen."

She rolled her eyes and then said, "I'm selling them on behalf of the Girl Guides."

"Really."

"So, how many? They're a quid each."

"What! A pound for these? Look, I'm sorry but I'm not interested."

She looked a bit disappointed. She then glanced around as if checking for witnesses.

"Okay, I'll throw in a blowjob if you buy a dozen. What d'ya say?"

"I'm not hungry thanks!" I slammed the door shut not exactly sure what had just happened. I was pretty sure that a girl pretending to be a Girl Guide had just offered to give me a blowjob. I really couldn't leave this area quick enough. The neighbourhood had gone to shit recently.

...JUST SOUTH OF HEAVEN/JIM ODY

Chapter Seven

"What a great day to be alive!" Dice shouted through the open van window as he pulled his ride up to my house. Hysteria was just a Def Leppard album it would seem.

The engine rumbled to a stop and was engulfed by a thick cloud of carbon-monoxide. The harmful gasses ventured up and away into the atmosphere from the exhaust. Probably knocking another few seconds off of the future of mankind. My Prius driving neighbour would be going into cardiac-arrest if he saw this blatant disregard to the environment. Dice may as well leave open the door to my freezer, turn on all the lights and then cut down my tree. Although the tree looked to have died a while back.

I had put my yellow tinted glasses on for protection from the sun's harmful rays. The same ones zapping through the hole in the ozone layer that Dice had just increased. I know Dice loves my glasses. It's in the way he silently shakes his head at me with jealousy. He knows not everyone can pull them off. Fashion isn't for everyone.

To me Dice's beat-up black van had either child-molester or bank-robber written over it in ink that only my cynically trained eyes could read. It run on hope rather than fuel.

I had to smile as Dice opened the door to get out of the van. He had the most hideous Union Jack seat covers I had ever seen in my life. Perhaps he thought people assumed him to be Polish.

"God save the Queen!" I sung loudly in my best out-of-tune Johnny Rotten voice, whilst trying not to smile. "You don't strike me as the patriotic type, man."

"Truth is they came with the van."

"You knock the price down because of them?"

...JUST SOUTH OF HEAVEN/JIM ODY

Dice turned the loud engine off. "Some women love 'em," he added with a sigh.

"Some women like big pants, but I wouldn't put them in my car."

"You're a fuckin' hoot. Anyone ever tell you that?" he grinned.

"Ex-girl friends have called me much worse."

"That doesn't surprise me, my friend. Oh, by the way it's not fancy dress tonight. Why're you dressed like Elton John?"

"This is my own style."

"That's Elton's style. This isn't the seventies anymore so say good bye to yellow brick road, and throw them away!" He was on a roll. He really thought he was a funny guy. He continued, "And you're currently single, you say?"

"I'm taking a break. True story."

"Here's a true story for you. Anyone who says something, and then adds *true story* to the end is usually lying."

"Not this time."

"That a fact?"

"True story."

"Saying it twice definitely makes it bullshit." We'd carry on like that for hours. Rarely either of us would end up crying. Unless we started pinching each other. Dice has a death grip.

"Seriously though, you like a hippy now or something?" Dice asks me as we walked towards my house. His jealousy held no boundaries.

"I don't know what you mean," I replied. "I look cool."

"Them beads were cool thirty years ago, now they're just old lady cast-offs."

"We haven't got a dress code, have we?"

He looked me up and down and said, "I think we might have now. We buy and sell antiques – not wear them!" He laughed loud and high pitched just like I remembered him doing at college. He'd cleared rooms as I'd recalled.

"Well, you're still the comedian, I see."

My clothes were not that old. My brown bell-bottoms had probably seen better days. It was questionable that my argyle patterned top hadn't had some old guy drop dead in it before I picked it up for a quid at a charity shop, but my white vest was Calvin Klein. It cost as much as my beat up leather jacket, which again I admit did look like the cow had probably had the crap kicked out of it before giving up its hide for my expense. A small price to pay for style I thought.

Curtains twitched up and down the street. Eyebrows raised and silent tutting helped the folk around me enjoy their day just that little bit more. There'd not been this much activity around this area for a while. The neighbours did enjoy being entertained.

"You wait until you meet Scaly Dave!" I said opening the front door to my two-bedroom house.

"Uh?"

"Scaly Dave, my fish. He's a great guy!"

"He's a fish!"

"Don't tell me you're a fishist."

"A fishist? You just made that up? Or is there an ever-growing problem of fishism that I'm unaware of?"

"Without fish there wouldn't be chips," I stated.

"I'm not sure that's entirely true. I see you still say the first thing that comes into your head."

"All I'm saying is wait until you meet him."

"Is he battered?" Dice laughed.

I stopped. Things had suddenly got very serious. The shit just got real. "Never fuckin' say that in front of him. He's very sensitive."

"Chill. He's a fucking fish, Caper. A fish!"

35

...JUST SOUTH OF HEAVEN/JIM ODY

"One day you will understand," I replied under my breath. A little disappointed with the situation, I pointed over to the fish tank. I had to smile. There in all of his wet and fishy glory was Scaly Dave himself.

"This is Scaly Dave!" I smugly said pointing to the tank with pride. It was like a parent unable to hold back their happiness any longer.

Dice pressed his face up against the side of the tank and nodded his head. "He's a fish alright."

"Dave, say hello to Dice." Scaly Dave didn't seem very polite today; he shrugged and swam around to the other side. He's a good judge of character. The jury was still out on Dice in his book. I couldn't blame him. He'd hated Jezebel (apart from the one time we'd sex in front of him by accident).

"I don't hear him say anything," Dice said.

"Ah huh. He's a little upset and unsettled about being moved. You two'll be friends, you'll see."

"I'm sure we will." Dave had heard enough of this tomfoolery and swam around to his special shipwreck happy place.

The plan was that we would spend the night here – maybe go out and get drunk - and set off for Cornwall tomorrow. I had planned on living with Dice for a couple of weeks, then as long as all went well, I would sell my house and buy another in Cornwall. When I say went well, what I meant was that neither of us had murdered the other.

I had already asked Scaly Dave what he thought, and to be honest he didn't object, so it seemed like this plan was a goer.

"Nice place you have here. What d'ya call your design, single-trash-chic?"

"I'm enjoying this time of solitude in this woman-free-zone." I threw a glance over to Dave who was eye-balling me.

...JUST SOUTH OF HEAVEN/JIM ODY

"Don't look at me like that, Dave. If they don't return, then the females are not deemed as regulars."

Dice looked at me strangely. He may even have been re-evaluating the situation. "What? D'you think he lifts a fin to help around here?"

Dice turned and busied himself with looking at my CD's. I still liked to keep them.

"Hey, Caper, d'ya see that email I sent you about the truths of life?"

I nodded and felt the goofy smile on my face. You could always rely on Dice to get the funny emails just as soon as he received them. "I sure did, buddy."

"Okay, admit it you tried to lick your elbow, right?"

I nodded. "When someone tells me I can't do something, then I am sure as hell going to try and prove them wrong."

"Yeah, I damn near strained my tongue muscles. It was like a dirty weekend in Margate I had once."

"Margate?"

"Yeah, Margaret in Margate. I'll spare you the details, but my knees hurt and my tongue felt like it was going to fall out of my head by the end."

I put my hands over my ears. "Too much details!"

He grinned and I gave him a knowing look and left it at that.

We had planned to go out on the town for a *farewell to Swindon* drink before my journey into a new place, new home and new job. We thought we'd go out in a couple of hours so that gave us time to order in a large Hawaiian pizza, and watch the first half of some football match even if they were in the lower leagues. Football was football after all.

We chewed the fat for a while, catching up on a thing or two by way of anecdotes and general put downs. I was looking forward to us working together. Unlike my last boss, I assumed Dice wouldn't be a fucking arsehole.

Then we decided that we were ready to unleash our own brand of awesomeness onto the town. This was of course a phrase that had not been used this side of 1993. I apologise.

Nevertheless, it was time to rock n' roll.

...JUST SOUTH OF HEAVEN/JIM ODY

Chapter Eight

Apparently, every dog will have its day, or so they say. However, the last time I checked I was not of the leg humping and crotch sniffing variety, with the impressive flexibilities of ball licking and tail chasing. And just who the hell are *they* anyway? *They* know and say too bloody much in my humble opinion, but then again, what in the hell do I know?

It was this sort of banal discussion I was having with Dice in a bar imaginatively called Booz. It was a rowdy establishment where alcohol was drunk in quantities rather than quality, and the morals of women were left at the door with the leering flattened-nosed door staff. Classy could never be used as a description for this place, mainly for fear of misrepresentation. No matter the weather, everyone adopted the rule to dress like it was the hottest day of the year. These reasons alone were enough to attract us. Bulky jumpers and large coats were never deemed sexy to me.

I wasn't always a fan of the music. Often it was a pulsating noise muffling the sound of broken glass. On occasion a song would come on that I would feel the need to sing along to. Dice looked slightly embarrassed, but within a few hours he'd be the first person at the karaoke bar next door looking to sing some Elton John number. It didn't matter what he boasts sober, he'd be singing *Candle in the Wind* at the top of his lungs and glancing up to heaven with emotion, with a tear in his eyes given half the chance.

When my lips began to buzz and my eyesight strained, I knew we were going to have a good night. We had been knocking back the beers whilst idly trying our luck with any ladies that we found mildly attractive. At college I'd learnt the fine art of averages, which is to say if you kept trying, eventually you'd succeed. At the start of the night we had only seen a couple of stunners, but two hours later those same faces had evolved into things of charm and hidden beauty. Dice was interested in a girl with a large nose and a mole on her cheek so big that I thought I could see its feet.

"You said she was, and I'll quote, *'fucking ugly'* when she walked in, mate," I pointed out, and this was true. He'd gone out of his way to describe her to me with huge sweeping arm movements. The same arm movements he should've been using to keep her away.

Dice seemed to think this over. With a smile and eyes that had given up opening all of the way an hour ago, he slurred, "I might have been a little hasty in my evaluation, Caperman."

"Mmm," I pondered out loud. "Nah, I think you were right on the money! I know you're no Tom Cruise, but she's *fucking ugly*! Okay, maybe I'm being unkind, perhaps she has an alternative look." Dice had looked odd as a teenager, but he'd grown into his looks with age. At best I'd describe myself as average. Alcohol provides me with a confidence that outdoes my looks. Sometimes it works. Other times not so much.

"I think she's got something," he said dreamily, and I knew then he was on that beer-goggled slippery slope of drunken lust – the sort that only ever ends in tears and dirty sheets. The fine line between having your arse slapped in pleasure or your face slapped in pain.

"She's got a fucking hairy mole, is what she's got!" I laughed. "People don't generally carry their pets on their faces. It's a good thing that she doesn't have a Great Dane."

"Ballistics. Logistics. You're being mean." He'd stopped listening to me. So, I just said, "ah-ha," as he got up and staggered over to her. I would've wished him luck, but he didn't need luck; he needed a cage. And a cattle-prod.

...JUST SOUTH OF HEAVEN/JIM ODY

Dice is of average build and around six-two in height, which makes him look skinner than he actually is. Standing next to the girl with the mole, he made her look a little dumpier than she would against someone stockier, say like myself for instance. But love is blind.

He was speaking with a lot of hand gestures, and surprisingly none of them seemed rude or by any way offensive. Add to this the fact she was smiling and her mole was so far up her cheek I had to wonder whether or not she could still see out of her left eye, I could only imagine the sordid lengths the poor guy was going to stoop to in order to get some of that dirty loving. He wasn't backing away, nor running for the hills, so I took it he was going to see this one out. The beer monster had taken him over and there was nothing I could do to help him.

And then he swooped in for the kill, albeit a little sloppy if I can be forgiven for such a trivial criticism. I carefully watched as Dice was trying not to be suffocated by the large furry creature on the side of her face, and I decided then he was on his own as I was coming over a little queasy.

Now completely inebriated, the rhythmic beat and flashing lights become mesmerising. I was nodding my head to some boy band I had no interest in. My vision almost kaleidoscopic. Alcohol pumped through my veins and made me do things I wouldn't do normally. I nursed another triple Malibu not feeling the slightest bit embarrassed when the barman asked me to repeat my order. A couple across the bar smirked. Fuck them. And their adult drinks.

Then with my tongue feeling fatter than normal, I saw her. And the weirdest thing was she was smiling at me.

I thought at first maybe my fly was down and Caper Jnr was hanging down my thigh for the whole world and his mother to see. He wasn't as it happens, and I was already trying to guess what defects she must have to be walking over to me still smiling. Maybe she was high. Or simple. Perhaps she wanted to murder me. Or she saw dead people.

"Hi, how're you doing?" I said probably a little too slow as I was finding my enlarged tongue was impairing my speech a little.

She showed me her pearly-whites and I have to hand it to her, she certainly knew how to brush and floss. Somewhere in this world there was a proud dentist ready to high-five the hygienist triumphantly.

Around her smiling face long golden locks that were almost platinum bobbed with each step. An athletic build under a vest top and hipster trousers that had me dribbling down my chin. She had slightly tanned skin and deep green eyes.

"Not bad," she said. "You?"

"I'm groovy." It slipped out. Too many episodes of *Scooby Doo* had ruined me.

"Are you local?"

I raised my eyebrows and over-gestured a shrug, then replied, "Yes, mam. Was my large forehead the give away? What about you?" She smiled at that and nodded as I wondered why I was just repeating the same questions back to her. I was being about as smooth as sandpaper-pants.

"So how come I've never seen you before?"

"Maybe you haven't been looking in the right places." There I was back in the groove. The Malibu had taken control and now I was as smooth as a badger's belly.

"Am I looking in the right place now?" she teased.

I leant back on the bar, downed my drink and said, "Lady, you've three cherries in a row, and I'd say you've just hit the jackpot!"

...JUST SOUTH OF HEAVEN/JIM ODY

She laughed and said, "You gonna buy me a drink?" to which I said, "You've just won the jackpot, so I think you can afford to buy me a drink."

"Nice. What're ya' having then, Buster?" said in a Mae West accent.

"I'll have a Malibu, Toots. Straight and hold the rocks, yeah?" I had more New York added to my slurring. Although, really I was shit at accents so it probably sounded more South African.

She had a job to keep a straight face as she said, "Where shall I hold them?"

And like a speeding bullet, I said, "Above the knee and just south of heaven." We both laughed at that.

My ex-girl-friend wasn't ugly by any stretch of the imagination, and I would almost say she was pretty in a sweet girl-next-door kind of way. However, this girl was by far the most attractive women who'd ever bought me a drink, and she was not of the sort of women that usually looked at me with anything other than contempt.

A few minutes later she handed me my poison and I had it down my neck quicker than a whore's draws. She'd joined me with necking what appeared to be a whiskey and black.

"What's your name?" I enquired whilst rubbing my chin and trying to look all Christian Slater from *Heathers*. I already had the slightly closed eyes and alcoholic arrogance now growing before me was a devil-may-care attitude.

"Janie," she smiled putting her empty glass back on the bar. "And what shall I refer to you as?"

"My name is Caper, but you can refer to me as The Captain."

"Well Captain, let's blow this joint and find somewhere else a bit quieter."

...JUST SOUTH OF HEAVEN/JIM ODY

"Like a church or a morgue?"

"If that's what floats your boat."

"Well, it's not the size of your boat, it's the motion of the ocean."

"Eh?"

"Nothing." I grabbed her hand, which was maybe a little forward, but you know what they say, if you don't jump in the pool, you'll never get a chance to drown.

I looked over at Dice who still hadn't come up for air, but was somehow aware of the situation. He was giving me the thumbs up sign, which turned into the universally approved 'Okay' sign. He might be handy if I ever meet a deaf person, I thought as I left the bar with an overly attractive blonde-haired girl. And a mind full of dirty thoughts.

Apparently, youth is wasted on the young, but it turns out drunken Friday nights also qualify too.

...JUST SOUTH OF HEAVEN/JIM ODY

Chapter Nine

"Where d'ya live?" she asked me as we got outside the bar. She clutched my hand tightly which made me feel good. Touching the body of someone new can often send electric shocks to your brain.

"Just down the road," I replied. I'd been knocking back shots of Malibu mixed with beer all night and the fresh air was bringing the blinkers down on the sides of my eyes. The all too familiar feeling of drunkenness washed over me, like a welcoming wave on a hot Hawaiian beach. I did my best to walk like I knew what I was doing. Apparently, this was a struggle. It shouldn't have been as I've been walking for years.

I was beginning to worry about silly little things my overly-active conscience was flipping up in my mind. The way alcohol sometimes makes me babble out sentences and then stop halfway through, so everyone is left wondering what the hell I'm going on about. Drinking so much didn't seem such a good idea now. I had the feeling she wasn't half as pissed as I was.

In recent years I'd been in and out of some fairly long-term relationships, so picking up random women down the local cattle-market was not something I was used too. I can't explain how it feels to stumble through your front door whilst grabbing at the clothes of a girl when you barely remember her name. Dopamine, adrenaline, testosterone, and alcohol had a euphoric effect on me as I began liberating her of her clothes. Flashes of unknown skin over unfamiliar curves left me breathless. Endorphins were raging around my nerve-endings with pure excitement. This was my drug. This was plunging the needle into my vein and feeling the high wash over me.

I don't need to go into what happened next but what I will say is that an hour or so later we were laid in bed naked. I had a smile on my face that almost went right the way around my head. I was feeling like the king of the castle and after a few things we'd done, the dirty rascal too.

She lifted her head from my chest. She pulled some rogue blonde strands of hair from her mouth and said, "I have a confession to make." Not the words that you want to hear in this particular situation, I'd wager.

"Ah-ha," I replied.

"I know who you are," she said.

"Eh?"

"I know your ex-girlfriend Trixie," she said with her big green eyes showing real sadness.

This was getting worse. "And yet you still slept with me?"

Her gaze was far off as she spoke. "Not everything she said was bad, you know?" She tried to make light of the situation that was becoming bleaker by the second. "She did mention that you were a Private Investigator."

This was news to me. She probably just called me a dick, but I decided to go with it. "Uh-huh," I nodded, mainly because I liked the sound of that. Caper J - PI. I was off thinking about business card designs when I realised she was talking again.

"…well, I need you to get me something. A pocket-watch."

"A pocket-watch?"

"Yes, I know roughly where it is too."

I didn't really know what to say. This girl was fantastic, but now in the afterglow of lust she had just asked a huge favour. I can't help but wonder whether this was the real reason she'd willingly came home and shed her clothes for me. I would help more women if this were the case. But I'd not come down in the last shower, so had to wonder.

"Why do you need this watch so much?" I asked after a long pause.

...JUST SOUTH OF HEAVEN/JIM ODY

She rubbed her eyes, and I wondered whether this was a feint of sadness or whether she was actually tired. Time had passed the witching hour a while back, but when she spoke her words were in defeat. "It's personal."

"She says naked in bed with a guy she knows nothing about. Caper wonders what's going on," I slipped into third-person mode. I always hate it when other people do that, so why I succumbed to this quite frankly escaped me. Euphoric hormones perhaps.

"I know it sounds stupid – and by the way my request has nothing to do with me being here naked – but I don't want to get into it. Can you help me?" She looked with pleading eyes and breasts peek-a-booing from under the covers. Her whisky-breath and smudged make-up tried for vulnerable. I was caught in her trap. I was going nowhere.

"I'll do my best," I said and she hugged me tightly, but what in the hell did I know about finding antique watches? This was where my roach-sucking side-kick Dice came in. Him of the ugly-bird-snogging variety, would be told to warm up on the side-lines and come on as a substitute.

With my head on the pillow, I looked up at the ceiling and glanced over at her. There was something about her. She felt it too, I could tell. Propping herself up on her elbows, she smiled at me and traced unfamiliar fingers over my chest. I looked forward to joking to Dice tomorrow about his choice in women, and trying to tell him how we were now going to look for a pocket-watch. Apparently, it was back in Cornwall at a nightclub called Heaven.

I'm sure he would want to hug me for bringing such adventure into his life like this. He didn't need to know about the danger. As she kissed me, and climbed back on top of me, it was the last thing on my mind too.

...JUST SOUTH OF HEAVEN/JIM ODY

Chapter Ten

The odour was strong in the morning air. Even the freshness of dawn was unable to remove it from existence. The things that rot and are rife with bacteria cling to anything and everything.

Rotting discarded food melts together in a multicoloured mush. A stream of urine flows by, the previous owners more than likely sleeping off a hangover someplace else. The only other smell comes from a guy huddled in the doorway of the closed-down shop. The stale-stench of his body surrounds him like some stinking aura. He's alive but his body, at times, goes through stages of death before alcohol springs it back to life.

You wouldn't notice by looking at him, but Dexter was a legend. He probably still is, but nobody on God's earth actually recognises him anymore. Years of living the playboy lifestyle and fronting the punk band Raping Jesus should have set Dexter up for life. With such hits as, *Suck my fat one*, *When the Queen goes down* & *STD's, the goat and me*, it was a shame that Dexter had sold his soul to the evil guy downstairs and had been left paddle-less up the proverbial creek of shyster.

Three marriages to three money hungry hussies had bled him dry. A full-house of addictions had only made things financially worse. It was not so much amazing as to the vast amounts of money thrown away, but the fact that Dexter was still alive and remotely healthy at all. Living on the streets is not a recommended option on most health plans. But when you start to know the bailiffs on a first name basis, and start asking them about their families, then chances are you are on that downward spiral. Before long, it will have you traipsing around with no

...JUST SOUTH OF HEAVEN/JIM ODY

more than the clothes on your back quicker than lightening bolts and laser beams.

Dexter was stood out on the corner of Fore Street, having been moved on from Station Road earlier that day. He was there with his string-less guitar and attempting to sing Free's *Alright now*, whilst making the guitar noises in between the lyrics. At midnight on a Friday night people just thought that he was drunk, which of course he was as he had been for the past twenty years. He'd sipped from discarded bottles and pint glasses all night, and only gave up a little after one a.m. when he saw someone put down half a cheeseburger on a wooden bench. This was heaven sent and therefore a gift, which he would hungrily accept.

Dexter was in his forties now and didn't look a day over seventy-one. This was mainly due to his beard, which was speckled grey and as wild as his youth. His weathered features had faced each of the elements thrown at him within the past five years of his liberated life and made him look like an older Keith Richards.

He had no long-term goals. Apart from staying alive. And some days, even that appeared to be unattainable. In fact, most days his will to live was lost after his last ex-wife had left him. Now he would slide his fingertips seductively over the shapely contours of a wine bottle, but the truth of the matter was it just wasn't the same.

He wanted more. He'd had it and lost it, but perhaps it was time for him to get it back. His last hurrah. His moment to shit or get off the pot.

Today was the first day of the rest of his life.

He sat up. Stretched up arms that bared skin from under his heavy-jacket and shouted loudly like Tarzan. A woman looked alarmed and ran for the first time in ten years. A guy looked worried and walked in the opposite direction.

...JUST SOUTH OF HEAVEN/JIM ODY

Fuck them, Dexter thought. He farted loudly and mumbled, "I will rise again!"

...JUST SOUTH OF HEAVEN/JIM ODY

Chapter Eleven

I woke up with a smile on my face. My mouth tasted of a woman's nether regions and my head was fuzzy. Then everything came rushing back. I looked over but I was alone.

I slowly sat up. I was naked and slightly sore. This at least meant it wasn't a dream.

I fully expected to see her still there. I was more than disappointed. The night had been too good to be true, and this only suggested to me that she considered it to have been a mistake. I felt a childish longing to see her naked body again. It felt like the opportunity had been snatched away forever.

I got out of bed, stretched and searched for my underwear. Walking around swinging all over the place was a feeling I could never get used to. I wasn't accustomed to doing it very often.

I pulled up my boxer shorts and stepped into my trousers. I then grabbed a T-shirt and walked towards the spare room.

It was empty. Dice was MIA. He'd probably been eaten by his lady-friend.

I searched my pocket and located my phone. I saw a number of messages.

Dice sent me the first one which was a text that simply said:
In the van!

Then a picture message followed of a pair of boobs I didn't recognise. I assumed them to belong to the girl with the mole on her face, although her face nor said mole were present. I had to concede they were very nice boobs.

I ignored the next ten pictures when Dice and his large tool appeared. I wasn't sure whether it was seeing him naked which made me uncomfortable, or the fact that instead of having sex he thought to take and send me pictures. It didn't bode well.

...JUST SOUTH OF HEAVEN/JIM ODY

Alcohol doesn't always agree with everybody. When Dice drinks, it doesn't agree with me at all. Here was the proof.

"Morning Dave!" I idly said not looking up from my phone. I saw a couple of messages from Janie.

The first one was simply:

Sorry, Caper.

I shrugged. I didn't even remember taking her phone number, but there it was with her name against it.

The next message was a picture message. I hoped it was her boobs. It wasn't. It was even more alarming than any of the ones from Dice.

Scaly Dave sat in his small tank with a worried look on his little face.

I looked up from my phone to where Dave's tank should be. He was gone.

Of course he was gone! He was here on my phone in all of his wet glory! In unknown surroundings!

There was another message:

I need that pocket-watch. Just in case you don't realise the importance, I've taken your fish. He will be returned when I get that pocket-watch.

So, there it was. Her throwaway words that hurt so deep. It made sense that she knew Jezebel now. They both clearly blew the devil in their spare time.

"Fuck!" I shouted. The last message simply said:

See you Captain. Don't forget about me. Toots. x

I opened the door whilst wrestling into my T-shirt. Still bare-footed I walked to Dice's hulk of a van that was blocking the sunlight from my house.

I opened the door and jumped in.

...JUST SOUTH OF HEAVEN/JIM ODY

"Dice?" It was at that moment that Dice and his lady-friend both made loud animal noises. As I saw flashes of flesh and swinging body-parts, I jumped back out of the van and slammed the door shut.

I stood there looking up the street as the postman wandered down whistling some happy tune by Phil Collins. He smiled and handed me a couple of envelopes.

"Nice morning for it!" he said in a friendly way.

"For what?" I replied. I couldn't help it, I felt the world was against me.

"Anything you want," he grinned. His smile was put on pause as the backdoors of the van burst open and the girl from last night got out zipping up her dress. That was bad enough. Worse was Dice following her completely buck-naked.

"Morning, Postie!" Dice said cheerily.

The postman nodded. "Right, well best be on my way," and was gone.

"See you soon, baby," she winked at him and walked off. He held up a hand by way of a farewell, which would've been better served covering up his manhood.

"You gonna put some clothes on?" I said squinting at the horror.

He nodded and then bent over as he reached into the van.

"Whoa! No better!" I said and escaped for safety into my house. When all's said and done, leaving this place was a good idea. There was a chance the neighbours might lynch me.

Dice soon followed me in.

"We've got a problem."

"Tell me about it," he jumped in. "She looked better last night. Saying that though, man, can she fuck!"

I held up my hands. "She took Scaly Dave!"

"Who, Nelly? How did she—"

...JUST SOUTH OF HEAVEN/JIM ODY

"Nelly? No, Janie! The girl *I* brought back!"

Dice then smiled lost in some memory. "Damn, she was fine. You did well there, mate. Hold on," the penny dropped. "She stole your fish?"

I nodded.

"What did you say to her?"

"I said we'd help to find a pocket-watch for her."

"So she stole your fish?"

I blew out my cheeks. "She wanted me to know how much she wanted the pocket-watch."

"Fuck, that's cold." Time stood still as we both shook our heads and scratched our chins. This wasn't the sort of conundrum we were expecting today.

My phone beeped which snapped us both back into reality.

It was a picture of the pocket-watch, and then a map of where it was.

I held up the first picture.

"This is the pocket-watch."

Dice grabbed the phone with greedy hands. "That is a beauty. I can see why she wants it."

"Is it worth much?"

Dice rolled his eyes. "A small fortune, my friend. You sure you want your fish back?"

"Not even funny."

"About that girl. You did know who she was, right?"

"I only know she was a friend of Trixie's and, if you hadn't noticed, was hot as hell!"

"That as maybe, but she's also married. Not to some dork, but to Darren 'Cutthroat' Collins the MMA fighter."

"Fuck a duck."

"Fuck a duck indeed, my friend."

I was then grasping at straws. "Isn't he inside for murder?"

...JUST SOUTH OF HEAVEN/JIM ODY

"*Was inside.* He's just been released."

"Fuck." None of this was a good thing. I pulled up the map and location of the pocket-watch on my phone.

Dice whistled. Not some jolly tune, or even some 80s pop like the postman, but in an *uh-ho* sort of way.

"It's the cellar of a nightclub in River town, called Heaven."

Dice walked up to me and looked in my ears. "Just seeing whether I could look all the way through."

"Huh?"

"Have you got rocks in your head, Caper? Heaven is owned by notorious gangster Big Al Capri. Why the hell would you want to get into his cellar and steal a pocket-watch?"

"You did see what Janie looked like, right? And she has Scaly Dave."

"Will that matter when you are dead as a do-do and buried in some unmarked shallow grave?"

I shrugged, "Well at least I'll have beautiful people at my funeral."

"Well, I guess," he said, but I don't think that he was convinced, and then muttered something about a barrel full of monkeys, but I was trying not to listen. He can moan better than any woman I know.

"Jesus. And to think I employ you now."

This could be the first testing part of our new working relationship.

...JUST SOUTH OF HEAVEN/JIM ODY

Chapter Twelve

My enthusiasm for leaving was slowly diminishing by the minute. But I looked at the sorry face of Scaly Dave on my phone and knew what I had to do. Dice sent me off to shower and rid the smell of Janie's from me. We both smelled like stale sex so he agreed to do the same. I got my stuff together and lugged out a couple of big bags full of clothes and things I couldn't be without.

We were about to leave when Dice said with a grin, "You travel light, Caper. You got your make-up bag too?"

"I don't need make-up, I have natural beauty."

"Is that what your mum said?"

"No, that's what *your* mum said, though I couldn't truly be sure that that was her exact words. She was on her knees with her mouth full at the time."

Dice shook his head in defeat. "Yeah, well, she has to earn a living somehow, my friend."

Dice put on some music that would scare people away and off we went. I threw a glance back at my house and wondered if I would ever see it again.

"You did it with her then," Dice enquired when we were coming up to the M4 junction.

I didn't need to confirm this. "She will be a great memory. I knew it was too good to be true."

"They usually are, mate. You get pictures?"

I looked over at him like he'd said something stupid. "Of course not."

"I did," he said proudly.

"I know. You sent them to me."

"Really?"

"Really." He seemed incredibly proud of himself.

...JUST SOUTH OF HEAVEN/JIM ODY

"She looked better naked, didn't she?"

"I'll give you that much," I agreed. He did have a point.

Yesterday, throwing in the towel to my day job seemed like the best thing. Today, my life was in a complete whirlwind. With love, lust, confusion, and fear all shaken up into one large cocktail of feelings, I should've had a large cherry on a stick up my arse and held an umbrella in the air. I could've had a title of *Death by seduction* tattooed on my chest. You could bottle me up and sell me to the masses.

"So, what do you think about all this then?" I tentatively asked Dice, who still hadn't committed himself on whether he was going to help me or drop me off at a truck stop and run for the hills himself. I assumed he'd stick around.

"Superman has kryptonite, and you my friend, have women." This was by no way a great revelation to me. The history was all there.

"Granted, but what can we do about it."

"Get you neutered. That would go a long way to solving your troubles. Luckily for you, I've been giving this some thought, what with the fact that because of your lustful shenanigans, this will no doubt drag me down into your fucked-up life. I will be forced to save your worthless arse once again..."

"I think it's the little things you say that mean so much to me," I slipped in.

"...Okay, now the details. As it happens, I am aware of the nightclub Heaven, and we may very well be able to get our hands on that pocket-watch and get your fish back. You might even get into her smalls again. This brings me nicely on to your choice of women. I think the most disturbing part of this whole arrangement is that we will become marked men. I'm a little concerned over a murdering fighter with the nickname of

...JUST SOUTH OF HEAVEN/JIM ODY

Cutthroat, so this is the tricky part. Do you think she will tell him?"

"That could very well depend on our success rate in regards to the retrieval of said pocket-watch."

"Uh-huh, at least you are realising that and not thinking that this is true love." I wasn't that stupid. Although I had thought about children's names. But only briefly.

Dice then put on a Black Crows CD that he adored. The soulful vocals and guitars kicked in with beautiful almost gospel back-up singers, letting it all pour from their musical hearts. I tapped my fingers and had to admit life seemed a little bit safer. Hell, I live life in the fast line. I fly as close to the sun as possible. I'm a success with the fairer sex every now and then.

"You don't have much luck with women, do you?" Dice said, suddenly bringing me back down to earth with a bang, crash, and a wallop.

"I don't know what you are talking about." Denial is usually best.

"What about Cally, huh?" He grinned.

I winced at the memory. "She was very attractive too."

"She also drank a bottle of vodka and thought you were her boyfriend. And you didn't even realise."

"I thought she could tell that I was shorter, uglier, and had two arms."

"Ha, ha! That's right, her fella only had the one arm after trying to juggle chainsaws! Well, it wasn't all bad, you still boinked her though, right?"

I frowned. "I don't think I've ever boinked anyone. How would you even do that?"

"You know what I mean. You got down and dirty with her."

I looked out of the window at the fields splashed with colour. The cows peacefully sat down thinking it normal that

...JUST SOUTH OF HEAVEN/JIM ODY

cars sped by in both directions all the time, and I said, "Yeah, but when she thinks you are someone else, to the extent of calling you that person's name, then it ceases to be such a great thing."

"She was hot though, huh?"

"For sure," I sighed, "She didn't even know who I was the next day though."

Dice looked over at me with a big grin. "You remember what she looked like naked?"

"Uh-huh."

"Then who gives a cheesy-pea? An image like that is worth a million." And you know what? I think that for once his weird and strange logic might just have been right. However fucked up that might be. I was getting fed up of sleeping with sexy girls who wanted nothing more from me.

As we got nearer to Bristol, I grabbed the tabloid newspaper that was crumpled on the floor and looked over the large headlines: *Sexy Sue's Sizzling Striptease!*

The story was about this week's hottest young star that upon turning the ripe old age of eighteen had shed her top and flashed her knickers. This huge news-worthy story had managed to make the front page, pushing politics, security breaches, and poverty to be lost further inside. It's a strange world we live in, I thought as I turned to pages four and five, which showed the aforementioned young lass in glorious Technicolor for all to see.

Dice looked over and smiled. "Alcohol and money are a great combination, huh?"

"And a nice taste in underwear helps," I agreed.

I was then drawn to a story in the bottom left hand corner with a wonderous title of: *Roy Rogers Robbers Raid Redruth's Royale*

As I read on, I learned that four men all dressed as cowboys had stormed into a small casino and made off with around

...JUST SOUTH OF HEAVEN/JIM ODY

£100,000. They even had gun holsters with guns, which they proved were loaded by shooting a couple holes in an unsuspecting wall. It probably moved when told to stay still.

"Have you read about these robbers?" I wondered holding up the page.

"Yeah," Dice replied with a smile that slowly spread over his face. "It's weird to think that that sort of thing happens, huh? It's hardly the wild west."

I folded the paper back up. "Thing is," I said. "It must take a lot of planning to do a robbery, and yet to me twenty-five-grand split four ways doesn't seem much of a reward, for all of that hard work."

"I suppose," Dice agreed. "But what I don't understand is the term armed robbers. Of course they are armed, else they would be disabled, right?"

"Ah-ha," I said wondering where this was going.

"Unarmed robbers would be an amazing feat, don't you think? Can you imagine four unarmed men wobbling into a bank and demanding money, without even the ability to point a finger at anyone?" He laughed. No-one laughs as loud at his jokes than Dice himself.

"I don't think that you wobble anywhere just because you don't have any arms."

"Standard balance issue, isn't it?" He seemed serious, which was a worry.

"I really don't think it is."

"You know what I mean. So anyway, that means armed robbers are in fact armed-armed-robbers."

"—or perhaps bi-armed robbers," I offered.

"Exactly. I think I should write in and complain."

"You do that."

...JUST SOUTH OF HEAVEN/JIM ODY

He tapped a beat on the steering wheel and said, "Impressive though, huh?"

"What, walking without arms?"

"No!" he said in a raised voice. "A heist in this day and age."

"It's hardly Ocean's Eleven, is it."

"Ocean's Four by the sounds of it. Well, I think they are brilliant."

"Or criminals."

Dice shrugged. He did this when we didn't see eye-to-eye but he didn't want to make a thing of it. He did it once when we were describing how attractive his mum was.

"Well, he's something else," he then added, changing the subject. "You heard about those men disappearing?"

"Where?" I said. I'd not heard.

"Cornwall. Over the past year a load have gone missing. No one knows where."

"How come I've not heard about it then?"

"I think they've only just decided that they might be connected. Previously they put it down to a number of single disappearances."

"So, what connects them?"

Dice pulled a face. "Fuck knows, do I look like a copper? They ate within a twenty-mile radius. They probably have something else too."

"Ah, some signature thing. Keep it out of the press to stop crazies confessing to it."

"You watch too many movies."

"Impossible. You can never watch too many."

"Good point."

...JUST SOUTH OF HEAVEN/JIM ODY

Chapter Thirteen

She smiled to herself as she wiped her sweaty brow. Digging graves was not her favourite part of the process for sure. But it was a necessary evil when dealing with the highs of her fantasies.

She was a woman who had strange tastes. What had once started as merely misadventure, had unlocked a door inside of her that should definitely remain closed and forgotten.

There was something about the innocence in his eyes when he looked up to her. He wore the white jacket and hat. The way he held tightly to the holder of the milk bottles. That jingle-jangle of glass on glass action sending chills up her spine, and lighting a fire down below.

Rodney had been his name. Not very sexy. Name or man.

At first, nothing special to look at. A want on his face and a nervous expectation tried to twinkle in his eyes. One of his eyes watered constantly. It was the one that wandered. He sniffed quite a bit like he might be coming down with something. But once he pulled on that jacket and straightened the cap upon his head, he became a real man. A hero to households throughout the land. His crusade to deliver the white-nectar of the cow to expectant folk was never-ending. A splash and a dash in tea and coffee. A shower over Cornflakes. He brought them the ability to wake up and start the day properly! Milk was god.

But inevitably, like all great things in life it could never last. Whether she met them online, groped them in a club, or simply offered them a lift on a Friday night when they got home, and when she had finished with them, they could never leave. Not because what she did was so bad, most had enjoyed it very much, but because the man upstairs would never allow it.

...JUST SOUTH OF HEAVEN/JIM ODY

He was big now. A strong and powerful man. He liked to have a new toy. But he was clumsy. Not matter what she said to him, he would never listen. Each and every time he'd break his toy. And she would be left to bury the secret in a shallow grave out the back. Never to deliver again.

...JUST SOUTH OF HEAVEN/JIM ODY

Chapter Fourteen

At one stage we'd been stuck behind a coach in the slow lane of the M5. Peering over the backseat were the designated teen rebels. They sported football shirts of whomever happened to be topping the Premier League over the past couple of years. At first, they just leered at us, then when that failed a reaction made obscene hand gestures, and finally they pressed bare buttocks against the glass. I could imagine the teachers deliberately sat at the front of the coach ignoring them in a hope they would get bored and behave. In my experience, this was incredibly unlikely.

"Pit-stop!" Dice declared as the sign for Taunton Deane services passed us stating that it was one mile away. This meant coffee, which of course was up there with sex and football.

In front of us the coach pulled in too. Typical. The gobby lads would be let loose on unsuspecting members of the public. Sometimes, you just wanted to punch them in the face. Morally, it was wrong, but cutting these cocksure lads down to size might even help them in the long run.

The sun was beating down and it was hotter than a leather suit in a sauna. If you discounted the windows, then the van had no aircon of note. We were both looking forward to getting some fresh air. Dice parked the van. We got out which was a bit like opening an oven door and getting inside.

I noticed Dice shuffling himself with his hand deep into his trousers.

"Mate, what are you doing?" I hissed, a family nearby looked shocked and herded their children away. The small boy was heard to be saying, "Why is that man playing with his pee-pee?" His parents tried to ignore him and they marched off at a rapid speed.

...JUST SOUTH OF HEAVEN/JIM ODY

"Dunno. I'm a bit itchy."

"Do you have to do it here?"

Dice glanced at the van. "I've been waiting for twenty miles to do this. Had I done it back on the motorway then we might've ended up in a pile up!"

"Okay. Good point. You've upset a family though. Can you keep your nut-scratching to a minimum in public places?"

We headed past the mobile stalls selling coffee and pastries towards the building. A group of lads stood around spitting and pretending not to be smoking. I recognised them from the coach, albeit they now wore their trousers correctly.

"Hey sweetheart!" One of them with a fancy footballer's haircut said as an attractive girl in her late teens walked by. She ignored them. Smart girl.

"Frigid!" he blasted back, and they all laughed at how clever he was.

Then they spotted us.

"Look, it's the benders in the van!"

Dice and I looked at each other unsure of how this sort of situation should pan out. It was only yesterday I'd been seen as a gangster. This was the full spectrum of a youngster's brain in action. I longed for yesterday again. A flash of tits and a hero's welcome. Not anymore.

Two of the lads had taken it upon themselves to act out their assumptions. One was bent over and the other was pretending to penetrate him. They whooped and screamed in fake orgasm.

"Look, they're jealous! They want some of our sweet young arse!"

Dice then exploded. "You fuckin' little dickheads. I'm gonna smash your fuckin' faces in!" But as he made a move towards them, a nervous and balding man with a cup of tea and a heap of concern waltzed out. He had to have been one of the teachers. No one else would want to engage with these louts.

"Now, now," he said, his green cardigan flapping open. "There is no need for threatening behaviour towards these young men." For a second, I thought he meant us, then I saw him looking at us like we were perpetrators and realised where his allegiance was.

"Come Dice, let's go."

We walked off through the automatic doors into the cooler building. The hustle and bustle of people surrounded by generic shops and eateries. I looked back to see the lads sticking up their fingers at us, and one of them dropping his trousers again. The teacher was off walking back to the coach probably feeling good with himself.

We got a couple of mugs of drinks – a filter coffee for me and a tea for Dice. He could never see the pleasure I received from a mug of bitter but sweet coffee, and also concluded that tea was far more British. We did both agree on double-chocolate chip muffins.

We sat down at the back of the coffeeshop and looked over at the mixture of society swarming around the place. It was like a food blender of demographics all meeting together in order to take a break, take a pee, and eat and drink.

"So, what's this club *Heaven* like then?" I said blowing on the top of my short medium roast of Colombia's finest coffee, which I suspected, had seen about as much of Colombia as I had.

"Aside from the owner, it's not a bad place. Music-wise it's pretty much a straight-out chart-music affair, unlike those other Happy-Hardcore joints that appear to be popping up all over the shop. It has two smaller rooms which play more specific music on different nights."

...JUST SOUTH OF HEAVEN/JIM ODY

"Happy-what? I'll bet there's no rock," I mumbled into my coffee before taking a large swig.

"Hardcore. It's fast dance music. Popular in the 90s. A sub-genre of rave."

"Okay," I said. I didn't. I was aware of people meeting up in cornfields or warehouses and taking drugs and dancing until the police broke it up. I'd never been into that scene. I preferred lyrics and guitars to computer generated beats. Maybe I was old before my time. I felt like a lyric from The Who.

Dice held his mug of tea up as if it was a winning trophy and he the captain of a team and said, "Well, that's where you're wrong my faithless friend. They play the classics as well as some of the new school too."

"Blimey."

"Blimey indeed. But of course, we won't be in there tonight as we will be outside for when it closes."

"Can't we go in beforehand?" I asked picturing scantly clad women jumping around to good honest rock music. That was more attractive to me than the bulging eyeballs and stone-faces of women on acid dressed in boiler suits.

"We'll see." Dice was good with making plans and following them through. I was there to pick up the pieces when they went tits-up, or he lost his shit, but for the most part his organisation skills were good to moderate. I preferred to take a handful of plans, chuck them up into the air, and then grab one like a magician with a card.

Dice got up to go to the toilets, and it was only then that I got a real good look around at what seemed to be quite a strange slice of life. In the corner next to me sat a spectacle that was truly only believable with your own eyes.

At times words escape me. This was one of those times.

...JUST SOUTH OF HEAVEN/JIM ODY

Chapter Fifteen

There are some strange sights in this big bad world. Possibly, none more so than two men and a woman all dressed up as the late Elvis Presley. Out on the town after dark this would be a little odd, but in the middle of a service station in the heart of Somerset, it was bizarre.

It's fair to say that all three had turned out to be nothing like their parents had anticipated. Maybe they would have hid their pink vinyl 45's and never mentioned about a place called Graceland, if their children were to honour and worship the memory of a dead singer so.

Pete Rowfield was the founder member of the *Official Unofficial Elvis Lives! Fan Club*. As he was the founder member, he got to officially change his name to Elvis Aaron Presley. That and the small fact that he was born on January 8th 1977. This was of course same month and day as the original Elvis, and also the year that the king died on the proverbial throne. He'd always felt a special bond with the late-singer. He swore blind that he was a re-incarnation of The King. A claim a little dubious seeing as he was eight months-old when he officially left the building. Nevertheless, he shrugged off this detail because sometimes late at night he could hear the mournful singing from a faraway voice that sounded an awful lot like Elvis. It was a sign. It was a comfort to him deep within his heart.

His younger brother, Wayne Rowfield decided that as his brother had got to have the surname of Presley, then he should also have it, what with them both being brothers and all. So, it was only natural that he became Aaron Elvis Presley. He liked

...JUST SOUTH OF HEAVEN/JIM ODY

Elvis (the singer), but more because his brother loved him. They were close and he loved that it was something they could share.

The third and final official member was Pete's (or Elvis's as we will now call him) girlfriend Roberta Torrence. As she too was as mad as a hatter with Elvis (the dead one – not the previously-known-as-Pete one), she changed her name to Presley Aaron Elvis. The truth was she was quite the rebel. She already had short hair and tattoos, so she quaffed her hair up, wore oversized gold sunglasses, and sneered a lot. Wearing a white t-shirt and turned up blue-jeans, the mere glance at her made Elvis hard.

So, to summarise, Elvis is going out with Presley, and is brother to Aaron. Aaron, secretly has a crush on Presley, but of course Elvis doesn't know. Presley doesn't know where she's going in life. Maybe she'll marry Elvis, maybe she'll disappear and listen to Prince, who knew? She just wanted some excitement in her life.

All three had been to the Elvis seminar in the Birmingham NEC the day before. They had sat at a desk clutching their leaflets for five hours full of expectation. They had unofficially recruited two people. One was an old man from Newcastle, and the other was a Punjabi girl from Leicester. However, it wasn't clear whether or not they would be changing their names, or if they were, what they would change them to. It wasn't hugely important, but it would rank them higher up in the fan club. Obviously.

Elvis thought he knew everything. Not just about the great messiah that is The King Elvis Aaron Presley, but just about everything else, and he would argue even if he knew he was wrong. He simply loved to have arguments.

Presley suddenly thrust her arm over one shoulder, grabbed her elbow, and started waggling her tongue out.

...JUST SOUTH OF HEAVEN/JIM ODY

"What the hell are you doing?" Elvis asked. It almost looked sexual and highly inappropriate for such a populated place. And in front of Aaron.

Aaron chuckled. "She's trying to lick her elbow!" Presley nodded whilst still straining her tongue and sending a shooting pain into her funny bone.

"Why would you even want to?" Elvis frowned. Sometimes he felt like the adult and these two were the kids.

"Because I said she couldn't," Aaron sniggered watching how the frills on her leather jacket were jiggling back and forth.

Elvis shook his head. "It can't be that hard." He tried and quickly realised that it was indeed impossible. Unless you had short arms, or an extremely long tongue.

Two minutes later and all elbows were safely on laps and all tongues had returned, unscathed to their respective mouths.

"You think that Elvis was really seen in the fruit and veg section of Tescos?" Presley asked Elvis.

He looked at her with eyes filled with horror. "Hell no!" Elvis replied almost disgusted that his girlfriend would even contemplate such a blasphemous act as doing his weekly shopping. "Tescos? In Carlisle?" He then added shaking his head, and making his large Elvis-like sunglasses shake, "Why the hell would he be in Carlisle? He's a megastar, he doesn't need to shop – let alone in Carlisle."

Aaron looked down at his cappuccino and said under his breath, "There's also the small fact that he's also dead."

"What the hell did you just say?" Elvis spat slamming his large fist down on the table and sending a glob of frothy milk onto the Formica table. Aaron remained staring into his cappuccino, imagining that he could jump in and hide under the chocolate bits.

...JUST SOUTH OF HEAVEN/JIM ODY

"I'm talking to you!" Elvis shouted slapping his brother on the arm.

Presley put her hand on Elvis's silk-shirt covered shoulder and said in a calming voice, "Come on, Elvis. You know your brother's beliefs. You can't expect him to agree with you all of the time, can you?"

"But this isn't some small little thing, is it? He thinks that Elvis Aaron Presley is dead! Shit, he is a member of the Official Unofficial Elvis Lives! Fan Club, and as a member of the Official Unofficial Elvis Lives! Fan Club, one would presume that you would whole-heartedly believe that Elvis lives, or else one could go fuck-themselves and make up their own sad fucking fan club called the Official Unofficial Elvis Is Dead And I'm A Twat Fan Club!"

Aaron, still looking suitably sorry with himself, then muttered, "Maybe I have already thought about starting my own fan club. I would already have half the membership of yours."

"Shut up, Wayne!" Elvis said sarcastically, knowing that this would upset his brother.

Aaron scrunched his face up, as if he had suddenly become possessed. "Don't call me Wayne. My name is Aaron."

"Yeah, whatever. You should be called Jesse after Elvis's dead twin. You're about as much use as him!" And with that he laughed out loud and slapped his silk covered thighs.

Aaron couldn't help it. The Elvis thing helped bond the two of them as brothers especially since his dad left them to go into porn, and their mum had moved in a lad younger than them both. He loved the music of Elvis, and for the most part the dressing up and everything else that went along with it. But was Elvis still alive? He didn't think so. But so what, *right?* Did that make him any less of a fan? People believed in aliens and dinosaurs and a

...JUST SOUTH OF HEAVEN/JIM ODY

whole host of other made-up shit. And of course, Presley was always around. He liked Presley. He liked her a lot.

I had been sat there listening to the arguments going on at the table of Elvis-faux's, and I was finding it hard to keep a straight face.

It was at that point Dice came bumbling back over. I say bumbling because he was off in some dream land and didn't see any of the Elvis's until he nudged the main one, spilling his coffee all down his silk jumpsuit.

"What the fuck!" Elvis shouted.

Dice turned around. "Sorry mate… What the fuck!" He noticed the three of them all dressed up. "This a stag-do?"

"What?" Elvis said standing up. He was a tall, even against Dice, and imposing guy.

"Stag-do. You know when you celebrate the ending of a life…hold the wedding; is one of you female?"

This was bad. Dice had a habit of saying exactly what was in his brain. It was the like the filter to his mouth fell out periodically.

"You had better shut the fuck up! You've ruined my clothes!"

"It's fancy-dress, you're bound to drop something down it! Dry clean it and you can take it back fine. It looks cheap anyway."

Elvis swung at Dice. I got up quickly. He could be an idiot, but he was going to help me get my fish back. I would be there for him.

Dice moved to the side and used Elvis's momentum to push him as he stepped passed. Elvis fell over and hit another man knocking his coffee over.

"Oi, Elvis, you wanker!" he shouted as Aaron went for Dice. I headed him off but not before Presley kicked him in the nuts. I

...JUST SOUTH OF HEAVEN/JIM ODY

pushed her. I wasn't proud of the move but it sent her flying. I helped Dice up and we ran off with our tails between our legs. It was not a good moment in my life.

With heavy breaths we couldn't get through the automatic doors quick enough. I turned back to see all three Elvises in hot pursuit. We burst through and almost fell over a lady with a pushchair. Inside was a kid about twelve.

"Did you see that?" I said as we ran.

"Lazy bugger!"

It was then that we saw the pink Cadillac. It was strange to see it so far away from Graceland.

And even weirder to see the group of lads kicking the grill and hanging off of it.

"Look it's the benders!" The cocky one shouted, and then noticed who we were running away from. "Fuckin' 'ell it's Elvis! And there's three of them!"

"Oi, get away from that car!" Elvis shouted.

We had crossed the road and headed towards the van when I stopped to see the Elvises no longer cared about us. One of the lads was still urinating on the wheel.

"I can't stop!" he was crying as Elvis was pulling him, and then Aaron and Presley were pulling Elvis and telling him to leave the lad.

We jumped into the van and with a rev, a cloud of smoke, and a bang from the engine backfiring, Dice started it up.

"What just happened there?" I asked.

"I spilt Elvis's coffee, you pushed a woman over, and we were verbally abused by some boys. Not the highlight of my life, if I'm honest! In fact, I will not even use it as an amusing anecdote in my autobiography."

"What would you call it? *To All The Boys I've Loved?*"

"More like, *Life is as bumpy as Caper's Mum!*"

...JUST SOUTH OF HEAVEN/JIM ODY

I rolled my eyes. "Funny."

Dice reversed the van but instead of leaving directly at the exit, took another circle of the carpark, slowing down at the pink car.

"So long, fuckers!" he shouted, as I slunk down in my seat. I looked back just in time to see three dead rock stars with angry red faces and swinging medallions looking like they wanted to kill us.

And a lad crying and doing up his trousers.

As we pulled out onto the M5 again, Dice turned to me and said, "I hated Elvis the first time. Imagine a life with three of the fuckers?!" I had to agree. More than one Elvis would've been a nightmare.

...JUST SOUTH OF HEAVEN/JIM ODY

Chapter Sixteen

It was no mean feat to successfully rob a casino, whether it is situated in a large city like London, or as in this case a small casino in the Cornish town of Redruth.

Randell Johansson was pondering this with pride as he sat down in from of his laptop and tried to come up with the finer details of his next master plan. This one he hoped would make him a bit more money than the last heist. Of course, what he really needed to do was find a way of keeping the money for himself. Splitting it with others was not a good thing. He was the one sat hashing out the details of the security system, the entrance to use, and the men for the job. His last crew was slick. That was great, but what he needed were a couple less diligent that he could micromanage. They would never understand the split of stolen cash and he could make more money. He had a further plan to leave the country there after. The trouble with hiring idiots was they were bound to squeal at some point. There was no way he was going to be caught and thrown to the perverts in prison. He would be nobody's bitch.

He was the brains behind the whole thing and after a diet of gangster and heist movies, it was obvious that this was his calling. His last cellmate told him as much, and no-one knows what it takes to be a master criminal more than a criminal themselves. He could see no fault in this logic.

What the national papers forgot to also mention was that the casino was closed at the time of the robbery, and the security guard on duty had left early when someone with a voice like Randell's had called in saying that said security guard's dad was in hospital. The stolen money was meant to be in a safe locked tight – and to be fair that was exactly where it was – but when you have been locked up with a guy that thinks safes are easier to

...JUST SOUTH OF HEAVEN/JIM ODY

crack than Rubik's Cubes then it means that no safe is safe (pun intended). Well, the complete truth was that Randell was able to crack open a 1975 Cleaverson double lock safe, but no other type or model, which was good because that was exactly what this one had been. It was the main reason he had chosen this place to hit. Very few of these models were still in use.

Randell Johansson was of Swedish descent, which was to say that his grandfather was Swedish and his grandmother had been a barmaid in the East End of London and was as Swedish as a union-jack wearing bulldog.

His parents moved with his grandparents to Stockholm when he was ten, leaving him with an uncle who was a bar-knuckle boxer and all round hardman. He gained his first tattoo at fifteen when he joined a local gang, and received a cross on his forearm in Indian ink as a mark of his commitment to the gang.

Randell was no idiot, which is a surprise due to his lack of education and his time spent in borstal. With his brains and his six-foot plus stocky frame it became clear that he had the ability to be persuasive and therefore a natural leader. Twenty years, and a dozen tattoos later, and here he was. His criminal success rate was mostly small petty crimes, until that big one: the casino in Redruth. But this next one, well, that would be different; this was what he had been building up for. The big one.

There would be no cowboy suits for this one, oh no; the last thing you want is to be given a stupid nickname, like the one from that newspaper: *Roy Rogers Robbers*. They sounded like cartoon characters. None of them were called Roy for a start. To think someone was paid silly money to come up with crap like that. It makes you question society.

Randell picked his mobile up and rang his man who was looking after the disguises. He was a slimy guy called Sammy Charles.

...JUST SOUTH OF HEAVEN/JIM ODY

"Sammy, it's me. Have you got the outfits yet?" He said getting straight to the point. He never understood why people spent time on small talk. He didn't care how the little shit was, he just wanted to know he could follow simple instructions.

"Who's this?" a small voice came back.

"IT'S ME!"

Silence, then, "...and me, would be..?"

Randell took a deep breath and wondered just how far he could shove his mobile down that little skinny runt's throat before he would realise. "Randell. It's Randell. Do you know now?" Frustration was clearly showing now. He had wanted simpler guys but this was stupid, or rather this bloke was stupid.

"Well, of course I know now, you just told me, but I didn't know before, did I?" The voice was no longer small anymore and had got slightly cocky. Randell wasn't quite the scary Godfather figure that he wanted to be – more like a big brother.

"Alright, whatever. Have you got the suits?"

"Yeah, see, I wanted to talk to you about that," he mumbled beginning to skate around what he was trying to say.

"Is there a problem with what I wanted?" Randell was working himself up to a migraine again, he could feel it. Being in charge was just a fucking stress. He wasn't sure the bigger cut was worth it.

"Just a small one. The shop has sold the boiler suits to someone else..."

"WHAT?!" Randell shouted. He had hoped that they could do this next heist dressed as his favourite band Slipknot, in boiler suits and masks, but as Sammy had decided to use some fuckwit-outfit to order the disguises from, then they were probably going to end up being fucking ballerinas or something.

"I SAID..." Sammy shouted.

"I HEARD," Randell shouted back, "WHAT YOU SAID!"

...JUST SOUTH OF HEAVEN/JIM ODY

"Oh, then why…"

"What are they going to do about it? We need something tonight. Are we going to get four identical costumes for tonight, that's all I'm asking?"

"Yes, they will provide us with something or our money back."

"What!"

"OR OUR MONEY BACK!"

"I heard. We don't want the *'or your money back'* line, as we need costumes! We can't very well turn up naked and slip in and out dressed like porn stars, can we?"

"I'd rather we didn't," Sammy agreed.

"Well, thank fuck for that. So, do you think you can sort out our lack of costume problem whilst I do the grown-up work, huh?"

"Yes, boss."

"Yes, boss, indeed. Now sort it." He cut the call, shook his head and dialled the number of the next guy.

Boston was a guy of average intelligence, or he would be if everyone who could read and write were suddenly wiped out in a major natural disaster. All he had to do was sort out the guns.

When his phone went off, he was looking at one of the guns he had just bought off a scouser with a crew cut and a face as innocent as a slapped arse.

"Yeah," he said in his Brummy accent. He wasn't from Birmingham, he was from Newcastle, but everyone told him they couldn't understand his Geordie accent, so he tried to perfect a West Midlands accent. Boston wasn't good at accents at the best of times, and his voice tempo and pitch were going up and down like a cheap whore. He sounded like a confused cross between Indian and Swedish. Now people told him that his Birmingham accent made him sound stupid. But you could only please some of the people all of the time and all that.

"It's me," Randell said hoping that he wouldn't have to go through it again.

"Uh-huh," Boston replied.

"Have you got the guns sorted out?"

Boston smiled and held up one of the guns proudly. "Sure have." And opened the clip to see whether it was full or not.

"Good man," Randell sighed with relief. Thank fuck one of them was switched on – even if it was the simple one. He was the sort of guy you needed. He didn't ask too many questions. Didn't speak very much. Looked big and mean and just got on with things.

And that's when Boston realised that there were no bullets inside. There would never be bullets inside, as this was a cap gun. A useless toy cap gun. It would only scare grannies and toddlers.

"Shit," Boston mumbled, and fumbled with the other guns to see whether the fucking scouse git had screwed him over on the others too.

"What's up?" Randell asked.

"Nothing, boss. It's just started to rain, that's all." All four guns were cap guns. He looked around his flat for possible replacements.

"It's sunny here." *Baseball bat?* Uh-uh. *French stick?* No, it's not sawn off.

"Oh, er, really. That's good." *Pillow?* No. *His mum's dildo?* She'd notice...

"Are you sure you're alright?"

"Yeah, peachy. I'll see you later."

"Sure, and Boston?"

"Yeah?"

...JUST SOUTH OF HEAVEN/JIM ODY

"Don't forget the guns, huh?"

"No chance. I can't wait to show them to you!"

Randell looked up the number to the last guy. He was called Princess and as camp as can be. Randell had met him in prison. At first he'd felt threatened by him, not physically, but because he was so confident and without a care. He was a real comedian and was a good addition to have in a gang. In his experience most people trusted a gay man. He didn't know why. The criminal world can be strangely acceptive of preferences.

Princess answered loudly. He always did. It was like he was the star of a show. "Hey Sugar, what's up?"

"Princess. Just checking out that our get-away vehicle is ready for action tonight."

Princess walked around the Pink Cadillac and wondered why two of the expensive tyres had been slashed, and one looked to have been pissed on. He'd only popped into the service station for a pee and this was what he'd found upon his return.

"Don't you worry yourself, boss. Everything is fluffy bunnies, I tell you. Fluf-fee Bunny-kins. Toodle-oo." He cut him off. *Shit, what was he going to do now?* He wondered. He thought about calling the AA, but these weren't tyres that would be held by anyone. They had to be imported in. That was a huge cost and also a long delivery time.

Randell looked down at his phone and wondered whether his choice of personnel was really chosen wisely, or more like they were the only criminals that weren't likely to kill him and run off with the money when this thing was over.

He said a silent prayer with unchristian words and begging, crossed himself for the first time in twenty years, and silently asked for forgiveness from some of his previous sins. Sometimes needs must.

...JUST SOUTH OF HEAVEN/JIM ODY

Chapter Seventeen

Dice began to fumble in his jeans. He jiggled around on the seat like he had a real issue in his trousers.

"Shit, you better get that checked out," I said and naturally moved a little further away.

Dice laughed and pulled out some squashed joint and a lighter. He rolled his window down, lit it and puffed away like it was going to give him some great revelation.

"You want some?" he said.

I held up my hands. "Nah, you're alright."

"Suit yourself," he said and then itched his nether regions. "You're right though. It's a bit red down there."

"Serves you right," I said. "Grabbing wildlife to fuck has its ups and downs."

"That supposed to be a joke?"

"The joke's on you now." He shrugged and refused to comment further.

Lenny Kravitz was on the radio shouting out a list of things his mama said over the music. It made you wonder whether she may've increased the list with other things our Lenny failed to mention - shouting being one of them.

It was at that point that a small dot behind us began to get bigger and nearer at a phenomenal rate. The loud engine sounded raspy and unwell but seemed to work just fine at bringing the white vehicle to Formula 1 speeds. It cut in right behind us.

"What the fuck?" Dice said gripping the steering wheel tight and clamping his freshly lit doobie almost flat between his lips.

Lenny Kravitz's mama also never mentioned anything about speeding. Nor swerving on the A30 duel-carriageway smoking weed.

...JUST SOUTH OF HEAVEN/JIM ODY

"What's going on?" I said suddenly noticing that Dice was alert and ready for something. That was never a good sign. I usually ended up getting pinched by a man or slapped by a woman. Neither did I enjoy.

"Your friends the Elvis twins," Dice said.

"They can't be twins, there's three of them. Elvis triplets is what you mean," I corrected. "I guess that wasn't their car then."

"Ya, think?"

"Or they stole another."

"What, just to chase us, numb nuts?"

I shrugged. I'd heard people do a lot less.

Rumour had it that the true Elvis Presley owned no fewer than five-hundred vehicles in his lifetime. I'm sure the King didn't drive any of them with the recklessness of a drunken mole, as was the driving skills on show of the car flying up behind them. The white Audi TT wove left and right, wanting to use its power to over or under take. Dice remained in the Fastlane, even though the van moaned at the speed. The dashboard shook like the hips from Elvis himself. I pictured the tyres smoking and bursting into flames at any moment.

I'm no expert but I'm sure that if the king was alive today, a German sports car would not be his dream choice of transportation. He'd go American all the way.

Dice looked to be doing a good job of looking at where he was going and keeping a watchful eye on the car behind. He saw Evil Elvis giving him a grin straight from the face of Beelzebub himself. A pure bad guy expression, of frowns and hunched over the wheel with menace. His car shot left on the verge where there was a light gravel coating.

Dice floored the accelerator as he saw the Audi's bonnet getting nearer in the passenger window. Unfortunately, the van didn't move as fast as both Dice and I willed it too. It may have

...JUST SOUTH OF HEAVEN/JIM ODY

been better if it had been the Flintstones vehicle and we could've pumped our legs for all we were worth. There was a sudden rattling sound coming from underneath which was never a good sign.

The car was gaining at such a rate as to be almost side-by-side now.

"Why don't you just hit them?" I suggested as it seemed like about the only chance we had of getting out of this alive, or more importantly to save face. No one wants to explain how they got beaten up by three Elvis impersonators. Especially if one of them is female.

"What, and dent my van? You've been watching too many films. This isn't *The Dual*, you know." Of course, this wasn't *The Dual*. *The Revenge of the Elvis Impersonators* was what it was, and I for one was hoping to be around for the sequel. I'd get the girl in that one. Maybe not lose my fish either.

Sometimes you have to know when to shit, and when to get off of the toilet, as someone once said, so I took hold of the situation (or the steering wheel as it's also known), and pulled it anti-clockwise. The van shot to the left, and there was a large bang of crunching metal as the car and our side panel made contact.

The rear view was poetry as the vehicle slammed its brakes on whilst turning the wheel so sharply that the front right tyre blew.

"That's not quite what I had in mind," Dice said taking a large drag of his joint. "But I guess it worked pretty well."

I tapped my head and replied, "Yeah, not just a brain-helmet, mate!" And Lenny Kravitz was happy to tell us of his love of American Women. Well, good for you, Lenny. Good for you.

...JUST SOUTH OF HEAVEN/JIM ODY

Chapter Eighteen

Janie had finished her shift at the Swindon café and had walked slowly through Queen's Park. She was stalling and wondering how this lovely bright day was going to turn into a storm just as soon as she got home.

Gerald 'Cuttthroat' Collins had already left three messages on her mobile asking where she was. And even though the first one had sounded as if he was genuinely worried, the other two had told a different story. He had told her what was likely to happen when he got his goddamn hands on her worthless-skanky-whore-ass.

He was also interested to know why there was a Goddamn fish sat in the kitchen eyeballing him.

Last night had been good, and for the first time in years she had realised what it must feel like to be wanted and desired. She had flirted and been made to feel like a woman. He was slightly cocky and his technique was sloppy with alcohol, but all the same it was great.

Did she like him? She couldn't say. Did she love Gerald? That was a real no brainer, of course not, but she was trapped. Maybe the pocket-watch was all she needed to set her free. He loved her for who she was, or rather what she looked like. She was a trophy wife. He loved her no more than she loved him. They were familiar, although even that was hardly true anymore.

She stopped and looked at some children feeding the ducks. They had not a care in their innocent little worlds. Too young to experience the shit hitting the fan of life. Their families were around them ready to smother them with love. All in a good safe and comforting way. So many choices still left for them to make and new experiences to enjoy. But then one day you meet a strong man who tells you what you want to hear, and he buys you drinks and treats you like a princess. But then he starts training and fighting. Becoming obsessed with being strong. Then he starts drinking, and before you know it, he realises that he enjoys this sport of rolling around and grabbing men so much that he wants to do it outside of the ring too. He pretends that it is to do with power and control but really, he's discovered that he has deep sexual feelings for men. He's so disgusted that he camouflages it with hatred. Then your world is filled with false sexual advances, and his interest for you no longer is there. He despises you and your feminine ways. He doesn't want a princess-bitch, but a prince to give his affection to. But of course, he will not let you go. He has to remain an alpha male. He cannot lose face.

Janie opened the front door with tentative fear. She'd only taken two steps into the house when she heard his pounding footsteps from upstairs.

"Where the hell have you been?" he blasted in his cockney accent as he powered down the stairs.

"At work," she spat back with defiance. She'd fight him all the way to the grave if she had to.

His face had already changed into a deep purple colour with his pent-up rage. "I mean last night!"

"I stayed at a friend's house." She tried to walk past him but he stood in her way.

"Which friend, huh?"

"Kelly."

He gave a sly smile. "Kelly, huh? Ya' left ya' work clothes there, but you didn't sleep there, d'ya?"

"What do you care?" she mumbled looking down at her black slip on shoes.

...JUST SOUTH OF HEAVEN/JIM ODY

"I'm ya husband! I never said that you could go out last night! Nor did I say that you could go off with some guy with stupid fucking beads and a fucking stupid name, did I?"

"What rights do you have to go and do what you do with blokes?" she spat back, but knew as soon as she had said it that it was a mistake.

"As your husband I have every right. And as my wife, you've none!" He slapped her hard across her cheek and the power knocked her off balance and onto the cold hard wooden floor below. She covered up just in case there was more to come, but as she looked up, she saw her husband had grabbed a large holdall bag. It was the one they usually packed when going away. He stared at her with hatred. Janie thought that it must be some of her stuff and he was kicking her out. She was about to feel relieved when he stopped and said, "I am gonna have ta kill that Caper Juggins now! I hope you was worth it 'cause when I've finished with him, he'll only be able to fuck angels in heaven!"

"You don't know where he is!" she said through the tears and running nose.

"Your friend Kelly told me that 'e was moving to River Town in Cornwall today, and my dear, that's just where I am going now, with me old friend Bomb." And with that he slammed the door and Janie was left in an eerie silence. She touched the side of her face which still stung like hell. Many tears had tumbled from her eyes and she hated herself even more for it.

Shit, she thought, Bomb wasn't just Gerald's friend - Bomb was a hit man. She had to warn Caper. But if she did that, then he'd never get the pocket-watch for her. With that, she'd sell it and disappear.

...JUST SOUTH OF HEAVEN/JIM ODY

Or with the pocket-watch she'd buy his silence, hopefully with a free divorce thrown in for good measure.

She got to her feet, ran to the door, and shouted after him, "He's getting that pocket-watch for you!"

He stopped in his tracks. "What did you say?"

"The pocket-watch. I told him to get it for you."

"And he's gonna do that. For you?"

"I stole his fish!" She tried to smile. Her mouth twitching and she sniffed.

"What?"

"That fish. The one in the kitchen. It's Caper's pride and joy. I've fish-napped it until he gets me the pocket-watch."

"Fuck me. How's he gonna do that?"

"I don't know, but he's going to do it for me!"

"What did you tell him," he sneered.

A couple more tears escaped down her cheeks and her face still hurt from the slap as she wiped them away. But there was something about the way he smiled. He was almost proud of her. "Nothing. I just said that he'd never see his fish alive again, if he didn't get it."

"He's even more retarded than I first thought. Why would he get it for you?"

"So I could give it to you, my husband. That's why I had to sleep with him, because I knew he would do it and then you'd be able to pay off that debt once and for all." Lying was never easy. But nor was the realisation that you were in this world alone.

"If he's true to his word, then he may just escape with some broken bones, but if he's empty handed, then God-forgive me for the sins that I may commit."

...JUST SOUTH OF HEAVEN/JIM ODY

Chapter Nineteen

The smell of rubber hit lingered in the air, and the dust from the dry muddy verge floated around before it settled. For a second, all three of them were in shock.

"You stupid bastard!" Elvis shouted, slapping Aaron on the head with his hand. His large ring catching him hard. "You can't drive for shit!"

"And you'd have done better, I suppose," Aaron replied, rubbing his head. "You can't even drive!"

"I can. I just haven't got a license!"

Aaron puffed out his cheeks. Elvis always thought he was the best at everything but actually it was just because he was older and bigger than everyone else. "Idiot," he muttered under his breath.

Presley giggled as Aaron slammed his fist on the steering wheel and leaped out of the car like he was going to pick a fight with the wheel itself. "I don't know why we had to go after them. So what if they ran their mouths off, those other little shits fucking around with the car were worse!"

Ignoring her, Elvis got out ready to taunt Aaron some more. "You're about as much use as a one-legged man in an ass-kicking contest," he mocked adding literal fuel to the fire.

"You're as much use as a no-handed man in a clapping contest!" Aaron replied.

"What?" Elvis said. "That doesn't make sense."

"Neither of you make any sense," Presley laughed.

Also ignoring Presley, Aaron threw Elvis a glare that clearly wasn't a let's-have-a-group-hug-to-settle-this gesture, and said, "If you don't shut the fuck up, I am going to slap you like the bitch you are."

...JUST SOUTH OF HEAVEN/JIM ODY

"Boys, boys, boys," Presley smiled. She was always the peace-maker. They made her laugh. They loved each other in their own way, but they did tend to get a little hot-under-the-collar with each other all the same.

"Shut up and change the tyre, woman!" Aaron then said. It was unclear as to whether there was any humour with it. He didn't mean to say it, but once it was out there, he had to pretend he did.

Presley snickered, "*Yeah*, right!" and looked to Elvis for support.

"Why not? You're all for equal rights, right? *Women should have the same opportunities as men, Elvis*, you say. Well, here is an opportunity to change a tyre and I will not stand in your way," he replied.

Aaron raised his eyebrows at the comment and then nodded, "It's a good point. I also appreciate you as a woman, and I'll allow you to change the fuckin' tyre too."

"Fine!" Presley spat as she stomped to the boot of the car. "One of you fuck-wits had better get the tyre out though. I'm not doing everything 'round here." She took back those thoughts. They were both idiots.

Elvis looked up the road. His mind filled with the dark van and the two wankers inside. Man, he wanted to get them back something rotten. They'd driven all the way to Birmingham in what now seemed like a wasted journey. He'd told the other two that there would be queues of people lining up at the NEC to sign up for their fan club. They could charge a joining fee and make so much money they'd go for a weekend in Blackpool. Maybe grab a show. See the lights. But no one had officially joined and so they'd left with their tails between their legs and come home. No lights, no show, and no Blackpool.

...JUST SOUTH OF HEAVEN/JIM ODY

They were a fine example of the youth of today each pulling their weight and trying to put one over on each other whilst dressed as a dead idol. It's this sort of scenario that parents weighed up in the *for* category when pondering over the word *abortion*. It was no wonder they never got invitations to weddings anymore.

A black non-descript car sped past. The windows blacked out. Inside a lone wolf on a mission to kill a man and collect an antique pocket-watch.

...JUST SOUTH OF HEAVEN/JIM ODY

Chapter Twenty

Barton 'The Bomb' Jones was a former lightweight boxer. His nickname came from the fact that he was dark in colour and would go off suddenly just like a bomb. Exploding with punches from all angles. He'd briefly had some success in the professional ranks before sustaining a broken eye-socket in his one and only defeat. The doctors told him that due to some nerve damage and scar-tissue, there was a chance he could go blind if he carried on. It took him a while to agree – he was turning his back on something he was talented at - but leaving sparring sessions seeing double each time told him soon enough he had to throw in the towel.

He walked out of the gym and stretched after an hour-long work out. If truth be told, he couldn't stay away from there and did everything but fight. He maintained his sleek physique by pounding the heavy bag and dreaming he was in the ring again. If the money was right, he even toyed with coming back for one last fight.

He had found a job that paid better than professional boxing. He was a self-employed hit man. He chose his jobs carefully, but the profession paid well.

He liked to repeat the title from an old heavy metal album called, *'Killing is my business...and business is good!'* although he didn't speak of his job very often. It paid to be discreet. His line of work had made him a shit load of cash, and the sort of respect that money can't touch, let alone buy.

On his self-assessment tax form, he was in the employment of Business Consultation, however Bomb knew as much about business management as he did fly-fishing. Which was that he thought fly-fishing was all about trying to catch flies, which from his experience was a hard and pointless task.

...JUST SOUTH OF HEAVEN/JIM ODY

He walked up to his new BMW saloon and jumped in without a glance in either direction. He knew there were people around, so it was all about looking cool. This one was a week old and still had that new-car smell.

The engine purred to the sound of Drum and Bass. For a brief spell the underground sound had been cool with those from the streets who enjoyed racing cars around abandoned car parks. The fast and tinny sounds of a snare drum being played faster than humanly possible. Huge fat bass lines that rocked the car back and forth. Then a haphazard synthesizer attempting a crude melody jumped around with random notes. It was somehow seen as impressive amongst peers and other like-minded youths many years ago. Bomb was an ancient 30 years old and was seen as an example of not hanging up your super woofer soon enough.

At 5'6" and built like an anorexic, Bomb wasn't huge. At first glance he didn't exactly put the fear of God in you, but he always had a sneer on his face that made him look just plain mean. In his boxing days he could *certainly* punch.

He was a strange mixture of things your mother hoped you would never turn into. Although he would never shy away from a fight, Bomb was a minority believer in ditheism. His two Gods were Sex, and in particular Janet Jackson. Every month without fail, Bomb religiously wrote fan mail to Ms Jackson, somehow assuming that she really gave a bag of monkey bollocks about his mundane mutterings. More surprisingly still, he actually believed that he would meet her and they would fall in love. She reminded him of a happier time in his life. He wanted that back.

The Hit-Man & the Pop-Princess.

He had more chance of snogging Bubbles the chimp, than even being in the same room as Ms Jackson. *But everybody's got to have a dream.*

...JUST SOUTH OF HEAVEN/JIM ODY

He glanced at a couple of underdressed young ladies as they made their way from the car park towards the gym, and was transformed into Mr Charmer. He figured he was a fool to wait for Ms Jackson.

"Hey, ladies. You want a workout? You come over here, I'll warm you up!" He shouted above his music through his car window. One of them had long blonde hair. She didn't have an ounce of fat on her body, and whispered something to the bigger built red head with a grin. They both waved and smiled.

Most of the time Bomb was focused. When he was on a job, he could sit in one position for hours. His eyes trained on the one spot. He'd barely blink or breathe. But add a scantily-clad female and he couldn't control himself. It was like he needed to liberate them from their clothes and have sex with them no matter where they were. He was a sex addict. Plain and simple.

Bomb had had this addiction for many years but didn't see it as an addiction – the classic attitude of an addict. He picked and chose his sexual partners at random and by no other means. He bored quickly of them when he'd had his wicked way. He lied to each girl with only the thought of getting them into bed on his mind – then the next day was filled with deep regret and guilt. The only way he got rid of the guilt was by going out and getting another girl again. A girl that wanted to be with him and would do anything he said. There was always one available. It was surprising.

Of course it is always a good argument that a sex addict isn't in fact in the wrong as they portray the classic characteristics of the evolved male Homo sapiens, whereby urges to copulate promiscuously is not *are* suppressed by cultural restraints, and it is us who spend a lifetime ignoring all sexual desires towards members of the opposite sex whence paired off, and so

...JUST SOUTH OF HEAVEN/JIM ODY

committed to a monogamous and loving relationship until death do us part.

"The backseat is big enough for three, ladies," he yelled again. "It takes two to tango, but three to please!" The blonde shook her head and looked up to heaven. The red head smiled and walked over to Bomb. Her face was fairly attractive, though she was packed into her orange lycra all-in-one quite tightly and it was obvious that she liked her cream cakes and donuts, but - *whatever*. Any port in a storm.

Bomb watched as her large breasts jiggled rhythmically with each step, almost shouting out to be let free from their prison.

"So, what are you offering, bad boy?" she said confidently leaning in the car window and showing a cleavage likened to the Grand Canyon. She knew his type. She'd had his type before, and spat them out quicker than they'd come.

"Get in and I'll show you. *Say*, are you a real red head?" he said with a cheeky little schoolboy grin.

"I think you're about to find out." She hated the gym anyway; there were many other cardiovascular activities that she found more highly entertaining.

As they drove around the back of the warehouse to a more secluded spot, Bomb said, "This sure beats stretches for warming up!" And as he turned to her all he saw was a large naked pair of breasts bouncing free, and he just had to smile. Life sure was grand!

And then his mobile rang and ruined it all.

94

...JUST SOUTH OF HEAVEN/JIM ODY

Chapter Twenty-One

Gerald 'Cutthroat' Collins was also known in circles that he frequented as Bulldozer. The name was perfection on so many levels. He was big built and could knock anyone or anything out of his way. He was also likened to a bull, insomuch as he didn't say a lot, had a short-fuse, and was hard to stop in his tracks.

Cutthroat took a last drag of his cigarette and flicked it with perfection at the feet of a guy who had just cut him up on Swindon's infamous magic roundabout. A huge design of five small roundabouts surrounding one large dominant one. Whilst it looked daunting and scary to most, it was actually incredibly efficient. Dickheads aside, most people were able to manoeuvre around it fine.

Cutthroat may well have let this pass on a normal day, but this was not a normal day. You do not expect your wife of six years to fuck some other guy, even if you prefer something a little meatier between your partner's legs than what she has to offer you herself. Vows were made for a reason. Cutthroat could see the difference between what he did and what she'd done. He was just fooling around. She was serious. He knew it.

So enraged was he, that he'd followed the boy-racer a mile and a half before the guy stopped at a local convenience store in Covingham. Cutthroat pulled his car up beside the shocked guy and summoned him out.

The guy in his late teens was making a fudge factory of his underpants as Cutthroat stood silently staring at him. The lack of sound hung in the air like a guillotine. It was worse than being shouted at.

"We've got a problem here," he started. The other guy stood rigid with fear. "Don't you think?" He walked up to the guy.

...JUST SOUTH OF HEAVEN/JIM ODY

"I-I-I'm sorry, mate," the guy mumbled. The fear was there for all to see. The machismo had run off the minute his car door opened.

"I believe you are – now! You didn't seem too sorry when you cut me up though, did ya?" Cutthroat grabbed the back of the guy's head. "Or when you put your foot down with little or no care for pedestrians or other road users."

"I-I-I-," the guy started.

"*Sorry?*" Cutthroat finished for him. "So you keep saying, but if you had lost control young man, you would have turned a child into mashed potato and ketchup. You're no chef and I'm no fairy fuckin' godmother." Cutthroat slapped him across the cheek. An act which brought more embarrassment than pain. If you get punched, you can brag. If you get slapped, you shut the fuck up. Cutthroat knew this.

Folks were really trying his patience today, but he was really going to enjoy getting that little fucker Juggins back. He had a pair of pliers with that lad's name written all over them. But first he had to teach this schmuck a thing or two.

The lad was expecting the worst and was beginning to feel the muscles in his bladder slacken when it happened.

Bang! Cutthroat fell to the floor like a giant sack of potatoes that had fallen from the sky, and began to snore loudly. You see, Cutthroat suffered from narcolepsy whereby he would fall asleep at a drop of the hat, and without warning. This was why he didn't like it when other people abused Her Majesty's Highway Code, because of course his driving license had been revoked a few years back for this very reason.

Okay, he had just been driving but that was a short journey. It was Janie's car. She wouldn't care, unless some little prick smashed into him, of course!

...JUST SOUTH OF HEAVEN/JIM ODY

This was why he needed Bomb, firstly as a driver so as he didn't end up in a car wreck, and secondly to make sure that he killed the guy. Life was rarely perfect.

It just so happened that Bomb was the best hit man around and owed Cutthroat a favour or two.

...JUST SOUTH OF HEAVEN/JIM ODY

Chapter Twenty-Two

Dice and I had been driving for what seemed like hours. Technically it had been hours. Four to be exact if you added the time we'd stopped at the services too. By the time we passed the sign saying we were now entering Cornwall, my backside felt like someone had given me a local anaesthetic without me knowing. I could've bounced up and down on a pin cushion and still felt no pain. I began to fidget around on my chair.

"What's up with you? Ants in your pants?" Dice said momentarily taking his eyes off of the road.

"Says the guy whose been scratching his nuts for the past few hours." I replied doing the buttock walk up and down the seat.

"Only another three quarters of an hour and we'll be there."

"So, what is River Town like then?" I asked realising that of all the places in Devon and Cornwall that I had visited as a child, River Town was not one of them. Cornwall was the last county in the south-west before hitting the Atlantic.

Dice spread his hands out as if stating the title to a play, and said, "A place of dreams and solitude, filled with laidback and big-hearted folk."

"Sounds good."

"The place has tripled in size over the past ten years."

Just then the sound of the Scooby Doo theme tune rang out and made me almost mess my trousers.

"What the hell is that?" Dice asked.

"My phone." I picked it up and noticed the one word - Bitch, and I knew who it was. I know it's childish to change the names when you split up, but hey, that's me! Big-Kid-Caperson-Poo-Pants-Booger-Nose-Pee-Pee-Head-The Third. So sue me.

...JUST SOUTH OF HEAVEN/JIM ODY

"Yes?" I said trying to sound as pissed off as I was. It's funny the way our feelings change so quickly towards past lovers and girl-friends. You start off full of love, lust, and happy emotions, and then when something happens that dissolves the relationship, the mere sound of their name is enough to make you bring up your breakfast and shake your head with regret.

"Caper, can we talk?" the small voice said, and I was surprised that she wasn't already shouting and swearing at me.

"What do you think we're doing now? Whistling *Greensleeves*?" I replied, ever the comedian.

"Let's meet up," she said.

"No can do, I've left town for a while."

"What!?" she said louder. "Where have you gone? How long have you gone for? You didn't say you were leaving yesterday!"

"I'm sorry," I said with sarcasm. "I didn't realise you were my mother."

"Well, I hope you don't fuck your mother!" She spat even louder and more aggressively. She was building up into one – I could just picture her face getting redder and redder. This punctuated our relationship. It was explosive. Either fits of rage or orgasmic convulsions.

"Besides, you're the one who flashed your tits at me and then slammed your door in my face."

"You like my tits."

"I never said I didn't."

"Come back. They miss you."

"Your tits do not miss me," I was getting side-tracked. She was using her voodoo on me again. I had to be strong. "Oh, and I almost forgot..." I paused – dramatically.

"What?" she said, the nice calm voice was suddenly back again.

"Good bye!" I shouted. Beep, I got rid of her with a single press of a rubber button.

Dice looked at me with his eyebrows raised, then looked at the phone as a hint.

"My nan," I said straight-faced.

"Your nan showed you her tits yesterday and now they miss you?" he replied. He wasn't convinced.

"Okay, you're right, it was Jezebel."

"I love it when you call her that, in that not-really-bitter tone."

"To quote you, *'I swear to God that I don't know what the Hell you are talking about most of the time,'*" I replied pretending to be toking on weed too.

"Yes, but you were saying that line in sarcasm, whereas I actually mean every word."

I grinned.

"Let's take this back a bit," he then said. "You never told me you were sniffing around your ex yesterday."

I was already shaking my head to that. "I wasn't sniffing at all."

"Then how did she manage to show you her tits? Was it an accident?"

"I went around her house to tell her it was over."

"When a guy does that, he usually ends up sticky with regret."

"Not me. She was stood at the door and flashed me her tits."

He glanced over at me, "She does have nice tits. If her personality was half as nice, then I'd tell you to marry her."

"But it's not, that's why I left."

"Shame, though."

...JUST SOUTH OF HEAVEN/JIM ODY

For a full minute or so I allowed the montage of her boobs to bounce, bob, and wobble through my mind. I'd dried my mouth many a time over those.

"What about that girl in college you used to follow around like a lost puppy?"

He was exaggerating. "What, Martha?"

"Yeah. You were obsessed with her."

"I was eighteen and she was hot. I'd have been the same if she'd only been plain-looking."

"Wasn't she into some funny stuff?"

I thought back. We were young. We were open-minded. It's just that in the end I realised I wasn't that open-minded.

"Was she the one with the brother?"

"Lots of my ex-girl-friends had brothers, Dice. It's quite normal."

"Yeah, but not ones who walk in on you humping their sister!" He laughed at that. He'd always found that to be funny. I'd probably traumatised the poor lad. He'd had learning-difficulties so I could only wonder what he thought about seeing my white-spotted arse pumping up and down between his sister's legs. He'd just grin at me and dribble milk down his chin. He loved the stuff. It was all he'd drink.

"In many ways she was one that got away," I said with a fondness I knew was born from nostalgia. I do remember the anxiety that crept into our relationship of wondering what she wanted me to do next. Public sex and cross-dressing soon had me calling time on our relationship. But she was that classic ex whose picture book in my memory bank I went to the most. She was exciting, and anxiety is one of those feelings that's debilitating and yet time dilutes it to a mild notion and vague recollection of not feeling great.

...JUST SOUTH OF HEAVEN/JIM ODY

"You should Facebook-stalk her. Unless you already have!" He winked.

"I've not. I don't go back. You know me."

"A missed opportunity, my friend," he mumbled as if it were high wisdom.

We were again caught up in our thoughts for a while.

"So, let me guess. Have you got a cunning plan yet?" I slipped in, whilst picking up a music magazine with a picture of an angry young man on the cover. He was currently the lead singer of the latest and greatest band. Adored by the anarchic youth of today.

"I've got a few ideas, but there's still time to iron a few things out," he replied and I had to smile. He liked to mull things over in his mind. He'd never admit it, but he was a reflector. He took in the details and wrestled them around until the answer bullied its way to the forefront.

He was a good planner. Shit at choosing a woman, but good at bringing a plan together. He was a younger and uglier version of Hannibal from The A-Team.

When I saw the sea, I got this strange feeling I guess everyone who lives as far away from the ocean as I do feels. The nearest I get to feeling sand between my toes is down the local Jewsons. They've banned me from lying out on a sunny summer afternoon in my Speedos and working on my tan. Apparently, it's bad for business.

The sun shone brightly and the sky was the bluest I had ever seen it. Visions of semi naked women rubbing themselves with sun tan lotion, Cornish pasties over-seasoned with black pepper, and ice-cream splattered around greedy faces, all filled up my mind.

In some ways I felt as though I was back home.

...JUST SOUTH OF HEAVEN/JIM ODY

Dice had put on the Beach Boys from his phone and I almost believed we had two surfboards in the back and were looking for the beach to ride the crest of a wave. Searching for a slice of salty wet utopia.

"You really need Scaly Dave back?" he then asked. This perhaps meant that his plan wasn't as water-tight as he hoped.

"You like your balls?" I replied slightly arsy.

"Okay. Not quite the same, but I get your point."

After turning into a long winding lane and getting so close to the sea that I was almost getting wet, a large wooden house became visible. It was idyllic. I'd be quite happy to see it as an Airbnb destination. Although, I had to wonder whether it was sensible to live in a house made from a material that rots easily. Especially in a part of the world notorious for its rainfall. The maintenance bill must be huge.

The porch was beautiful, and you could be forgiven in your disappointment of a lack of hammock and rocking chair ready to whittle wood on. I listened very carefully but heard no harmonicas playing. It was then that I was glad at how things had panned out. It was strange to think this was going to be my new home, even if it was short term. This would be the benchmark to what I wanted, albeit on a smaller scale.

Swindon seemed a lifetime away from this place, though that could have had something to do with the fact that I couldn't remember seeing a roundabout for the last twenty minutes or so. It's also true that without the usual hustle and bustle you've become accustomed to, you can feel dreamy, and anything that seems the total opposite will have you questioning where you have been laying your hat, so to speak. A gorgeously large wooden house with a sea view on the year's sunniest day will certainly have you wondering about things. The need for the stuff left behind. I was certainly debating this, amongst other things.

"Who else lives here?" I asked. "This place is truly amazing."

"Uncle Fresno," Dice said with a sly grin. Then, "You'll never have met anyone quiet like him."

"*Uncle Fresno*, huh? Interesting name," I said. "Is there a story behind it? Isn't he the guy you were shipped off to at college?" Dice didn't respond for a while and just smiled like he was off on some daydream. Just when I didn't think that I was going to get a response, he replied, "There is always a story with Uncle Fresno. And yeah, he took me in. But we don't talk about that time." I shrugged. I didn't need any kiss and tells.

We pulled up next to a dark black 1978 Trans-am complete with golden eagle on the bonnet. It was just like Burt Reynolds' vehicle in the movie *Smokey and the Bandit*.

"Love the wheels," I said all big-eyed and with a drooling mouth.

Dice turned off the engine and the Beach Boys stopped singing about 'doin' it again,' and said, "I thought you would, Caperman. I just thought you would."

"You know me so well." I got out, grabbed a bag and followed Dice up to the porch.

Dice pounded on the large front door, which rung some nice glass wind chimes into a random melody. They looked like folk art panhandled or owned by most people in these parts.

Just then an arm thrust around my throat and pressed a blade of a knife, clearly not made for buttering bread, against it. It was that point of time I was lucky not to empty the contents of my bowels into my jockeys.

"Friend or foe?" a deep American voice bellowed from what seemed like the pits of hell.

...JUST SOUTH OF HEAVEN/JIM ODY

"*Is this a word association game?*" I said unsure.

"Smart-ass," the Barry White voice replied, though without words that were meant to woo me.

"*Uncle Fresno!*" Dice said rather loudly. "How ya' doing?"

"I'm doin' fine, Dyson." The knife was withdrawn from my neck rather more slowly than it had appeared there. "Who is this joker?" Uncle Fresno asked.

"This is Caper. He's my new partner, and I'll tell you later what the plans are," Dice said as Uncle Fresno led us into the house. I thought it a little strange that he wanted to tell Uncle Fresno so quickly about our troubles.

"What the hell have you got there, son, a make-up bag?" Uncle Fresno said to me pointing at one of my bags.

"Told you," Dice whispered nudging me.

"Clothes. I have a habit of changing them when they get dirty," I said.

"That right," he was dismissive of me. I could see the family connection to Dice.

"Ah-huh," I replied. Well, there wasn't really anything else that you could say to that.

Uncle Fresno looked to be around sixty, with long grey hair tied back in a ponytail. Although he was clearly over the hill, and halfway down the other side, there seemed to be a fair bit of muscle packed under his leather waistcoat. He was certainly weathered, but looked like a cool hippy to me, even if I had yet to see him crack his face. Maybe he was still getting over Vietnam.

The house was quiet and dark. Sunrays rested diagonally from the window to the floor, stealing their own spot. The house smelt floral like your Grandma's purse, and there were antiques everywhere.

...JUST SOUTH OF HEAVEN/JIM ODY

"I thought I heard voices," a female voice said from a room beyond my view. I was pleasantly surprised, when I saw the face that matched the voice. Standing about five-ten, she looked like a model, even dressed in dungarees and a flannel shirt. She looked a bit like one of the Walton boys after an impressive sex change, though even more attractive and feminine. I had no idea where she fitted into this strange picture, but she certainly made it more pleasing to my tired eyes.

"Skylar, how are you?" Dice asked embracing her.

"Feeling better now I know you're in one piece," she sighed deeply. You could see in her eyes that she had real love for Dice. I thought Dice had only been away for a few days but it appeared to me now it had been much longer.

"You know me. I always come back in the end." She then caught my eye and threw me a polite smile, which I was happy to return.

"And who is your friend," she asked, pulling away from Dice and giving me the once over.

"This is Caper. He's my new partner."

"How are you doin'?" I said as politely as possible, whilst trying to remain a little Clint Eastwood too. I felt again like I was meeting a blind date for the first time. You know, a little nervous, a little unsure of the procedure, and a feeling that she was disappointed but putting on a brave face.

"Fine, thank you," she replied then turned her attention straight away from me. I had the feeling that I had blown it. It sure as hell was not the first time that I had done that in this lifetime – and I had a sneaky suspicion that it wouldn't be the last time either.

I then remembered Janie. It was presumptuous and possibly even foolhardy to feel guilty, but it was there. Sat prodding at my conscious anyway. Besides, she'd stolen Scaly Dave. I'm not sure whether or not I could forgive her for that.

"Your boy can sleep in the back guest room," the deep voice of Uncle Fresno said flatly, gazing suspiciously at me. I thought it had been an act on the front porch. I now suspected it was just a prelude to what he really wanted to do to me.

"No, he's all right. *Trust me.* He's got the room at the front of the house," Dice said. Uncle Fresno glared at me and looked me up and down with what could be mistaken for real contempt. I checked my flies just in case they were down and my dick was hanging out. As it happens, nothing of the sort was amiss downstairs in the trouser department. That was always a huge relief.

"I'm all right," I said, stupidly thinking what I said would have any ounce of persuasion at all in the decision of this old yank. *What was up with the back guest room?* I thought. Maybe the sheets hadn't been changed or something.

The house was nice. It smelt of wood and vintage things. There was an underlining whiff of oil that greased the parts of mechanical things, and of course incense.

I looked around as Dice nodded to me to follow. I'd had better welcomes in my life.

...JUST SOUTH OF HEAVEN/JIM ODY

Chapter Twenty-Three

Cutthroat and Bomb met in the Covingham Hen public house. It was a spit and sawdust pub with more boarded up windows than ones with glass. It was filled with old-timers sipping bitter and moaning about the smoking ban, youngsters spending the government handouts or cash earnt via illegal activities. But there was something familiar about the place that kept them coming back. They were surrounded by friends, or known associates as they'd be legally described.

Over a couple of beers, they decided to set off for River Town straight away. The place wasn't big so they should be able to find the two idiots quickly.

"Caper Juggins, huh?" Bomb said. "I hear he got sacked yesterday for calling the management a bunch of nazi bastards, or some such. Not just that, but he smoke-bombed the presidential suite and defaced the top knob's Aston Martin. Kid's got balls, alright. Although, he was a corporate puppet for many years so he can't be all that bright."

"Sounds like you wanna date him," Cutthroat said with disgust. "Where'd you hear all that?"

"Our Shelly's girl Theresa. She works with a guy called Fun Mike and he was party to it all!"

"He was there?"

"Well, he was in a meeting at the time, but his mate Ben told him, as he'd heard from Donna."

"Donna?"

"Dollar Donna. The girl who charged a quid for a hand-job at the Christmas party."

"Oh her," he raised his eyebrows. "She made fifty-quid, I heard, right?"

"Yeah, but was off work for a week with RSI. Weak wrists."

...JUST SOUTH OF HEAVEN/JIM ODY

"I can imagine."

Bomber carried on, "He's some sort of hero now."

"Fucking typical. Those boring office twats find anything exciting."

"True that."

Cutthroat took another sip and then said, "What about this Dice character; what do you know about him?"

Bomb shrugged. "Not much as it happens. A bit of a wheeler and dealer, looks kinda funny, but that's about it. It's his uncle that we've got to be careful of. Fresno Santos is an American-Latino from Cuba originally. He grew up in Florida and came over here twenty-years ago when he married some bird from Southampton. She died of a heart-defect a few years back. He's a bit of an inventor and has his place booby trapped. Or so I've heard."

"Where does he live?"

"Who Dice or Fresno?"

"Both."

"They live together. Although there is a chance that Dice has another place somewhere else, but the rumours are a little sketchier. Sounds like he has more than a few secrets."

"Well, that's just flamin' great then isn't it? Why is it that my slut of a wife decides to shag a guy running off to the house of a maniac?"

"Thems the breaks."

Just as they got out of the pub Bomb pulled out an envelope which he carefully smoothed before slipping it into the nearest post box.

"What's that?" Cutthroat asked pointing to where the envelope had just disappeared.

Bomb frowned, "A letterbox?"

...JUST SOUTH OF HEAVEN/JIM ODY

Cutthroat looked up to heaven and shook his head. "No, not the post box, the thing that you put in the post box – and I don't mean an envelope."

Bomb suddenly smiled, or rather beamed, and looked off into a place unseen by others. A place where dreams came true and fantasies were attainable.

"That was an invitation to Janet Jackson. She is going to come to my cousin Porky's Bar Mitzvah."

Cutthroat took a deep breath. Bomb wasn't that stupid, but sometimes he got caught up in these silly things. He probably still believed in Santa. He then said, "Where do I start here?" He placed a hand on Bomb's shoulder and started off slowly and carefully. "Firstly, what makes you think Janet Jackson cares about a streaky piece of piss as yourself enough to get into a private jet and travel the eleven or so hours to accompany you to a family get together? Which then leads me nicely to your cousin Porky, and the small matter that you don't have a Jewish cousin named Porky, right?"

Bomb suddenly looked serious. "Well, he's not a proper cousin."

"So, what is he then? To you I mean?"

Bomb took a deep breath and then replied, "I got friendly with a girl called Claire. Man, she was stacked and firin' on all cylinders, if you know what I mean! And when she licked my—"

Cutthroat held up hand for him to stop, "I don't need these details. Just who Porky is to you."

"Well, he's her cousin."

"Okay and you have known her for how long?"

"Three days."

"And you have met her how many times in those three days?"

"That was the only time."

...JUST SOUTH OF HEAVEN/JIM ODY

"And of course, you have been faithful since, right?"

"Sort of." Bomb was smiling now.

"What does sort of mean?"

"There were only two others since. I turned down the third."

"My, my, what will power you have."

"Not really, she was fucking ugly. Besides I shagged her last year."

Cutthroat shook his head and placed the thumb and forefinger of his left hand over his tiring eyes, and concluded, "So you met a girl, who invited you to her cousin's Bar Mitzvah, you sleep with two other girls, turn another one down – who was fucking ugly – as some dumb sort of token gesture, and then invite a famous pop singer to accompany you."

"Uh-huh," Bomb nods. "Sound's about right."

"What do you think Claire will say when you show up with said singer?"

Bomb holds up his finger. He has obviously thought this one through. "Threesome, I hope!"

"Really?"

"She likes Janet Jackson, so will be so overjoyed that I have brought her along that she won't notice me slipping in my tongue every once in a while!"

"This is a joke, right?"

"Not at all. I might even set up a camera and sell it to the papers. I might go viral having sex with Ms Jackson!"

"Oh, my poor search engine."

"Piss off. I've never nodded off whilst having sex."

Cutthroat ignored him. "I can't believe her Jewish cousin is called Porky."

"I guess at least no-one will eat him, huh? Although, I think it might be a nickname." And that was the smartest thing that he had said all day.

...JUST SOUTH OF HEAVEN/JIM ODY

"Right then, Bomber. Let's get goin'," Cutthroat said as they got to Bomb's car.

"Hey, what are you doing? I have just got to go see some young honey for half an hour. I'll meet you back here then."

"Son, this is my life we are helping out, not yours, and you wanna go play rumpy-pumpy with some two bit whore called Claire!" Cutthroat shook his head in contempt.

"I can't help it if I'm such a hit with the ladies. And I've never paid them a penny, *they want my love for free!*" he said proudly. "And it's not Claire, it's Bonnie."

"And who is Bonnie?"

"That would be Claire's mum." He grinned proudly.

Cutthroat shook his head unable to believe what he was hearing, and then added, "It's going to be some Bar Mitzvah! Does she also like Janet Jackson?"

Bomb shook his head and kept smiling his cheesy proud grin. "Nah, can't fuckin' stand her. She prefers La Toya."

"Figures," was all Cutthroat replied.

Cutthroat made a mental note to find out the date of this Bar Mitzvah; it sounded as though the guests would make the ceremony of a young Jewish lad coming of age a hell of a lot more interesting.

Cutthroat also thought about the other guy. His name was O'Donald. He didn't know any more than that. He was of Irish descent and always wore black. Even his car was black. He lived in Taunton and was already in Cornwall staking out the club.

He and Bomb would look to get that pocket-watch. But if for whatever reason things got out of hand, Cutthroat was happy in the knowledge that O'Donald would shoot that fucker Caper and his fucking side-kick.

O'Donald had been a sniper in the army. He'd done two tours. Or so the stories went. But no one really knew. He was a mystery. He was hard to track down and would cost half of the worth of the pocket-watch.

His orders were also to shoot any witnesses. It would be a clean job. That he could be sure.

...JUST SOUTH OF HEAVEN/JIM ODY

Chapter Twenty-Four

I was ready to take a nap right about then. The journey had been long and the day was somewhat exciting, but I could think of nothing better than an early night snuggled up, the window open with the cool sea breeze gently whispering over me. I loved this part of the country. Everything was done at a slower speed.

Dice showed me to my room. It was bigger than I was used to, though maybe a little bit clean and magnolia for my tastes. But there was a large double bed and a cheap CD player on the dresser. So really, I could want for nothing.

I slipped out to the van and brought my two large bags in. One was filled with clothes and the other with CD's and a handful of books I hadn't read, along with a couple of my favourites.

It's very easy to feel home sick, and even easier to feel silly about it, so I slipped on a CD that would make me feel better, and take me back to a time of happiness. The CD of choice was Poison's 'Look what the cat dragged in,' by no means a musical classic, but the familiar tunes of young love, sneaking out and pretending to be cool was what I loved back when I was thirteen and had the whole of my life ahead of me. It's easy to think that back then if you could've seen just how far you had got in twenty-odd years, then you may very well have been filled with regret and disappointment, and certainly of a willingness to do things differently. But in truth it's been a lot of fun getting not very far in this life. My only true regrets are that I didn't worry so much about the consequences of my actions.

Uncle Fresno shuffled in to my room and gave me his evil eye again. Silent, he looked accusingly at me. I wondered whether he was trying some Jedi-mind trick on me.

...JUST SOUTH OF HEAVEN/JIM ODY

I wanted to compliment him on his house. "You look nice," I said as an ice breaker and realised from his look of horror what I'd just said. "I mean your house. Your house is nice."

Uncle Fresno looked at me like I'd just asked to see his wrinkly old todger and replied in absolute amazement, "You're fuckin' strange."

Just as I thought I couldn't feel any more uncomfortable, Uncle Fresno came shuffling over purposely as if ready to make an attack on me with the absence of witnesses.

"You brandish that knife again and I might be forced to kick you in the nuts and run like a girl!" I smiled - albeit nervously.

Uncle Fresno sneered at me and then said slowly and a bit too calmly, "Son, you wouldn't have time to piss your pants and call for your mommy!" *Christ*, I thought, *here we go*.

Uncle Fresno reached into the pocket of his slacks and pulled out a pipe. He then pulled out a pouch of what was probably tobacco and proceeded to push it into the pipe with his wrinkled thumb. I sat waiting for him to come at me again.

"Who the hell are these glam girlies, Pretty Boy Floyd?" he asked still not cracking his face anymore, and I had to smile. The fact that he knew about the glam music genre was pretty cool, but the fact that he had heard of Pretty Boy Floyd was even better.

"Poison," I replied.

"Ahh," he said as though that explained it. "These bastards had that annoying song, '*Unskinny* something-or-other'..."

"*Bop*," I corrected. "*Unskinny Bop*."

"...that's it, along with that *Cherry Pie* song by Warrant, collectively ruined music of the early nineties. I thought I'd escaped it by leaving America and coming over here, but it turns out you Brits liked it too! Give me some Motorhead, The Stones, or Metallica any day. Thank fuck Nirvana came along and sent those sissy-boys packing!"

"Is that a fact?" I said. I loved Americans; they were less snobby when it came to music. They'd hum Dolly Parton and then bust out MC Hammer like it wasn't a thing. Over here you were meant to only listen to one genre per person. It was some stupid unspoken law.

"Son, that's a Goddamn fact. What did you think I liked? Elvis fucking Presley?"

"For the love of God, I hoped not."

He looked through a handful of CD's I had and even took a quick look at the back of a couple. I felt like I was being investigated. I probably was. He looked up at me then smiled, "You take good care of Dice, uh-," he clicked his fingers trying to remember my name.

"Caper," I prompted.

"-Caper - uh, yeah. He likes to live a life of danger. Just let me know you've got his back." I could actually see love and hurt in those old eyes. He looked like he'd really lived life well. There was something a little Nick Nolte about him.

"I've got his back," I confirmed.

Uncle Fresno got a lighter out and flipped the cog with his thumb producing a flame likened to that of a flamethrower.

"Jesus, you like fire?" I asked raising my eyebrows to the large dancing flame. "Last time I saw a flame like that it had a large homemade dummy on it and half a village around waiting for the fireworks to go off!"

He smiled wisely at me and said, "Fire is a wonderful thing. We use it to keep warm, to cook with, to get rid of rubbish and for its own favourite use - to destroy. Don't ever be fooled into thinking that we control fire - no - fire lets us use it. When it wants to use us, there is nothing we can do but either admire the great force that it is, or try our damnedest and fight it." He sat back and took a long suck of his pipe whilst we both pondered this fact.

He looked across at me again and I could tell he had another burning question to ask. When he spoke, it was hard to detect if there was any humour in his voice. "Why have you got your Granny's beads 'round you neck? Truth is I wasn't trying to scare you earlier, I was going to rid you of them damn girly things," he pointed with his pipe at my beads.

"You don't think they're cool?" I pressed.

"Cool is one letter away from fool, son," he mumbled and sucked his pipe long and hard this time. Smoke danced up to the ceiling, as he asked, "You one of them transvesty-things?"

I laughed out loud at that. "No, I'm not," I replied when I finally quit laughing.

"You got small girlie wrists and a thumb ring," he stated.

"What does that prove?" I replied raising my voice just a little.

"Ah!" Uncle Fresno chuckled. "You're a girl, disguised as a dumb fuck!"

"You ever thought about doin' stand-up at a comedy club?"

I was just thinking up some pearls of wisdom to share with Uncle Fresno, now he clearly wasn't going to slit my throat, when the aching feeling in my bladder told me that it was about time I emptied it.

"Hey, you got a john around here?" I asked getting up.

He pointed out of the door, which was not surprising seeing as my bedroom had no en-suite. It wasn't considered good etiquette to urinate out of windows around these parts. "Take a right, down the landing and it's the first one on the left."

"Cheers," I replied because my mum always raised me to be nothing if not polite. Speaking of which, I knew I had to call her and let her know I was safe. She loves me. She shows this in the way she threatens to kill me often.

I had just left the bedroom when my mobile went off, I looked down and the name had my heart beating almost out of my chest. Janie.

"Hi Janie," I said trying to remain calm. "How are you doing?"

"Caper, my husband knows," she said desperately and a little too worried for my liking.

I tried to be light-hearted, "And he doesn't mind?"

There was a pause that sounded a bit like she was taking a big gulp of air. "He's going to kill you, Caper. You have to get that pocket-watch, then you could try denying it…"

"I've done judo, you know," I said, and it was true, though not since I was eleven but that was beside the point.

"I don't think he cares about a cuddling martial art. His mate doesn't care either what with him being a professional hit man and all that!" This was worse than I thought.

"It's quite a tough discipline, I'll have you know. I was a junior blackbelt. Hold on, *what?* A hit-man?"

"A hit-man. You know, like a guy who kills people. Look the pocket-watch is a in a large box with brass handles, an oak finish about the size of a body, with velvet lining."

"That doesn't sound like a box so much as a coffin to me."

"Yeah. That's it. It's in a coffin."

I rubbed my forehead and nearly pissed my pants there and then. "I have two guys, a professional fighter and a professional hit-man after me, and my only chance of survival is to break into the cellar of a notorious gangster and retrieve a pocket-watch from a coffin – it's not exactly another day at the office, is it?"

"Look, be careful, Caper."

...JUST SOUTH OF HEAVEN/JIM ODY

"Thanks, but I wouldn't count on seeing me alive again." I was getting a little Jack Dee with her, but life wasn't exactly a major giggle-fest at that point in time. "How's Scaly Dave?"

"Who?" She sounded confused.

"My fish."

"He's fine."

"Can you put him on the phone?"

"What?"

"Scaly Dave, can you put the phone up to the tank?"

There was a second or so of silence before she huffed. "Here he is."

"Dave? Are you there? Hang in there, buddy. Hang in there."

I heard the phone move. "Anything else?"

"I'll have fries with that," I grinned as I said it.

"D'you always joke when you're nervous?"

"Mostly."

"Okay then. Be positive."

"No offence, but the grass is a little greener on your side of the fence right about now."

She was silent again, and I was a little worried maybe I'd upset her – even though I was the one being hunted and likely to have his balls swung in the air by some bad dudes before the day was out, but there you go, women can be sensitive. And mean.

And then she said, "I guess so."

"Are you going to see me again?" I then asked thinking this was maybe the last time that we may speak for a while – if ever again.

"As long as you stay alive. I've a fish to give you."

"Good answer." And that was that.

...JUST SOUTH OF HEAVEN/JIM ODY

Chapter Twenty-Five

Sammy was on the phone to the costume shop again, and his heavily sweating palms were making the job of holding the receiver all the more difficult.

"Hey, Mr Piper, it's Bob again." He was using a false name but of course they wouldn't know that.

"Bob Di Niro? Robert?" the croaky voice replied.

"Ah ha. Bob. That's right." Why did he always do this?

"You talkin' ta me?" the guy said in a strange accent. Sammy wasn't quite sure what that was all about. Maybe it was a new thing taught on one of those How-to-keep-your-customers-happy seminars – Accents, and how to impress.

"I suppose so. There isn't anyone else here," Sammy pointed out.

"Then who the Hell else are you talkin' to?" the guy then added with a chuckle.

"No one, I think we established it's only the two of us."

"Then you must be talkin' to me!"

Sammy then remembered what he'd rung the guy for. "So, what about those suits that you promised me? You got them yet?"

"Ahh, yeah the suits," his voice slipped back into a slightly Northern accent again. "What do you want suits for anyway?"

"Do you question everyone that buys a costume?"

"No, not all of them."

"So, have you got them?"

"The one's you wanted?"

"Yes."

"No."

"What do you mean, no? What have you got then?"

"I've got you four identical suits of the finest quality."

...JUST SOUTH OF HEAVEN/JIM ODY

"Ah ha, and what do they look like?"

"I'm Popeye, the sailor man," he sung and added, 'Toot toot' at the end.

Sammy couldn't quite believe this. "You want us dressed as sailors."

"Not sailors. Popeye."

"What's the difference?" Sammy said raising his voice.

"Popeye was a hero! You want to be a hero?" Sammy did want to be a hero – but sailors? Come on, what was Randell going to say to that?

"You little fucker," was all he could think of to reply.

And then the guy started with the accent again, "Forget about it!"

"Forget about what?"

"Never mind. Look, these outfits are identical. You'll look great at your stag-do, or whatever the fuck you're doing."

"Sailors..." he mumbled shaking his head.

"Popeye, sir," the guy corrected.

"Okay, when can I pick them up?"

"In an hour, sir. Do you want the pipes and hats too?"

"Damn right I do! You got tins of spinach too?"

"What?" the guy said with shock.

"You said they were Popeye, so surely you have tins of spinach, right?"

"You can pick them up from Tescos. We can't hold tins of produce on account of health and safety."

"Not real ones, prop ones," Sammy added. "It'd be a nice touch."

"So would getting a handjob, but you don't get one of those either."

"Fine."

"Okay. See you later."

...JUST SOUTH OF HEAVEN/JIM ODY

When Sammy got off of the phone he was feeling a little down and decided that the only way to feel better was to ring the other two of his criminal cohorts, and hope they too were a sack of shit when it came to unorganised crime. Sammy had visions of retiring early and counting his cash on some exotic island. At this rate he'd be stacking shelves at Iceland.

Princess was sure to be doing fine, but Boston, well, he was sure to be fucking up his plans. Hell, with him the engine is always running but there's never anyone behind the wheel.

Boston's phone rang and rang without answer. Boston had just received an email stating that it was impossible to lick your own elbow. For the first fifteen minutes Boston had been trying to do this, and for the last fifteen minutes Boston had been trying to unhook his bracelet from his earring, which had somehow managed to get entwined whilst he was thrusting his tongue out at the spider web tattoo on his left elbow. His arm was beginning to ache, and every time it dropped it pulled at his earlobe. This was an issue he hadn't been expecting today.

Sammy cursed at his mobile and rang Princess instead. Whilst conceding that the big pussy was bound to have everything in hand for his boss. God, he hated the cocksucker.

"Hey, Princess. How's things?" he said through gritted teeth.

"Are you talking through gritted teeth?" Princess asked.

Sammy gave a nervous smile he was happy that Princess couldn't see. "Don't be daft. I'm sucking on a sweet."

"A sweet what?"

"What! No! I wasn't... I mean..."

"Okay, Mr Cranky-Pants. I'm joking. Chill out. Also, I am fine, thank you awfully for asking."

"Good. Good. You got the getaway car alright?"

"Well, it's in hand, Sammy-boy." That sounded like a good old honest-to-god cover up. A huge lie, so that was good.

...JUST SOUTH OF HEAVEN/JIM ODY

"Something wrong, Princess?"

"No, no. Everything will be F-I-N-E – fine. How are our ghastly suits?"

Sammy couldn't help but chuckle. "Probably more to your liking."

"Oh, yeah. I love big baggy boiler suits. They have padded knees?"

"What?" Princess loved to wind Sammy up.

"Never mind."

"Okay, anyway, gotta run. Smell you later!"

"Toodle-oo, Scooby-Doo!"

It sounded promising but Sammy still needed to ring Boston just to make sure that he was in a worse state. It was a bad state of affairs when you didn't always have to succeed, you just had to be slightly better than the other two. He tried Boston's mobile again, but it still rang and rang. Of course, Sammy wasn't to know that poor Boston, in trying to unhitch his bracelet from his earring, had now caught the bracelet on his right hand in his eyebrow ring. As his left hand didn't reach around to his earring, his only choice was to pull his right hand as far as his eyebrow ring would let him and try to free his left wrist bracelet from his ear. And then with his free left hand he could set about freeing his right wrist bracelet. Boston's time was running out as he was due to do a three-hour shift at Beninni's Pizzeria in an hour before meeting the rest of them.

He was beginning to think that this crime lark was an awful lot of work.

...JUST SOUTH OF HEAVEN/JIM ODY

Chapter Twenty-Six

After I'd relieved my bladder I went down to the kitchen where I could hear Dice talking excitedly to Skylar.

"...she was a stunner, wasn't she, Caperman?" he said as I walked in. I'd heard tales of fabrication before, but his abilities to stretch the truth were quite impressive.

"Who? Janie?" I said, as she was the only lady besides Skylar that I could think of that could be labelled as a stunner.

"No, Caper! God, it's always me, me, me with you, isn't it," he smiled mockingly shaking his head in fake disgust. I didn't detect any sarcasm, so I had to assume he'd deluded himself.

"Then pray tell, my eagle-eyed women-scout, just who is this stunner that I am meant to be backing you up with?"

"Greta," he said like it was obvious and I would feel so stupid as to not remember this vision of beauty.

"Who?"

Dice looked at Skylar, "Not only does he like women's jewellery, but he's unobservant and incredibly slow."

"I have never met a girl that has said, 'Hi, my name is Greta.' Where might I have met said angel-winged innocence?" I pressed.

"How about last night?"

"How about, your description uses some creative license."

"The forked tongue of jealousy speaks loudest," he said.

I grabbed my phone. "You sent me pictures of her naked, so let Skylar be the judge.

"Oh, let me see," Skylar grinned.

"Nope! Why've you not deleted them yet, Caper?"

"I was asking myself the same question. I didn't go sending you pictures of Janie, did I?"

"Janie?" Skylar then looked interested.

...JUST SOUTH OF HEAVEN/JIM ODY

"She stole his fish!" Dice laughed.

"Back up," Skylar said with hands out. "Fish?"

"I met a girl last night. She came back to mine. We had sex and she stole my fish."

"Seriously, she stole your fish!"

Dice then started laughing loudly. "Maybe she thought it was an elaborate fairground game! Fuck the sorry-arse guy and win a fish!"

"Not funny," I said shaking my head.

"It's actually a little funny," Skylar agreed and she high-fived Dice.

When they had stopped doing a stupid dance, I turned and said to Dice, "She told her husband."

"Well, there's a revelation!" Dice shouted a little too loud in my book.

Sklar added, "Ooh, you bad boy!"

"No, you don't understand," I started. "He's after me—"

"Figures," Dice cuts in.

"And wants to kill me—"

"Also figures."

"And has a hit man after us too—"

Dice looked over all wide-eyed, "Oh, now it's *us*, huh? Shit, that's a whole lot of trouble." He shook his head and then said, "You know what? Greta might've been ugly—"

"Trust me, she was."

"But you don't see no hit man after me, do you?" He had a point, I guess.

"Well, you do, but not because of her. You'll probably have the RSCPA after you because of her. Besides you've been itching your nether regions ever since."

"Coincidence."

...JUST SOUTH OF HEAVEN/JIM ODY

Then in came Uncle Fresno. "What's all this about ugly women, hit men, and itchy parts?"

Skylar was still finding the situation amusing, something that I certainly was not. "Well, this dumbass here with the shaggy hair is where you'll find the ugly woman and itchy nuts, and Mr Girlybeads there is where you'll find the hit-man. I say throw 'em both in the cellar and let them fight it out to the death!" She roared with laughter; I concluded that I was going off of her, and fast.

As Fresno rubbed his chin you could hear the sound of stubble that seemed to be a little later than five o'clock. "For a pair of business partners and friends, you two don't seem to have gotten off to the best of starts," he stated. "A hit man could really be bad for business you know. Itchy nuts can be bad for your health. It brought a lot of good men down in 'Nam." His mind wandered off to another place for a while. Then just like flicking a switch he was back. "It's lucky for you I'm here."

Dice then piped up, "And what the hell are you going to do, old man?"

"I'm not scratching them for you, that's for sure. They new?"

"What, my nuts? No, I've had them since birth!" He made that awful laughing sound.

Uncle Fresno shook his head in disbelief. "And you wonder why you only attract ugly women."

When Dice stopped laughing, he then mumbled, "They are new."

"They might be too tight."

"What?"

"Aside from dirty women, another big cause of itchy nuts is underwear that's too tight."

...JUST SOUTH OF HEAVEN/JIM ODY

"You didn't see her," I added. This got a glare from Dice. I thought it only best to show Uncle Fresno the picture.

He nodded. "Her face is odd, but she has a nice body."

"That's being nice."

"She knew what she was doing." Dice winked. I glanced at Skylar who rolled her eyes.

"Well, that's something," Uncle Fresno said. "Go change your smalls and you might be okay. If not. get yourself to the clinic."

"Will do," Dice winked again. He was doing a lot of winking. It didn't suit him.

"I'll help you out with these bad men, I suppose."

I was surprised at this response, as there seemed to be no humour, but as I looked, Fresno was chuckling. He then said slowly, "Son, I may be as athletic looking as Ozzy Osbourne on a bender, but I've still got brains and if I get to go toe-to-toe, then I'll be all Anthony Joshua on their asses!" To prove this, he threw a couple of jabs and did an Ali shuffle.

"Yeah, I hear ya," Dice conceded. "Loud and clear."

"You young bucks," he laughed. "Ya think that you can take on the world. Look, you got a couple of hours, I'll have a plan by then."

"Here he goes," Dice said sarcastically.

"Look, you little fuckers," Fresno said which I was beginning to realise was his way to sound overly aggressive. "There are some weird folk around here. More weirdo than you two! You hear about the men disappearing?"

I nodded. "Dice was telling me."

"It's the sea air. Makes some folk go crazy!" He even made a crazy sign with his finger in a circular motion around the side of his head. "Then there were those fucking idiots who broke into that casino!"

...JUST SOUTH OF HEAVEN/JIM ODY

"They are Dice's heroes," I said.

"Figures," Fresno agreed. "Why the fuck were they dressed as cowboys?"

Dice looked like he was about to say something, but then appeared to consciously decide against it. That was unusual for him.

Fresno made a point of grunting loudly, and off he went.

"So, here's another thing," I said. "The pocket-watch is in a coffin."

"Well, that's just great then. Is it big enough for two?" I think that sarcasm was starting to get the better of him. Maybe he could be an after-dinner speaker.

So I said, "I think that sarcasm is starting to get the better of you."

Skylar picked up a glass from the side and filled it with some cola. "You two are funny, you know that?" We both said nothing. I'd spent many years staying out of confrontation and to now be burdened with what seemed like a death-sentence was a scary prospect.

"Let's go watch some TV," Dice then said, like this might be the big answer to everything.

"You want to watch TV?" Again, I knew Dice was mulling things over, but I wanted action. I wanted to get to that club, get that pocket-watch, get Scaly Dave back, and go and hide someplace that didn't allow thugs, hitmen, or ugly woman. I wasn't so sure about Fresno sorting out our plan of action, but I guess I was going to have to roll with the punches on this one.

We were watching a music video where a young black girl was gyrating her body extremely well to the fast beat of the song. It was in a quite erotic and mesmerising way. It detracted my concentration from the song, which may or may not have been a good thing.

...JUST SOUTH OF HEAVEN/JIM ODY

I felt the burden of it all. I didn't know what to do.

I wished Scaly Dave was here. He would know the answer. He'd tell me my options.

...JUST SOUTH OF HEAVEN/JIM ODY

Chapter Twenty-Seven

The 'Graceland' sign at the end of the drive may have pictures forming in your mind of large mansions, landscaped grounds with blooming gardens, and sunny days in Memphis, Tennessee. This 'Graceland' was a white cottage halfway between Falmouth and River Town, Cornwall. The grounds were best described as abandoned and other than daisies and dandelions, no other flower had been spotted since a clump of daffodils in 1987. Even they'd decided not to return the following spring, and it had been concluded that they were most likely Missing In Action.

Elvis stood over the purple felt-covered pool table with the cue stick in his hand and wondered whether it was possible to hit the number 9 ball with his cue ball. Aaron had unintentionally snookered him with two of his balls. The only hope he had was with the help of at least two cushions, and although he had indeed successfully completed harder shots than this before, neither time had he actually meant to do it.

"Good luck, honey," Presley said suppressing a chuckle. Sometimes it was good that Elvis was put in his place, whether or not the other person realised that they were doing it.

"You make your own luck in this world," he said as he leant over the table and rested his chin on the smooth wooden shaft of the cue. His idea was to send the ball down past the two covering balls and towards the right angle of the corner where it would hit one cushion, bounce off onto the other one, and gently roll up to his number 9. Not only would it hit it, but it would come to rest so close to his ball that Aaron would have to also play off the cushion to hit either of his remaining balls.

The king was singing out about going to a party at a county jail. It blasted out of the speakers from a large jukebox which

...JUST SOUTH OF HEAVEN/JIM ODY

was situated in the corner of the room. It had a large Elvis figurine on top dressed in a white jumpsuit and holding a microphone out in front of him. It was Elvis's pride and joy. He'd bought it at auction for £500, and spent another £200 doing it up. He thought it was worth it. Presley thought the money might've been better spent on the house, but she wasn't about to bring it up.

Elvis's ball missed Aaron's two balls, hit one cushion and hit the other before rolling just short of his number 9 ball. It came to a stand still in perfect line for Aaron to slot his ball into the middle pocket. Aaron did this and with two shots still left had screwed back hitting the black 8 ball close to the pocket. This left him in line to slot his remaining ball into the far corner pocket.

"Wanker," Elvis said as Aaron knocked in the black ball and won his third game out of five.

"Thank you very much!" Aaron said with a lip curl and a shake of his hips. "Looks like the pizza is on you, Elvis!"

Presley walked up to her defeated boyfriend and kissed his cheek. "Never mind. You were unlucky. Anyway, I'll have cheese and tomato, thanks!"

Their house was owned by Elvis and Aaron. Their parents had given them the money to purchase it a few years earlier. Presley had now lived there for a little over six months. She stayed over one night and never left. Her parents didn't much like Elvis and disowned her. She didn't seem to care, although Aaron had seen her sat alone crying a couple of times. Elvis said she was better without them. Aaron wasn't so sure. Presley remained tight-lipped. She had plans. Not all of them included a dead singer.

Aaron walked over with the handset to the telephone and slapped it in his brother's hand, whilst making the letter L with

...JUST SOUTH OF HEAVEN/JIM ODY

his thumb and forefinger against his own forehead and saying loudly, "Loooseeeer!"

***

Over at the pizza parlour of Beninni's Pizza, Boston had just started his shift and was thinking reluctantly about the lack of weaponry for the night ahead. This was why he gave the first customer a pizza that hadn't even been cooked, and was now oblivious to the ringing telephone. He didn't have much going on in his head, but what he did have was a heap of worry.

Beninni's Pizza was about as Italian as the British national anthem. Beninni himself was actually a middle-aged guy called Ben Drove, though was also known as Dover (as in Ben Dover), or Diddy (as in "Ben drove." "Did he?"). Each employee took turns making the pizzas, answering the phone, and delivering the pizzas.

It was now Boston's turn to answer the phone. He was stood in front of the phone. His sole purpose was to only answer the phone, but as he was deep in thought, he was not able to complete his duties sufficiently.

A loud trill made everyone but Boston stop. "Does someone hear something?" Dover asked looking at Boston then looking at the phone as a hint.

Tubs, the overweight co-worker of Boston was about to give a customer his change, but at the last moment withdrew his money filled hand and looked over at Boston too. The customer was left with his empty hand out waiting for his change.

"Whatever is that noise?" Tubs said and the phone rang on and on.

"D'ya think I could get my change?" the guy said almost with humour.

...JUST SOUTH OF HEAVEN/JIM ODY

Tubs placed a hand to his ear. "You'll have to speak up over the phone, sir. If someone got the phone then I'd be able to hear you and give you back your change, but someone doesn't seem to realise that they have one single job to do, which isn't brain surgery? Is it, sir?"

The guy shook his head and looked beckoningly at Tubs' change filled hand, almost trying to use telekinesis to make it jump into his own. "Uh, no," was all he said.

"But look at him, huh? All he has to do is pick up the fuckin—" He noticed a woman who had just walked in. "Excuse my language, madam – but no, he just stands there in a trance."

The phone kept ringing. "I can't stand to watch this," Dover said and walked past the phone. He went out the back to where a newspaper sat. He picked it up and turned to the centre pages to see what might be on the television later.

"And still it rings," Tubs states looking at the woman now who's a lot more attractive than the guy waiting for his change. The guy was also getting redder in the face with rage.

"Can I have my change?" he said with anger.

Tubs turned to him. "Did you just say that with anger? Perhaps through gritted teeth?"

"Maybe. Now, my change…"

"What do you mean maybe? Do you not know how you speak? Tell me, sir, are you able to answer a phone? I'm beginning to have doubts!"

"My change!"

"Boston! Will you get that phone?"

Then the lady with blonde hair so bleached that it was almost white piped up, "Are you serving here, 'cause I could always go someplace else, you know?"

"What's your problem?" Tubs said annoyed. What was it with people today? Does no one have any patience anymore?

...JUST SOUTH OF HEAVEN/JIM ODY

"GIVE ME MY CHANGE!" The guy was now leaning over the counter and trying to grab it from Tubs.

"Sir, step back from the counter; you are invading my space which is a public offence within the confounds of this pizzeria."

And the phone kept ringing. And ringing.

Back at 'Graceland,' Elvis was starting to get a little pissed off. Not only did he lose at pool, and then have to ring for pizza, and pay, but no one there was answering his call. What was it with these people? Did they not have the ability to answer a phone? Were they retarded?

He looked at the phone like it was its fault, huffed and tried again.

Back at Beninni's, Tubs was asking this very question. "Boston, are you retarded? Can't you just pick up the phone? Please. There you go, I even said it nicely!"

Then suddenly the glassy-eyed look suddenly shone with a light and Boston came to life. "Is that the phone?"

"Well, Hall-a-fucking-llu-yah. He's alive!" The guy was still leaning and grabbing for his change.

"That's it!" Tubs said, snatching back the pizza. "Under section 12, line 5 of our safety regulations, I am using my rights to refuse to serve you, sir. You were warned!"

"But I've paid you! You have my change in your hand."

"Too bad, sir. You should've thought of that before you started grabbing and groping over the counter. You're lucky I don't do you for sexual conduct!"

"WHAT?"

"Yes, sexual conduct!"

The guy in disbelief turned to where Dover was now sitting with his feet up and staring at the topless model on page 3. "Hey, you back there! This guy won't serve me!"

...JUST SOUTH OF HEAVEN/JIM ODY

Without taking his eyes away from the naked breasts, Dover replied, "Were you leaning over the counter, sir?"

"He's got my change!"

"I repeat, were you leaning over the counter?"

"I was trying to get my change."

"Well, there you go then. I'm going to have to ask you to leave now." Though he still remained transfixed with the girl in the paper with legs like a young gazelle and come-to-bed eyes.

"B-but I haven't…"

"Do I have to call the police?"

The guy slammed his fist down on the counter and stormed out.

Boston picked up the phone. "Beninni's Pizzeria – for the perfect pizza around, Beninni's the best in town, home deliveries or walk in to buy, our prices and quality will make you smile! Good evening, my name is Boston, and how can I help you?" All he heard was the dialling tone. "Some people are just so impatient!" He said slamming down the phone.

Tubs handed the woman her pizza and she handed him a twenty-pound note…and then the phone rang again, but Boston was back in his trance.

"Do I hear the phone ringing?" Tubs turned to Boston.

The woman shook her head, looked up to heaven, and said, "Keep the fucking change, you idiots!"

"Charming," Tubs said under his breath.

It took another ten minutes before Boston was able to answer the phone to Elvis and successfully take his order.

...JUST SOUTH OF HEAVEN/JIM ODY

Chapter Twenty-Eight

Dexter loved pizza and he had slowly been working his way around the fast food joints in River Town for the past couple of years. He'd had a scam going which worked every time and was really just going back to times before take away shops or corner shops or any kind of place which required a transaction between two willing parties.

It wasn't entirely true that Dexter didn't have a home. Currently his place of residence was an old abandoned wine cellar in a warehouse next door to the nightclub, 'Heaven,' though in truth the whole of River Town was his home.

So, stashed away he had himself a phone book and a postcode book, both of which he had on long-term hire from the local library, without their knowledge, that was. He was a regular visitor to the library. They had the best toilets. There was no place in town he'd rather take a shit.

The scam was basically ordering a pizza and then mugging them. Dexter would spend twenty pence on phoning the fast food vendor of his choice from a secluded phone box. This was the hardest part as most phone boxes had been taken away now. Some were even houses for free books! Dexter, after the greetings and pleasantries would give them a name, telephone number, and the address and then on demand the post code. Sometimes they wanted the postcode and then wanted Dexter to match the address – fine. Sometimes they even asked for his telephone number so as to ring him straight back – fine, he gave the telephone number of the public phone box that he was using.

The trick was to either pick an address nearby or try and find a secluded spot not too far away. He sure as hell didn't want to work too much for his food. He would get a job if he wanted to do that.

...JUST SOUTH OF HEAVEN/JIM ODY

On the occasions he wasn't able to afford the twenty pence, then he would have to forget about step one and go straight to step two: Delivery-Boy Mugging.

Ethically this wasn't entirely legal and would certainly be frowned upon by most levels of society, and certainly by the laws of Her Majesty Herself, but at the end of the day Dexter had to eat, and just who was losing out? The shops weren't going to miss one pizza in a night were they? The delivery person wasn't usually harmed too much as their mopeds weren't exactly grease lightening, so when they were pushed off, or noosed off with rope, or hit with an old boot, skidded on oil, etc. they were usually dazed long enough so as Dexter could make off with the pizza.

Today had been a long one for Dexter. He had stood on the corner of Union Square all afternoon singing songs like AC/DC's *You shook me all night* and Free's *Alright Now*, along with a couple for the ladies like Britany Spears' *Hit me baby One More Time* and Aqua's *Barbie Doll* – it was important to sing songs for everyone to enable him to have the most chance at making money. In fact, the latter songs always brought him in more money. It almost made him sick. Did they not appreciate music anymore? His hands hurt from strumming his string-less guitar and his throat hurt from the vocal ranges of oral gymnastics that he'd put it through. When you go from Lemmy's gravely throat rasping and whiskey-soaked vocals of *Ace Of Spades* to the high-pitched harmonic alco-pop vocals of Aqua, well, you really are asking for it, even if you were a professional like Dexter.

Despite the blood and guts he put into his busking, he had around fifteen coins in total from the afternoon's work, and then when he came out of the local convenience store with his bottle of cider clutched tightly in both arms, all he had left was

...JUST SOUTH OF HEAVEN/JIM ODY

seventeen pence. So he was going to have to switch to plan B – straight to the mugging.

When you have no money, you have to sometimes rely on statistics and patterns to enable you to profit the most, like what songs bring in the most money, what street to sing on, what time of day and also the information that helped him right now: This included, what the most common route from the pizza parlour was.

Twenty-five minutes passed before the deep chugging sound of the 50cc moped came around the corner a lot slower than the sound would have you believe with a large guy huddled over the handle bars, head down and elbows in the air in some comical cartoon pose. He looked like he wouldn't look out of place in the Mario Kart game.

Boston never did like deliveries. In truth he wasn't a great fan of answering the phone nor serving the customers, but since last Monday night when some idiot had lassoed him and pulled him right off of the moped, he was now very cautious. He was almost ninja-like as he scanned the horizon looking for some Clint Eastwood, Man-with-no-name type attacking innocent people trying to earn an honest living. Of course, if the heist came off tonight, then he may never have to ride one of these death traps again.

That's when he felt the rope around his body, and he only had time to mutter the words, "Oh, crap!" when he felt himself stop in mid air as the moped carried on in front of him. He hit the ground with a heavy bump which knocked the wind out of him, and by the time he looked up all he could see was a guy in a black baggy jumper, baggy trousers and most notably a KFC bucket on his head as a disguise making off with his pizza. The very same one he was due to deliver to a guy by the name of Elvis. What a weird day this was turning into.

...JUST SOUTH OF HEAVEN/JIM ODY

Watching this spectacle was Cutthroat and Bomb who were on their way to get a pizza. They both looked at each other speechless and started laughing. It was the funniest thing they'd seen in a long time!

"Fair play, buddy!" Cutthroat shouted as Dexter turned, tipped his KFC bucket, took a bow and ran off in to the night with his pizza under one arm and his half bottle of cider in the other.

"What's the world coming to?" said the Hitman looking at the big guy getting to his feet and hobbling over to his moped.

"Bomb. There are no honest gentlemen left on this earth."

"Lord, ain't that the truth." And off they went to Beninni's pizza for a large Hawaiian pizza and some garlic bread.

...JUST SOUTH OF HEAVEN/JIM ODY

Chapter Twenty-Nine

To say that I had rumbles of hunger in my belly would be an understatement. I was beginning to wonder whether these people actually ate, and that the talk of supper a while ago was a joke at my expense.

I was just about to broach the subject of food when Skylar's pretty voice rang out from the kitchen like the sweet angel of mercy, telling us that supper was about to be served. I looked across at Dice who was fast asleep. Typical. It was so laidback he could relax even with our impending doom hanging over us.

I was so hungry at that point that I would have pushed women and children out of the way to get to the food. A wanted man has the weight of the world on his shoulders and must eat as much as possible to gain the energy to fight to the death – or run and hide for hours until the world is a safer place.

I sat down opposite Skylar, with Dice next to me, Uncle Fresno at one end and an empty place at the end nearest to myself.

I was just musing to myself that this was probably for somebody's imaginary friend when a blond lady in her late thirties walked in. She was the same build as Skylar and could easily pass as her older sister. I wasn't quite sure how she fitted in to this strange little gathering but was getting used to surprises. I concluded that since being around Dice I had encountered a handful of very attractive ladies – as opposed to ex-girl-friends that felt the need to sleep with my friends.

Uncle Fresno then cleared his throat, which I couldn't help but turn my full attention to him. Then he spoke, "Caper, this is Sian - my beautiful wife." At first, I was shocked, but then after a little thought I was not surprised. The old codger had something

...JUST SOUTH OF HEAVEN/JIM ODY

about him. He had a charm of a man who knew the world, and one who had fought half of it and won.

I was snapped out of my daydream by a swift elbow to the ribs from Dice.

"Nice to meet you, Sian," I said smiling at her politely. I couldn't help it, I turned and winked at Uncle Fresno in a *Good work, fella* way. Thankfully he saw the light side of this and smiled back.

Sian was probably used to comments and I had to give her credit with what she said next. "I know it's hard to believe, but I'm quite a bit younger than Fressy." She grinned. *Fressy!* I had to chuckle.

You look so cute, my baby Fressy!

I had sick perverse images in my mind I was struggling to shake. A wrinkled body entwined with smooth skin. Breathing apparatus and Viagra, when I replied. "*No!?* I thought you were High School sweethearts!"

Sian smiled as she passed over the potatoes to me.

"Yeah, Grandad over there sure likes the young 'uns!" Dice sniggered. This was certainly a strange family, but I couldn't help but feel at home, and suddenly growing old didn't seem like such a bad idea. They laughed and joked, but underneath I saw a great deal of respect.

As the humour died down Uncle Fresno changed the subject completely.

"What d'ya think about that casino getting done over then?" he said, though I wasn't sure whom it was aimed at.

"*The Roy Rogers Robbers*?" I replied after no one else said anything. I looked at Dice, but he was too busy eating.

"I heard there was no one there when it was broken into," Skylar then added. "The papers failed to mention that as it didn't sound so Hollywood."

Uncle Fresno was frowning at this. "How do you know that?"

"PC Rogers—"

"I bet he does!" Dice cut in jabbing me in the ribs with his elbow, like this was the funniest thing since the first *knock knock* joke. Sometimes I felt embarrassed for him. No one else smiled.

"Yeah, well, don't you be getting too cuddly with him..." Uncle Fresno trailed off, sounding as if he was being vague on my account. Maybe he had something illegal going on here, who knows. The guy looks like he not only knows every trick in the book, but probably wrote the book himself too.

"Don't you be worrying about who I'm cuddling," Skylar said with a sly grin then looked at me. I returned the glance with a smirk but couldn't help feeling a little jealous at the thought of some bobby frisking this fine young lady.

It was strange that I was having such mixed feelings when it came to the handful of females that I had come into contact with recently. Janie was still where my strongest feelings were at, but she'd stolen Scaly Dave. And I think the thought of being hunted down was taking the sugary edge off of the romance. A romance that seemed all the more one-sided.

I realised that Fresno was talking again, but it was directed at Dice.

"What d'you reckon, Dice? A bunch of pussies them robbers?"

"They were caught, were they?" he said still not looking up.

"Lucky, is what they were. They should be more careful next time."

Dice looked up and shrugged. "If there's a next time."

Fresno took a sip of wine, and asked, "You don't think having been so successful they'd not try again?"

...JUST SOUTH OF HEAVEN/JIM ODY

Dice took a bite of steak, chewed for a second and replied, "Some might. Some of the crew might know better."

Frenso nodded. He seemed satisfied with the answer and let the subject be.

I tucked in to my steak and potatoes like a starving young orphan. This was certainly nice nosh. I ticked this off as another good reason to stick around, and not click my heels together in order to go back home.

Thinking back, it is weird that I had an appetite because I was still as nervous as a fox on the day of the hunt, but I for one had never been one to lose his appetite over a small thing like life or death.

After a while Uncle Fresno put his cutlery down and spoke up. "You boys could try leaving before the club opens, you know. I spoke to Troy earlier who says that he's sure there's a coffin in the cellar of that club. Rumour has it there is more than a pocket-watch inside if you know what I mean." I could certainly imagine – it wasn't a hard sum: Gangster plus Coffin equals Body.

"O-kay," Dice replied. I think he was suddenly a little worried about having to rummage around a dead body for a pocket-watch.

"Right, and what you want to do is go in the warehouse next door, go to the left-hand wall and follow it half way along where you will see cardboard on the floor. Pick this up and you will find a doorway to the warehouse cellar. Take the stairs down to the small room and find the fireplace, which shares the chimney with the cellar to the nightclub.

"A chimney in a cellar?" I said.

"These weren't always warehouses. They were part of a huge building split into flats. It was in recent years these were all knocked through to make larger rooms."

...JUST SOUTH OF HEAVEN/JIM ODY

"Oh, okay."

"Anyway, there is your doorway. Simply keep quiet. Go in, find the pocket-watch, and get the hell out of there. Easy."

"You want to show us? You use words like *simply* and *easy* like this will be simple and easy," Dice said.

Fresno chuckled, "You wet-ends. No, I don't want to show you. This is your problem, not mine." He turned to me. "You alright with this, Caper?"

"Me? Oh, I'm just dandy with this," I said and Skylar and Sian both laughed at my sarcasm.

I felt like I was having my last supper, that's how I felt.

...JUST SOUTH OF HEAVEN/JIM ODY

Chapter Thirty

Bomber finished up his last piece of pizza and laid back on the hotel bed full up from the fast food. He knew he would probably be hungry later.

"Not bad," Cutthroat said from his single bed. "Not bad at all."

"What's the plan then?" Bomb said pulling out his gun and a rag, and then proceeding to polish the gun's shaft.

"Do you have to do that?"

"What? Polish my gun?"

"Yes, of course. They could have cameras here, you know."

"You're fucking paranoid, you know that?"

Cutthroat shook his head. "I'm cautious, and there's nothing wrong with that."

"I guess," Bomb said putting his gun back in his jacket.

"It's a waiting game. We know where our boy's living, but we have to wait for him to get the pocket-watch, and then we nail him."

"What? *Fuck him*?"

Cutthroat rolled his eyes. "No, kill him."

"Ah, okay. That makes more sense. If he's got the pocket-watch, do we have to kill him?"

Cutthroat shrugged, "I don't know. We'll see. He still fucked my wife, pocket-watch or not."

"What if he hasn't even bothered to get the pocket-watch?"

Cutthroat hadn't even thought about this as he presumed that Caper and Dice would be scared enough to get the pocket-watch. Janie had said that she thought he was stubborn. She knew his ex who said he was an arsehole. It didn't bode well.

"We skin the little fucker alive," he sneered.

...JUST SOUTH OF HEAVEN/JIM ODY

"Righto, boss. Let's order some porn."

"You want to go out to that club?" Cutthroat asked.

Bomb smiled, suddenly his mind was filled with half naked young women, gyrating along to the popular sounds of today. "Damn right, I do," he said. "Damn right."

"Okay, give it an hour and we'll hit the town."

"You gonna get yourself a nice young man, huh?" Bomb flippantly said.

"What?"

"A nice young man."

"I'm not gay, you know."

"Come on, pull the other one!"

"Why do you think I'm after this little fucker?"

"He's cute?"

"No, he slept with my wife. You see I'm married. Gay people don't marry people of the opposite sex, do they?"

"Well, that's not entirely true, is it?"

"Well, in my case it is."

"Okay, whatever."

They both sat there in silence for a few minutes.

"I don't care if you are," Bomb then added.

"Shut up."

Bomb shrugged, it didn't bother him. He moved on in his mind and instead thought about the sexual encounters that – if you pardon the pun - lay ahead. He wished his pleasure was the sole reason for this trip. Cutthroat sat stewing over what Bomb had said.

What the hell was the little cocksucker talking about; he wasn't gay, was he? So what if he enjoyed the company of men, that was just a bit of fun, wasn't it. If they got naked then so what? Standard drunken shenanigans. And so what if he hadn't had sex with his wife for over a year and didn't think of her in that way anymore? That was most likely due to the fact that she had let herself go, right? He'd only met a couple of men for someone to talk to. What happened after that was just a bit of bonding. It made part of him angry when he thought of their naked hard bodies. It really made his heart race with rage. He liked getting angry, that's why he had grown hard.

"I'm not gay, you know!" Cutthroat spat out suddenly. He almost regretted it as soon as he heard himself say it.

Bomb looked over at him and held his palms up in innocence. "It's nothing to do with me, man. I just assumed that with all of that fighting lark, and the rumours…look, I couldn't do it, is all I'm saying. I love naked women too much…" he wasn't sure where he was going with this now.

"What rumours?"

"Forget about it. Okay?"

"No, tell me."

Bomb took a deep breath. "It's quite well known that you've gone off with men before. It doesn't matter. Sometimes the most alpha of males are like it."

"Whatever. I don't have to deny anything."

"I'm not asking you to confirm or deny it. Do what you want."

Cutthroat paused and stuttered. "Okay."

"Look, to be honest, what I really like is…" but he was snoring before his chin hit his chest. Bomb looked at his cheap watch and ordered a porno called *Legless In She-attle* which boasted a female lead with a wooden leg. This would have to do before he got his hands on the real thing later.

...JUST SOUTH OF HEAVEN/JIM ODY

Chapter Thirty-One

He sat completely still.

The view from the top of the building opened out to a panoramic view of the club. Below, the dolled-up ants scurried around in drunken masses. Either pawing at each other sexually, inebriated friendships, or in an aggressive fashion.

The whole place was huge and whilst he'd done all the recon he could, he'd only been given the location yesterday. He'd been on call for this assignment whilst intelligence sourced the location of the pocket-watche's whereabouts. Getting information of building layouts was not easy. He'd hacked into the local government website for the original plans from when it was a huge residential block of apartments. Then he'd found the updated planning proposals for converting to an entertainment establishment.

Details of the cellar were sketchy at best.

He looked through the viewfinder at the attractive ladies, whilst maintaining a view of the rest of the building. Mixing business and pleasure.

He slowed down his breathing. This was normal and quite relaxing. He'd once sat in the same position for twelve hours straight. His only movements were from his breathing and blinking. He was focused within enemy territory. Any indication of him being there would've been his death sentence.

He'd killed three men that day. They weren't his first and they wouldn't be his last.

This wasn't even on a tour.

This was as a civilian.

Some days he didn't think of himself as being human. He was a machine doing a job for the highest bidder. A machinery.

...JUST SOUTH OF HEAVEN/JIM ODY

Chapter Thirty-Two

Night had fallen around us. There was an electricity in the air. The sound of laughter and fun can be heard. Drunken hysteria and testosterone fuelled the youths parading around the streets. They owned the night.

We were sat in Dice's van in a dark alleyway contemplating the right time to make our move. I was finding it hard to concentrate due to the adrenaline and fear pumping around my body. The nerves were sending confusing signals to my bowels. I was not feeling the best.

You can prepare yourself as much as possible for something like this, however until you're actually sat there, then believe me you haven't got a clue. I wanted to be a million miles away from here. I wanted the troubles from life to be taken off my shoulders whilst I floated in a pool. Preferably, one with a bar. With beautiful women swimming around me.

Linkin Park was coming out of the speakers. The music was turned low and we were left with our thoughts.

Dice fumbled deep into a bag and threw me some leather gloves. "Put these on," he said. This simple act once again underlined the illegality of what we were about to do.

Janie was indeed a very attractive young lady, and I guess this was the flipside to that pleasure. To be honest if it wasn't for Scaly Dave, I think I'd have bailed. No woman was worth this shit. Breaking into the property of a gangster with the intention of stealing something of obvious value in order to give to another gangster and his hit man friend just seemed stupid. All of this on the slim chance that this may very well keep me alive and see the pretty young lady again. I had a rock on one side of me and a very hard place on the other.

...JUST SOUTH OF HEAVEN/JIM ODY

Maybe if she'd held a banner in the pub that night explaining these very small things, then I might not have been so keen to take her back to my humble abode and get down and dirty. If I'd had Scaly Dave with me, he would've known. He feels it in his waters. It's like a gift.

"So, let me get this straight," I start. "We go through the fire grill from the old warehouse next door?"

"Right."

"We locate the box, spring it open, grab the pocket-watch and run like hell in the night?"

"Right, again."

Dice opened his door and got out. "Let me just take this unique opportunity to say that in the few hours we've been partners, you've certainly made the job a little more interesting, although you've given me a pang of woe at the loss of my old boring mundane world."

"You're welcome, Dice," I grinned nervously. "It couldn't have happened to a nicer person."

For a guy who had only found out about this job a few hours ago, Fresno sure as hell knew a lot about this place quickly.

First, he knew about the abandoned warehouse next door to the club, then he was able to plan going through the fire grill for us to get our bounty.

As the black veil of night settled down over the town, the warehouse was in pure darkness. This was our cue, and we half-jogged in like a couple of idiots pretending they were in an action movie. Dice flipped on the switch of his torch and I nearly shit my pants there and then. Dice found this amusing and placed the beam on his face, pulled his best Boris Karloff face and laughed a wicked laugh.

"Dick!" I spat and slapped the back of his head.

...JUST SOUTH OF HEAVEN/JIM ODY

Everywhere shadows jumped and hovered and I had this chilling feeling we were not alone. The storyline of a dozen horror films flashed through my mind like an old cine film – none of them with happy endings. This was a stupid fucking plan.

Dice picked up a large cardboard box that had been flat packed. We both jumped as something scuttled away into the shadows. A dampness surrounded us. A fetid smell hung in the air. It was a mixture of rotting meat and death.

Below revealed some concrete steps going down into a black hole.

"After you," he said pointing to the steps with the beam of the torch.

I raised my eyebrows then after a pause replied, "Piss off! I'm not going down there without the torch."

Dice handed me the torch. I was left wishing I had said something else. In fact, anything else.

As I got to the bottom, I realised I was in another room. The room smelt even worse. It was like a public toilet. One that had never been cleaned. There seemed to be a lack of air ventilation which only caused the smell to be thicker and almost make you gag. A dirty pair of hands wrapping itself around my windpipe. I scanned the room with the beam of the torch searching for the fire grill.

Suddenly I saw him.

A tramp sat staring at me, a half empty bottle of something sat next to him. He was finishing up a pizza and had a KFC bucket with what looked like eyeholes pushed through the sides. Then I saw Dice stride past me.

"It is not your time yet, my child!" He said in a booming voice to the tramp. A little *too* booming if you ask me. "Hide your eyes, my child and I will let you live." He carried on.

...JUST SOUTH OF HEAVEN/JIM ODY

The tramp put the KFC bucket on his head, which was strange as now he had covered all of his face besides his eyes. He pulled his knees up to his chin and grabbed the bucket with both hands. He covered his eyeholes as he was told, and begun to rock back and forth. You'll be amazed at the things drunk folk will believe.

Dice pointed to the right of me and as I shone the light there, I saw a wooden filing cabinet.

Dice mouthed to me to push it to the side.

It was easier said than done. It felt like it was filled with concrete, and made a horrible screeching and scraping sound. Finally, I got it moved a few feet. Revealed behind was a small gap in which a grill could be seen.

Dice got down on all fours and pushed the grill. It remained stuck fast.

"Shit!" He mumbled. He sat down and with both feet kicked it as hard as he could. It shot out. He looked at me with a smile, but this was no time for congratulations. He proceeded to go through. It was a bit of a squeeze but he was through in about ten seconds.

As I got down on my hands and knees, I was a bit worried about the tramp behind me as I had my ass in the air and felt incredibly vulnerable. I pushed my head and shoulders through the gap.

Dice had hold of the torch again and as he shone it around, I was amazed at all of the junk that was in the cellar. There were chairs, bikes, TV's, bookcases, golf clubs, fire extinguishers, computers, mattresses and boxes! Oh, yes there were hundreds of boxes.

"You see a coffin?" I asked in a whisper. Dice was busy looking around, picking things up and moving things here and there. I guess the antique dealer in him was shining through and I

...JUST SOUTH OF HEAVEN/JIM ODY

was wondering whether he was going to try and walk off with a load of other items too.

"Not yet, I don't," he said rifling through an old wooden tea crate.

I was feeling a little claustrophobic down there in the thick darkness. Not because of all of the stuff, but because I knew there was no quick escape. If we were caught in here, we'd little chance of getting out alive.

Dice picked up a battered paperback. It had once been white but was now an off-cream with a blue picture of a jetty going out into water. It was called *Lost Connections* and written by some hack writer. It was a shit book. I'd tried to read it once when an ex-lover had it sat by her bed. She loved it. She never did have any taste.

"Leave that for the rats," I said to Dice. He threw it over some boxes where it hit something large.

"That's it!" Dice suddenly proclaimed pointing the beam over to a large shiny black box.

We fought our way through the sea of junk until we got to it.

"You think this is it?" Dice asked.

I shrugged. "Fucked if I know. Open it up."

"You open it up."

We looked at each other. I blinked first.

"Fine." At first my fingers slipped before I was able to open it. We both held our breath. I tried again. It was useless. The lid was glued shut, and you could smell it. I had to wonder just when and why it had been glued.

"Perfect. It's glued shut," Dice said without sarcasm which dumbfounded me, as I was wondering what was so perfect about it being glued shut. The thing looked as though it could hold Andre the Giant, it was that big. How the fuck were we going to get that out of here?

...JUST SOUTH OF HEAVEN/JIM ODY

"So what does that prove?" I said. "It being glued I mean."

"That there is something in here that someone doesn't want getting out." I walked over to it, and besides the size was extremely impressed with the finish. When I died (and that could be soon) I wanted my coffin to be like this.

The moon could be seen through a small window, which must've been on pavement level outside. Just how we were going to get the coffin up and through the window was going to be somewhat of a challenge.

"It's a nice coffin, isn't it?" I remarked, and it really was.

"It's a bloody nice coffin! The best coffin a man could wish for! Now help me lift it."

I grabbed the nearest end and we struggled to lift it a couple of feet. "Jesus," I said. "How big is this fucking pocket-watch?"

"Maybe it's the size of the clock around the neck of that rapper. You know, the one from Public Enemy."

"Flavor Flav," I said.

"That's the one!"

"Maybe."

We managed to get it the ten feet to where the window was, and then we scratched our heads at how we could lift it the six feet we would need to get it out of the cellar window.

Dice dragged a large crate over and jumped up on it flinging his arms in the air. I was just thinking he was about to shout, 'I'm the king of the world!' when he pushed at the window. It didn't budge.

"*Use the force, Luke!*" I whispered loudly referring to the classic *Star Wars* movie.

"Shut-the-fuck up!" was all I received by means of a reply. Another push and the window came free. That was the wonder of age and neglect. No matter how strong it was in youth, when aged everything becomes weak. Dice triumphantly jumped down

...JUST SOUTH OF HEAVEN/JIM ODY

and grabbed the other end of our large lead-weight coffin. I was beginning to think it was filled with concrete.

Well, we'd huffed and puffed and just short of blowing a house down, had hefted the coffin up and half way through the window. My back screamed in agony, but we were almost there.

Dice then turned to me, clearly blowing and said, "Caper, go bring the van round here."

"What a minute," I replied. "I'm not going back past that old tramp."

Through the moonlight from the open window I could see Dice shake his head with a smirk. "Righto, I'll go. Now, *will you be alright on your own*?" he said sarcastically.

"Yes, I'll cover my eyes so as the monsters can't get me."

I didn't realise just how dark and alone I was until Dice had gone through the fire grill and I was left on my own. My imagination kicked in and I had a hundred thoughts racing around my head. I thought of the club owner whom was clearly not a churchgoer and the things he might do to us if he knew that we where trying to ship out a coffin from his premises.

It then occurred to me this was probably the most illegal thing I'd ever done, and only now whilst in the darkness under the moon, on my lonesome did I now question the right and the wrong of this whole deal. The most frightening thing was when I thought about everything that was wrong about this, I thought about the naked acts of last night and could somehow justify our actions here. With an x-rated *Robin Hood* theory my conscience still remained clear. Or clear-*ish*.

I heard the van start up and get nearer as my face was lit by the reverse lights. And a thick dark cloud of poison from the exhaust. It was then I realised there were a couple of holes in the coffin. What sort of an undertaker puts holes in the design of his coffins?

...JUST SOUTH OF HEAVEN/JIM ODY

It wasn't long before Dice was grabbing on the other end of the coffin and we managed to pull it all the way out. He held open the window and with a little bit of coaxing, I was just able to pull myself out of the window. The thought of going the long way in the dark sure fuelled my want to get out of there and I was glad that I'd recently lost a stone in weight.

I had just got my leg out when...SMASH!

I accidentally kicked the glass and it broke into a thousand pieces.

"Shit!" We both exclaimed together and heaved up the coffin like it weighed the same as a large shoebox. We pushed it into the back of the van and I jumped in with it. I fumbled with the back doors as Dice started up the van and we headed off into the night.

I felt relief wash over me.

...JUST SOUTH OF HEAVEN/JIM ODY

Chapter Thirty-Three

"Whooo-aaa!" Dice shouted in elation. I also felt the adrenaline turn into relief. I was still anxious to have the pocket-watch in my hands.

"Hey, Caper? Open that thing up."

"What with? My dick?" I jested, almost giggling out loud.

Dice fumbled with something then held his hand out with an object. "Try this."

I grabbed the shaft and realised that it was a knife.

"Why didn't you take this into the cellar?"

"I sort of forgot."

"Some lights would be good," I said straining to see anything.

Suddenly the van was lit with a bright red glow as ten small red bulbs gave off their crimson light.

"Nice lights," I chuckled. "Is this so your girlfriends feel at home?" I then noticed a blow-up mattress in the corner. *And who says romance is dead? He sure thinks of everything, doesn't he!*

I slid the blade along the gap and heard it cutting through something. When I got all the way around, I pulled to open the stiff lid. But stopped.

I was somewhat loathe to open the coffin as you never really know what's inside, or rather you do know what's inside and I certainly didn't much want to come face to face with a corpse.

The contents of the coffin made me sit back quickly with a start. This was a first.

It sure as hell wasn't just a pocket-watch but we had guessed that by the weight.

I couldn't believe what I was looking at, but then again it seemed so natural and obvious.

"What's in there?" Dice asked aware that I had opened the coffin.

"It's," I started, "a body."

The large guy was dressed in a black and white suit. He was laid as still as you'd expect a dead man to be. His skin was pale and his eyelids thankfully closed. *Jesus,* I thought, *this guy has been murdered and glued up in a coffin.* Then I saw the bottle of pills and the note.

Dice had stopped the van and was making his way to the back when I threw him the bottle and began to read the note. It said:

To whomever it may concern,

Sometimes in life you have got to stop and realise that you can be no more. You have won all of your fights until there is nothing left to win. The fortune teller was right when she told me that I had done just about all in life I could do, and that the best work for me was on the other side.

I have taken enough pills to help pass me over to the side that needs me the most.

Yours

Travis
P.S. Sue, Please don't be sad it really is better this way.

"Travis, eh? Who signs off a suicide note with *yours*?" Dice half-heartedly joked.

"Well, I don't think he was thinking straight when he wrote it, mate," I replied. "There's probably enough pills left for you." I tried to make light of the situation.

...JUST SOUTH OF HEAVEN/JIM ODY

After a minute of us staring at the cadaver, Dice said, "Make sure he's dead."

"*You make sure he's dead.* I don't want to touch a dead person."

"It's not contagious! And anyway, you found him. It's your right to make sure he's dead." It was true, we should find out whether or not he had fully passed over to the other side, I mean, the glue did seem to be only recently set, but the thought of the cold skin under my fingertips made my stomach feel like a heavy hangover.

"Go on," Dice pushed.

I slowly bent over and pushed my two fingers closer to his neck.

I touched him. Then it happened.

Travis bolted upright, just giving me time to pull my head out of the way, and proceeded to vomit all over my trousers. "Bastard!" I shouted and slapped him. I'm not usually the violent type, but this bugger had just played dead and showed me his last supper. *Not to mention that these were my favourite trousers!*

"Who the *fuck* are you?" Dice said. "Count *fuckin'* Dracula?"

Travis wiped his mouth and then replied, "Eh? Where am I?"

Now with the red lighting and the hostile reaction things can't have looked good for someone who thought they were about to make a transfer over to the other side.

I had to smile as I replied, "You are in hell, son. Did you really think they'd let you upstairs?"

"B-but, I - uh," he stuttered unable to say anything comprehendible.

He looked over at Dice for help, who nodded back to him whilst saying, "You sure shit up a rope my friend. What were

...JUST SOUTH OF HEAVEN/JIM ODY

you expecting? Horns? Fire? *Uh-ah* my man - this may as well be heaven to what will soon happen to you!"

The sorry bugger sat there, his eyes all wide open like a startled bunny and unable to move, his mind was racing with horrific thoughts this was plain to see.

Anyway, being the nice guy I am, I just had to tell him the truth - let's not forget that this is a big built guy.

"Hey, Count Travis?" I said, getting his attention with the mere mention of his name.

His eyebrows dipped as he then questioned, "How do you know my name?"

Dice then jumped in before I could say anything. "The devil knows all his children's names!"

"Dice, shut up," I said throwing him a half glare which he responded to by sticking out his tongue in defiance. I turned back to Travis. "It was on your suicide note. This *is* your suicide note, *right?*" He nodded.

"Well, you ain't dead."

"Oh, shit!" He spat, genuinely disappointed with this fact.

"We found you, unexpectedly, I might add—"

"Are you gay?" he suddenly said to me, which seemed a somewhat bizarre thing to blare out.

"No, are you?" I replied back quickly.

"I'm not the one wearing the beads!" Travis then smiled. Dice was in stitches.

I felt hurt, though I was getting used to the fact that my beads weren't anyone else's cup of tea. They'll be back in fashion one day.

"Okay," I started. "Let's talk about stupid people, shall we? Stupid, is to give up on life and wanting to take your own. Stupid, is to not take enough pills and gluing one's self inside a coffin."

...JUST SOUTH OF HEAVEN/JIM ODY

"What about the airholes?" Dice threw in.

"YES!" I said slapping my wet thigh. "Why put air holes in the coffin? If you are trying to kill yourself, you're not supposed to be able to breath when you are dead!"

Travis looked hurt and disappointed. *"I didn't say your beads were that bad,"* he mumbled in his own defence. "That glue smell isn't good for you, ya'know. I had to have the holes 'cause it smelt so bad."

"I don't believe this," I replied. Dice had tears rolling down his cheeks and was trying to keep balance with laughter.

"Anyway, you shouldn't have kidnapped me," he said looking up showing the whites of his eyes, like some lost puppy dog.

"We didn't know you were in there did we?" I said.

"Yeah, some dick glued the lid on, thus making it hard to open!" Dice chuckled.

Travis shrugged then replied, "Yeah, well, normal people don't go around taking coffins, is all."

"Maybe you're right," I said. "Maybe we should have been at home laid down in our coffins poppin' pills, waiting for the glue to dry and sucking air through our little holes like you - a normal person."

Travis got up and dusted himself off. "I think I'll be going now," he said as he opened the back door. He jumped out into the night and ran off.

Dice scrambled to the door and called after him. "Remember to walk against the traffic, you don't want to be killed!"

I looked inside the coffin, but apart from the note there wasn't anything else. No pocket-watch to be found anywhere.

"Shit, there's nothing in here!" I exclaimed remembering the original plan and reason why we had unwittingly kidnapped a well-dressed failed suicidal idiot.

...JUST SOUTH OF HEAVEN/JIM ODY

"Damn it!" Dice said opening the back doors again. Travis had disappeared. Swallowed into the night.

"You think he's got it?" I asked.

"I doubt it. He wouldn't have wanted to take that thing to the grave with him, would he?"

"Who knows? So, are we off back to the club then?" I really didn't want to, in fact I would have been happier to face my ex-girl-friend, and let her attack me with a pair of pliers.

Dice glanced at his watch and slowly shook his head. "Can't. Club's due to open in twenty minutes, place will be crawling with bouncers and security."

"So what now, Batman?"

"We go back home, grab some sleep and come back here for about half three. Club will be closed and no-one else should be around." Dice wrinkled his nose like a little bunny rabbit and said, "Besides you smell like puke!"

"Yeah, funny that," I replied, looked at the wet patch on my thigh and tried to will it away. It wouldn't go and the smell had me thinking I might make a similar patch on my other thigh.

It wasn't long before we were pulling up outside Uncle Fresno's wondering what the rest of the night would hold for us.

...JUST SOUTH OF HEAVEN/JIM ODY

Chapter Thirty-Four

Back at 'Graceland' the three Elvis lovers were sat around doing their usual thing of watching Elvis movies. They'd start off sat quietly and before long they'd all be up singing and dancing to all of the songs as and when they appeared in the films.

"Can you believe how long that pizza took tonight?" Aaron said when they had finished. "I was beginning to think that we'd never get it."

Elvis was then smiling at the memory of the large delivery guy who appeared to be dragging his leg as he shuffled to the door with the two large pizzas. "I can't believe that he made up some lame excuse that he got mugged on his moped!"

"By a tramp with a KFC bucket on his head, no less!" Presley added. They all chuckled at that. You'd think he'd come up with a more plausible story than that! The guy had seemed very sincere about the incident. He'd even given them the pizzas for free with a free two-litre bottle of lemonade, by way of an apology.

"Anyone for another drink?" Aaron asked as he walked out to the kitchen, but was met by two shaking heads as a response.

"I think I'm going as *Blue Hawaiian Elvis* tonight," Presley said nodding to herself.

"That right?" Elvis replied. "I think I'll put my gold jumpsuit on."

"Nice," Presley said and nodded.

Aaron walked back in whistling a tune that sounded very similar to Cliff Richard's hit *Living Doll*.

Suddenly everyone stopped what they were doing. There was a sudden tension in the air. This was not good.

...JUST SOUTH OF HEAVEN/JIM ODY

"That sounded very similar to Cliff Richard's lame song *Living Doll*, Aaron," Elvis said accusingly.

Aaron placed his drink down. "Uh-ha," he said and started to sing it further. *"Got myself a crying, talking..."*

"What the fuck are you doing!?" Elvis shouted.

"I thought that was pretty obvious."

"You don't sing Cliff Richard's songs if you are an Elvis fan, do you?" Elvis added turning red with anger again.

Aaron looked at Presley who shrugged a non-committal way. "Why not?"

"Because Cliff Richard thought he was Elvis Aaron Presley, with all of his stupid songs and silly films. He was a wannabe – nothing more!"

"Cliff is still alive and loved by grandmothers across the country," Aaron stated.

Elvis flew across the room at him and suddenly they were both rolling around on the floor not really doing anything that would prove that one was better than the other. They looked more like gay lovers than fighting brothers.

"Alright boys," Presley said and pulled them apart when it was clear that the only thing that was happening was they were both getting red in the face and sweating.

"Consider yourself out of the fan club, Cliff! Yes, that's right, you no longer have the right to your former name anymore, and will now be known as Cliff!"

"Piss off, then you no longer have the right to be called Elvis anymore, and shall now be known as Chicken-fucker!" and off they went again, rolling around and trying to choke each other with their medallions. Swept back hair was no longer smooth but tousled in a dishevelled mess.

Once again Presley stepped in. "Elvis, say sorry to Aaron."

"Sorry, Cliff."

...JUST SOUTH OF HEAVEN/JIM ODY

"Up yours Chicken-Fucker!"

"Shut up! Both of you!"

Elvis got up and swept his palms through his hair and mumbled, "I'm going to get changed then if we're still going out tonight."

"Me too," Aaron agreed and off he went, leaving Presley to wonder just how in the hell she'd got caught up in this. She'd dated a computer geek for a year. He was boring as hell, but last thing she'd heard he was making a lot of cash. That said he only liked to have sex every month and insisted on ejaculating on her buttocks. He never once tried to make her orgasm. Maybe Elvis wasn't so bad after all.

...JUST SOUTH OF HEAVEN/JIM ODY

Chapter Thirty-Five

Princess knew there was no way he was going to get two new tyres for his pink Cadillac. The tyres were special and would take a week to order and arrive in stock. He had hours before the shit went down later that night. He needed an alternative set of wheels that could be used as a getaway car. Princess didn't have another set of wheels and although the other stooges did, there was no way he was going to go running to them with his panties in a wad, and hope that they would help him out.

Just then Princess' mobile started ringing to the tune of *YMCA*. Princess always liked to let it ring for a while just so as anyone around who was completely blind or as thick as shit would know it was his phone and he was the gay and very proud.

"Princess' gay hotline, for all your homo needs," he boomed out in his usual camp singsong voice.

"Hey sweet-heart, it's Tiger," the deep Yorkshire voice replied.

"Well, my big cuddly beast! Is it a gay day for you today?"

A slight chuckle from the other end was replied by, "It's always a gay day here, sweet-heart. When're you going to come back down to the club, huh? You need to think about bringing your cabaret act back from the dead. There is not a day that goes by when some young sailor doesn't ask about you."

"For real?"

"Uh-huh. Now what do you say?" It was then that Princess remembered Tiger had a car he would let them borrow. Sometimes a man has to use his femininity to its full capacity.

"How about you do me a favour, and then we can maybe talk about me filling in a slot down at your club."

"Uh-huh. And pray tell what do I need to do in order to get my slot filled, you sweet thing," the voice had gone up an octave.

...JUST SOUTH OF HEAVEN/JIM ODY

"I need to borrow your car – and I'm not just talking about the backseat, lover boy!"

"You mean Bessie the Bitch?"

"Indeed I do."

Tiger paused and mulled this over. "And you'll fill in my slot?"

"We'll see where the mood takes us when I bring her back, yeah?"

"Okay. When d'you want her?"

"Well, handsome, like a leg wax and a facial I need it yesterday, but bring her over now and today will be the gayest day ever."

"Sure thing."

The car was a pink convertible mini with large eyes as headlights and a smiling face around the grill.

Randell was going to freak when he saw it, but then Princess didn't know that along with their pink getaway Bessie the Bitch, they were to be dressed as sailors and carrying cap guns for weapons.

Life was all about bluffing and conning your way through from birth to death.

...JUST SOUTH OF HEAVEN/JIM ODY

Chapter Thirty-Six

As you can imagine we were feeling like a pair of old socks that had been trodden on one too many times. We had to go through the unsuccessful events at the cellar with Uncle Fresno and the sexy temptress twins. All it did was spell out what failures we had been. We left our balls out by the door. It was going to be a time of ridicule. We were almost pushing the other forward to enter the house first.

There was laughter as we entered, but this was from Sian trying to lick her elbow. It seemed they'd got Dice's email too.

It didn't take long for the smiles to die down as we pissed on the parade.

Dice stood at the sink in the large kitchen and put the kettle on. Uncle Fresno, Sian, and Skylar sat at the large table waiting for a re-telling of that night's events. The fact that we were there without the pocket-watch spoke volumes, however there was a chance that we still had an ounce of self-esteem left so they were poised ready to tread on it further.

I sat down at the table, opposite Skylar and adjacent to Sian, feeling as uneasy as one could when your failings are repeated in front of two attractive ladies and a hard to please old man.

"So, we plan to go back there again about three-thirty," Dice said handing out the now made coffees. It almost sounded plausible and like a well thought out plan. The added biscuits did seem like a bit of a bribe, if I'm honest.

"Seems you too both defy all scientific logic," Uncle Fresno smirked. "How do you struggle with a large coffin and not think to open it in the cellar?"

Both Dice and I looked at each other, and were at a loss for words on that one. It would have been a lot easier, but not as

...JUST SOUTH OF HEAVEN/JIM ODY

easy as asking Travis whether or not he knew the whereabouts of the now infamous pocket-watch.

"Beats me," Dice replied. We had hoped the response was sufficient.

"Well," Fresno started. "Don't be surprised if when you finally get back tonight, me and the girls are murdered in our beds."

"Don't be so melodramatic, Fres. You know you've got more than enough things that will stop them before they stop you."

Fresno then looked up at me and one of the evilest grins I've ever had the pleasure of seeing appeared on his weathered face. "I do, don't I?"

After the coffee, Uncle Fresno grabbed a large decanter of brandy and poured out three glasses full of the amber liquid. Dice and myself had been omitted from this, due to our early morning task. Or, if you ask me, due to our complete failure - which was fair enough, though I really could have sunk a couple, if only to calm my nerves.

As the night matured, the jokes and stories got bluer, someone was brushing my leg again. Both Sian and Skylar were smiling at me every time I glanced and I really couldn't tell which one it was. I smiled back at both and continued to feel awkward. I'm a master at that.

Around eleven, we all hit the hay, as my old neighbour – Harry 'The Hay-hitter' Samuels - used to say. I was certainly enjoying myself here and couldn't wait for the worry of the pocket-watch and more importantly Janie's husband to free themselves from my mind.

In my bedroom, I laid down on my bed. It was slightly harder than I'm used to but comfortable nevertheless. The idea was to rest up, or just grab a couple of hours sleep. I'd already

...JUST SOUTH OF HEAVEN/JIM ODY

wrestled whether or not I should bother trying to snooze. You often felt like three shades of shit on two hours sleep rather than pulling an all-nighter where your body just adapts.

As usual, my mind wandered around a number of subjects. Some were to do with danger and possibly ending up dead soon, and others relived sexual exploits from the dirty footlocker in my brain. Then things mellowed and I thought about a girl I'd not given much time to in many years. Her name was Shelly.

Shelly was a petite and shy girl who I remember telling me one night that she thought that sex was violent. This, I had thought at the time, was a strange statement to make. An ex-girlfriend of mine once said that sex was a roller-coaster ride of passion and lust bound together by pure love. And a schoolteacher once confessed that she thought sex was an interlude of animal instinct between a lifelong show of love. Both better descriptions than Shelly, I thought, lying there still.

But for a moment, I thought about Shelly and her statement.

Fucking was violent. It wasn't about feather-like touches, and stolen kisses. It was grabbing and thrusting. Two people together in body but separated in minds. Grunts, clenched muscles, bites, and bodily-fluid explosions. A release. Sometimes a regret. Sometimes a moment quick, gone forever but edged in our psyche.

Neither one was in control. It didn't matter, and I thought about the one time Shelly and I had been in this very situation. Once again, I was overcome with guilt.

Shelly and I had been at the same party. I had been eyeing up this girl so far out of my league that it was an insult to her that I was even bothering let my look linger; she was *that* stunning. Obviously, she looked down at me like I was a spotty faced pervert who had his trousers around his ankles and was threatening to piss in the punch – three out of four wasn't bad.

...JUST SOUTH OF HEAVEN/JIM ODY

After I'd mumbled a hello to her and her friends had laughed until their make-up ran, I gave up on the Hollywood ending and scuttled off outside to the water fountain for some fresh air.

Shelly was sat with her head in her hands. She had a face as green as a Martian, and mumbled she was the ugliest girl there. This was rubbish as I had seen a couple of bloaters that had to be kept away from the desserts for fear of turning the cream sour. I told her as much and she'd smiled, albeit in consolation.

She wasn't ugly, she just hadn't taken full advantage of her potential like some of the others. She had eyes like pools of innocence, unlike the girl who had forced me out there with my tail between my legs. However, we'd both drunk more than we should've, and when I slurred something about her being fine looking to me, she grabbed my hand and dragged me off to her dad's garage just at the end of the next street.

Amongst tools and storage boxes, and the smell of wood and oil, we had kissed hard and ripped at our clothes like they were on fire. I'd thought I was amidst the heat of true animal passion. It was only later on that it dawned on me that to an onlooker - like a child spying on a dog performing a sexual act to a bitch in heat - I would have looked as though I was trying to hurt her. At no time did we caress, nor cuddle - for which I now feel ashamed. Her need was a moment of want. Mine was a sexual release. We connected through low self-esteem.

Makes you think though, without love - *sex is violent*.

I said a silent prayer for Shelly before drifting off to sleep.

...JUST SOUTH OF HEAVEN/JIM ODY

Chapter Thirty-Seven

Charles 'Chalky' Perry played the guitar in a local Country & Western band called Wagon Wheels. He was one of the best black County & Western guitar players in UK. In truth there weren't that many, but that shouldn't take away just how good he was. Had he wanted to play a more popular genre, then he may've been selling out arenas around the country, and possibly the world.

His parents got him guitar lessons as soon as they saw him picking at the strings of an old Gibson that was lying around. For weeks he played and played until the metal strings had made his delicate fingers sore.

Chalky wanted to play rock music. Not growly, angry morbid stuff, but good old rock 'n' roll. His dad, however, was a major Country fan, and frowned upon his son wearing bandanas and chains – but thought it fine that a six-foot-three black man should wear a cowboy hat, tight crotch hugging Wranglers and a rodeo shirt (frills an all) like himself.

So instead of going for his dream, Chalky let his father live out his Nashville fantasy through his son. Chalky knuckled down and became a very talented Country & Western guitar player indeed. However, when said father ran off with an eighteen-year-old barmaid from Dagenham, Chalky decided that the Country & Western scene could go screw itself. He left his home in Chalstern, a small village just outside of Newbury and went to live with his mum in River Town, Cornwall instead.

He still played guitar for a couple of local bands and often played at his uncle's club, but at this particular moment he was working as an Entertainment Entrance Executive. This was a job

...JUST SOUTH OF HEAVEN/JIM ODY

known elsewhere as a Bouncer, or Doorman. The club he worked at was called Heaven, and his uncle was Big Al.

Chalky stood at his uncle's desk and stared at him with pride. This guy had done well for himself, and Chalky then felt a little guilty he'd not made the effort to see him more throughout his life.

Big Al sat back in his large leather swivel chair, the throne of all swivel chairs, and puffed deeply on a Cuban cigar. Plumes of pale-blue smoke curled up to the ceiling. He said, "Chalky-boy, you got that thing in them eyes of yours, you know?"

Chalky looked back puzzled. "What's that? *Grit?*" he replied.

"No, you arse! Hunger. Hunger for success. I know about your little thing you had goin' before," he paused and waited for Chalky to respond. You see a while back in Chalky's younger, and more foolish years he'd gone ram raiding in Northampton – Just the once – but once was enough to get whiplash from a bad manoeuvre by the driver, so the £500 he made, was at a price – two weeks in a neck-brace to be exact. Plus neck pain throughout the winter months ever since.

"Eh?" was all he offered, showing you never admit anything until you know you have no way of getting out of it.

"You know. That whiplash thing. How d'ya do that? Huh? Straining between the legs of some honey? I don't think so, *eh Chalky-boy!*"

"Yeah, well, mum thinks I—"

"Your mother is a good women. You know I'd never tell her." He paused, first as if in thought, and then to articulate the words he'd found in his head. He made a show of looking around the room at the fine art collection decorating the walls, and then

173

fanned his hands out. "You like my club?" A rare air of pride escaping from the large black man.

Chalky beamed. "Damn right I do, man. This place is cool."

Big Al liked that. *Cool.* Yeah, it was just that.

"I could have a job for you here, you know," Al then said, "Apart from playing the odd set. I hear that you are the best black Country & Western guitarist in Britain. I'm proud to be related to you." It was hard to tell the sincerity of the last comment. Besides, he hated it when people added his colour. He was the best Country & Western guitarist period.

"Job? What, bouncin'?"

"No, Charlie Chalk. And you're not a Bouncer, you're an Entertainment Entrance Executive. Don't you forget it! We both know that although you are the finest Entertainment Entrance Executive I've got, you have much more to offer."

"Really?"

"Damn straight. You think Bronson could do anything else except punch drunks and feel up loose women? No!" He had a point. Bronson was peaking at any level of work potential. His days were numbered if any one of the inebriated women complained about him and his wandering hands.

"What sort of job are we talking here?" Chalky was curious, as he wasn't entirely sure his uncle's income came solely from the club's admission fee and beverages. But his uncle would see him right, and he respected Chalky's mum. She was his sister after all.

"We'll talk later. Now get out there and show them who's boss!"

Chalky grinned like a kid who had realised he'd made the school football team. "Oh, one question, Al?"

"Yeah?"

...JUST SOUTH OF HEAVEN/JIM ODY

"What the hell is the deal with the chicken-head? I keep seeing staff walking around wearing a huge chicken-head."

Al laughed out loud. "These kids! They are a great bunch of guys 'n' gals! You know old Travis-" Chalky looked blankly and shook his head. "-the guy who went home ill tonight, the most unlikely Christian devotee you could wish for—"

"Ahh, the guy who organised them strippers? Said he would only have them if they dressed as nuns and crossed themselves when they were fully naked. He said it was to seek forgiveness from Jesus Christ himself."

"That's the guy!" Chalky chuckled as he remembered the large built guy stressing how important it was to do these actions in order to receive full redemption. Half of the strippers had thought that redemption was an official certification to strip in public wherever and whenever.

"Well, he said that if any of the staff were seen resting against anything, then they are seen to be keeping their nest warm, thus the chicken-head!"

"Surely bouncers aren't going to be taken seriously with a chicken-head on though, right?"

"Chalky, if I was to take the piss out of a six-foot-plus chicken, who's got arms like battering rams, I would expect the chicken to kick the shit outta me, if he didn't, I'd know he was a pussy," Al winked, then added. "If you don't lean, you won't have to worry, right?"

Chalky smirked, shook his head slowly and walked out.

At the bottom of the stairs he walked through the large double doors and out into the club. Through the sea of young girls trying to look five years older than they were, and blokes trying every mating ritual open to mankind, Chalky saw a large chicken-headed barman dancing back and forth, unsuccessfully trying to spin bottles like Tom Cruise. It was a hard enough trick

...JUST SOUTH OF HEAVEN/JIM ODY

to do at the best of times, but with impaired vision due to the chicken-head, then it was a complete disaster. Chalky had to laugh to himself. Maybe this was what it was all about, right?

...JUST SOUTH OF HEAVEN/JIM ODY

Chapter Thirty-Eight

When Cutthroat walked into the club for the first time he was struck by just how young the females looked. Bomb was grinning like a little boy with a porno mag, and didn't know which way to turn. Every direction flashed cleavages and long naked thighs. All dressed up to look older than they were, whilst dirty old men snuck in trying to look a lot younger than they were. It was like a perverted maths equation of ages.

Cutthroat jabbed him in the ribs with his elbow. "Remember why we are here. And how old they probably are."

"Yeah, I know," Bomb almost whined, whilst wondering whether his partner had got laid in the past year. "Are you celibate?" he said frowning with his hands held out like he *needed* to know.

"Don't you be worried about my sexual prowess, you just keep ya mind on what we gotta do, right?"

Bomb rolled his eyes, "Alright."

Cutthroat had thought about them splitting up to find Caper and Dice, but this was too much like a recovering alcoholic searching a wine cellar. He was more interested in his addiction than the job in hand. He scanned the surrounding dance floor at all the bouncers. Thankfully they were all dressed the same in their smart fucking suits. He couldn't help it but he hated bouncers. The way that they stood there like they were the big bad boys; stick them in a ring with him and we'd see just how big and bad these boys really were, he thought. He pictured one of them laid out on the canvass, tapping like mad as Cutthroat administered a Guillotine neck-lock on to him.

Smiling to himself he turned around to Bomb and almost saw red as the little twerp was stood ten feet back giving mouth to mouth to a thin rake of a girl, clearly not wearing underwear.

...JUST SOUTH OF HEAVEN/JIM ODY

Bomb quickly pulled away and tried to mouth something about seeing her later and hurried over to Cutthroat.

"Hey, I been thinking?" He said wiping his mouth.

"Before or after you were checking her over with your tongue?"

"Huh?" Bomb frowned and Cutthroat nodded over to the young lady who was now rubbing up against a guy that looked thoroughly petrified. His mates were laughing their heads off at him.

"Oh, no. Whilst I was doing that – see I was multi-tasking! Why don't we find the boss of this joint and tell them that someone is trying to rob them?"

Cutthroat thought about this. "But what would that do, apart from us look stupid in front of a fuckin' gangster!"

Bomb was then distracted by a girl that could easily be a glamour model. She was a Barbie doll fallen off of the Instagram production line with bleached blond hair, bright make-up, short skirt, and large breasts that didn't move when she walked.

"Look at that!"

Cutthroat clicked his fingers in front of Bomb. "Hey, focus you little fucker!"

"Right, right. We speak to the boss, he sends someone to look out for our boy, he turns up, 'cause let's face it your missus—" he trailed off as Cutthroat raised his hand. "Well, you know what I mean."

"Then what?"

"Well, either we offer to give him a good kicking whilst lightening the load of his pockets of said pocket-watch, or else the guys here will be appreciative of our efforts at stopping such nasty criminal acts as B & E that they will let us have the pocket-watch."

...JUST SOUTH OF HEAVEN/JIM ODY

"The pocket-watch is worth £500,000, do you think that they will just give it to us?"

Bomb shrugged. "It's the best plan yet." And sadly, this was indeed the case.

"Or we mention it to no one. Wait for Caper Boy-Wonder to get the pocket-watch, and give him and Dice a good kicking. Nick the watch, and fuck off into the sunset!"

"What, together?"

"It doesn't have to be."

"Maybe."

"Whatever. We'll go with your plan then."

...JUST SOUTH OF HEAVEN/JIM ODY

Chapter Thirty-Nine

Randell was sat in his velvet smoker's jacket and puffed from his antique mandarin coloured pipe. He blew out the smoke without inhalation. The pleasure was totally in the ability to be able to do so, and not the choking and morning hacking that came with the intake of filter-less smoke.

He was currently in his study wondering when the rest of his motley crew were going to arrive. Of course, when I say study, I actually mean the corner of the lounge that pretends that it's a study because it has a copy of *The Wind in the Willows*, *On The Road*, and *The Shining*, which of course are the only three books that Randell has read, aside from a Roald Dahl when he was at school, and the adventures of Billy Blue-Hat and his buddy Roger Red-Hat. And of course, when I say lounge, I do in fact mean lounge/diner. The complete truth was just as Randell didn't live in a quintessential town-house, neither was this a stately manor. Randell had these in his sights, but currently he resided in a mobile home.

He couldn't stand tardiness and sipped at his sherry whilst wondering whether or not he should put on some music to suppress his anger. It was times like these he wished he enjoyed classical music, not just because of the soothing tones of violins, flutes, and clarinets, but because, well, it went with his attire. The trailer was just until tomorrow when he would have the cash to maybe buy the little cottage twenty miles away with fields where he could shoot pheasant, grouse, duck, and whatever other animals chose to trespass on his land.

Not for the first time he wondered whether he should've kept the crew from the last job.

...JUST SOUTH OF HEAVEN/JIM ODY

The doorbell to his mobile home didn't work so, Princess finally tapped on the window to let him know that he and the others were outside.

Boston had arrived first, fifteen whole minutes ago and had tried the doorbell no less than twenty-six times. He was very patient, and not once thought to bang on the thin tin door. Sammy had arrived after the twelfth ring and had suggested that he pushed harder on the small plastic button. Perhaps it had been a question of pressure, rather than a lack of sound. He did this for another fourteen times until Princess ran around the corner and asked them what the two of them were doing fighting over who pushed the bell. Princess concluded that maybe the bell didn't work and they should tap on the window instead. Boston and Sammy both nodded in agreement. It seemed like a sturdy plan. They then argued who was going to tap, until frustrated, Princess took charge and did the honours.

"You lot are late!" Randell said swinging open the door and storming of into the trailer. He took off his smoker's jacket like he was about to administer a fatal beating to each and every one of them. Why should he bother dressing up for them when they didn't have the common courtesy to be on time?

"I've been here nearly twenty minutes," Boston whined.

"Well, you're not much good sat out there are you?"

"Your bell doesn't work," Sammy stated.

"So why didn't you tap on the window?"

"We did," Princess added.

"What before then?"

Sammy and Boston looked at each other like they wanted the other to answer. "Not really," Sammy mumbled.

"What do you mean, not really? Either you did or you didn't. Which is it? Boston?"

...JUST SOUTH OF HEAVEN/JIM ODY

"It wasn't me," he said as if he had just been accused of humping the neighbour's dog.

Randell rubbed both eyes with the thumb and forefinger of his right hand. "It wasn't you, what?"

"That did whatever you just said."

"Which was?"

"Tap the window. That was him." He pointed to Princess, who smirked and shook his head.

Randell took a deep breath and said slowly, "I know it was him because when I opened the curtains I saw his big gay face smiling back at me."

"Ahh, right."

"Right, well, let's forget it. Sam, my man, where are our outfits." Sam picked a large holdall bag up. "In here boss."

"Good, good. Boston, you got the guns with you?"

"Ah, ha. Sure have, boss. Right here. Good ones too. I think you're gonna like them. In fact, I think you'll well and truly love them!"

"Okay, let's not start beating off over it. Princess you got the wheels?"

"Ready to roll. Like me, it just needs filling up!"

"Where is it?" Randell asked looking outside past the other cars.

Princess smiled and said, "You see that large van over there with the little dent in the side?"

"Uh-huh. God, good. For a minute I thought-" he noticed Princess's face, "-shit. What?"

"Well, next to it is a cute little mini. You see it? It's got cute little eyes as the headlights!"

"Jesus f'ing Christ!" Randell said, and that wasn't a good sign. "What the hell do you call that?"

...JUST SOUTH OF HEAVEN/JIM ODY

"Bessie the Bitch," Princess added quite seriously, whilst Sam was unzipping his bag. "But we could come up with another name?"

"Our f'in getaway car even has a name! Bessie, no less! It's pink, it's got eyes as headlights, it's small enough to put in your pocket, and it's likely to be the most memorable getaway car in history! If one more thing goes wrong, then I am going to shoot somebody!" Randell shouted stamping his left foot with every word. Sam zipped the bag back up and tried to hide behind it. Randell saw his little mime and raised his eyebrows at him. "And what, may I ask, are you doing?"

Sam looked at both Boston and Princess who without moving seemed to somehow take a step backwards leaving him vulnerable and open. "Checking the zipper, boss?"

"*Checking the zipper, boss,*" Randell mimicked. "And why the fuck would you need to do that, huh? The bag is staying here."

"Uh, yeah, true."

"Show me these great outfits, will you?"

"What, now?"

"No, fuckin' Christmas. Of course now!"

Sam opened up the bag again and pulled out the navy-blue trousers, the crisp white and blue top, and the little white hat. He handed them over to Randell with his head bowed down. He didn't want to see the look on his face.

"What the fuck is this?" was all Randell said. His face was now an interesting plum colour.

"The outfits."

"Please tell me we are not going dressed as sailors?" Both Princess and Boston tried hard to suppress sniggers.

"Popeye, boss. We will be dressed as Popeye."

...JUST SOUTH OF HEAVEN/JIM ODY

"Oh, well that's just fine and dandy then isn't it? For a minute there I thought that you intended us to go dressed as queers in our little pink gay-machine, but no, you had us dressed as everybody's favourite fall guy, Popeye, who if I'm not mistaken is in fact a sailor man, is he not?"

"I guess so," Sam mumbled.

"You guess so? Well I know so, and I hope to god that you have four cans of spinach in that bag or we are well and truly fucked."

"Yeah."

"Yeah to spinach, or yeah to fucked."

"Fucked. I did ask about the spinach but apparently due to health and safety—"

"I don't want to hear anymore," Randell said looking up to heaven. "Boston, get them nice guns out, if they are pea shooters or catapults then you had all better run."

Boston gulped, wiped his brow and took out one of the guns, and handed it to Randell, whilst repeating as many Hail Mary's over in his head as possible.

Randell looked over the gun carefully, but thankfully not carefully enough because he was in fact scared of guns and quite frankly wanted nothing to do with them. "Good man!" he said as he handed it back. Boston was relieved so much that he relaxed and accidentally farted slow and deep for a good three seconds. There was then much waving of hands in front of noses as a smell from Beelzebub himself attacked all nasal passages within a two-mile radius.

Randell was pissed, but it would have to do. He looked at the scared faces in front of him, and then at the shithole he lived in, and knew like the old Elvis song, it was now or never.

Fuck it, surely nothing else could go wrong.

...JUST SOUTH OF HEAVEN/JIM ODY

Chapter Forty

The Prodigy were pumping out hard and fast beats whilst the singer boasted about starting fires. The dry ice was thick in the air and it was getting hard to see. Not to mention breathe. He could see where the talk of fires had come from.

Cutthroat glanced at a tall black guy too smartly dressed to be anything other than staff. He recognised him, mainly because he was famous. It was Charles 'Chalky' Perry, the fantastic Country & Western guitar player, and nephew of the proprietor Big Al. Weirdly, Cutthroat felt a little starstruck. He could just mention a few things to him and see how he took it. Maybe get an autograph.

He looked behind him and was thankful that Bomb was following. He gave him a little jab with his elbow and pointed to where the big guy was stood - leaning against a pole.

Cutthroat turned to Bomb and grabbed him by his shoulders.

"You see that guy there, standing against the pole?"

Bomb nodded but he clearly didn't recognise him as the guitar virtuoso he was.

"He's one hell of a guitar player. Man, he can make that thing sing!"

"So, what's he doing here as a bouncer? Shouldn't he be on stage someplace?"

"You heard of Big Al?" Cutthroat tried. Sometimes talking to Bomb was like speaking to a slow child.

"Of course. He's the gangster who owns this joint."

Cutthroat nodded enthusiastically. "Exactly, and that guy is his nephew, so we can speak to him!"

Chalky didn't realise that he was resting against the pole until two things happened. Firstly, someone tapped him on the shoulder, and then a large chicken-head engulfed his world as it was placed on his head. Everything went dark, and something smelt funny. A cross between musty and sweat. The music was slightly more muffled. The whole experience was slightly uncomfortable. He turned around just in time to see someone running off. At least he thought that's what he saw. The eye-holes were meshed and only in line with the eyes of someone with abnormal features.

The grinning barman got back to the bar as he high-fived two colleagues. Then he noticed two guys stood looking very serious at him. He wondered whether they were lost.

The first guy was tall, white, and muscular. He spoke in a cockney accent and said, "You're Chalky, right?" The small guy was black, dressed smartly, and couldn't seem to fix his eyes on anything for more than a few seconds. That was until his eyes came to rest at the back of a young lady wearing a white dress that in the lights turned transparent.

"I'm Chas the fuckin' Chicken. Who wants to know?" Chalky said. These guys didn't look like comedians, nor were they sexy young ladies, so quite frankly they were already in his presence far too long. He didn't like this guy's attitude or the way his little mate was ogling at that girl – still.

"A friend. And, er, you play a mean guitar... I just thought I'd let you know," he replied, in a very awkward way. Chalky wasn't sure what to make of it. He could tell he was a confident guy, but when he spoke to him, he seemed slightly intimidated. Maybe he had a childhood experience with a chicken. Or a crush on guitarists.

"All Chalky's friends were given names at birth. How can I tell him you're looking for him if you don't know it?"

"Ha-ha, yeah funny. I'm Gerald," the guy said calmly, then his little friend managed to take his eyes off the girl's thong wearing buttocks long enough to add, "Just tell us where the fuck

...JUST SOUTH OF HEAVEN/JIM ODY

Chalky is and we won't have to kick your fucking head in." His mate looked shocked.

"Calm down, mate. He's going to tell us."

Chalky smiled in his chicken head. *They couldn't see, right?* "Tell your son, if he doesn't start showing me some respect, he's not going to see his twelfth birthday."

The big guy threw the little guy a glance as if to tell him to button it, and then said, "Excuse him, he got caught auditioning his finger puppets by his mum. He's still a little pissed off, if ya know what I mean."

"He'll stop doin' it when his dick falls off."

The guy paused ready to go at it from a new direction. "Look, I'm not looking for no trouble, I just need ta see Chalky. Er, you."

Chalky could see these boys were trouble. You wander around these clubs long enough and you can spot them a mile off. "I'd really like to help you boys, but Chalky went home sick today, he's not expected back for a few days."

"Is that right?" the big guy said. "Okay, sorry to bother ya." The two men walked off. Chalky scuttled out the back. It was never good to be wanted by lowlifes.

Cutthroat looked down at Bomb. "That was him. Those hands have slid up and down a guitar neck with real poise."

Bomb sneered, "What the fuck! You went all weird talking to him. You want to fuck him or something? He was a Cocky-twat; if I've got any bullets left, then I'm writing his name on one and sending it special delivery to his head." Then a girl dressed as The King – Elvis Presley, took his attention. She had on a blue jumpsuit, which was open, and showed skin from her neck to the large glittering buckle. She winked at him and suddenly he was off following like a long-lost puppy.

"Oi, where are you going?" Cutthroat shouted.

...JUST SOUTH OF HEAVEN/JIM ODY

Bomb turned his head and shouted, "Look, she needs my love."

"An Elvis impersonator? In Cornwall? You really are sick."

"I ain't nothin' but a hound-dog," he sung, whilst grabbing his crotch in a rather suggestive manor.

"Fuck!" Cutthroat exclaimed as he looked at his watch. *He's got twenty minutes, and then he's dead!* Cutthroat thought as he saw Bomb sucking the life out of this girl and his hand creeping down under the buckle. How the fuck did he do it? He didn't even utter a word to her.

He turned to the bar and ordered a whiskey. He needed something to loosen him up. Especially if he got to speak to Chalky again.

When Chalky walked back into his uncle's office, he was met by a man laughing out loud hysterically. "Jesus, Chalky," he said through his laughter. "I don't know whether to pluck you or fuck you!" He was off again, holding his stomach and rocking back and forth like he was a granny in her rocking chair minus knitting needles and wool.

Chalky removed his chicken-head and wiped his sweaty brow.

"What's up, son?" Al said as he saw Chalky's serious face.

"I just had two guys asking for me. Thankfully, I was wearing this!"

"See, not such a bad thing after all, huh?" Al replied. Chalky nodded. "All right, give me a detailed description and I'll get Bull onto it."

Chalky still looked a little concerned. "Should I tell mum?" He was surprised how strange that sounded; he hadn't had to say that in ten years.

"No. They go anywhere near her house, Bull will take them down," Al said very seriously indeed.

...JUST SOUTH OF HEAVEN/JIM ODY

"You mean—" Chalky didn't want to finish the sentence. Al nodded and they both knew what he meant.

"Okay," Chalky said and walked away from his uncle's office.

At the bar, Elvis saw the guy walk over and order a whiskey, and wondered what his story was. He nudged Aaron who almost spilt his Budweiser down his shirt, to show him that they might be about to have a little fun.

"What are you waiting for?" Elvis said nudging the guy.

The guy looked at him, swallowed his shot in one and said, "Where's the fancy dress party? Now piss off!" Then held his hand up for the barman again.

"What did you say?" Elvis said. Aaron walked round to this guy for intimidation tactics and eye-balled him.

The guy turned around and looked both of them up and down, then replied in his cockney accent, "Neither of you two looks like big breasted bitches, so piss off!"

Aaron ran his hands through his sleeked back hair then mumbled, "Screw this idiot, let's go and find Presley."

"We're watching you, buster!" Elvis said peering over his large Elvis sunglasses.

With that the guy grabbed his shirt and pulled him close, getting a large chunk of Elvis's gold-plated medallion. With his other hand he slipped the gun barrel from his waistband and without anyone else in the club noticing, he stuck it into Elvis's flab-covered six-pack stomach.

"If you wanna step outside an' discuss life, let's do it. But I don't think you really wanna start shit with me - *Elvis!*" The guy said through gritted teeth. "You want to go meet your idol?"

Elvis went pale and held his hands up. "Cool. Cool. Have a good evening." He skulked off, mumbling to himself, "He's alive anyways," and Aaron looked at him confused, but worried.

...JUST SOUTH OF HEAVEN/JIM ODY

Bomb was dancing away with this female Elvis and his hands had been to the edge of the unknown, but there were still things that were considered taboo in the public eye.

His plan hit him as his fingers were teasing over this girl's very tight trousers. Montell Jordan was boasting from the speakers about this is how we do it, and Bomb smiled to himself as he kissed her neck once more.

He pulled his head away and removed his hand from her crotch. The look in her eyes told him that she too wanted the rest of the world to disappear for a while. He grabbed her hand and walked her away from the darkened corner towards the toilets. It was never a romantic gesture, but sometimes you had to work with what you've got.

As they got there, he pushed the door open and she happily followed, a twinkle in her eyes and a big smile on her face.

It's always a strange situation when you are in mid flow and a female walks into the toilets. Some men try covering themselves, others feel compelled to flash off whatever they are blessed with, whilst others carry on like this happens to them all the time.

Like a true gentleman, he kicked open the door to one of the stalls and let her go in first.

After a couple of minutes, which always passed like seconds to Bomb, her bra was undone and her tight silk trousers were sat high on the ledge, away from the urine-soaked floor. He stood with his hands on both side of the cubicle as she sat on the toilet seat, taking him full into her mouth. It was a good thing that she no longer resembled Elvis F-ing Presley, as anyone barging in, might think he was a fairy. He didn't want that. It might give Cutthroat ideas.

Suddenly, there were a couple of large bangs on the cubicle door.

...JUST SOUTH OF HEAVEN/JIM ODY

"Come out from there!" Boomed the voice.

Bomb looked above to see the face of another fucking Elvis looking shocked, but hardly *all shook up*!

"Presley, what the fuck are you doin'?" he said, though it was pretty obvious to everyone around. Someone had a mobile and was filming it.

Presley grinned and pulled her large dummy out of her mouth so as to speak. "I'm checking this guy for testicular cancer!" She giggled, and then carried on like that answer would suffice.

"What, with your mouth!" He replied dumbly.

"Yeah, best way. More sensitive than the hands."

Bomb felt a little uncomfortable, to say the least. Presley pulled her bra down and, since Bomb had removed is hand from her, she stepped into her trousers with a sigh. She even mouthed *sorry* to him. He shrugged and pulled up his trousers. He fucking hated being blue-balled.

There was one thing that really pissed Bomb off, and that was when he was unable to finish the girl he'd started. He was full of rage. The cubicle door flew open and then, slap his ass with a dandelion, there was another fucking Elvis Presley glaring at him with contempt. It was like some Twilight Zone episode: *When Elvis Attacks!* He really must watch for people spiking his drinks.

The white suit Elvis then spat, "You're dead, mate. That's my woman!" He swung a huge fist at Bomb, who saw it the other side of Christmas and stepped to the side. He swung one of his specials, which caught the guy on his jaw with a large crack, sending his Elvis sunglasses flying through the air. The guy's eyes were already rolled up in the back in his head before he hit the ground.

Bomb sure could punch.

...JUST SOUTH OF HEAVEN/JIM ODY

And dead rock icons cock-blocking him would only make things worse!

Voyeur Elvis, clearly not wanting to stand and exchange punches after his mate's shortcomings, grabbed Bomb from behind and tried to use his bulk to wrestle him down to the floor. There was one thing that Bomb knew, and that was if he heard the DJ playing some wanky Elvis, he was going to pull his gun out and shoot every motherfucker singing or dancing to it.

As an Entertainment Entrance Executive, you were taught to know when a fight was in progress. The mixture of fear and excitement filled the area, as onlookers longed for violence and bloodshed. People just loved to be in the thick of things, smelling the whole blood, sweat, and tears of these scuffles. They hoped to see sights that would make them wince. They hoped someone got killed or maimed. It would make a wonderful anecdote to relive over biscuits and weak coffee the next day at work.

Chalky saw the looks of males as they came out of the toilets, grabbing mates and heading back in. This meant one of two things: either a fight or the voyeurism pleasures of two people having sex in a cubicle.

The way they grinned and did that strange pogo jump of excitement, suggested a sudden rush of adrenaline. So, when four lads piled back through the doors it was obvious that there was more going on than a horny couple putting on a show.

Chalky charged in, pulling and pushing his way through. Clearing a path of bodies within seconds like they were nothing. Slipping and sliding on the pooled urine on the floor. He found the small black guy from earlier giving a good impression of a bucking bronco rider to some guy dressed as Elvis. Another Elvis, looking less plump was led out on his back, his white jumpsuit soaking up piss like a sponge.

...JUST SOUTH OF HEAVEN/JIM ODY

"Break it up!" Chalky shouted pushing gawkers out of the way.

The small guy was swinging the other Elvis around and just as you thought he was going to stay there forever, over he went with a loud thud. The small guy, now spitting and breathing like a rabid dog, turned to the second dazed Elvis, and was about to knock his lights out when he noticed Chalky. He turned and threw one of his specials, which connected with Chalky's jaw. Throwing him off balance.

Now luckily, Chalky had been in enough scraps and scrapes to take a punch. It was an occupational hazard having drunken fools swinging at you. Add alcohol and suddenly everyone thinks they're Anthony Joshua.

It's a strange feeling to be stood in front of some psychopath who wants to kill you. As they squared each other up, Elvis jumped up, like a coiled cobra, and kicked the small guy over when Chalky charges in. He hears shouting as another bouncer bundled in too.

Within a minute the three guys and the young lady are escorted out of the toilets towards the fire exit.

Cutthroat sunk another whiskey and looked at his watch again. He was just about to go and look for his little prick of a sidekick, when he saw him. Two big burley bouncers were carrying Bomb and the two Elvises from earlier out towards the fire exit.

What's the stupid sod done now? Cutthroat thought as he walked purposely over to them. Then he recognised one of the bouncers.

It was Chalky. Now minus the large chicken-head.

And they were heading to the side exit.

There would be no witnesses. Should things go south.

...JUST SOUTH OF HEAVEN/JIM ODY

He placed his hand on his gun and followed them through the *No Entry* signed doors.

Maybe it was time to ignore his hero and collect.

...JUST SOUTH OF HEAVEN/JIM ODY

Chapter Forty-One

For the first mile, things were quiet in the small pink mini. Randell was fuming and so angry he couldn't look at anyone else in the car. The tension was thick. The nerves were on edge. It was safe to say that nobody was having a good night. All of them wondered whether this was actually worth going ahead with. Nobody wanted to bring it up.

Princess couldn't help it. He'd been wanting to put the radio on for a while. His hands would hover close to the stereo, but like wanting to grope a new lover, he bottled it and pulled his hand away.

This time though, he threw caution to the wind and went for it.

The radio suddenly blasted out The Bee Gees singing *Staying Alive*. It was an awkward moment. Then Sam noticed Randell tapping along to it. He nudged Boston. When the chorus kicked in Randell, Sam, and Boston sung along. Princess smiled and joined in too. Before they knew it, the tension had all but evaporated and they were jigging along and singing loudly. John Travolta would've been proud with the flair shown by men stuffed into a small automobile, and still able to bust a move like a pro.

The evening suddenly got better. Perhaps this might work after all.

Until the blue lights appeared in their rear-view mirror.

"Oh, shit," Princess said. "The fuzz."

He pulled over into a bus stop. Careful to drive around the glass where local hoodlums had smashed it up.

The copper walked up with a swagger that oozed confidence. Princess wound down his window.

...JUST SOUTH OF HEAVEN/JIM ODY

"Evening, gentlemen," he started. "D'you know why I pulled you over?"

Princess shrugged. "No, officer. Did I do something wrong?"

"You were speeding, sir. This is a residential area. A small child might have been running out into the road after a football, or some such toy. Very dangerous."

Randell wasn't happy with this. "It's in the early hours, no children are out at this hour, Mr Pol-ice-man."

"You know where children are, do you sir?"

Randell took a deep breath. This was the problem. The police always wound him up and then before he knew it, he was doing gymnastics in the back of a riot van on his way to a cell. "Just saying, is all."

The policeman then looked in the back at each of them.

"You boys been drinking?" he said knowingly.

"Nope. Not a drop," Princess said proudly. He wanted to stick it to this copper. Sam and Boston froze in silence.

"Really? Then why might you four all be dressed as sailors, might I ask?"

"Popeye!" Sam said loudly from the back. "We're not sailors, we're Popeye!"

The policeman scratched his chin and got out his notebook. "What, all of you? You've not been drinking but all decided to dress as sailors. Sorry, my mistake, Popeye."

All four men nodded and looked in different directions. Each of them, in their own individual way, blamed The Bee Gees for making them relax, boogie, and get caught by the police.

"Yes, we were coming from a party."

"What sort of party was it?" the policeman asked.

"Dress up," Boston said. "You know, fancy-dress, an' shit."

...JUST SOUTH OF HEAVEN/JIM ODY

"And you all chose to dress up the same? You all fans of Popeye?"

There was a silence. No one knew what to say or how to respond to that. It was easy to see how people confessed to things they didn't do.

"You've all gone quiet. You run out of spinach?" he laughed at his joke.

"Haha. Good one," Randell said in a way that suggested he thought anything but that.

"Okay, how about I see your license, sir?" the policeman said to Princess.

He huffed and slipped his wallet out of his pocket. He glanced up, as if to question, and then thought better of it. He slipped it out and handed it over.

"Godfrey St. Cheese?" he said, which set Sam and Boston into childish giggles.

"Did you have to say it out loud?"

The policeman looked at the two in the back trying to compose themselves. "Did they not know your name?"

"They don't know me by that name," he said looking down at his wallet.

"Ah-ha. And what name do they know you as?"

"Princess."

The policeman looked confused. "Not sure that's much better, if you ask me."

"I'm not," Princess said back quickly.

"Okay. Okay. Calm down. I won't be a minute." He walked back to his police car to check the license.

Randell was shaking his head. "This is unbelievable! What a fuck up!"

It seemed to take an age before the policeman came back. He was tapping the license with one hand onto the other.

...JUST SOUTH OF HEAVEN/JIM ODY

"Is this your car, sir?" he asked Princess.

"No, I borrowed it from a friend."

"So, you have permission?"

Princess nodded. "Correct. You can check with him, if you like."

The policeman nodded slowly and narrowed his eyes. He was thinking about his options.

Suddenly his radio went off with an excited voice needing assistance in an escalation of violence.

"Barry?" a voice behind called. "We've got a call. Deacon's Jewellers. Armed robbery!"

"Right. You boys stay out of trouble," he flipped the photo ID back at Princess, pointed a finger and rushed off.

"Fuckin' hell!" Randell said slamming his hand on the dashboard.

They sat in silence not sure what Randell was getting excited about.

"Did you hear him?" he said when he noticed the puzzled faces around him.

"No," Princess said when everyone else remained tight-lipped.

"Someone else is robbing the place we were about to rob!"

"Fucking liberties!" Boston said.

"Exactly," Randell said. "Well, that's fucked things up for us hasn't it!"

Princess turned the engine on but sat there unsure what to do.

"Get some music on."

Princess hit the button, but at a lower volume. It was Adele.

"Shit," Boston said. "Like things couldn't get any worse."

"Yeah, complete wank. Turn it over or turn it off," Randell agreed.

...JUST SOUTH OF HEAVEN/JIM ODY

That's all you need. Bloody Adele.

"I'm hungry," Boston said.

"Fuck it, let's go get a kebab or something," Randell said. "We'll sort out what we are going to do from there."

Princess turned the channel over and was met by the cat-strained sounds of Celine Dion. Out of the frying pan into the bloody fire.

It was becoming increasingly clear that Randell was not thinking that luck was on his side tonight. The only thing worse than Adele was Celine *bloody* Dion.

...JUST SOUTH OF HEAVEN/JIM ODY

Chapter Forty-Two

I woke up to someone nudging me. I hated that. A smell of an unknown place had me momentarily confused. Through the darkness I could make out a figure.

He looked mean and angry and certainly like nobody I had ever seen before in my life.

Behind him two other shapes emerged, turning into ugly men who clearly didn't want a hug.

The bedclothes were ripped off of me and two very strong pairs of hands grabbed both of my arms and pulled me out of bed.

My head was booming and feeling light. Pain shot through my skull as a bright light shone in my eyes.

I didn't know whether I had just passed out, because I was now strapped to a small wooden children's chair. My chin was almost on my knees – and my dick was almost in my mouth.

The guy looked deep in to my eyes. His pointed features were so devil-esque, right down to a pointed beard, I thought maybe Fresno had finally killed me.

I felt naked, and when I looked down - I found I was.

I heard someone walk behind me and then I saw her back.

It was the same back that I had seen back in Swindon. She was saying something to this devil-guy, so softly I couldn't make out a single word. Then I heard, "Ask him."

The guy clicked his fingers and a large meathead strode over and handed him what looked like a drill. I hate being forced to do DIY jobs at the best of times, but being woken up to do so seemed mean. I'd never be able to grip a nail properly.

His eyes looked deep inside me when he finally spoke, "Was she good?" he asked. It felt like there was no right answer.

...JUST SOUTH OF HEAVEN/JIM ODY

My heart was trying to get out of my chest, and I really wanted to phone a friend on this question, though I don't think it was worth anymore wealth than my life. There really could be no correct answer to this question.

"She's a very beautiful woman," I replied, trying to sound grateful as opposed to boastful.

He didn't seem unhappy with this answer, although he wasn't giving me kisses on my cheek either. He spoke again. "Tell me. When was the first time you met her?"

"Yesterday," I replied. My response came out a little too quickly and desperate. Under the covers my fingers were crossed.

"Is that right?" he pressed, though in a way that sounded like he thought I was speaking shit. I nodded anyway. I even smiled. Perhaps he couldn't sleep and just wanted to know this. He might kiss me good night and leave.

There was a horrible pregnant pause. He might have been eyeing up which of my limbs to remove.

He looked at his drill and pressed the large orange trigger a couple of times. He was showing me it was charged up and worked fine. I was happy for him. I hate it when the battery is too low to finish a job.

I didn't know whether or not to compliment him on his drill. It was a nice big one. Not the biggest I'd seen, but I'd imagine it would do the job. I decided that it might be wiser to take his attention away from it.

He walked slowly up to me and said, "Okay, enough of this pussy footing around. You and Dice went to get my pocketwatch. Now where is it?"

I wasn't expecting that. I stuttered and stammered saying, "Uhh, I," and "But, we, uh,"

"Well?" He demanded and started to push the trigger on and off, on and off. It was still working.

"Caper!" He shouted. "Caper!"

It was then that I woke up and heard the alarm next to me, sounding a lot like the drill. Then I saw Dice.

"Caper," he said, "were you asleep?"

"No, I was miming how your jokes make me feel."

Then he frowned, "Shit, you naked under there?"

"It was hot. Anyway, what's it to you?" I mumbled.

"Alright then, Mr Grouchy!" he said shaking his head.

Thank God I'd been only dreaming. I really thought my goose had been cooked!

We needed to get that pocket-watch or we were going to be inside a body bag - Dice's words, not mine. Through all of the excitement of it all, it now hit home like a baseball bat to my skull. This wasn't about adventure. This was about life and death.

"So," I started as calmly as possible, "what if the watch isn't at the club?"

"Let's not worry about *what if's*," he replied as I pulled back the covers and slid out with my back to him. I grabbed my faded denims – the ones without vomit on them - put them on then got my funky floral shirt. I know how to dress – don't listen to what anyone else says. Jealousy is an ugly thing.

"You look pretty rough, man," Dice said frowning at me. I gave him a smile that said, *cheers,* and shrugged my shoulders.

"My fish has been taken, I lost my job, and I have a hitman after me. It's not surprising I'm not full of giggles, is it?"

"Hey, you'll need that," he said pointing to the knife on the side.

...JUST SOUTH OF HEAVEN/JIM ODY

"What?" I said, looking at it for the first time. It hadn't been there when I went to sleep. Someone had come in and left it there.

Dice looked at me funny but I remained quiet.

"What's with you?" he said.

I picked it up and looked at it, then replied, "Nothing." It had a handy leather pouch and strap, so I reached under my trouser leg and strapped that little sucker on. I'd seen it in a movie. I didn't expect it to feel so uncomfortable.

We walked out of my room. I had a strange limp. It was no good, I had to re-attach the knife. That's when she walked out of the bathroom wearing a tight silk nightdress. She smiled sweetly at me, and then said, "What time is it?" As I looked at my watch, I heard Dice reply, "Half two, go back to sleep, Cindy."

She walked past us to her room.

I was dumbstruck. Who was that? Uncle Fresno had himself an open house. Maybe the old bastard was a pimp!

"Who is *that*, and where did she come from?" I said in a whisper turning to Dice.

He rolled his eyes, then replied, "Cindy - she's a cousin of Skylar, and before you start thinking anything, she's only eighteen!"

I shook my head at that. I had no interest in girls more than ten years younger than me. It seemed weird for starters.

"So, what's she doing here," I asked. The old guy had a lot of women around him.

"Her parents thought it might be a good idea that she was under the watchful eyes of Uncle Fresno, Sian, and of course Skylar. She's - *how shall I put it* - a wild-child, to say the least!"

"And this is the best place for her?"

"You'd be surprised."

...JUST SOUTH OF HEAVEN/JIM ODY

Chapter Forty-Three

The man looked through his telescopic lens. He tried not to be distracted.

It wasn't everyday you saw three people dressed as Elvis Presley. Did they not know he was dead? Surely they listened to more up-to-date music than that old fart.

He looked up and down the street. At one stage he saw a man stumbling around with KFC bucket. There really was a whole mix of people out tonight. It must've been open day at the funny farm. He made a sound that to others might've sounded like wind, but it was in fact a laugh. He allowed himself this small pleasure.

Things were getting heated down there.

Nearby a girl was flashing her boobs. He wasn't sure what she was trying to achieve by this, although he did conclude from his lens that she was incredibly ugly. Hiding her face with her sparkling top whilst baring her assets was a great marketing move on her part. A lad with a huge round belly and small piggy-eyes looked more than interested. Had they been football teams, they would both have come from the lower leagues.

He scanned back to the bouncers at the club. There were lots of hand gestures. Most obscene. He saw Cutthroat and that other prick who thought he was the top hitman around. The fucking idiot!

He scoped him and thought about pulling the trigger. He applied a little pressure. Then released his grip.

Then flirted with murdering him again.

He felt himself get hard.

...JUST SOUTH OF HEAVEN/JIM ODY

Chapter Forty-Four

Chalky chucked the fighters out along with the female Elvis. He'd seen many things in his time as an Entertainment Entrance Executive, but nothing quite as strange as three Elvis impersonators fighting in a toilet cubicle.

All three men gave him their own evil stares, especially the little prick whom had thought he could out punch him. His face looked kind of familiar. Barton someone. Had some stupid nickname. Bang, Bash or something.

The female Elvis had a strange look on her face. It was like this was as much fun she was going to get without batteries and a big plastic cock. She looked to be suppressing a smile.

Chalky was about to walk back in to the club when the bouncer next to him fell flat on his face. He turned around to find the cockney guy from earlier give him an evil grin.

"Chalky, the brilliant guitar player," he stated with a consolation sigh.

Chalky shrugged. This guy clearly recognised him so pretending wasn't going to get him anywhere.

Bomb walked over to him then said, "This prick just fuckin' threw me out!" He then looked over at the other two guys and said, "You can shoot those two Elvis wankers!"

Cutthroat shook his head and frowned, "Shut the fuck up! Just for a minute!"

The Elvis in the white jumpsuit with piss-stains then piped up, "Shoot that little twat, he was shaggin' my missus!"

Then the other Elvis added, "Yeah, that just ain't right, man!"

Cutthroat rolled his eyes up to the place he knew he would never go and shook his head. "Okay, next person that speaks when not spoken to is getting shot, got it?" This was typical.

...JUST SOUTH OF HEAVEN/JIM ODY

Every time they got someplace, Bomb got distracted by females. This inevitably got them into trouble.

There were a couple of nods. The girl huffed and looked bored. Considering she'd just cheated on her boyfriend, she didn't seem to understand what it meant for the trio's dynamics.

"That goes for you too, sweetheart!" He said noticing her. He then turned his attention back to Chalky. "D'ya know why we're here?"

"You haven't got a date?" Chalky replied deadpan.

"I'll let you off on that one, due to who you are. We need something and you have it. I really don't want to shoot you."

"I thought you were a fan. It's a bit of an odd situation we find ourselves in. If I can be candid with you, I don't want you to shoot me either."

Cutthroat nodded. "It's not ideal." He smacked him with the barrel of his gun, splitting Chalky's nose. "But we have a job to do."

"Really. And what is it you want?"

"We are after a pocket-watch located in the cellar of this club."

Chalky grinned. "Good-fucking-luck on that one! You should see the shit down there. Here's a few words for you: needle in a haystack!"

"Don't you have it?"

"No, you said it yourself it's in the cellar. I have no idea whether or not it is indeed where you say it is. I for one am not looking for it!"

"You fuckin' well are!" Cutthroat raised the gun and pointed it at Chalky. Eyes narrowed. Sweat beads formed. Muscles twitched.

***

...JUST SOUTH OF HEAVEN/JIM ODY

The guy was still watching from above. He wanted to pop them both.

It would be so easy.

And then he felt the tickle.

He looked down and saw the biggest spider he'd ever seen in his life.

He hated spiders with a passion. He was bitten by one that had escaped from school. Some huge tarantula.

He jumped up and shouted!

***

Someone shouted from above.

Cutthroat was distracted and Chalky jumped at him. Cutthroat's arm shot up in the air and the gun went off. Firing off a shot into the sky.

***

The bullet went straight through his eye and deep into his brain.

The war veteran of two tours, master sniper and deadly hitman fell down dead. The blood leaked from the hole all in his face and pooled over the roof.

All of the deadly situations he'd found himself in, this would not have been how he would've expected to die. He didn't have time to even consider this. His lifeless body came to rest.

His soul wisped up and out into a place beyond this world.

***

...JUST SOUTH OF HEAVEN/JIM ODY

Cutthroat fell to the floor. Chalky was about to punch him when he noticed something incredibly peculiar.

His eyes were closed. He was asleep. Fast asleep.

"Shit!" Bomb said stamping his foot in frustration.

"What the fuck? He knocked out?" Chalky said amazed.

"Asleep, probably."

"What?!"

Bomb let out a huge sigh. "He's narcoleptic."

"What? Shags dead people? Sick bastard!"

"No, you fucking idiot. He falls asleep at the drop of a hat sometimes."

Bomb then grabbed the gun. "Ha! Right, who's first?"

A huge form appeared from nowhere. A crackle of electricity forced a squeal as Bomb dropped the gun and fell to the floor. Big Al appeared behind him grinning from ear to ear and holding an electric baton.

All three Elvises bolted as fast as their tight silk trousers would allow them off into the night. Whatever internal problems their fan club had, they'd look at it later.

"Who the fuck are these two pricks?" Big Al said.

"They mumbled something about a missing pocket-watch."

"This look like fuckin' lost and found to you, get them the fuck out of here!" Chalky and another couple of large guys grabbed the two fallen men and carried them around the side of the building. Fists and boots swung a few times, before the two men were left there.

As they got to the end of the alleyway, Presley started to laugh. "What...a...rush!" she squealed as they came to a stop.

"I can't believe you, you little slut!" Elvis spat. "You didn't know him from Adam and you were doin' that to him!"

Aaron nodded his head in agreement. "Yeah, specially as you're seein' Elvis an all."

...JUST SOUTH OF HEAVEN/JIM ODY

Presley rolled her eyes up to heaven as if this was all some big joke and nothing to do with hurting these battered egos.

"We ain't *married*," she said pleased with herself. "You've never once told me I couldn't do that, so how can you now tell me off for it?"

Elvis looked perplexed by this. "I didn't think I had to." He threw a glance at Aaron.

Aaron frowned. "I would've thought it was an unspoken rule that you wouldn't blow some other guy. I'm with him on this one."

"Really?" Presley said in mock amazement. "Where I come from, it's the norm."

"What, Penzance?"

"Exactly."

"Shit," Elvis said. "I didn't know."

"Well now you do."

Elvis paused taking in this new information. He then screwed up his face. "I'm gonna get that Chalky-boy! I'd get that little dick that you were blowin' if he wasn't gettin' it now!! Ha! Ha!"

Aaron joined in with the laughter. "Yeah, he won't be worth shit for no umph, umph," he motioned with his hips suggestively. "Not in a big body cast!"

Presley had stopped smiling, but her grin came back as she retorted, "Had a bigger dick than the both of you put together!"

"Ain't never seen mine," Aaron said under his breath.

"Wouldn't want to, either!" she replied. Aaron looked crestfallen. He'd had fantasies about her for as long as he had known her.

"Let's go back home," Aaron then said trying to change the subject.

...JUST SOUTH OF HEAVEN/JIM ODY

Elvis smacked him on the arm. "Piss off! We're gonna get that big mouthed Chalky!"

"What's the point?" Aaron replied yawning. He just wanted to go back home, slip into his Elvis pyjamas and forget about the day.

Elvis gave him a look like he'd just started on his admiration for Sir Cliff again.

"He tried to diss us, man!" He said. "We ain't letting him get away with that!"

Presley giggled, "You ain't black, Jamaican Joe!"

"Shut up! I've still not forgotten about what you did neither!"

She pulled a face. She was bored and wanted excitement. She'd get away with it. She'd let him feel up her tits later and he'd forget his own name.

"Okay, so what are we going to do then?" Aaron said unenthusiastically. Really, all he wanted was a cocoa and then his bed.

"Easy, we just wait for him to finish work, follow him home and BANG! We nail him!" Elvis grinned as if he had just come up with the best plan ever.

"Whatever," Presley shrugged. She'd rather go and meet up with the black guy again, and finish what they'd started.

"'S'pose," Aaron added. They headed back to their car to wait until closing time.

...JUST SOUTH OF HEAVEN/JIM ODY

Chapter Forty-Five

My eyelids were heavy. It had been a long day and going to sleep for a couple of hours proved to have been a bad idea. Dice was as bright and breezy as normal, and had stayed up.

I was busy trying not to nod off as Dice was chanting along with some rap band about going *Chicken hunting* and tapping the steering wheel like it was a snare and bass drum rolled into one. He must be a riot at karaoke. The band were rapping enthusiastically and unperturbed by the explicit lyrics their mothers would hear them say.

"Hey, Caper! Wake up, man," I heard suddenly which made my heart kickstart. I wiped the line of drool that had escaped from the side of my mouth and rearranged my trousers a touch.

I quickly discovered it was neither morning nor was I in bed with an attractive Asian girl. We had stopped and there was a girl laughing at me through the van window before her friend took her off. Not the most idealistic scenario in the world. I watched them, and then saw her bent over emptying her stomach contents all over the pavement. I'd consider that to be karma.

"I'm awake," I said. We were in the back alley near the club of Big Al. "I sure hope that thing is here!"

"It will be. It will be," Dice replied though with no real conviction. It was like we had been given a large box marked *straws* and now we had the opportunity to grasp as many as we could.

Considering the fact this was England, and it was such an unearthly hour, the air was still fairly warm. It was nights like this I thanked God for global warming. Or summer nights if nothing else. The shine from the moon gave us our only light which was a lot brighter than my optimism at finding the illusive pocket-watch.

...JUST SOUTH OF HEAVEN/JIM ODY

I got out and we were just about to make our way to the building next door when we heard a confidant female voice.
"Hey boys. You lookin' for a good time?"

...JUST SOUTH OF HEAVEN/JIM ODY

As we both turned around Dice said, "Why? You got golf clubs and a Ferrari?"

Her smile turned sarcastic. "Ha, fuckin' ha!"

She looked like she'd come out of the night club broke and was thinking of the best way to get her taxi fare. She wore tight hipster trousers, and a top that might've been out of the kid's section. She had suffocated breasts and a well-defined stomach that sported a jade coloured jewel. She threw a glance at me, looked me up and down, and said, "What about you?"

"Eh?" was all I was able to reply. I'm not used to women throwing themselves at me, even if they expect me to pay for the pleasure.

"Oh, sorry. You two are both -uh-" she whistled a couple of times, "-*together*?"

"What!" Dice and I both spat together.

"Well, it's just those beads...and—"

"What *about* these beads?" I said acting hurt, twisting them with the thumb and forefinger of my left hand. I pulled them away realising this in itself wasn't a very masculine thing to do. It wasn't being accused of being gay that bothered me, it was that so many people were giving me shit for my beads. I thought they were cool. Why could no one else see it?

Dice laughed and then added, "Yeah, take them things off, will ya? I'm beginning to get the impression those are what've been holding you back, man."

"There's nothin' wrong with the beads—"

"*If you're an eight-year-old girl!*" Dice laughed in a Groucho Marks impression, complete with jumping eyebrows and the holding of an invisible cigar. He was enjoying this. The girl looked at him and smirked, then looked back at me and tried to conceal her amusement.

...JUST SOUTH OF HEAVEN/JIM ODY

"It's not just the beads. I mean. *Two guys*, *late at night* and a *big van* in a *back alley*? Even the Pope would think that you two were sneakin' a little game of hide the sausage. You can't blame me," she added with her dainty hands held out, her palms up.

"I tell ya one thing," I started. "I'd have better taste than him." I pointed to Dice.

"Shit," he replied. "I had such high hopes for us, Nancy-boy!"

"Sorry to interrupt," she said. "Are you interested or not? You could show me exactly how much of a man you are."

"How much?" Dice asked, though I couldn't help but think he was just interested in what he could get. He didn't strike me as the type to run off with any whore who gave him her price list.

"Depends on what you want," she said fluttering her eyelids. *Like that's gonna help*, I thought. What she doesn't realise is that once a man has decided he wants to sleep with the chosen women, she is now in the position to be able to call his mum a bitch, tell him he's a lowlife scum, crash his car and spend his money, and the very second she removes her clothing he will be there panting like a dog and ready to go. Men can be extremely sad.

"What about whatever is most popular, and then I can give you one of them hug things for a couple of minutes, and you can tell me how good I was."

"I'd hug you for three minutes," I replied. "And give you a back massage." As soon as I said it, I was full of regrets. This was really getting sad. When you start pissing-contest haggling to solicit a wannabe whore, then you know it's time to go home.

"She ain't gonna want no back massage from you," Dice smiled. "She'd be searching for your change and kicking you out as quick as your performance!"

...JUST SOUTH OF HEAVEN/JIM ODY

I nodded and replied, "It beats me why your mum can never change a fiver."

The girl cleared her throat to get our attention. We both looked over at her.

"Is this for both of you?" she asked.

"No way. I don't want him watching me. He'd probably video it," I said, though I had no intention of paying a woman to sleep with me. "He sent me pictures of himself and some girl last night!"

"Why'd he do that?"

"Dice? Care to elaborate on that?"

He shrugged again. "I was pissed and she had nice boobs."

"It's extra to film," she said like this was a normal request. "And my boobs are great."

We both glance at her chest, then just as quickly looked away. It was a natural reaction.

"Look," she said in frustration. "Are you interested or not?"

"It's a no from me," I admitted.

"Yep, me too."

"You're not cops are you," she suddenly said. "I was only joking."

"We look like cops?" Dice added.

"Not really."

"Well, there's your answer to that then."

She shook her head in frustration. "Oh, screw you. What the hell are you doin' here anyway?"

"Waiting for you to light up my life with propositions of good free loving!" Dice said with a wink.

"Well, nothing good in life is for free."

"Air and water," Dice said.

...JUST SOUTH OF HEAVEN/JIM ODY

"Whatever," she responded. I was surprised she was still here. I'm sure if she was a hooker she'd know where to go to get actual clients and not a pair of clowns yanking her chain.

"Look, lady. We've got some business to attend to," Dice said which put his foot in it.

"What? In an old building?" she pressed. "You into real estate?"

"Yeah, something like that," Dice replied, clearly trying to keep his mind on the job.

It truly was a predicament. Dice and I both felt it. We *had* to find that pocket-watch. But here was a mildly attractive young lady, who was clearly interested in the fine art of lovemaking, even if she was trying to free us of our cash. We had both told her clearly we didn't have any money, but here she was still asking questions and flirting. I didn't know whether to feel aroused or sorry for her. She clearly had no place else to go.

"Oh, sounds interesting. What's the business?"

"Nothing much," Dice replied, but this time a little more seriously. "It's not for young ladies."

"Fine!" She said hurt, turned and stomped off slowly.

"Hey!" I called, but she had clearly made up her mind to leave us.

Dice looked at me and frowned. "What the hell was that all about?"

"We are just so *damn* attractive!"

"Even if one of us has got girl beads around our neck."

"Piss off," I replied.

Then Dice started laughing. When he was more composed, he said through giggles, "Last time I saw beads like that, *Google* had misunderstood my search criteria. I clicked on a link that sent me to a video of some girl inserting similar beads into another girl's anus!"

...JUST SOUTH OF HEAVEN/JIM ODY

"*Google's* fault, you say."

"Yes, your honour," he nodded.

"You can't always blame the search engine," I replied, and we left it at that.

...JUST SOUTH OF HEAVEN/JIM ODY

Chapter Forty-Six

Chalky grabbed his coat and touched his split nose cautiously. *Damn*, he thought, *that's going to hurt like hell in the morning.* Heavy footsteps got louder behind him and he turned around and saw Big Al.

"Hey, Chalky. Bull's going to be outside your house tonight making sure everything is alright just in case those bozos try anything again."

"Cheers, Al."

"Before you go, can you do Bull a favour though and secure a window that has been broken in the cellar."

"The cellar?" Chalky didn't like the sound of that too much. For a big guy he could get the jitters every once in a while.

"Yeah, shouldn't take five minutes to just bang up a piece of plywood over it."

"You've got someone looking out for me outside of my house but you're sending me down to the cellar on my own?"

"You're not scared are you?" Big Al grinned. He wasn't taking any of this seriously. In his mind his nephew could take care of himself. Okay, he got into a bit of bother, but that was part of the business. Those two numbskulls were long gone by now. Probably halfway back to London, or Swindon, or wherever else those pricks came from.

"Of course not. Just checking with you."

"Okay, then."

"Okay. No problem."

At that same time, Dice and I were creeping around in the dark like a pair of weirdos. We were in the building next door hoping we weren't about to be mugged.

"This place is bloody creepy," I said as I felt my way to the hidden staircase. "I think I feel my bowels moving!"

...JUST SOUTH OF HEAVEN/JIM ODY

"I think I can smell your bowels moving!" Dice laughed. He could be right. Dinner wasn't sitting well with me now.

We pulled up the cardboard and walked down the stairs slowly. We were met by a smell like no other.

"Jesus, I really can smell your bowels, man!" Dice said in a loud whisper. "I think you ruined another pair of trousers!"

"That ain't me, this time," I replied. And it wasn't. Honest.

As the glow of Dice's torch searched around the room we found the reason for the smell.

The tramp.

He was hunched over with his trousers and pants off, gripping a copper pipe and making a noise that sounded as if something was trying to go up, and not out, of his arse.

"What are the chances of that," Dice mumbled.

"Damn right," I replied. "A tramp shits, *what?* Once a week, maybe once a fortnight?"

"Probably less often than that, my friend."

"And we manage to come, catch him in the stinky act."

"If he had waited ten more minutes—"

"Fifteen - max."

"—we wouldn't have been subjected to this Godawful sight."

"Yeah, makes you wonder whether the hand of lady luck is just spanking our bare behinds."

And as if in defiance there was a sound likened to water splattering on concrete. Our friend Mr Tramp let the contents of half the bins he had scavenged from reappear as if by magic. Not too mention the large Hawaiian pizza he'd procured hours before.

Dice didn't even bother with his *pretending he was God* routine. He shone the light to the gap and we jumped through into the cellar like there really were ghosts and goblins after us.

...JUST SOUTH OF HEAVEN/JIM ODY

Some sights and smells were certainly sent by the devil himself, and that was one of them, I truly believe.

I was beginning to wonder whether it was a sign for me to turn back. Run from the horror. Escape from this excitement to the mundane world there was before. An easy world of immature workmates and psychotic ex-girl-friends. I realised there really wasn't much in it.

I'd already had myself a little adventure, but was sure there was more to come. Besides, I couldn't leave Dice up to his neck in this. We were a team, a partnership, and for the first time in my life I wanted to follow something all the way through, from start to finish.

And I wanted to get Scaly Dave back.

...JUST SOUTH OF HEAVEN/JIM ODY

Chapter Forty-Seven

Dexter wasn't feeling too hot. He didn't know whether it was the sadness of leaving, especially since the two intruders had come back, or a dodgy burger and the whiskey he had downed earlier that day. The pizza was fresh so it couldn't have been that.

The smell was so strong he was almost glad he was leaving!

He'd tried telling himself he'd gone this long with only these two people finding him, then who's to say he could go that long again without being found? Then they'd come back and put the final nail in his coffin - the bastards! He didn't think they were aware of their actions but wasn't that like the youth of today. They only cared about themselves. And looking good on Instagram, whatever the fuck that was (he'd heard some girls giggling about selfies, although assumed it was something to do with masturbation).

Maybe he should find another club, he thought, and seek residence around that. He mused at maybe finding a strip club where he could see the young ladies go into the back door, and he could fantasise about what they might look like naked. His sexual urges were few and far between and becoming less and less as the cold weather and long nights brought on more desires revolving survival. Surely not one woman on this planet would give him the time of day- even if he had the money. He couldn't blame them, he was hardly a catch anymore. In fact, they were more likely to catch something from him than anyone else.

He felt in his pocket for his lucky penny and gripped it tightly whilst listening to the mumbled voices in the next room.

Just what the hell were those two up to?

...JUST SOUTH OF HEAVEN/JIM ODY

If only he had money. He'd buy a cane and dress dapper like a gent. He'd love to collect antiques and show them off in a big house.

...JUST SOUTH OF HEAVEN/JIM ODY

Chapter Forty-Eight

"So remind me again, what exactly are we searching for?" I asked. I remember there being some wooden box. We'd got all excited about a coffin and assumed it to be that. It was more than likely some small box we'd tripped over.

I could hear Dice rummaging through something or other. Knowing him, he was probably distracted. I'd hate to think what would happen if he found some old Playboys down here. I'd need a gun to move him.

I just hoped he didn't find that shit paperback again. If he did, I'd probably go and throw it in the tramp's shit so no one would have to endure its contents.

"There must be another coffin in here," he said, although he was looking in boxes, so I'm not sure he remembered just how big that fucking thing was earlier. My back did, that's for sure.

I stumbled away from Dice and in the beam of the light, searched over all the junk. *Who the hell collects all of this stuff?* I wondered.

Dice followed me over to where I had found an old pool table.

"I think we might come back for this!" He grinned.

I looked past a motorbike helmet and found some boxing gloves. I had to put them on and pretend to spar a couple of rounds. It was just one of those things. Letting off a bit of steam.

Chalky walked down the large staircase to what seemed like the bowels of Hell. His eyelids were becoming heavy and he thought of curling up to Leigh-Ann in a nice warm bed. Mama wouldn't mind, he thought.

He saw a cheap football on the bottom step and couldn't help but kick it as hard as he could.

It hit a bucket with a metallic *clang!*

...JUST SOUTH OF HEAVEN/JIM ODY

"What the hell was that?" Dice asked standing still with a cowboy hat on like he was Billy the kid. It actually fitted him just fine.

"I didn't hear anything," I said getting my imaginary opponent on the ropes and getting ready for the knockout punch.

I could see Dice had got a gun out, and that lone act brought icy cold finger of fear down my spine.

But not as bad as when the door was suddenly swung open!

The door knocked Dice off of his feet and sent the gun flying through the air, like shit off of a shoe. I didn't see it however, as I was throwing a one-two in the face of the large black guy who had just turned on the light.

I realised this wasn't a good idea about the time that his large tub-thumping fist made contact with my right eye and sent me sprawling on my backside.

He picked up the gun and then spoke in a way that was hardly polite.

"Fuck that hurt! Twice in one fuckin' night!" He shouted then asked, "What the fuck are you doin' here? And who the fuck are you?" He demanded.

"One question at a time," I said. "I think I'm seeing double, which is pretty damn unfortunate as you ain't no Playboy playmate!"

"And you're no boxer, which is damn unfortunate for you, again." Then he looked at Dice.

"And *look* at Clint Eastwood here!"

I could see that Dice clearly wasn't used to being on the losing side, where as me, well, that was the only side I knew.

"We're missing something," Dice mumbled.

"I should say," the guy said. "A couple of brains, if you ask me!" He paused, looked at us both up and down, and shook his head in amusement.

...JUST SOUTH OF HEAVEN/JIM ODY

"The cowboy & the boxer. Sounds like some sort of movie doesn't it? And what's with the beads? You some lentil lickin' hippy?" he laughed. Everything's funnier when you're the one with the gun, I thought. I, *myself*, wasn't finding this situation particularly amusing, or rib tickling at all, in fact quite the opposite. The joke will be on him when people are selling these beads at a tenner a time. I bet he'll be the first in line.

One look at Dice told you that he felt as though some well-endowed male had just taken him up the backdoor. I waited for him to get us out of another fine mess Laurel & Hardy style.

"So, the question is what do I do now?" he mused out loud.

"You could close your eyes, count to, say, a thousand, and we could run off like bitches and hide," I offered, feeling my eye, which hurt like a bastard, by the way.

"Okay," he said. "Speak again, bead-boy, and I will pull your tongue out so far you'll be able to pleasure a women in the next room."

"Could be handy," Dice replied.

The guy shot a glare at him. "That goes for you too, Clint." Dice held his hands up as if to say, '*okay, okay.*' I was glad that Dice was showing more face now.

"You are lucky this is my first day," he started. "If Travis hadn't gone home ill, then—"

I put my hand up and said, "Can I speak?"

"What?!"

"We saved that boy's arse tonight," I said.

"Yeah, silly sod tried to kill himself!" Dice jumped in.

The guy looked confused, and it was only then that I saw the blood pouring from his nose; sadly enough I felt guilty, even though my eye hurt like Hell still.

"What are you talking about?"

I looked up at him, "This Travis, he a large guy, right?"

...JUST SOUTH OF HEAVEN/JIM ODY

The guy nodded still looked sceptical.

"We found him in a coffin in here earlier, he had taken some tablets."

"Yeah, we got his suicide note in the van!"

The guy smiled then said, "If this is true, then you might just still be alive to remember what it feels like touch a pert pair of titties, of course if you're lying, then well, you can't imagine what will happen. I think we should go see Big Al—"

"Wait a minute," I said. "You want to know why we risked comin' here?"

He was growing impatient. *"Go on."* he muttered.

"Your friend Travis has got an antique pocket-watch, except he doesn't realise he's got it—"

The guy then held his hands out, "Here's an idea, why don't you try not speaking in riddles?"

"Okay," I said. "We got word that this pocket-watch was here in a large box, or coffin. We came here and borrowed the coffin which had your boy inside."

"We thought he was dead!" Dice said.

"Yeah, right up until the bastard puked on my trousers!"

"Weren't they your favourite trousers, Caper?"

"They were. They were these really nice—"

"I don't give a fuck about your trousers, carry on."

"After we got him out of the coffin—"

"He had glued himself in, you know!" Dice jumped in.

"Well, he ran out of the van like a pervert with a porno!"

"With our watch!"

"Yeah, with our watch. If we don't get that watch by tomorrow lunchtime, we're dead. Also, it won't take long before your boy is tracked down and as dead as a cast member of *Dads Army*!"

"The movie?" He looked confused.

...JUST SOUTH OF HEAVEN/JIM ODY

I shook my head. "No, the programme."

"There was a programme?"

I took a huge deep breath. "Forget it."

"Yeah, you want three deaths on your conscience?" Dice finished.

"What the hell are you talking about?" The guy said. I didn't think he was buying it. "I will be doin' my job, which is what my uncle would want."

"Your uncle is Big Al?" Dice asked.

"Yeah, so what?" he replied.

"Come on, man," I said. "Let us go and we will give you a share of the profit."

"It's a funny idea," the guy smiled, though I think it was more in sarcasm. "I let you go and I will never see you again, right?" *Ahh, I see were he was going now,* I thought.

"You can come with us," I said.

"We need you with us anyway. We need to find Travis," Dice said. *Good thinking, my son!*

The guy stood there thinking this over. Perhaps mulling over whether or not to turn us in to the psychiatric ward that we had obviously escaped from.

"What sort of money are we talking about now?" the guy asked.

As the boxer, I looked at the cowboy whom shrugged, then replied, "How does a grand grab you?"

The guy kept a straight face like he was used to haggling. "How about I shoot one of you and get a bigger share?"

"Go fuck up a tree!" I coughed out behind one of my gloves.

"What was that?"

"How about three?" I replied smirking.

227

...JUST SOUTH OF HEAVEN/JIM ODY

"Three-grand? Done," the guy said suddenly smiling as I shrugged at the Dice. He shook his head and looked up to heaven.

"So, you know where Travis'll be?" I asked.

"Yeah, I know where he'll be alright. We'll find him and be back home before I turn into a fuckin' pumpkin."

And just like that the deal was done.

...JUST SOUTH OF HEAVEN/JIM ODY

Chapter Forty-Nine

It was late. Most nights I was dribbling into a pillow. Sometimes into the chest of a fair maiden. Not too many times was I messing around in a dark cellar.

To say I felt a little uncomfortable was a hell of an understatement. Now, if we didn't find that bloody antique pocket-watch, we not only had some unknown guy wanting to make us deader than the proverbial dodo, but we now had this guy throwing us to Big Al and his henchmen. It was almost quite impressive to get into even more trouble than we were in before.

I was beginning to come around to this guy Chalky. He seemed like a straight up kind of a guy. That was right up to the point of him telling us about the two strange dudes who were also looking for something in the cellar. This didn't bode well. It told us that Janie's husband wasn't letting us go and get the watch ourselves. If he got it first, then we had no bargaining tool to get Scaly Dave back. Worse still, they might just go ahead and kill us.

"You know, we'll just go find the watch and give you your share," I said. "Stupid us all getting killed, right?"

"Yeah, nice try," he said. It was a shame he'd not come down in the last shower. He had a lot more brains than his job would suggest.

"You box?" Dice asked. I thought it was a bit late in the day to be shooting the breeze, what with the fact that we were trying to stay alive and all. I now realised just how short and un-athletic looking I was next to these two. Dice was tall, though not particularly big built, but he did have large arms that looked like he'd been stretched by them as a kid. I made a mental note to lift a few weights in the future. Maybe get myself a punch bag and mitts. Chalky looked like he spent a lot of his spare time knocking heavy bags off the ceiling.

"Sure do," Chalky replied, and off they went with their boasts of first round knockouts and powerful quick combinations that made Mike Tyson look like a fat ballet dancer trying to pirouette. For the record, Dice boxed when he was fifteen for about a year. I'd not heard about any knockouts before tonight so concluded it was all bullshit.

As we got to the van Chalky turned around and asked me, "Do you box?" I think it was just out of politeness.

"No," I replied. "But I slapped a girl once in infants school when she took my *Panini* football sticker album!"

"Were you wearing those beads back then? I bet you wondered what changing room to go in for your P.E. classes!" Chalky laughed.

"You're a fucking hoot. You mark my words," I reminded them. "These are gonna be all the rage!"

Dice smirked at Chalky, "Shit, I'd rather wear leg-warmers and sweatbands again!"

Chalky began to laugh too, and I felt a little out of it. These two were suddenly BFFs, whatever that meant.

Just when I thought life couldn't get any worse it did.

The Scooby-Doo theme tune rang out loud.

Dice looked up to heaven then grinned a broad *check this out* chuckle. Chalky just looked amused by the two of us.

The words on the screen were the same. BITCH.

I punched the button and said in a non-friendly way. "What!"

"Caper?"

"No, Herman fucking Munster. Do you know what time it is?" Again, I was not amused. Why do people ring you at such ungodly hours and then wonder why you might sound a little pissed?

"Yeah, well, you needn't bother coming back." I heard sirens in the background at her end. If there was one thing in life I'd learnt, the sound of sirens was not a good sign.

"Why, what's happened?" I said suddenly worried. I had visions of my mum laid out. For a moment she let me hear the shouting in the background and the whining sirens.

Then she spoke slowly. Carefully. Crazily.

"That's the sound of firemen." Pause. "They are trying to save your house—"

"WHAT THE HELL HAVE YOU DONE?" I shouted down the phone. The smiles dropped from the faces of Dice and Chalky.

"I sort of set it on fire!"

"What?" It was still sinking in.

"Oh, and another thing—"

"What?" I tried to remain calm.

"Fuck off!" Beep. She was gone.

"What a stupid bitch!" I spat.

"What's up, Chuckles?" Dice asked.

"That stupid bitch—" I started pointing at the phone like she was inside, "—has just burnt my house down!"

"Oh, little pig," Dice said shaking his head. "The wolf finally got you."

"The wolf blew the house down, he didn't burn the fucking thing down like that heartless bitch!" I was fuming.

Dice turned to Chalky. "He went to see her yesterday and she flashed him her tits."

"So, how does he go from that to her burning his house down?"

...JUST SOUTH OF HEAVEN/JIM ODY

"A miscommunication," I said running my hand through my hair. All of my stuff gone up in flames!

"I'd say!" Chalky said.

"They had a *dare-I-say* fiery relationship," Dice said in a whisper.

"I can hear you."

Chalky turned to me and said, "You wear those beads, and you wonder why you attract weirdos!"

"Looks like you're stuck with me now, partner!" Dice smiled. How can they both find this funny?

"What about my Alice Cooper records?" I said looking at the floor and shaking my head in disbelief.

"What, vinyl?" Dice asked.

"Damn right."

"*Blasphemy.*"

"Yeah, long live the Coop," Chalky added.

Dice frowned at him. "What?" Chalky replied.

"You like Alice?"

"You say that because I'm black?"

Dice looked nervous. "No, because most people think The Coop is dated."

"Well, I know music. In fact, some say I'm one of the best Country & Western guitar players in Europe! Have you not heard of the band *Wagon Wheels*?" Chalky asked like they were as big as Abba.

Dice looked at me. I shrugged then we both said in unison, "No."

"Yeah, well, we're big in Oxford," he stated and continued to look glum.

"I'm sure you are," I said, with a hint of sarcasm – then I remembered my situation.

...JUST SOUTH OF HEAVEN/JIM ODY

For a moment I wondered whether it was like a sign. My last route of retreat had been stopped. The bridge burnt. What have I got to go back to in Swindon now? I didn't miss the magic roundabout or the self-destructive football team. At least here you could drive more than a hundred metres without hitting a damn roundabout - they had junctions and traffic lights. It was all so very novel here.

Of course, there was my mum.

"I had a girlfriend who burnt all of my underwear when we split up," Dice said.

"Really, I hardly think desecrating a well-worn collection of crusty Y-fronts is on par with a burnt down house, is it now?" I added.

"Why'd she do that?" Chalky asked. He was more interested in Dice's woes than mine.

Dice threw his hands out in a stupid act of wonder. "She's female," he sighed. "Why should there be a reason!"

"So, what am I going to do? If you *don't mind* me being a little bit selfish and worrying about my little predicament," I demanded.

"Beats me. Wouldn't want to be in your shoes, my man." *Cheers, Dice.*

"Yeah, real bummer," *No shit, Chalky.* "Good luck with that one." *Cheers.*

I sat in the front seat of the van and Chalky peered over my shoulder. He'd given up his act of holding us hostage a long time ago which eased the tension somewhat, and it was good to have a third person to help save our lives. I had a feeling that he found us as threatening as a toddler having a tantrum, and actually took pity on us.

"Jesus, that's some coffin," Chalky said feeling the smooth cold oak under his fingertips.

...JUST SOUTH OF HEAVEN/JIM ODY

"Bloody nice coffin," I agreed. It really was, you know.

"If I don't make it," Dice said with a smile. "Put me in that thing."

"You leave me in the shit, and I piss on your body before you make it into that," I said.

"What's the lining like?" Chalky asked.

"Take a look," I said, as the lining was even more impressive than the oak finish. It shouldn't really matter. I know your body is laid down against it until eternity, but it wouldn't really matter if it was lined with stinging nettles. That said, it was a lovely lining.

Chalky opened the lid to take a look.

"BOO!" Shouted the figure as they bolted upright. *Shit, not again!* I thought.

Dice swerved the van at the sudden commotion. The tyres squealed like we were in some police chase.

The wannabe whore from earlier sat there smiling and pointing at our white faces.

"Did I scare ya?" She giggled.

"I think I'm a couple of pounds lighter, I'll tell ya that much!" Chalky replied taking a deep breath.

I shook my head at her and said, "Okay, now might be a good time to ask you what you are doing in the coffin."

"I was sleeping," she said as though this was a perfectly acceptable answer. "Your voices woke me up!"

"Oh, I'm sorry," I replied sarcastically. *I like sarcasm.* "Maybe we should have been quieter, just in case someone had broken into our van."

"*My van*," Dice added.

"—his van. And taken residence in a box for the dead."

"Are you pissed off with me?" she said sweetly, flashing her eyelids like she had done earlier.

...JUST SOUTH OF HEAVEN/JIM ODY

"No, I must have forgot to put the sign outside saying 'All Welcome.'" I saw Dice grinning. He then added, "You not have a home to go to?"

"Sure, where do you guys live?" she replied, and I was beginning to wonder whether she really was new at this game.

"I hope your meter ain't running?" I said.

Dice smirked again. "Yeah, good point."

"I was only joking about that," she said without conviction.

"You didn't seem to be joking when you were asking to do all kinds of freaky-shit to us."

"I'm not sure I did."

Dice then spoke up, "In my mind you did!"

I realised that Chalky had been pretty quiet since she popped out.

"You alright Chalky-boy?" I asked.

He raised his eyebrows then replied. "Yeah, guess. It's not everyday that a young lady jumps out of a coffin at you."

"Ain't everyday a guy points a gun at you," Dice added.

"Yeah, and *you* weren't packing?" Chalky grinned.

"Yeah, but Dice threw the gun at you. You didn't throw yours back, *did you*?"

Chalky scratched his head. "Remind me again why I'm here?"

I had to say it. "About twenty-eight years ago ya mama decided that you papa could get jiggy with it and nine months later..."

"Ha-fuckin'-ha!" He replied seeing the funny side.

"Where can we drop you?" Dice said looking in his mirror at the girl.

"Nowhere. I'm coming with you guys."

"But you don't know where we're going," I said.

...JUST SOUTH OF HEAVEN/JIM ODY

"You like to talk, don't you?" she said to me. "Do I make you nervous?"

"What?" I said, not because I didn't hear her, but because I didn't understand what she was getting at.

"Do you fancy me? Is that it?"

I paused a little too long, and then said, "Dice kick her out here, she's annoying me."

"You like to joke, but you are shy around women," she said calmly. Chalky chuckled.

"I ain't dropping her off, she sounds like too much fun."

"She ain't insulting you!" I said.

"I'm not insulting, I'm observing," she added matter-of-factly.

"You wanna get back in the coffin and observe your eyelids again?"

"You *want* me," she said slyly blowing me a kiss.

I looked at *Chalky* for help. He seemed to sense this, shrugged and gave a look like I was on my own. *Well, thanks!*

"So where are we headin'?" I said changing the subject.

Dice laughed. "You'll love it! Tell 'em *Chalky*!"

"Peepin' Tom's Pleasure Dome," he said in a flat tone like everyone knew it.

"I presume it's not a kebab van then?" I said.

"Strip club!" Dice whooped like a drunken teen.

"Ya' still coming, Toots?" I said to our female guest.

She shrugged. "Why not?"

"You like naked girls?" I asked her, trying to make her uncomfortable.

"Who doesn't?" she replied, clearly not embarrassed.

Dice then piped up again. "Sorry, where have you been all my life?" I was beginning to see why he didn't have a steady girlfriend.

...JUST SOUTH OF HEAVEN/JIM ODY

Chapter Fifty

Randell had polished off the large donor kebab. He'd bought it from some greasy van that was parked in the shadows of an old car park. The woman selling them was cute, and he worried about her safety. But there was something about her he couldn't put his finger on that suggested she knew how to handle herself. She probably had a baseball bat and a gun back there,
The salty food had him guzzling down the last of his cola. He belched loudly. He was stuffed. The truth of the matter was these idiots were going to get him banged up again in Her Majesties Pleasure, if they carried on. Last week he'd successfully completed a job albeit with a different crew. He'd been wary then, but they'd come through fine. He figured that if someone slipped up then they couldn't be pinned on any other job, so doubt would creep into any investigation. It was a gamble, but then crime was based around not knowing. His mistake now was relying on these clowns to use their initiative. The car was a joke, and the outfits were stupid. Thank fuck the guns seemed okay.
He looked over at his crew. Sam was balancing a chili between his nose and upper-lip, wiggling it around like it was some sort of spicy moustache. Boston was chucking chunks of chicken in the air and catching them in his mouth like he was in a fucking circus. And Princess was sat down with a napkin out and some wet-wipes, cleaning his fingers every time he touched something new. They were hardly *Ocean's Eleven*.
"Check this out!" Boston said chucking a lump of poultry high into the air and then moving around in a circle ready to catch it. He did but it shot down his throat.
"Urgh!" He screamed in a strange low baritone voice. The chicken had lodged itself down his windpipe. Princess grabbed

him from behind and tried the Heimlich manoeuvre, although it looked like he was dry humping him. Sam flapped his arms around and mumbled, "Shit, shit shit!" The chili remained stuck to his face.

"Fuck," Randell said looking at the idiots. Boston suddenly spat the chicken out onto the floor. He and Princess fell to the ground in the excitement.

If their heist hadn't already been ruined, then this spectacular portrayal of loonies on release was enough to have him running away from crime forever. Randell knew this job, and others could wait. He had been greedy and sloppy in his plans. There would be other jobs and other days. And hopefully by then, he'd have other men recruited too.

"Any of you boys milkmen?" the lady in the van then said out loud.

"Huh," Boston replied.

"Milkmen. You know, delivers the milk?" She grinned.

"Nope," said Sam. "We'd be off to work soon if we was, wouldn't we!" He laughed. He liked that response.

The lady nodded, and closed up the van. "Shame," was all she muttered.

***

She looked at them. If only one of them had been on their own.

She could sweet talk the most devoted man to twist off his wedding band and follower her into the back of the van. She didn't care about kebabs and burgers. It was a job. It paid okay. But she got to meet such interesting people.

...JUST SOUTH OF HEAVEN/JIM ODY

She glanced at her watch. She'd go back into town and hang around in the shadows. There was always some lonely sap looking for some sexual release.

***

They were just about to get back into the car when four lads all pissed up came into the light. They walked in the strange way the Oasis' Gallagher brothers did, all cocky bouncing from one foot to the other.

"Aye-aye! What the fuck have we got here!" The Liam Gallagher of the group said. His hair was even in that same sort of messy but styled-look at the aforementioned singer.

"Hello, Sailor!" Another whooped.

Randell fucking hated men sometimes. "How about you fuck off," he said in no uncertain terms.

"Here we go, Sailor-boy has got some balls on him!"

Boston snarled. He didn't mind confrontation. He preferred it to a hug and a cuddle. "I suggest you run!"

"Look at Mr Steroids over there! I bet your cock is the size of a fucking pimple!" They all laughed at that. Alcohol boosting their confidence. One of them was wearing an anorak which made loud swooshing sounds as he gestured with his hands.

Sam opened up the bag and pulled out one of the shotguns. "Say hello to my little friend!" He shouted. The smiles dropped off of their faces.

"Alright, alright!" Gallagher said holding up his hands. "No bother. Just having a fuckin' laugh, innit?"

They disappeared in a quick jog.

"Thank fuck for that, Sammy-boy!" Randell said. "In arm-to-arm combat I probably would've killed a couple of them. I can't have a murder-rap as well."

...JUST SOUTH OF HEAVEN/JIM ODY

Princess looked at Sam, who didn't look convinced, rolled his eyes and tried not to laugh. *"Really?"* was all he could say.

Randell nodded. "I did so when I was in the Special Forces."

"What SAS?" Sam said. "Special Forces is American."

"I was born in Kansas," Randell said looking off past the car park to the bars.

"Like Dorothy?" Princess said. Sam coughed to suppress his laugh.

"Sure."

"Only, I thought you came from Kettering?"

"I did. Just after Kansas."

"Just like the alphabet," Princess added.

"What?"

"If you put the two in alphabetical order, then Kansas would be before Kettering, right?"

They all looked at him. That's when Sam accidentally pulled the trigger.

The sound of a loud, but less than scary, cap-gun bang could be heard.

"What the fuck was that?" Randell said looking at Sam.

Shocked, Sam shrugged. "I dunno. One of those things you throw onto the ground that makes a sound."

"No one threw anything," Randell pointed out.

"Weird," Sam said looking to change the subject. It looked like Boston had royally fucked them with the guns too. "Shouldn't we be getting a move on?"

Randell stared at him from a few minutes. That was it. If he hadn't already decided, then that would've been the last straw. Even their weapons were shit.

"No, abort mission. I need a rethink."

"Really," Boston said. He sounded like he'd been told to leave the toyshop. He hoped it wasn't down to the guns.

...JUST SOUTH OF HEAVEN/JIM ODY

"'fraid so."

Sam and Princess looked relieved. Perhaps this wasn't the life for them. It was funny, but Randell was thinking the exact same thing too.

...JUST SOUTH OF HEAVEN/JIM ODY

Chapter Fifty-One

The large neon sign rang out the desperate and embarrassing words of *Naked Girls*. It was like it was the only thing they had to draw you in. In fairness, it probably was.

I'd never had the urge to go to a strip club. Maybe it was the stigma of desperation and perversion. Or maybe I just never had the bottle. Part of me was now happy that I was here through the necessity of staying alive rather than to beat off in the shadows surrounded by other sad men.

"He comes here?" I asked as I jumped out of the van and looked at the boastful tagline *More than just Breasts!* Well, that was reassuring, I thought.

"Almost every day of the year," Chalky said.

"I thought he was religious?" I said naively. You see to me, I was brought up to believe all priests where pure goodness; Dice once told me that monks had the bold patch on their crown due to fellow monks stroking their head whilst they were received oral sex. Dice has a strange and perverse take on religion.

Dice looked up to heaven and shook his head. "Bless him." Condescending bastard!

Chalky smiled, then said with a straight face, "I knew a vicar once. He used to audition the choirboys by making them kneel in front of him. When it comes to a vicar, just 'cause he's kneeling, don't mean he's praying!" Again, I didn't think this could be used as a liberal brushstroke to religious beliefs. Perhaps more so a window to Dice's sordid mind.

"That's sick!" The female of the group said. It then struck me that I didn't even know her name.

"So are you going to tell us your name, or am I going to have to look in your underwear to see whether your mother's sawn a tag there?" I jested.

...JUST SOUTH OF HEAVEN/JIM ODY

"Their ain't enough material for a tag!" She giggled. "But be my guest."

I noticed that Dice was striding ahead. I think the thought of naked women was too much for him. I would have liked to think he wanted to find Travis quickly, and save our bacon - but I know Dice.

"It's Amy," she said almost sweetly, holding out her hand.

"Caper," I said shaking it.

"That's a funny name. Your mum not like you?" She smiled.

"Something like that," I replied with a deep breath. Everyone was a comedian when it came to my name.

The place was a huge out of town eyesore that might've looked better placed in the seedy parts of Vegas. I hadn't realised there was such high demand for this smut in sleepy Cornwall. It appeared I was wrong.

The large squared-off building had a carpark filled up with every vehicle you could think of. The demographics seemed large and wide for this place. Neon signs and coloured bulbs of lights dangled from every which way with no finesse. It wasn't really what drew in the crowds and we all knew it.

The bouncers gave Amy and me a strange look as we walked past. They probably thought she was here to audition and I was just a dirty pervert.

The smoky atmosphere engulfed us as we walked into the large dark room. The interior looked like a nightclub after a bar room brawl, but then did the clientele really give a shit about fancy seating and expensive decor? They wanted the naked women dancing as close to them as possible, and whizzing around the metal poles like an attractive hyperactive chimpanzee. That sounds derogatory towards women, but really that was what men saw them as. Just sexier and less hairy.

...JUST SOUTH OF HEAVEN/JIM ODY

AC/DC thumped out their classic *You shook me all night long*, and the regulars cheered knowing which young lady danced to this particular number. The girl in question waltzed out in a dress as tight as my Uncle Pauley on a piss up, shaking her large assets to the drumbeat whilst we guessed how much they must have cost.

I looked at Amy who had her face screwed up in a look that suggested she didn't share the regulars' feelings of lust and satisfaction. So, whilst she agreed to liking naked women, even she had her own taste in them.

"You sure you want to be here?" I asked her.

"Oh yes, I love to watch dancing sluts with fake tits," she mumbled. I looked around trying to find Dice, Chalky, or our friend Travis. I realised just how many men ended up here in the small hours. It was quite sad. I wondered how many of them had their own women at home, alone, wondering where they were. I had expected stag-dos and collections of men, but apart from a couple of parties, there were a lot of single men stood on their own. They might've come in a large gaggle, but each had filtered out to be by themselves. It was slightly creepy.

We fought our way to the bar where I saw Chalky had managed to get the attention of the barman.

"Nice girls, huh?" the barman said pointing one of the ordered bottles up towards the stage.

Chalky shrugged. "Yeah, not bad."

"Not bad?" The barman was less than happy with that response. "If you can find more attractive women in any other club, I will give you free drinks for a week. We have black dancers too!"

"I like all women. Just because I'm black," he began but then took a deep breath. It was no good getting into it with a guy who wet the lips of perverts for a living. Besides, he was

...JUST SOUTH OF HEAVEN/JIM ODY

unaware of any sort of club like this outside of London, and wasn't interested in arguing.

With a "Humph!" the barman wandered off to a wily looking guy who gave the impression he may have left his mac at home tonight, along with his extensive porno collection and hand cream. Even the bristles on his chin looked dirty.

"Hey Chalky? Where's Dice?" I asked, relieving him of a beer.

He pointed to a dark corner where a cage held two girls wearing nothing but g-strings. One was thoughtful enough to be checking the other for lumps in her breasts. I thought that was nice.

Dice was leaning in and pushing notes in their underwear like there was no tomorrow.

I felt the large knot in my stomach as I thought about that.

Had he given up? Had he decided to spend his last night in the living shoving his savings in strange girls' knickers? I couldn't think of too many other things I'd rather be doing, so I suppose I had to hand it to the guy.

As we walked closer to Dice, a beautiful black girl bent over and kissed him on the cheek. It wasn't that she was friendly, but rather in response to him shoving another couple of notes in the small material that covered any modesty she had left.

"Dice? Rob a bank?" I said pulling up a chair and watching the cute backside of the black girl wobble away.

"What?" He suddenly looked guilty. Then he looked at the notes and grinned. He then winked at me and handed me a note. I looked at the tenner. It looked just like a regular ten-pound note. Except the Queen was winking.

"What the?" I mumbled.

245

...JUST SOUTH OF HEAVEN/JIM ODY

"Great, eh?" Dice said beaming. "I always carry a wad just in case I end up in a place like this. Can't use 'em any place else. They never know until later."

"But that's fraud," I said posing the question to myself as much as to Dice.

"Why? I'm not using it to buy drinks. I'm only pushing it down bras and g-strings."

"But those girls will probably end up taking a share of your Mickey Mouse money home as wages. Does that not bother you?"

He shrugged. "I never thought of it like that."

Chalky was smiling between slugs of beer.

Dice snatched the fake tenner off of me and went to put it with the others. I caught him off guard. "Hey, give us all some then," I said.

"What? But? I thought you were taking the moral stand point?"

"What I said was true. Don't mean I want to agree with it though. What do you call these fake things?" I had heard about them before.

"Beaver leaves," Dice smirked and handed Chalky and myself a couple each.

"Want some?" he then said to Amy.

"I think I'll pass," she said like one of the lads. "This is fun to you? Pushing fake cash down dirty pants?"

Dice and I looked at each other and grinned. "Sort of."

Amy didn't seem impressed by this. Though she made no effort to leave.

Chalky got up and stuffed his funny money in his back pocket. "I'm goin' to see if I can find Travis - and maybe find a home for these!" He patted his back pocket and winked at us all.

...JUST SOUTH OF HEAVEN/JIM ODY

The music changed to a Guns N' Roses song called *Rocket Queen*. A flame haired girl of around twenty strode out wearing a small white bikini and proceeded to kick her legs up to the ceiling - it really was a sight. I only realised that I was staring hard when Amy tapped my jaw closed. She was a stripping contortionist.

...JUST SOUTH OF HEAVEN/JIM ODY

Chapter Fifty-Two

Cutthroat and Bomb had turned up to the club just as Chalky was getting into a van. Not just any van but the one owned by Dice, the friend of that wife-fucker Caper.

"What the fuck?" Cutthroat said. "Since when were they tight?"

Bomb shook his head slowly. He couldn't believe it either. What if they had been in cahoots all along?

Bomb brought the car around as Cutthroat kept eyes on the van. He smiled to himself. He liked that phrase of keeping eyes on something. It sounded like he was in *Starsky & Hutch* or some such programme.

The van had just turned the corner when Bomb turned up. Cutthroat jumped into the passenger seat and off they went. God, what he wouldn't give to be able to reach out with a flashing light and place it on to the roof, as they skidded around corners and took out unsuspecting storage boxes.

They almost lost sight of the van a couple of times. Had it been rush hour then there would've been no way they'd have kept up with them. As it was the van stayed in their sights right up until a red light brought them to a standstill.

"Shit!" Cutthroat said.

"Hold up," Bomb then said. "They've gone to the strip club!"

"What the fuck are they going there for?"

"Who fucking cares!" Bomb had a smile broader than Broadway as the neon shone in his wide eyes.

The light turned green and Bomb almost screeched the tyres with his excitement to get into the large carpark.

"I think I've arrived at my utopia," Bomb said as he stared at the sign saying *Peeping Tom's Pleasure Dome*.

...JUST SOUTH OF HEAVEN/JIM ODY

They got out. Bomb was skipping like a kid going to Disneyland.

"All welcome at the gates of Shangri La!" He sang and smiled at the bouncers, who didn't know what to make of him.

"Shut the fuck up, Pee Wee," Cutthroat said.

Bomb threw him a look, but he was too pumped up for naked flesh to truly care.

As they walked in, Bomb felt his heart beating out of his chest in expectation. He knew he was obsessed, but so what? Enjoying the pleasures of the flesh was a natural thing.

The flame haired girl on stage had now lost her bikini - both top and bottoms - and was doing some sort of Yoga that a clothed Jane Fonda might or might not be proud of thirty years ago.

"Keep your head on things," Cutthroat warned Bomb, but knew it was like talking to a little kid. He'd may as well had spoken to him in Welsh for all the good it would've made.

"Yeah, yeah," he said bewitched and spellbound by the dancer.

"Try and look out for the three dead-men-walking, right?"

Bomb was already walking away; his eyes were locked on the dancer and her incredible moves. His eyes were mesmerised and he was licking his lips.

Cutthroat scouted quickly around the room, but in the dim light he could barely see faces. He then decided to make a little money. This place was perfect. He spotted the first young lady that was walking around. As he looked at her young face and strangely solid figure -not fat- just more natural, he amused himself as to what their job title might be. They walked around and did anything suggested for money, be it serve drinks, table dance or a private show. The best thing was they walked around with notes hanging from their bras and panties. Now there was quite a few members of security employed to watch out for people like Cutthroat - but there truly wasn't anybody quite like Cutthroat.

He caught her eye and motioned her over with a quick raise of his eyebrows. His baby-blues shone out pound signs that money-grabbing bitches just can't resist.

"What's your pleasure?" she said, all smiles. Her eyes were dead. He could be anyone. He hated that.

He looked her up and down as if overwhelmed with everything on offer and unable to make up his mind so quickly.

"How about I dance a little for you whilst you make up your mind, sugar?"

"Okay, sounds good," he replied in his best shy boy routine.

She began to twist and shake to the music just like a true Rocket Queen. She turned around for him to undo her bra. In a quick motion he unsnapped the catch with his right hand as his left brushed out a twenty pound note from her g-string. She turned around unaware, revealing a large drooping pair of breasts, which looked well handled, almost like a dog-eared book. He wondered just how many fingers had thumbed through her pages.

Cutthroat brought out his wallet and pulled out a ten-pound note. Her face lit up as if she had never seen it before. As she stepped close - almost touching- Cutthroat slipped the ten in the front whilst slipping another twenty from the back at the same time as he slapped her bare buttocks playfully.

"We must do this again," she said putting her bra back on. "I hope it was worth it."

Cutthroat gave his best look of gratitude before replying, "More than you'll ever know."

She looked back one last time and added, "Maybe you'll want more next time."

...JUST SOUTH OF HEAVEN/JIM ODY

Cutthroat felt the forty pounds in his pocket. "I think I will," he replied wondering whether he should have taken another twenty. Life was all about the line of greed and trying not to cross it.

In the club the signal was shocking. That said, throughout Cornwall weak mobile signals were seen as a positive. Chalky couldn't get one bar to appear no matter how hard he shook it. Luckily the club's 80s décor included a bank of phones out the back.

Chalky put the handset down after leaving a message on Leigh-Ann's mobile telling her he was working late. He was sort of. He said he would crash at Big Al's so as not to wake her or mama up. He forgot to mention that he was in a strip club. It was a need to know type of deal.

He still wasn't sure of what to make about the story of the pocket-watch but he was having a little fun. He'd not had this since the last *Wagon Wheels* tour. God, did he miss it, even if the groupies were old women. The prospect of this being somewhat financially beneficial added the proverbial cherry to the topping of the night. Leigh-Ann wouldn't give two-hoots when he had a load of cash for her.

Dice and Caper seemed the strangest pair since *Laurel & Hardy*, and it was hard to see exactly where in society these two belonged.

And the girl? What was that all about? Say what you want about these two clowns, they knew how to have fun. They had some sort of magic that made you question why a young attractive female might latch on to them and follow them from here to a make-believe land without question.

He looked over at them and saw them laughing at something and suddenly wished he was sharing the joke. They seemed to think they had hitmen after them, but the two idiots from the club couldn't take a hit out on a cub scout, and looking at them they really didn't seem to care.

Chalky's only regret was that his own attractive female wasn't here with him, tugging on his arm showing everyone that she was his and he was hers. This would never be the sort of place she'd come to. He wasn't sure whether that was a good or bad thing.

As the redhead from the stage walked closer to him, he felt the guilt before she winked. He gave a nervous smile and looked away, agreeing to keep his money in his back pocket. He suddenly didn't want to touch the smalls of another woman.

He got out his packet of *Camels* and lit one with his metal Zippo lighter. He took a deep drag and thought about Leigh-Ann telling him they would be the death of him. And you know what? Maybe she was right.

Fuck the smoking ban, he thought. There wasn't a person here who gave a shit.

...JUST SOUTH OF HEAVEN/JIM ODY

Chapter Fifty-Three

"Well, this is fun," Aaron mumbled from the backseat of the car.

Presley yawned. "He's right. Let's forget about it and go to the hotel. I need my sleep!"

Elvis threw the door open in enthusiasm, which made both Presley and Aaron jump with a start and take notice. "Give me five minutes," he said grabbing his mobile like it was a deadly weapon.

"Where the hell is he going?" Aaron whined when he'd gone.

Presley gave a non-committal smile and replied, "Beats me."

Elvis was pissed. It had been a fucking ball-ache of an evening. Of a few days if he was honest. First, they'd been unable to get more members of the fan club, and then his girlfriend sneaks off to blow a stranger at a club! He was seething at the memory. He jogged down the back street and realised just how unfit he was. His lungs began to burn and his chest tightened like the invisible man was giving him a bear hug.

With a loud "Urgh!!" he shouted out in anger and kicked a chicken container as hard as he could. He then stopped and tried to count to ten. Then he carried on to twenty. By seventy-five he was feeling a little better.

He couldn't believe that Chalky still hadn't come out yet. *Did he sleep there?*

It was then that he heard a couple of blokes cackling in some deep throaty way. He looked around for a place to hide. He knew he was dead if it was Chalky or one of the other bouncers.

The only thing in sight was a kebab van that sat silently on its own. Uninhabited.

It was his only chance.

...JUST SOUTH OF HEAVEN/JIM ODY

He made a sprint to it as if it was his saviour. He made a grab for the back door as the two men came into sight, and was surprised (and thankful) to find it unlocked.

He jumped in head first. Skidding to a halt, he waited for the men to disappear.

As the voices got quieter Elvis let out a sigh of relief. He was about to make a move when the back door clicked shut.

Someone had locked it.

Elvis was now worried - but not half as worried as he was when the driver's door opened and closed, and then the engine started.

He thought about shouting. Maybe banging on the side, but these actions might scare the driver and smash the vehicle into a large lorry. He didn't want to die in a kebab van. That would be one of the worst places to die. Apart from on the toilet.

Where the hell was he going?

The kebab van rumbled down the street. The suspension was old and hard. Elvis realised this was a stupid idea after all, and suddenly wanted to be in the hot tub back at Graceland. He wanted Presley in there with him. He'd forgive her and she'd peel off her bikini.

Elvis got his mobile out and pressed a couple of buttons until Aaron's number came up, then pressed 'SEND.'

Thankfully his signal was flicking from one to two bars. Strong for these parts.

On two rings Aaron answered. "Elvis, where are you?" he said.

"I'm in a kebab van. Someone has locked me in—"

"Was it Chalky?"

Elvis's heart sank. Maybe it was. Shit, he could be in more trouble than he thought.

...JUST SOUTH OF HEAVEN/JIM ODY

"I dunno," he replied, looking through a gap in the side of the van. "Looks like we're heading out of town. We have just gone past the Burger-King drive-thru."

"Right, we are on our way."

"Okay, don't ring me in case the driver hears. I'll call again in a few minutes."

"Righto." They both hung up.

Presley looked confused at Aaron. "What the hell was that all about?"

"Elvis has only gotten into a kebab van, and someone has locked him in and driven off!" It was almost funny.

Aaron jumped into the front seat and started the engine.

"But, how are—" Before Presley could finish, Aaron replied, "I don't know, let's just try and find him." He slammed the gearbox into first and left a twin pair of skid marks in the street, as he sped off like a formula one racer.

"The stupid git," was all Presley could mumble as they looked out for a kebab van with live meat in the back.

After a beat Aaron then said, "Why did you do it?"

"Do what?" she replied but knew exactly what he was on about.

"The guy at the club. You went off with someone you've never met before and—"

"Sucked his cock."

"Yes, that."

Presley shuffled in the seat. Perhaps the guilt was making her uncomfortable. She didn't really know what to say to Aaron. He was a mummies-boy. He probably just needed a good fuck by a strong woman. Although, he'd be one of those guys who would cry after. He'd thank you first, hold you tight and cry. She hated that. She preferred men that chucked her clothes out of the window and told her to fuck off. You knew where you were with them.

"Elvis is cool," she started. "You are both great. The fan club is great."

"But?"

"But I wanted a bit of excitement. The guy grabbed me and suddenly I didn't want to stop him. I know it wasn't right, but come on, if a girl grabbed you what would you do?"

"Probably piss myself."

"Okay, bad example."

"He loves you, Pres."

She nodded. "I know."

"He acts like an arsehole, but he's got a heart of gold. You've hurt him."

The silence of speech hung in the air as Aaron sped down the roads.

***

It had been a strange night for Travis.

Tonight, was the night he was sure he would never return from. He had planned this night for weeks. Tonight, would be his last night alive, and he was feeling somewhat disappointed with the events earlier. No one actually wants to die, they just don't want to live anymore. He'd come to terms with that and then those two idiots had freed him from the coffin. They were basically graverobbers. Yes, that's what they were. No better than Ed Gein. He should be lucky his head hadn't been scooped out and made into a fruit bowl or some such item.

What were the chances of someone finding him in the basement? What sort of weirdos go snooping in a basement and steal a coffin! I mean, is no-one's property safe nowadays?

...JUST SOUTH OF HEAVEN/JIM ODY

After leaving the van and the two strange dudes, Travis decided that he would go to the other place of worship in his life - *Peeping Tom's Pleasure Dome*. It was almost a sign.

A few hours had passed and after speaking to some of his regular mates, and gaping at that flesh from the pretty young things, he decided that he might go a little further tonight.

So here he was, pulling up his trousers in one of the back rooms. He was a little lighter in cash and a bit less horny than twenty minutes ago. His cheeks were flushed and a couple of liquid ounces of him were pooled on the floor. He hoped the cleaners were on more than minimum wage.

The girl had told him to ask for Foxy, if he should want a repeat performance. He thanked her and toyed with that very idea, then wondered whether he might like to try a different flavour next time. She'd been accommodating. Gentle at first and calling him Corporal. He liked that. She had a strong grip and a wonderful rhythm.

He grabbed his jacket and walked out grinning like a schoolboy.

It was then he remembered the teddy bear in his pocket. It was a stupid idea - but what the heck - it wasn't his bear.

"Hey, Foxy," he said. She turned her redhead around and grinned as she saw the bear.

"S'that fo' me?" she said giving a coy look of innocence.

"Yeah," he stuttered, "Something to remember me by."

"You're welcome, sugar."

***

In the main area of the club, the drinks kept rolling in. We sat back and watched the delights in front of us. Amy had a comment for each of the girls, which kept me amused. Dice sat with large eyes and I was beginning to think we might have to drag him out kicking and screaming.

"Jesus, look at that slapper," Amy said as a girl with bright green hair walked out. "She trying to be noticed or what?"

"I noticed her," Dice said not taking his eyes off of her. He was watching her so closely his head was bobbing up and down with her large breasts.

"That's great to know," Chalky added.

"Dice, stop nodding. You're like one of those dogs that old people used to put in the back of cars."

"What?" he said frowning but still looking like a stalker.

"Never mind."

Amy was shaking her head whilst saying, "I bet she thinks that her stupid hair will take your eyes away from her thunder thighs."

"Eh?" I said. I thought her thighs looked just fine. I never did understand that phrase. Was it a way of saying she was heavy-footed?

"Last time I saw legs that big, they were on a large grey animal with a trunk!" She laughed.

"Meow!" I said.

"I think her thighs are just fine," Dice said echoing my thoughts. He'd still not taken his eyes away from her or her thighs. We obviously had the same opinion. When I looked across, Chalky was also nodding in agreement.

"If you think you can do any better, be my guest!" I said. I was convinced that she probably would look a hell of a lot better than the rest of them. I was sort of warming to her.

"Come with me and I'll show you," she said slowly, looking straight into my eyes. She was tricking me, I could feel it - but I couldn't look a pussy. I took a sip of my drink then replied,

...JUST SOUTH OF HEAVEN/JIM ODY

"Okay, then." I waited for her to laugh at me and tell me she was joking.

But she didn't.

She stood up and said, "Come on then," and held out her hand. I looked over at Dice and Chalky. Dice was catching flies in disbelief and his eyebrows were so far up his forehead, I was waiting for them to get lost in his hairline. Chalky grinned maybe expecting her to still make me look stupid. It wouldn't take much.

I took her hand and started to follow her, feeling like a teenager at the local disco after the popular girl had finally noticed him. My heart was pounding out of my chest, and my trousers were starting to feel two sizes too small. It must've been the heat.

Then Dice's voice ruined my night.

"Caper, there he is!"

I turned around and mouthed "Who?"

"Travis," he said nudging Chalky nearly off of his chair. *Shit*, I thought and looked across the crowded place.

There he was wandering out of the door, unaware of what we were going through, the bastard!

And off we went like a bunch of shoplifters barging innocent folk out of our way.

With half naked women all around and our quick funny walking, the DJ could have played the *Benny Hill* theme tune and we wouldn't have looked out of place.

...JUST SOUTH OF HEAVEN/JIM ODY

Chapter Fifty-Four

Elvis had been doing his best not to fall into one of the cupboards. The floor was filthy and almost put him off ever having a kebab again in his life. All around was withered lettuce, bits of onion, and tomato pips. He looked out of the crack again as he felt the gears change down, and was surprised at what he saw.

He grabbed his phone and tapped a couple of buttons that had Aaron's phone ringing within two seconds. Presley answered.

"Where are you?" she said with desperation.

"We're pulling into the car park of *Peeping Tom's Pleasure Dome!*"

"The strip joint?" she spat back as if he had chosen it.

"No, the shoe-shop! Yes, the fucking strip joint!"

"Okay then. We're about ninety seconds away."

"Hurry up."

"We are. Don't go anywhere!"

"Ha fucking ha!"

***

Travis squinted as the brightness of the moon shone into his eyes. Why he'd looked directly at it was beyond him. He took a swig from his hip flask and tried to focus. He really shouldn't have downed that after all he'd drunk that night. He wasn't sure he wanted to go home to bed, but what were his choices? He even thought about lying out on the soft concrete below.

"Hi, how are you?" a female voice said from his left. He turned and saw a young lady with dark black hair and bright red lipstick smiling at him.

...JUST SOUTH OF HEAVEN/JIM ODY

"Not so bad," he slurred, hoping she didn't notice that he was drunk.

"You want a ride?" She asked and pointed to her van.

A kebab van.

Travis looked at her muscular legs and thought of them tight around his middle. "Sure," he replied and swayed over to her. He could sure murder a kebab right about now too!

Imagine that, he thought, *a lift in a kebab van.*

He walked over to the passenger's door and opened it whilst looking up and down the side of the van.

A kebab van, he chuckled to himself again, shaking his head. What a fucking day.

***

We'd burst out into the car park and saw Travis talking to someone.

"Who the fuck is that!" Dice said loudly as we all spied Travis getting into a kebab van *of all things* with a young lady.

We sprinted over to Dice's van and jumped in like we had just robbed the place. Real inconspicuous like. Maybe next time we'll all wear a stocking on our heads and carry sawn-offs. Only a bunch of idiots would do something like that.

***

Aaron skidded his car into the car park of *Peeping Tom's Pleasure Dome*. He almost rolled it. He tugged on the handbrake like he'd seen in the movies and it had slid sideways before a little wobble almost sent it over.

"Is that it over there?" Presley said grabbing her seat for safety and pointing to a white van over the other side of the car park. It was pulling out onto the exit road, its red lights glowing into the night.

"Yeah, I think it—" Aaron was interrupted by a large black van reversing back out and into them. It caught the corner of Aaron's front bumper and skidded them around in a forty-five-degree angle.

"What the—" Aaron spat slamming his brakes and holding his hands in the air. "Fuckin' idiots!" His car was taking a real bashing today. He probably shouldn't have been driving, but what the fuck.

***

"What was that?" Dice said looking over his shoulder then at his wing mirror.

"I think it was another car," I said, "Maybe we could go around cars in the future!"

"Wise-Arse!" He replied.

Chalky shook his head in disbelief. "I can't believe you are not stopping."

"We will probably not see Christmas if we lose that van, and you've now developed a conscience?" Dice added.

"Don't listen to him, Dice. I'm hoping for a bike from Santa this year!" I put in. Amy giggled, so that was good.

Maybe we'd still find time to dance for me before the night was out.

And then my phone buzzed.

"Here we go," said Dice.

It was Janie sending a text.

Have you got the watch? X

"She added a kiss at the end?" Dice said. "She stole your fish, set her husband on to you, and still gave you a kiss?"

...JUST SOUTH OF HEAVEN/JIM ODY

Chalky then gave me a strange look. Not the first of the night, and it wouldn't be the last. "Fish?"

Dice was enjoying this. "Yes, so as you will recall his ex rang earlier to say she'd burnt his house down."

"Ah-ha, I do remember that unfortunate event."

"Well, Romeo here slept with a woman last night who stole his fish this morning. She is the reason we are here trying to get a pocket-watch so as her husband doesn't kill him."

"Us," I added.

Chalky grinned. "This guy. He small and black?"

I shook my head. "I don't think so. I never met him."

"He fall asleep at the drop of a hat?" Chalky then asked.

Dice smacked the steering wheel. "Yes! That's him. He was some MMA fighter and developed narco-something. He just falls asleep at random times!"

"Ah, yes. The prick pulled a gun on me earlier tonight!"

"You should've killed him," I said.

"He did this to my nose," Chalky pointed to the cut on the bridge. It didn't look too bad. I think he got off lightly. "The fucking prick was about to pull the trigger and fell asleep. I ain't seen nothing like it!"

"Jesus Christ!" Amy said.

"Ain't no need for that," Chalky scolded.

"Sorry."

***

Bomb sat on the chair and looked closely at the redhead closing the door behind her. She smiled and walked up to him with a look that could be almost mistaken for lust. She was clutching a teddy bear, which was strange - but not unheard of.

...JUST SOUTH OF HEAVEN/JIM ODY

"My name's Foxy," she whispered as she leaned over to him, putting the bear's head next to his ear like it was speaking the sweet words. Sort of off-putting really, Bomb thought. He wasn't into Teddy-porn.

Until he heard the ticking.

Mr Bear seems to have swallowed a timing device. An antique timing device, he wondered. Or a bomb.

Merry fucking Christmas, Bomb, he could almost hear it say.

"How much?" he said.

"Fifty," she replied.

"And for the bear too?"

She gave a cheeky grin. "You can do him for free!"

"Maybe I want him more permanently."

"If you're good enough, you can have the bear, the memories, and my knickers for an extra tenner."

If only she knew, Bomb thought. "Done," he replied ready to go.

Then added, "What sort of knickers?" Like it really mattered.

"Small, sexy, and nice to touch. Here, take a feel."

Talk about ha'penny and a bun...

If this had been a cartoon, then you would've been able to see the steam shooting out of Cutthroat's ears. He had just witnessed Chalky and friends running out of the club, however his partner was nowhere to be seen. It didn't take a rocket scientist to tell him where the little shit was at, either. Seriously, when this was done he was getting him castrated. It was the only way.

Cutthroat ran out of the entrance which seemed to get the attention of the bouncers. They hadn't battered an eyelid when the other four ran through earlier, but deemed it unusual that a single person be running. What a hullabaloo!

Cutthroat had seen them get into the van and had jotted the registration number down on a ten-pound note. He grabbed his phone and rang a friend in the know.

On the sixth ring a tired voice answered. "Yeah?"

"Hey, Barney. How are ya' mate?" Cutthroat said like it was a Sunday afternoon.

"I was asleep, actually. That's what normal people do," he said stubbornly. "So, to answer your question, not very well. What the fuck d'you want at this hour?"

"A yeah, funny one. Look I need to know a name and address of the keeper for the following vehicle—"

"Hold on, let me get a pen." Cutthroat gave him the reg and promised him some compensation on his lack of sleep - if and only if, the information was of use to them.

Barney would take about quarter of an hour to get the information, so Cutthroat headed back into the club to see if his partner had raised his ugly little head yet.

He once again thought he might just cut the little bastard out of this deal once and for all. He'd already had a narcoleptic episode tonight. It was very often he had two or three spells, so he probably could put a bullet in the head of the little shit and live happily ever after.

He looked over at the newest dancer. It seemed as though she was in the twilight of her pole dancing career, which was to say she looked experienced and weathered. He tapped his hand to the beat of some rock anthem and glanced around at the sorry sight of men starring and pretending not to be touching themselves under tables.

...JUST SOUTH OF HEAVEN/JIM ODY

As he put a fresh cigarette between his lips, he saw the grinning face of his AWOL partner appear in his vision - holding a Goddamn teddy bear. What the fuck.

"Where the..? What the..?" Cutthroat had so many questions, he didn't quite know where to start.

"I can explain this," he smiled as if it was the best trophy a man could win. "Mr Bear has something in his tummy!"

"Are you retarded?"

"That's not a nice thing to say."

"I don't give a fuck about Mr Bear."

"Hold on. I don't think you're understanding the situation correctly. Mr Bear has something ticking in his tummy. A time-piece, shall we say."

Cutthroat took a deep drag of his fag and thought back to the cellar. *Of course*, he thought, *the pocket-watch!*

"That it, you think?" Cutthroat asked.

Bomb frowned and chuckled, "How many other fuckin' bears can there be with a ticking tummy!" He had a point.

"How do we know it's the watch? And how did it get here?"

"Maybe they dropped it. Or maybe the bear called an Uber?"

"We missed them you know," Cutthroat stated, ignoring the last bit.

"So what are you still doing here, then?"

"He jumped in a van with three others..." Ignoring Bomb's rant.

"Four, altogether? Where do all these people come from at this unearthly hour? Don't they have homes to go to?"

"...I dunno. There was Caper with beads around his neck, His mate Dice, that big fucking Chalky, and the other was a girl that would have you droppin' your draws again for!"

"*Yeah?*" The sickening look of lust was all too apparent in Bomb's eyes once again.

...JUST SOUTH OF HEAVEN/JIM ODY

"Yeah."

"And we're still standing here for what reason?" Bomb said whilst fidgeting with his crotch.

"Barney's running the plates."

"How is Barney? He okay now?"

"He was tired and pissed at being woken up. What d'you mean okay now?"

"It doesn't matter. If he didn't tell you, then you don't need to know."

"No, go on. What is it?"

"It's personal. It's better coming from him."

"Whatever."

"Right, let's get another beer and stare at some more at these fine women." Bomb smiled already moving towards the bar.

"You twat!" Cutthroat said, but Bomb was already gone.

...JUST SOUTH OF HEAVEN/JIM ODY

Chapter Fifty-Five

As Aaron got out of the car, he saw the van speed off in the same direction as the kebab van. He looked at the front tire and noticed that the bumper had bent and one of the jagged pieces had split the tyre.

Not again, he thought. *Maybe I should get shares in Dunlop.*

"Tyre's flat," he said throwing his hands in the air as if casting a spell like a wizard.

"What!" She shouted and jumped out of the car to look for herself. They'd already used the spare earlier.

"Well, that's us fucked then!"

"What a night."

Aaron looked out along the road that once had seen a kebab van bouncing around. Somewhere inside, Elvis was hidden and heading off into the great unknown. Then Aaron's phone rang.

"Are you following?" Elvis whispered with hope.

"Not exactly," Aaron replied looking at Presley with wonder, and thinking that maybe he should lose his voice with a bout of laryngitis.

"What do you mean!" Elvis demanded whilst fighting to keep his voice low.

"Some van backed back into us and punctured our tyre. We have no spare now, do we!"

"Shit," Elvis said. "I'll ring back later, and you had better be ready to go by then!" The phone went dead. Aaron wasn't sure what Elvis expected him to do. If he could go shit a spare tyre, then he'd be a magician.

"He's not a happy bunny!" Aaron said to Presley.

"Yeah, gathered that," she replied.

Aaron stood there with one hand on his hip and the other straight out to the side in a parody of a pissed off tea-pot.

...JUST SOUTH OF HEAVEN/JIM ODY

"What're we gonna do now?" he said.

Presley shrugged, then after a moment's thought added idly, "Why don't you try to buy someone's spare tyre?"

"Huh?"

"Look around you. This place is packed with cars. Each car has an owner that is in there watching naked ladies and throwing around tens and twenties like confetti. I'm sure they would like some extra queen's head to spend on the pleasures of the flesh!"

Aaron nodded in agreement. "I think you're on to something."

They pushed the car into the nearest space and flipped to see who would go and try to purchase the spare.

"I think you should," Aaron offered. "Being a girl an all."

"Very observant. I don't think that it's a great idea that a female should stand outside a strip club offering the local punters cash and following them to their car. They might rape me!"

"You could suck their dick too," he mumbled.

"What was that?"

"The luck here's with you."

She narrowed her eyes. "Hmmm, I think you're about to get a fat lip, Buster!"

"Oh, I love it when you call me Buster." He flipped the ten pence piece up in the air and chanted, *heads* under his breath again and again.

Presley caught it and flipped it over onto the back of her other hand.

The Queen looked unimpressed and unmoved by the importance of her appearance and remained poker-faced.

"Best of three?" she tried.

"No chance! See ya', Darlin'!" Aaron giggled like an immature teenager.

"Piss off," she mumbled as she got out of the car.

...JUST SOUTH OF HEAVEN/JIM ODY

Aaron stretched over and tapped her backside. "You might want to use your charms, if ya know what I mean!"

Presley glared at him with contempt and gave him a two fingered salute.

Just then a pink Mini came skidding into the car park. It stopped and three guys all dressed as sailors got out. The stood looking up at the place like it was the answer to all of their dreams. Men were so sad. The driver waved and drove off before she could approach him.

"Hi!" she said to them trying to look sexy.

"Woman Elvis!" one said with a grin.

"Sailor boys," she said fluttering her eyelids.

The big built one was already jogging with one with blond hair as the last one said, "Horny sailor boys!" And they were gone.

...JUST SOUTH OF HEAVEN/JIM ODY

Chapter Fifty-Six

"Well shit in a shish-kebab, this boy's motoring," Dice said as we found it hard to not let their back lights fade out of sight.

"Shit in a what?" I said.

"Don't you be picking at what I say, Caper," he chuckled. "Not with them beads on."

"You like my beads," I demanded. "You are just in denial."

"I like them," Amy said.

Dice laughed at that. "You thought he was gay!" He laughed again pounding the steering wheel.

"I was only joking," she paused and said with a straight face. "I think I was in denial..."

Dice swerved the van at that. "Shut up!" He shouted through tears.

"...Yeah, I think I was just disguising my jealousy."

"You *are* a girl though," Chalky added with a laugh.

"Shut up, before I crash this damn thing!" Dice said again through his laughter.

"Just saying what I feel," she added again.

"You go girl!" I added and we high-fived. It was a sudden shock of hysteria brought on by the excitement of the night. Dicing with death will do that to you.

Dice turned to me. "What did you put in her drink, man? First she wants to show you her donuts, then she thinks your beads are cool—"

"I never said they were cool. I just mentioned that I liked them!" She grinned.

"Okay. Point taken." He looked ahead and we saw the kebab van take a sharp turn to the left and head down a country road with hedges looming up either side.

...JUST SOUTH OF HEAVEN/JIM ODY

We were going faster than the roads should allow. I knew how a Rally driver's co-pilot felt being shaken side-to-side without the ability to be in control.

Then suddenly we dipped down, and the hedges retreated to give us a wide view for miles. It was quite breath-taking.

The full moon glinted romantically on the sea. It twinkled like a million magical stars. Sparkles of hope from wishes granted all over the world. I would have loved to have stopped there, sink a few beers with a lovely woman. A campfire and some canoodling would follow. After making love for hours, we'd sit with a blanket around us and watch the sun come up. But, staying alive was a little bit more important right now. I smiled to myself and made a note that when I knew I no longer had a bounty on my head, I'd come back here and live out this fantasy.

It would more than likely be alone.

"You think the mist is going to come down all of a sudden?" Chalky said looking up into the black sky like he might be expecting to see E.T. The famous silhouette flying over the full moon on that God-forsaken bike.

"If it was one of those movies, surely you two in the back should either be makin' out or smokin' grass!" Dice said.

"Sorry, you're not my type, sweetheart!" Chalky said to Amy. "And I left my stash at home."

"Shouldn't we have some rock band thumping out some teenage angst?" I offered.

Dice nodded to the glove compartment. "Good shout, my man." He hit a few buttons and suddenly Marilyn Manson was screaming out about *Beautiful People*. Beauty was subjective after all.

***

...JUST SOUTH OF HEAVEN/JIM ODY

Back at the club, the guy's face lit up as he stumbled out of the doors and set his eyes on the hopeful face of Presley.

She looked at his wavy hair and the stubble on his chin and wondered whether he had had a hard day or a hard life. He could have been any age from thirty to sixty, she really couldn't tell. Though he was stumbling, he was still one of those idiots that would try and drive home.

"You got a car?" she said fluttering her eyelids at him.

He smiled at her then mumbled in a thick Scottish accent. "Yeah, but I ain't drivin' nowhere. I bin drinkin', see?"

"You got a spare tyre in your boot?" she then added.

...JUST SOUTH OF HEAVEN/JIM ODY

He gave big grin and replied tugging his trousers, "No, just my tight buttocks in these, lassie!" He laughed out loud to that and slapped his thigh like it was the joke of the year.

"I mean in your car," Presley pressed, none too pleased with his attempt at humour.

"Aye, I got me-self one of 'em too!" He roared again, but at what it wasn't clear. "Ya follow me, missy." And off he went in a swaying meander that was somehow like a slow dance.

***

Travis wasn't sure what he was feeling at this point in time. He sat in the front seat of the kebab van and listened to a haunting song called *Years Ago* by Alice Cooper, about a man who still thinks he's a boy. He could actually feel the shivers going up and down his spin like some icy cold digit. Out here in the middle of nowhere the thought of what it was like to still think you were ten years old, when in fact you are grown up, was even more scary.

The young lady hadn't said much to him, except that she had a surprise in store for him. This made him nervous. The last time he was told that, a young girl by the name of Dixie had taken him to her flat. He had licked her tits like they were chocolate muffins but when he went in for the honey pot, he found out one big reason why her name was Dixie. He developed a cough and excused himself from her flat forthwith.

He'd made a mental note to question women a little more before he went off with them. He then realised he'd ignored that completely tonight. Again. He glanced over at her. She didn't look like she was hiding a big cock. But then neither had Dixie.

This woman seemed quite feminine. Her bright red lipstick and beautifully made up face made him wonder whether she'd really been out selling kebabs and burgers tonight.

...JUST SOUTH OF HEAVEN/JIM ODY

The young lady turned to Travis with an evil twinkle in her eye and said, "You know what would be really nice?"

Travis had his own idea, but wasn't sure that hers was in anyway similar. Despite that he replied, "What?"

She reached behind her seat and pulled out a long white coat and handed it to him. "Put this on, will you?"

She wants to play doctors and nurses? Travis thought until he saw the hat. *United Dairies* was printed on the cap. *A bloody milkman!?*

"You like milkmen?" Travis said confused.

"Ooh, yeah," she replied in an orgasmic purr. *Whatever,* Travis thought and pulled on the coat. He then realised that the strange rattling noise was coming from four empty milk bottles under his seat. At that point he wasn't sure whether she was a vixen or a loon. *Sexy or simple*, it sounded like a new television show on Channel 5.

The town was a long way behind them when the kebab van pulled into an old pub car park on the cliff side. The pub hadn't been open to the public in years and was as welcoming as the house in Amityville. It was a fair size for a country local and had probably once been a hotel or inn. A place for people from the city to escape to.

***

Dice whistled as the old pub came into view. He slowed down and killed the lights.

"Nice place," I said with sarcasm. "To be murdered."

"At least the coffin will feel at home," Amy whispered as Dice pulled into a gateway and cut the engine.

We sat there almost holding our breath as the engine made the odd clicking sound as it settled.

Dice turned around and said, "What the hell is a kebab van doing out here?"

...JUST SOUTH OF HEAVEN/JIM ODY

"Private job?" I grinned and looked up at the pub. All the windows were black and my eyes kept telling me that ghosts and goblins were going to leer out at me. I kept expecting to see the woman in black.

"This place is dead," Amy said.

"Hey, you alright, Chalky-boy?" Dice suddenly said.

With a yawn Chalky replied, "Yeah, I think I've had all of the excitement I can handle. I need some sleep."

"Ahh, bless," Amy said patting him on the shoulder.

"What the fuck is Travis wearing?!" Dice said stunned as we stared at the sight in front of us.

Travis the Milkman got out of the kebab van - empty milk bottles an all! He couldn't have looked any funnier if he'd been holding a three-foot dildo.

"If a chef gets out the other side, and a fireman bursts from the back, then I am going to piss myself!" Dice chuckled loudly, and for a moment I almost believed they would.

We saw the young lady get out of the other side, disappointing us at not being in fancy dress too.

"You sure we're not all dreaming?" I whispered, but I don't know why I was speaking so quietly. Maybe it was because without the music blasting, and the engine, all I could hear was breathing and the sound of beating hearts. And the smell of fear.

"Now what?" I said, almost afraid of what Dice was going to suggest.

He smiled. He was enjoying this strange pantomime that had gate crashed my life. "We go get that pocket-watch!"

"We are putting a lot in an assumption he has it," I pointed out.

"He must have it," Dice said. "Where else would it be?"

"It's still a risk."

"Off we go then," Dice encouraged.

"What, all of us?" I said, and kind of hoped that would be the case, or better still everyone except for me.

...JUST SOUTH OF HEAVEN/JIM ODY

"No, it'll only take a couple of us, someone has to stay with the van on look out. If we all go, they might think we are starting a party."

"Right, well as I'm comfy," I said, "I'll stay here."

"Me too," Amy said. "I'm going back in that coffin."

Chalky then came alive. "Don't look at me, I ain't going in there! I should be in bed, man. Besides I've got a split nose thanks to him," he said nudging my back.

"I said I was sorry, man." Jesus, some folks sure hold a grudge.

"Yeah, well, show us how sorry you are and go get that god-damn watch, so I can get home."

"Dice, you should go, man," I offered. "It is your plan."

"I've got it!" Dice exclaimed.

"Don't give it to me," I jested.

"Cards." He ignored me.

"What?" We all said in unison.

"*We will settle this with a game of cards*," Dice smiled like he was demanding some dual.

I looked at him like he'd just spread a rumour about me and his dad. "Do I need to remind you that if we don't get this watch, we are going to have to run like bitches? I don't think we have time to indulge in a spot of Black Jack, do you?"

"I was thinking more of Amy an' me, playing strip poker. You know, she'll strip and I'll poke-her!" Dice laughed.

"That's just crude," Amy said deadpan.

"Says the girl who offered us sex earlier."

"Why do you think you are single, again, Dice?" I said.

"For that," Amy added. "I think you should go, *Dice*. By the way, what a fucking stupid name you've got." I wasn't sure whether or not she was serious.

"Besides," I said. "You let Travis go in the first place."

Dice raised his eyebrows. "What? I didn't see you running after him."

...JUST SOUTH OF HEAVEN/JIM ODY

"Well, if you hadn't been playing the devil..."

"Shut the fuck up!" Chalky said loud enough for kangaroos and koalas to hear. "Let's go get the fuckin' pocket-watch, yeah?"

We all nodded in agreement.

Dice got his playing cards out. Each one depicting a different pose from a naked young lady. It must have taken some time and skill to think up the fifty-two poses. And just when you thought you'd seen it all there were the two jokers. All I can say is they were just plain rude.

Amy stared at her hand of cards, amazed at what some women would do for money. "You're quite a pervert really, aren't you, Dice?" She said and I found Chalky and myself nodding our heads - whilst looking closely at our own hands. Some of those things I would probably never see again in the whole of my life.

...JUST SOUTH OF HEAVEN/JIM ODY

Chapter Fifty-Seven

Travis walked through the large oak door into the pub and was hit by a strong smell he couldn't quite put his finger on. The place wasn't as rundown as the outside. It was filled with antiques as old as father time. It was hard to see where this young lady fitted into the picture. Maybe a hoard of cats would appear and kill him. He'd had her down as a cat-lady. One with a milkman fetish. Perhaps she'd offer him a saucer full.

"You want a little drink before we start," she said and cast her hand out towards a large drinks cabinet. It was likened to a small off-license store.

"Sure," Travis replied. He wondered whether he'd had enough of the devil's water for the night, but what the fuck? It would be rude not to. There was still a part of him that wanted to leave. Rip off the coat and drop the bottles and run out of the door.

But he stayed.

"Name your poison," she smiled and took off her jacket.

"Scotch would be great."

Travis watched as she picked up a large bottle half full with golden brown liquid and sloshed a couple of inches into a small glass. She turned around holding the glass as if it was the sacred golden goblet and said, "What's it worth?"

Travis was intrigued by this mysterious woman. He usually picked up young bimbos that were dressed like street whores and were happy to be shown affection of any sort. He'd seen a number of one-bedroom flats, the cramped backseats of a few small city cars, trashed student digs and even their parents' double beds, but never had he been taken out into the English everglades to such a large and abandoned house-cum-pub. By now he would've already had them on their back, naked, screaming, and clothed again. He would be on his way home forgetting their name and deleting their number from his phone.

...JUST SOUTH OF HEAVEN/JIM ODY

He gave her a blank look to the question. She perched on the edge of the large oak table so her skirt rode up and flashed lime green knickers at him.

"You want this?" She demanded thrusting the glass forward. He wasn't sure. He wasn't used to this.

He nodded anyway.

"Pray for it," she said.

He bowed his head and closed his eyes.

"Is that how you pray in church?" She demanded with the authority of a teacher to a naughty schoolboy.

He shrugged. As she pulled up her skirt to her waist and slipped off her panties, he realised that he should be on his knees and breathing through his ears.

"That's it, Mr Milkman," she said as he knelt down. "Pray long and hard for redemption, my sinner!" She shouted. And the scotch was forgotten about.

***

Back in the car park of the strip club, Presley was about to commit murder.

"What do you mean, you can't find your keys?" Presley said fuming and at the end of her tether.

The guy patted his empty pockets again as if he might have missed them the first twenty times of looking. "They were here a minute ago, lassie," he said with a shrug. "The wind has taken them, so it has!"

"I suggest you find them! And do I look like a fuckin' dog!"

"You look to me like a fine young lady - *is what you look like*." He reached out and placed a hand on her hip.

"Get off!" she shouted and slapped him good and hard.

"Screw you, darlin'!" he said and stormed off.

"Bastard!"

...JUST SOUTH OF HEAVEN/JIM ODY

He stuck two fingers up in the air at her in defiance and carried on walking away in his drunken dance.

***

In the back of Dice's van things were tense.

I had lost the first game thanks to the absence of the *Ace of Hearts*, (which I'm sure was missing by the way) and things were looking pretty glum. Dice hadn't mastered the art of a poker face, and Amy was playing her hand like it was going to save her life. Which it probably was.

And then there was Chalky. I had my suspicions he played once a week, puffing on a Cuban with one of those banker's visors on and wearing sleeve clips. Just to piss us off he shuffles the cards so skilfully that he can make a single card jump out and land face up every time. I imagine he spent many hours alone as a child mastering this trick. It probably got him laid more than once too.

I wish I hadn't played so much with the Top Trump cards as a child. That said, I do know shit loads about cars, bikes, and trucks circa 1985 - but fuck all about this specific game that we were playing.

Amy put down her hand of a pair of aces (minus the Ace of Hearts, I might add) and a pair of tens with a three. Dice threw his hand down in frustration, which was a pair of twos, a seven, a five and a Jack. I placed my Full House hand of three fours and a pair of queens and was feeling quite confident when Chalky laid his Royal Flush hand down and gave a big sigh of relief. He had won twice now and therefore would stay in the van. Our rules were this: Two would stay in the van and two would go to the house. Either the first two who won two games would stay in the van, or the first two to come last would go to the house.

...JUST SOUTH OF HEAVEN/JIM ODY

Two games down and Chalky had won twice and Dice and me had come last once each. Amy was sitting pretty with no wins, but no defeats.

Chalky sat the next game out but treated us to his remarkable shuffling techniques once more and spun each card out to us whilst dealing.

***

Back in the carpark, Aaron could see that Presley wasn't exactly having great success in finding a spare tyre. He searched around the parking lot for other options.

Then his phone rang. *Shit.*

He really couldn't be done with speaking to Elvis now. He toyed with telling him that everything was fine and they were on their way - but he would never buy it. Aaron couldn't lie for shit. So, he just ignored it.

Then he heard a voice.

"You got a problem, pal?"

Aaron looked around to where the soft male voice had come from.

"Yeah, we got a-," he paused as he saw that the guy was wearing a dress, "-flat."

The guy smiled, amused that Aaron wasn't expecting a guy in drag. "I got a spare you can have."

"Um, thanks," Aaron replied uncomfortably looking around for Presley to come back. He was beginning to feel threatened, though he wasn't sure why.

"Come over to my van," the guy said, then noticed how the colour drained from Aaron's face. He laughed then said, "I'm not looking to jump you! I'll bring it over to you if you prefer?"

Aaron now felt even more stupid. "No... I...it's alright I'll come over. Thanks."

"Do I make you nervous?" the guy said.

...JUST SOUTH OF HEAVEN/JIM ODY

Aaron gave a false laugh. "No, don't be dumb…'course not. Why would you?" He was now waffling. A sure sign of nerves.

"You never seen a man in a dress before?"

"Not really, no."

"Not really? What does that mean? Either you have or you haven't!"

"I mean, eh, only on T.V." He then realised what he'd said and quickly added. "Television, you know, um,"

"I'm familiar with a television."

"Right. Of course."

"I'm not gay by the way," he said suddenly like this mattered.

"You're not?" Aaron said in the same surprised way Neil Armstrong's parents did when told them he wanted to go to the moon.

"Just because I wear dresses doesn't mean I'm-" he winked twice and made two clucking sounds with his tongue at the same time, "-I'm no beaver leaver! What d'you think I'm doing here?"

"Eh, fashion ideas?" Aaron said nervously.

"Ha! Fashion ideas! Yeah, I like that!" The guy grinned amused and walked away to where his van must be. Aaron couldn't help but notice the guy's hairy legs as he walked with an unfeminine side-to-side swagger of a man. He concluded that the guy wasn't trying to be a woman, he just liked to wear a dress. In a lightbulb moment he was stunned with this notion.

***

Still on his knees with a tongue working like a piston, Travis couldn't help but think something was going to attack him from behind. He hadn't considered this to be how his day would end. It was awkward, and he wasn't enjoying it half as much as the last time he had done this.

...JUST SOUTH OF HEAVEN/JIM ODY

When she suddenly screamed like a banshee or a woman in labour, Travis didn't feel the usual satisfaction that engulfed him with encouragement. In fact, he was too scared to stop and look up for fear of her sprouting hair all over and howling at the moon. The chills on his back were for real and he kept thinking that a pair of balls were going to appear on his chin. That would really top off this nightmare.

After a long hard exhale and squeal, she pushed his head away, and for a split-second Travis thought that she was going to pull her knickers up, then her hand vigorously motioned back and forth like she might have a terrible itch where his mouth had just been.

Travis knelt back with his glistening mouth open wide with disbelief and felt the most sense of inadequacy he had ever experienced in his life.

For what seemed like an age, she writhed around and made noises likened to animals on their deathbed. Travis wiped his face, stood up, and stretched his legs. She carried on building up and up into quite a crescendo.

When the finale finally reached its climax, Travis realised why she lived so far away from anyone else. Her final scream would have anyone dialling for the emergency services, and the following panting would have her arrested for being plain obscene as an act of auditory perversion.

He looked and stared at her and couldn't help being aroused. Her black hair was stuck with sweat to her forehead. She had pulled her top up and pushed her bra over her small breasts amidst the heat of her personal passion to gain greater euphoric pleasure and lead her to her own private nirvana.

It was at that point that he heard something bang from the room above him, and his heart missed more beats than you'd think was medically possible.

They were not alone.

Someone or something else was in the house.

...JUST SOUTH OF HEAVEN/JIM ODY

***

Back in the van I was ready to spit the proverbial dummy. Cards were a bloody stupid game. I've always had that in the back of my mind, however this was all too apparent now as those bastard aces had caught me out again. I fucking hate aces. They sit in the pack like they own the place. They don't even have a proper value. They think they're cool because they don't have a face on them either. Well, screw you, aces. Screw you!

I sat back and stared at the red lights and wondered how I could have lost two games before anyone else. I wasn't looking forward to going up to that big house alone. I tried using my Chinese mind tricks. These had a surprising amount of success throughout my life. Proof was hard to come by, but I knew. Boy, did I know. Each incident couldn't purely be put down to coincidence. I was hoping that Dice would come with me as I felt he would do a lot better in a fight than Amy.

But you never know with a woman. Sometimes, they can be a real wildcard.

...JUST SOUTH OF HEAVEN/JIM ODY

Chapter Fifty-Eight

Elvis was sat fuming in the kebab van. His back against the cold stainless steel. Why wasn't Aaron answering the phone? This was hardly his idea of fun!

He looked through the crack in the side of the van and saw a large building. He'd already heard the sound of the waves crashing against the rocks, so he knew he must be near the edge of the cliff.

It had been one long night and he was beginning to question just why he'd bothered to come here at all. He was bound to run into Chalky again. Why get yourself killed in the process?

He could speak to someone and get him beaten up. Rally around the troops. Except, truth was he didn't know anyone. It was just one of those things he heard in movies. All he had was Aaron and Presley. His other mates slipped away when he began to be obsessed with Elvis.

He looked over at the side window and saw a padlock. These things were easy to pick. He'd seen it a done a million times in movies. You pop in something small, twist, and *pop* it flips open and you look smug. He pulled out his penknife and clipped open the small thin metal instrument, the one that baffled most people as to its existence, and preceded to wiggle it all around. He tried it clockwise, anti-clockwise, and then tried stabbing and swearing, but the lock remained intact.

He fucking hated kebab vans.

***

Travis was humming to himself when she finally wiped her forehead and pulled her bra over her large breasts. She smiled at his amazement. "You not used to the sight of a satisfied woman?"

...JUST SOUTH OF HEAVEN/JIM ODY

Travis tried hard not to stutter when he said, "No, I guess that was a little different from what I see everyday."

She pulled up her knickers and wiggled her skirt down. When she walked forward, she strode with large purposeful steps. "You want to see upstairs?" she teased.

"And what's up there that might interest me? You got a pool table or a Playstation4?" Travis stammered realising he still didn't know her name.

She gave an evil grin as she looked from the floor, slowly up his body to his eyes. "My bedroom."

She took his hand and led him out of the room. "Don't forget your bottles," she said. He reluctantly picked them up and followed her out to the large staircase. All of the while he was thinking if he wasn't so turned on at that point, then her fruitcake persona would have him running back to mother in the blink of the eye.

"What's your name?" Travis asked as they climbed the stairs in the dark. The steps were deep and carpeted. He almost tripped a couple of times.

She paused for a second and said, "What does it matter?"

"It would be a shame not to know," he smiled in a way that was genuine. He also wanted to add it to his little book. He had a list of all the girls he'd slept with. There were a couple without names and it looked weird. He didn't like that.

She laughed at that, not used to sincerity. "My name is Martha, *if you must know*."

"Pleased to meet you, Martha. My name is Travis."

"Hi Travis," she replied with a disinterest. A month from now she'd have forgotten it. There would be other milkmen.

Paintings of men's faces could be made out in the moonlight all up the side of the staircase. The strange thing about the men was that they all looked fairly young. They were out of place with the tops of their three-piece suits just visible.

...JUST SOUTH OF HEAVEN/JIM ODY

At the top of the stairs, a long dark corridor ran left and right. Travis felt his heart beating fast and remembered what someone had once said about fear and lust producing similar reactions to your body. A racing heart rate, heightened awareness in senses, dilating pupils, goose bumps, sweating, and so on. The only difference was the aching feeling in his crotch. A dormant beast of lust now awoken.

"I need the bathroom," she said. "Go on down to the end room on the right." She pointed towards that direction.

Travis was wondering whether this was really worth it and he took small careful steps along the corridor. He thought about running out of there and back to the strip joint. He never thought he'd be running scared into *Peeping Tom's* and looking to release his lust on one of those sweet young fillies.

When the floorboard creaked Travis nearly released the contents of his bowels into his pants, and his heart almost broke a rib. Of course, he was also lucky not to drop his milk-bottles.

When realising how foolish he was at being scared of his own shadow, he carried on to the last door on the right.

The door with the red light spilling out from underneath.

He pulled his milkman's hat back and wiped his brow, replaced it and with one hand clutching the milk-bottles, he opened the door with the other.

His mind was racing with a number of things. He was thinking about how his life was looking up. He'd gone from looking to leave this world, to being caught up in some woman's fantasy. He thought about kissing Martha on the traditional area of the body. The one below her nose.

He swung the door open and walked in tentatively, and was met by a lonely eeriness. If this were a movie then cinemagoers would be slipping down in their seats, waiting in anticipation for something to jump out at the idiot walking into the unknown.

...JUST SOUTH OF HEAVEN/JIM ODY

He saw the small single bed sat in the corner. It was strange because the size of the room made it look even smaller than it probably was.

A single light gave off a glow that cast large looming shadows.

The wallpaper was floral and dated. Small areas had been scratched desperately with nails.

Then two things happened.

First the door clicked behind him. His head swung around and saw an elaborate locking system with a red-light flashing.

Then he heard a similar clicking sound from the other side of the room. He swung his head towards the closet in the corner.

The door swung open and a man sprung out. He was half crouched like an ape with arms that extended out menacingly.

He looked at Travis. His wild eyes scanning him from head to toe. They spied the bottles and the outfit. His lip curled up at the corner in a sneer. Crooked yellow teeth looked like they wanted to taste him. He let out a piercing primal scream and ran at Travis either to give him a big friendly hug, or to taste his heart and kidneys.

Some people sure hate milkmen.

...JUST SOUTH OF HEAVEN/JIM ODY

Chapter Fifty-Nine

"How about another game?" Dice said staring with contempt at the black woman pictured on his card. She had an uncomfortable look on her face, which was hardly surprising seeing as how she was sitting on something a lot smaller than a chair and shaped more like a truncheon.

"Uh-uh!" Amy replied with a cheeky grin. "You two have fun, yeah?"

Chalky picked up the cards and flicked through them again. This time he bent the pack and sent them in an arc over his head from his left to right hands. Another time it would've been impressive. "Yeah, we'll keep the van warm, lads!"

It was the thought of the unknown that made me feel so uncomfortable. Dice didn't look enthusiastic for life anymore, and for a guy usually so fearless this was a worry. We could both think of things or people we'd rather be doing.

I tried to remain nonchalant and blasé about the whole situation. This started as a feeling, but like wind it escaped with nothing but air. "Let's go get the pocket-watch back, Dice," I said trying to muster up something likened to courage, in a whimpering battle-cry.

"Yeah, what's the worst that could happen?" Chalky asked with a snigger.

Amy shrugged then added flippantly, "They could die, I suppose?"

"That's true," he replied deadpan.

"Yeah, real nice!" Dice said, and out we got.

The night was turning into morning, and with it was quite a cold wind that creaked the pub sign and swayed the trees all around us. The sea looked choppy with plenty of white capping the waves. Cross winds had us losing balance. With acts that were almost mischievous, it pushed us and ran around us like annoying children. I was suddenly filled with the notion that

...JUST SOUTH OF HEAVEN/JIM ODY

maybe it wasn't vortexes of air that was doing this, but the ghosts of children playing in the witching hours of the night. Unseen and unnoticed. Left to play in peace. I shivered with the cold and the feeling of lost souls kissing my cheeks.

***

Over in the car park, deep inside the kebab van that rocked with wind, Elvis was having problems with the padlock. He had tried everything, including calling it *an f-ing stupid useless piece of crap*. This appeared not to help either. Of course, this was silly as it wasn't a piece of crap, and even a five-year-old knows there's no F in padlock.

Then suddenly it hit him.

No, it *actually* hit him.

The key fell from above and hit him, making him flinch and cut a bit out of his hand with the metal pick.

"You bastard!" He swore under his breath. *This truly was a night to remember!*

Then as if hit with an epiphany, he realised what it was. He grinned as the key slid nicely into the lock.

With a beautiful click, the padlock sprung open. Elvis then proceeded to try and open up the window.

Outside, and across the windswept car park, Dice looked at me then said, "You truly blow at cards, you know."

Yeah," I replied. "And you're not exactly shit hot at them either."

"I am on my own," he mumbled like this was a reason.

"I don't wish to know what you're good at on your own!" I retorted then bent down and picked up a lump of dry mud and tossed it at him. It was immature, but Dice was hardly the epitome of maturity.

As we walked passed the kebab van, Dice decided to get me back and picked up a chunk of mud the size of a football and lobbed it at me with all the strength in his huge arms. I ducked, but didn't need to have, because his shot was high, wide, and not so handsome.

***

Finally, Elvis pushed open the window and heard a couple of jovial voices getting nearer. He dropped the side down as carefully and quietly as possible, so as not to be seen.

He should have looked up sooner.

If he had, he would have seen the large clump of mud heading straight for him. It was on the crash course with his face.

Elvis glanced up just as the object made contact with his forehead - straight between his eyes.

BAM! His world went black as he fell back unconscious. Laid flat out on his back exactly where he started a few moments ago.

***

"*Easy!*" I said realising how much that would've hurt, had it made contact with my head. Dice looked bewildered, realising there must've been a rock in there somewhere.

"Sorry, mate," he said. "I didn't know there was something in the mud."

I was surprised at the sound when it hit the kebab van. It didn't sound like it hit the side but as if something fell down. That said, the wind was loud, and the van was rocking. Mother Nature was having fun.

We walked up to the door and were surprised not to see an ugly ass gargoyle doorknocker.

"You think the *Munsters* or the *Addams Family* live here?" Dice mused, motioning me to ring the bell.

...JUST SOUTH OF HEAVEN/JIM ODY

"I dunno," I replied. "Ring the fuckin' bell." I was a bit tense.

Dice flipped his middle finger up at me in defiance and said, "You were the first one out in cards, *you* ring the fucking bell."

I reached for the bell. "I want to see all four fuckin' aces, *mate*," I said, sounding like he pissed on my birthday cake and shat on my presents. I knew there were never four aces in that pack.

"They are *there*, I'm *telling* you!" He tried to sound hurt, but came off sounding faker than the breasts and acting skills in a porno.

The bell *bonged*. Probably an everyday sound in the middle of town around lunchtime, but in the small hours of the night, and in a weird looking place, it sounded spooky.

The night had been so full of surprises I was sure that I'd been celebrating my birthday on the wrong day for the past however-many years.

And as the door opened, once again I couldn't believe my eyes.

From the van I hadn't been able to see her face, but up close there was no mistaking her.

What a small fucking world. What were the chances of that?

...JUST SOUTH OF HEAVEN/JIM ODY

Chapter Sixty

"Where the hell is he?" Aaron said as Presley sat drumming her fingers on the dashboard. It was more annoying to Aaron as there was no particular rhythm.

"Maybe his battery ran out?" she added yawning.

Aaron shrugged. "I suppose we should go looking for him then."

The guy had tried to change the tyre but the tyre size was all wrong. They thought that was it, when the guy phoned a friend. Luckily, his mate turned up and changed the tyre for them.

"That should be it, mate!" the happy guy said springing up. Considering he'd been woken up to come and change a tyre, the guy seemed strangely upbeat. "I bloody love Elvis Presley!"

"Really?" said Aaron.

"Sure do!" And there you had it. Another member signed and sealed for the price of a spare tyre.

The guy with the dress had gone when his mate turned up. He was off to meet one of the dancers who was finishing her shift. He reckoned they were dating. A lot of the clientele assumed they were in a relationship with the dancers. It was an occupational hazard.

The guy was called Bobby and had spikey black hair and a mouth like Mick Jagger. They swapped numbers and he skipped off into the night.

"Another member!" Aaron said triumphantly.

Presley stretched and mouthed, "Whatever."

Aaron started up the car and proceeded to go where he thought Elvis and his ride had gone. It was a stab in the dark. Or dawn as it so happened.

Some Madonna song was playing on the radio. Aaron tapped his own fingers on the steering wheel. He hoped Presley noticed the correct rhythm he was tapping out. The banal words washed over him. He'd never liked Madonna. He didn't trust her.

...JUST SOUTH OF HEAVEN/JIM ODY

He stared over at Presley and wished they could both spend the night together - *without Elvis.*

***

She looked me up and down with a huge smile on her face.

"Caper, what a pleasant surprise," she said with real surprise. I could feel Dice looking at me like he had just found out I was dating Scarlett Johansson. His mouth was wide open, not only catching flies, but birds and small aircraft too.

"Hi Martha. How are you doing?" I said mechanically whilst trying to take it all in.

She nodded and then said, "You gonna give that girl her beads back, or what?"

"Still got the same sense of humour," I said.

"Yep. You still got a bizarre taste in clothes." She grinned, and then so did I, when it came to the bizarre, *and clothing*, this girl took the biscuit, swallowed it in whole, and then shat it out right in front of you like it was perfect etiquette.

Martha, Martha, Martha.

This could either make matters better or a lot worse. You see Martha and I used to be a couple. Back in school we were an item. We grew together and experimented together. We did a lot of things I have never even wanted to do again, and a few things I've done time and time again. Back at school and college it was cool to be experimental - all part of growing up - we said. We believed it.

Martha Preston was a girl who scared the butt-flake cakes out of a lot of people. She was a bit of a bully, but I dug her strong personality and different ways. She was a challenge. She was mean and feisty, but man did she know how to have sex.

Then one time at the school disco whilst dancing to *Bon Jovi* singing *Livin' on a prayer*, or *Europe* with *The final countdown,* she grabbed my arm and took me outside. We'd had a nervy

...JUST SOUTH OF HEAVEN/JIM ODY

game of dare. She dared me to hold her. I dared her to kiss me. So, she dared me to touch her breasts, and so the game went on, getting better and better by the dare until we were fully acquainted with each other's body parts and had forgotten whose turn it was.

We dated on and off for about three years. It was always on her terms, and then we drifted apart for no particular reason. Well, in god's honest truth she was starting to get into some real freaky shit. She was good, but she wasn't that good. I made excuses and left her to her own devices. And when I say devices, that's exactly what I mean.

She'd always remained in the back of my mind, and here she was looking like she had just walked out of a brothel. That grin and twinkle in her eye looking to grab me and fuck me twenty ways to midnight.

"I think you should pinch me, because I have dreamed too many times that you'd turn up at my door late one night," she said.

Then Dice cut in. "You ain't dreaming, darling. I can smell his feet from here!"

"I'm not your darling, Chief!" She stated almost turning her nose up at Dice. He wasn't used that that. He looked hurt.

I smiled, but didn't really know what to say. I was well and truly overwhelmed with emotion.

My mind flashed back to the afternoon at her house when we both lost our virginity. I had slipped on a glow in the dark condom that had been in my wallet for about five years, and she had suggested closing the curtains and getting under the covers, just to see whether it worked. I made the glowing member bob up and down and dance the fandango before we started what we were there for.

We'd oo'd and ah'd together for a whole minute, then later had sat giggling and listening to Billy Idol. It had taken a long

...JUST SOUTH OF HEAVEN/JIM ODY

time after that for me to sing out loudly with *Rebel Yell*, without thinking about that damn glow in the dark rubber!

But that seemed a million light years away from where we were that night on her doorstep.

A fresh sweet smell lingered from her strange house.

A smell like, what was it?

Vanilla. Yes, that was it.

***

Cutthroat put his phone away and set out to find Bomb, all the while thinking about ditching the little runt and running off without him. Cutthroat could feel his blood boil and the adrenaline pump harder and faster around his tensing body. To reverse the effect, he tried to focus on the incredibly thin oriental girl wiggling along to a Vandals song entitled *Ape Drape*. He might've been misguided into thinking the song was too fast to dance to, yet had this gyrating mover twisted and turned like a possessed spinning top. This was probably the reason why she didn't have an ounce of fat on her body, with buttocks firm enough to crack walnuts in the festive season.

Cutthroat was about to give up on his sidekick when a voice from behind him told him exactly where he was.

"Hey, partner. Still on your Jack Jones?" Bomb grinned holding up a girl who looked as though she had been riding the white horse a little too much. Her eyes could barely focus enough to acknowledge a new presence or change of scenery. Her face was as vacant as someone losing consciousness, leaving her with a stupid half grin like she was the local village idiot on her yearly night out.

"You still a fucking useless prick?" Cutthroat replied.

Bomb tried not to look embarrassed, but in front of this semi-comatose woman he could have revealed to her that he was the *Yorkshire Ripper,* and she would still have had that stupid half grin on her face.

"Yeah, funny one!" he replied.

Cutthroat looked from the corpse-like girl back to Bomb and shook his head; his fingers were itching to pull the knife on him, and maybe her, just to get rid of that stupid half grin. Instead he said, "I've got the address; ditch Janis Joplin here, and let's go."

Bomb turned to the girl like she was his childhood sweetheart and said, "I've got to go, Sugar. Work, you know?"

She nodded. "You an actor, yeah?" she asked in a sleepy little girl voice, full of awe.

"No, he's a fucking fool!" Cutthroat grinned evilly.

"Look, I'll see you tomorrow, yeah?" he said to her as she gripped his arm and looked even more lost than before. If, of course, that was at all possible.

"Where...you...going?" she mumbled again through eyes that could barely see. She wasn't quite getting this concept of leaving.

"Work, baby. I've got to go."

"You...going? An actor, right?" she asked again like this was the craziest thing ever, and something that people never did.

"She's fucking whacked out on Scooby's, ain't she?" Cutthroat said. "Just leave her. She might understand then!"

"Aren't you just the nice guy," Bomb said showing a sensitive side for what seemed like the first time ever in his life.

He turned back to her with his face full of concern again. "Yeah. Like I said, work. I've got your number though." He wiggled his phone at her.

"You calling me now?"

"Tomorrow, sugar. Tomorrow."

She seemed to be adding this up in her mind, but her two plus two was coming out at twenty-two. "You...gonna...buy me...a drink?" she asked.

...JUST SOUTH OF HEAVEN/JIM ODY

"Can't. Gotta go." Bomb fished around in his pocket and pulled out a crumpled fiver. He threw it at her. "Get yourself another drink, yeah?"

Cutthroat raised his hand in the air. He just couldn't choose which one he wanted to hit first, Tweedle Dumb or Shorty Dumb-Ass.

"Have...you...got my...number?" she asked and her words seemed to be fading as quickly as her brain. Cutthroat was sure that if you looked real hard, you could make out the *Power Low* words flashing in her eyes.

"Yeah, right here!" Bomb held up his phone again.

Cutthroat grabbed him by his collar and pulled him towards the door.

"What the fuck, do you want to mess with a coke head like that?" Cutthroat asked him.

Bomb stopped as they got out into the parking lot and grabbed his crotch. "You ever fuck a coke head?"

"No, I haven't!"

Bomb grinned again looking like his mind was flashing pornographic images through his memory bank. "Seriously, they are the best. Fast, hard, and so intense!"

"Alright, I get the picture!" Cutthroat said holding up his hands. "And take your hand off of your cock for at least five minutes! You think you can do that?"

"Look, the little general is tired. Have a heart!"

"Shut up and get in the god-damn car!" Cutthroat said as pissed off as ever. This was not professional. It never would have happened if he had been on his own. That's a fact!

***

"Well, don't just stand there, come on in," Martha said looking deep into me. Then she looked over at Dice. "I've got a good mind to make you stay out there!"

...JUST SOUTH OF HEAVEN/JIM ODY

"I'm house-trained!" he replied, not making things a million times better for himself.

"I'm impressed," she mumbled, summoning us in. "You don't look it."

I still couldn't decide whether I felt any better now knowing it was Martha.

"Look, Martha. We came here for a reason," I began. This was hard, as I was sure that she thought I had been looking for her for years and now I had finally found her. How do I begin to explain that I noticed her drive a kebab van here, and a guy dressed as a milkman, whom I know to be called Travis, get out and walk in here with our pocket-watch?

"Go on," she said eagerly. *She's expecting a ring*, I thought. No, surely not with Dice here, *right?* I then realised how stupid I was being.

"Are you on your own, here?" I asked, looking around at all of the antiques that looked like a lifelong collection of two or three generations.

"No," she started. "I live with my brother."

Dice nearly dropped a large china pot that he was looking at. "Travis, your brother?" he said.

"No," she replied sternly. "Be careful, that bed pan is a hundred and thirty-three years old!"

"Urgh, a piss pot!" he said screwing his face up and putting it down so quick you might've thought that it had been freshly used.

"What about now?" I asked.

"What about now, what?" she answered confused.

"Who else is here now, he means," Dice said wiping his hands over and over again on his trousers.

"Just me and my brother who is asleep at the minute." There was a sudden tension in the air.

Dice and I were both thinking the same thing. What the hell has happened to Travis the Milkman?

...JUST SOUTH OF HEAVEN/JIM ODY

Chapter Sixty-One

Dexter shuffled along the back streets of town, his eyes peeled for a new place of residence. It was hard when you were homeless. There wasn't an abundance of vacant homes calling him. There were no slick estate agents for vagrants stood in shiny suits with arms held out to piss-stained corners.

He almost broke into a jog as he spied the KFC bucket sat alone. It magnetically pulling him in closer and closer. His mind already indulging in a finger-licking fantasy of grease-dripping proportions.

His luck was changing as he counted three untouched pieces of chicken begging to be devoured.

"What have we got here?" a voice rang out behind him. Dexter turned around to see two men and two women heavily intoxicated with alcohol and looking for some fun.

"I don't wan' no trouble," Dexter mumbled through his chicken. He didn't give a shit about getting a stomach ache, he was going to eat as quickly as he could. That was one of the first things you learnt living on the streets. Everybody wants what you have. Even if it smells like shit and is covered in urine.

"You buy that chicken?" one of the guys in a *Ben Sherman* shirt asked.

"Found it."

"It ain't yours then, is it?" the other guy with an *fcuk* muscle top on stated.

"Finders keepers," Dexter mumbled back. That was the motto from the streets.

"What did you say?" Ben Sherman said.

"Give up the chicken, Bum." fcuk.

Dexter chose his words carefully so as not to aggravate these already hostile gentlemen. That's why he replied, "Fuck off, you dumb inbred fuckwads. It's my fuckin' chicken. Go get your own!"

...JUST SOUTH OF HEAVEN/JIM ODY

Fcuk muscle top ran at him, taking the words to heart.

With one big punt, he kicked the chicken bucket from Dexter's hands so high, you could imagine the man on the moon ducking, thinking: first it was a cow, now chicken in bread crumbs, what ever next?

"Then I guess none of us will have any then, huh?" He grinned as if this answer to the equation was likened to Einstein's theory behind relativity.

The two girls whooped and clapped as though their hero had once again surpassed their expectations with another dashing act of bravado.

Dexter, obviously not too impressed, hocked a large green loogy from the pits of his clogged lungs and flung the flying gobstopper sized ball of phlegm through the air like a missile. It came to rest on the tip of Fcuk's nose.

The girls stopped their laughing and Ben Sherman decided that enough was enough, it was time to kick some ass.

This was five minutes of pain and suffering on Dexter's part.

Two teeth, one shoe, and his trousers down, Dexter was left counting his balls to make sure they weren't missing. He chuckled to himself that at least his platinum credit card was in his other pair of imaginary trousers.

He still needed to find a place of residence, but now his criteria were a little different.

Would he find a place with a dentist and a tailor? His mouth throbbed and blood dribbled down his chin like he was a vampire. At no point in any teenage girl's fantasy had a vampire ever looked so bad.

That was life on the streets.

He wandered aimlessly through the night.

The fact you have no home can be a problem. The fact you have *no trousers* is a really mixed bag of monkey nuts. Dexter was realising this as he ambled along with the worry that at any moment, one of his nuts was going to fall out of his ten-year-old

...JUST SOUTH OF HEAVEN/JIM ODY

Y-fronts and peek-a-boo an innocent passer-by. The law took a dim view of it too.

Street people can have a strange sense of logic, and one of these was even stranger than normal. The sight of a raggedy-man laid out in the middle of a main road, missing his trousers, and actually thinking that a vehicle would rather stop than run him over was a little optimistic. The sight of a half-naked man with his balls peek-a-booing alone would be enough to run the silly sod over in anyone's book.

Dexter led out still.

His heart was beating fast. Not with the nerves of being run over, and thus having some poor God-forsaken paramedic have to scoop his dirty-ass up off of the asphalt, but because of his KFC bucket that was stolen from him. *His* bucket. *Finders-fuckin'-keepers!*

...JUST SOUTH OF HEAVEN/JIM ODY

Chapter Sixty-Two

For years I had lived such a boring and mundane life, and now all of a sudden in one day and night, I had had more fun and excitement than a paedophile in a playground. It was absolutely bizarre.

"What is that sweet smell?" I asked. The smell was very strong like someone had sprayed a whole can of air-freshener about five seconds before the door was opened to us.

She reached out and touched my cheek, then replied, "Vanilla. You like?"

I was already blushing, I don't know why, but I could feel my face burning up.

"Ain't that the smell of cyanide?" Dice added.

She rolled her eyes, then turned to Dice and spitefully said, "Are you really thick as pig shit, or what?"

"I guess I'm mistaken then, o'wise one!" he said in a dopey voice. They weren't seeing eye to eye.

"That's almonds," I corrected. "And it's the taste, not the smell of cyanide."

"We can experiment if you want?" Martha said to Dice, and I wasn't entirely sure that it was a joke.

Many a true word spoken in jest, I thought.

"See, that always got me," he started.

"What's that, syphilis?" I grinned - Martha giggled.

Dice looked momentarily hurt, and I had to wonder whether he was used to not always being the centre of attention. He carried on, however, "How do we know that tastes like almonds, if it's a poison?"

Martha gave a false look that she was thinking real hard about this, then said, "I think...I...don't... *give a flying fuck*!"

"Let's get out of here," Dice said hurt.

I paused, again trying to pick my moment.

...JUST SOUTH OF HEAVEN/JIM ODY

Not knowing what to say, or even how to say it, I suddenly spurted out, "Martha. Where is the milkman?" She looked nervous then replied, "You bin drinkin'?"

"Seriously, Martha."

"He's asleep upstairs," she said quickly. *Too quickly*, in my book.

I looked down and rubbed my temples. It had been a tiring night and I longed for a bed to sleep in. "The guy's name is Travis, and he has something of ours."

"He didn't look as if he had anything," she confessed.

Dice then jumped in, "Well, he didn't look like a fuckin' milkman when we last saw him - so I guess life is full of surprises!"

"Can we just go see him?" I asked, maybe fluttering my eyelids just a bit.

Martha thought this over, and then said with a sly grin, "I really don't want to wake him up - he can get so grouchy."

She wanted something. I'd seen that look before.

"What would make it easier?" I asked, dreading the response.

She licked her lips all around and replied in a whisper only I could hear, "I think you know what I want."

I pulled her close and whispered in her ear, "Not with him around."

She smiled and nodded, then turned to Dice. "You wait out in the study."

Dice looked confused and a little intrigued.

I hoped that the study was sound proofed. This could really put our friendship back a step or ten.

Martha showed Dice to the study, and I waited and wondered what the hell I had let myself into. Sometimes life's full of choices, and I was left with two: a bad choice or a not very good choice. The words *rock and a hard place* came to mind.

...JUST SOUTH OF HEAVEN/JIM ODY

Two minutes had passed when she returned and threw the outfit at me.

"Put it on then, Sweetie!" she said with the giggle of a schoolgirl and a popsicle.

As I slowly put the outfit on I thought about the last time she had called me Sweetie, or Sweet Susie as she used to nickname me.

I would like to take this opportunity to say that this outfit did not turn me on in the least bit. For starters, the knickers don't have a pouch large enough for little Caper, if you know what I mean, and the small silk string was quite uncomfortable slicing my ass cheeks apart. I never understood the point of underwear that went up your arse, rather than covered it. Even if I normally found it sexy to look at.

The stockings again were awkward, and the high heels were too narrow for my feet. The bra seemed like a waste of time if you haven't got any tits, and the skirt made me think that a dozen squirrels were going to come flying out to ambush me and rid me of my uncomfortable nuts. I then added the blouse and tie, then *Hey Presto!* I was a schoolgirl - Martha's favourite fantasy, and certainly not mine! This was one of the reasons we'd drifted apart.

Martha looked at me with large round eyes like I might be a blank cheque and stuttered, "Y-you look gorgeous!" All right then, why don't you just rid me once and for all of my ego. I couldn't have felt any worse if a four-year-old ran out and beat the crap out of me with a feather and a fountain pen.

So, it really says something when you have to dress up as a woman to be found attractive - I just prayed to God that Dice, Chalky, or especially Amy, didn't came bursting through the door at any moment.

***

...JUST SOUTH OF HEAVEN/JIM ODY

Dice, ever one to listen to other people's orders, was quite frankly bored shitless in the study. He was sat in a big comfortable leather chair. Which was indeed comfortable – that wasn't the issue. He had stared at the picture on the wall, which depicted a RNLI lifeboat in an emergency rescue on rough, choppy waters in a race-against-time mission to save lives. However, try as he may, Dice couldn't find any naked women, or even a cheeky mermaid, so his attention span remained short.

Sod it, he thought and silently opened the door.

He had no interest in what the hell Caper was up to. He just wanted that damn antique pocket-watch. And a good night's sleep. As much as he would like Caper to think he was used to these little adventures, the truth was this was the most adventurous thing he'd done since dressing up as Casper the friendly ghost and scaring the local kids in a highly non-friendly manner.

He snuck out of the study and along to the room where Caper and Martha were. From where he was, he couldn't get to the staircase without going back into the main room.

He was about to open the door and wonder who the pretty schoolgirl was, when he heard a voice growing louder and louder.

"I'll just check on your friend," she said, and Dice bolted back to the study, as quietly as possibly, on the balls of his feet.

He had shut the door and sat back in the leather chair, and was once again searching for those damn elusive mermaids, when the door opened and Martha nodded her head approvingly.

"Good boy. Glad you're obedient."

Dice returned a *'ha ha'* look and a wry smile. "Just like a dog."

Martha left the room.

Dice then figured that she wouldn't expect him to move so quickly, so he got up and slowly opened the door again.

...JUST SOUTH OF HEAVEN/JIM ODY

He looked down the hall, and when the coast was clear, he walked quickly and quietly towards the room.

He could make out Caper's voice and then Martha's, this helped him gauge exactly where they were in the room.

***

Martha had now got her headmaster's cape and hat. Then when I saw her produce her cane, I knew it was show time. I really hadn't missed this. The pain from that very cane was suddenly very real indeed.

"So why have you been sent to my office, you naughty little girl?" she bellowed. I felt so stupid that my shame was almost real.

"I was caught in the toilets, sir," I replied. Yes, she was the he, and I was the she.

"And what, might I ask, were you doing in there that might warrant you to be sent here in disgrace?" I hoped that Dice was going to save me now. I was ready to swallow my pride and show my shame.

"I was caught with another girl," I replied in a small voice, knowing how much Martha enjoyed this scenario.

Dice couldn't believe his ears when he got close enough to the door to understand what was being said. He almost toyed with the idea of staying where he was and listening.

He snuck into the room on his hands and knees, headed straight for the bar. From there he would be able to crawl out of sight and around to where the staircase was situated.

He tried to ignore what was being said as this was beginning to make him chuckle, and he wasn't sure just how much longer he could suppress a giggle.

Although the pub hadn't been open to the public in years, there were still stacks of clean, gleaming glasses, and a fresh stock of lager and bitter on tap, as well as a couple of coolers full of soft drinks and mixers.

This place was obviously open to some sort of business, more private than public, however.

The crates, along with some of the pipes, made for quite an obstacle course. Add to that a sticky floor that all pubs get when covered with drops of alcohol, and Dice had to move slowly so as not to make a noise. Not to mention his knees hurt like hell now.

***

Elvis's first thought upon opening his eyes was that he had been mugged. His head felt as though a keen cricket batsman had used it for target practise. His neck felt stiff and all the way down his back seemed to ache.

He thought he must have been left for dead.

Then he remembered, rubbed his eyes, and made a grab for his mobile.

On the third ring, Aaron answered.

"Elvis?" he asked unsure, almost scared. *The spineless shit!* Elvis thought.

"No. Long John Fucking Silver!"

"Where are you?"

"Sat on a beach in the Caribbean, with a couple of big titty bitches, a pina-colada, and a hard on!"

"Ya, shittin' me?" he said. *The dumb shit actually thinks I am*, he thought.

Elvis laughed then replied, "No, I'm in the car park of some pub, hold on..." he put his head out of the window and stared up at the large creaking sign that shined brightly by the light of the moon. "...Hell's Kitchen. You heard of it?"

...JUST SOUTH OF HEAVEN/JIM ODY

Elvis heard Aaron mumble the name to Presley, and then thankfully she was saying, yeah, she got pissed up there one time when she was seeing some bigtime hustler dude.

Elvis thought, *so fucking what?* but kept his feelings to himself.

"Be there in about ten minutes."

"Yeah. Just hurry the fuck up."

Click, they were gone.

***

"This strikes me as being a little odd," Bomb said, as they pulled up outside the trailer park. "This guy drives a big van and lives in a trailer that's not much bigger than his van. What the fuck's up with that?"

"Look, fuckwit, I don't care if he's butt-fuckin' chickens, or wrestling the bold-man, just as long as we get that tape back and finish off Chalky and his lil' bitch!"

"Okay, groucho! But where's the van?"

"Maybe he parks it someplace else."

The trailer was the smallest and most run down in the whole of the trailer park. Quite frankly, if the *Three Little Pigs* had been huddled in here, then the *Big Bad Wolf* would only have had to fart to blow the house down. It was that small.

"You think they are all in here?" Bomb asked as the turned off the engine and looked at the small flickering light in the window.

"Fuck knows. We are about to find out."

The small trailer park was mostly full of old people - retirees, which should have made Cutthroat and Bomb act more inconspicuous. Everyone knows old people sleep nearly twenty hours a day, however, if there is a slight noise then all members of the neighbourhood watch team are curtain tugging and noting down registration numbers and striking features, along with

...JUST SOUTH OF HEAVEN/JIM ODY

times and dates like true detectives. If you think I'm lying, then just look at Miss Marple and that woman from *Murder She Wrote*. Not one spring chicken there. Then there's Sherlock Holmes & Dr Watson, not exactly sprightly young men, eh? Inspector Morse, he even died.

You see, we overlook the fact that when you get to a certain age there are more things to life than bingo, bowls, drinking tea and remembering the war. When we reach that age, we too will become O.A.P.P.I.'s - Old Age Pensioner Private Investigators. You may forget to turn your cooker off, or wet yourself a couple of times a week, but you will remember with complete clarity the registration number of the Ford Focus TD 1.6 that was parked outside number 31 for forty-three minutes, on the twelfth of this month.

So, Cutthroat and Bomb got out with their guns in their hands, clearly pretending to be double glazing salesmen using bullying tactics again.

Cutthroat couldn't be arsed to go through the usual pantomime of who will knock on the door, so he banged it twice, as hard as he could.

The gruff voice shouted out, "Nobody's in right now. Please leave your name and number after the tone, then fuck off - Bleeeeep!"

Cutthroat frowned at Bomb whom found this highly amusing, then replied, "Glad you got a sense of humour, 'cause you'll piss yourself with laughter when I blow out your God damn door and fire a muthafuckin' bullet in you, wise-arse. You've got three seconds to open this fucking door, or I will keep my promise!"

"Who are..."

"One."

"...you. What do you..."

"Two."

"...Alright! I'm coming!"

...JUST SOUTH OF HEAVEN/JIM ODY

The guy was overweight by close on six stone and judging by the stain on his vest, he'd had pizza for his supper. He clearly wasn't expecting company. Had he been, he might have chosen a cleaner pair of boxer shorts to wear half mast. Thank god his vest was the size of a single duvet. That said, why this guy hadn't been fast asleep was also a wonder.

"You Richard?" Cutthroat asked, "Owner of a large black Mercedes Van..." he rolled off the reg number.

"Nah, I'm Terry. I sold that van to a guy name Dice, or something stupid like that. I did have the van in my stage name of Richard Suckar. Most people called me Dick." He paused. He hated it when he had to spell it out. "Dick Suckar! Get it!"

Bomb laughed out loud, but Cutthroat remained deadpan. *Who did this twat think he was?* he thought.

As Bomb pushed past him into his pig sty, all became clear.

The film playing on the television certainly wasn't made by Disney. Neither were you likely to recognise any of the actors. Two young men were performing such pornographic acts upon each other that even Bomb had to look away in disgust. It was fucking rude.

"Any chicks in this?" he asked.

The guy gave a little smile. "No, none at all. Isn't that just a thrill?"

"Fuck that," Bomb replied, "I need to see some knockers and a nice wet beaver. Hey, Cutthroat, this more your stuff, eh?"

"You fucking prick," he said touching the knife in his back pocket. *Go on*, he urged in his mind to Bomb, *just keep that shit up.* He did keep glancing at the TV.

"Maybe I should leave you and old Mr Sucker here alone, eh?"

With one big swoosh the knife flew through the air and thudded straight into Bomb's right thigh.

"You bastard!" he shouted, dropping his gun in pain and shock.

...JUST SOUTH OF HEAVEN/JIM ODY

Dick, clearly was a supple guy, and was bent over clasping the gun before you could say *Where shall I park my bike?*

"Shut the fuck up, you little faggot," Cutthroat said.

"Hey, I never said anything!" Dick said hurt.

Cutthroat turned to him, "I wasn't talking to you, Fairy-Fuck, I was talking to that little queen!"

"Are you one of God's sensitive little boys?" he said as camp as you like.

Bomb glared at him. "Go get yourself a dirty whore, will ya."

Dick screwed his face up. "Ugh, how repulsive, you vulgar little man."

"This is where we go solo, you little prick," Cutthroat said. "I've put up with your shit for too long!"

Bomb went for one of his legendry upper cuts, but the minute he shifted his weight onto his injured thigh, he felt the sudden jab of pain shoot around his nervous system, attacking him from all angles.

Dick jumped in. "You leave him you bully," he said to Cutthroat, as Cutthroat was ready to deck Bomb down once and for all. "I've a good mind to call the police!"

"You do that, and I'll turn you into a hermaphrodite - *very slowly!*" Cutthroat's eyes turned into pure evil. He looked with total disgust at Bomb and said, "I should kill you."

"Fuckin' faggot!" Bomb screamed in anger and pain.

"Just leave," Dick said trying to show some balls.

Cutthroat turned his glare towards Dick, who backed away with worry. "Write me down the address of your friend."

"Uh?" Dick said clearly raking his brain to think of whom Cutthroat was talking about. Cutthroat could sense this and urged him on with, "The fuckin' van, you twat. Who you sold the fuckin' van to!"

"Uh, right," Dick replied with a little embarrassed smile.

...JUST SOUTH OF HEAVEN/JIM ODY

One minute and three seconds later and Cutthroat was gone. Bomb was trying to make a fast exit, but knew he needed medical assistance - unless he left the knife in.

...JUST SOUTH OF HEAVEN/JIM ODY

Chapter Sixty-Three

The staircase was large and wide, and looked like something you might find in a large stately home - not a country pub.

The paintings were ghostly and Dice could feel twenty pairs of eyes raping his soul as he made his way slowly up each step of the way.

When he got to the top, he glanced at both sides up and down the landing. The musty smell of old carpet and mahogany lingered in the air.

That's when he saw the light spilling out under the door.

It invited him to gate crash the private party from within. He could only imagine what was going on in that room. It drew him closer with an invisible magnetic pull.

***

Martha had walked around me with authority. She sat on top of the bar and gave me her evil, well-practised look of somebody in charge. I wondered how many others had played this stupid charade with her. Albeit, our stupid charade. And that gave me the answer. Probably only me.

She looked down at me drinking up the situation. A small smile played on her lips. I wondered how many times she'd longed to be in this situation again. She was pondered a thousand things that she could and would do to me. Then when she spoke, she spoke slowly and hard. "Touch me." Demanding. But underneath there was hope and a fear that I may not respond.

An onlooker would never guess we hadn't seen each other in eight or nine years, and not played this game in maybe ten.

Just like figure skaters, or tennis partners, we knew our roles and each other's strengths and weaknesses - this itself made me feel nervous. I wasn't much of a person to relive lovers. Once removed from my life, I'd never ventured back before (aside

...JUST SOUTH OF HEAVEN/JIM ODY

from her). Suddenly, and perhaps briefly, I understood the fascination of doing somebody again for old-times-sake.

I stood up but every movement was uncomfortable due to my member being suffocated in the pair of small panties, trying as he may to escape his silk and lace prison.

"Touch me now." This time it was in desperation. The hardness in her voice had disappeared and had been replaced by pure lust. For a minute I thought she may have also been wondering whether or not we could both go with it like we had so many times before.

I was overcome with a want to have her naked, and a picture book of acts we had performed in the past was suddenly flicked through quickly in my mind's eye. A montage of the debauched.

Her impatience had her on me. I felt her kissing my neck and I realised that I was cupping her breasts like a human bra. From that point on I was lost in a hazy deep filled lust.

***

Elvis sat on the side of the road staring at the van a hundred metres away. It sat innocently in the gateway of a large yellow rape field. It seemed such a strange place to park. Almost like it didn't want to be seen.

He wondered whether it was a couple of horny teenagers making out together. Out of sight and out of mind of parental guidance. He mused at whether it was boy and girl, or boy and boy, or girl and girl - you never could tell nowadays. It certainly didn't bother him either way. He had his own feelings he wrestled with each day.

The humming of an engine could suddenly be heard, and when the twin beams cut through the night, Elvis got up and hoped that it was his ride.

This little adventure had ended abruptly with his *kidnapping*, and now that he was free, he was happy to give up on that

...JUST SOUTH OF HEAVEN/JIM ODY

Chalky guy for tonight and lay his head down on a nice soft pillow and sleep a sleep of a thousand dreams. You really can have too much excitement in one night.

The car slowed down and Aaron was peering out worriedly, not too sure of Elvis's mood.

Elvis jumped in the back seat and said, "What a night. Let's go get some rest."

Aaron gave a nervous laugh at that, and Presley said, "So who wants to share the bed with me?"

Elvis was resting his head on the side of the door and all ready to drop off into the land of nod. "He can," was all he could manage.

"Right, then. Aaron, it looks like it's your lucky night!" She said slapping him gently on the thigh.

Aaron's pulse quickened and his mouth became dry, his eyes found it hard to concentrate on the road. His mind wandered into his daydream fantasy that he had been going over and over, ever since the first time Elvis introduced him to Presley.

Presley-long-legs, he called her in his head. Even if she was kidding, the fantasy would keep him going on a little longer.

***

As Dice put his hand on the door handle, red light was already spilling out. He had this feeling wash over him that he was all too familiar with.

Danger.

The pocket-watch was in this room. He knew it. Dice was already feeling a little uneasy at going inside. I was downstairs catching up on old times with an ex-girlfriend in a way that needs no words. And Chalky and Amy were outside in the van picking their noses and wondering just what the hell they were doing there. They had probably started up the van and were heading out towards Newquay by now.

...JUST SOUTH OF HEAVEN/JIM ODY

Dice was aware at how he was stalling, and couldn't remember the last time he had held on to a door handle for this long without trying to open it.

After a deep breath and a wish from lady luck, he turned the handle and was surprised to hear a clicking sound. He swung the door open and stepped inside.

And there was Travis...

...JUST SOUTH OF HEAVEN/JIM ODY

Chapter Sixty-Four

Aaron couldn't help it, his eyes kept catching the twin mounds of Presley's chest in his peripheral vision. Though the road was ahead, all he saw and pictured was Presley. Maybe it was the late night. It made him drunk with desire. Perhaps it was seeing just how quickly and easily he'd seen her go off with another guy. Add those words she'd said and somewhere in his mind he saw them both together naked and happy.

It was only when Presley suddenly shrieked, that Aaron stood on the brakes so hard that the tyres screamed in pain at the friction from the tarmac.

There was some crazy old man led out in the road! The stupid bastard didn't even have any trousers on. *Maybe this was so he didn't mess in them when someone came close to running him over*, Aaron thought, his heart pounding out through his chest.

Aaron and Presley simultaneously jumped out of the car and ran around to the front bumper.

"Didn't think you was goi' ta stop," he smiled with a grin that had as many teeth missing as present.

"What the hell are you doing here?" Aaron demanded. "I could have run over you!"

"Ya nearly did, ya little hooligan!" he replied uninterested in anything else.

"If you didn't want to be run over, then what were you doing in the middle of the road?" Presley asked a little flustered.

"I was waiting for some kind folk to stop – I wasn't expecting his and hers Elvis impersonators, but then I'm just a simple man," he said rubbing his dark whiskers with his dirty fingers.

"What do you want?" Aaron asked glancing at his watch, wanting to be back at Graceland with Presley right about then.

...JUST SOUTH OF HEAVEN/JIM ODY

The chances of that were going the way of an anorexic's belly by the second.

"I lost my home tonight, and some young hoodlum took me chicken—"

Presley jumped in, "Tugged your chicken?"

"I don't want to know—" Aaron said with an angry frown. "That's disgusting."

"Took! Not tugged! I'm not a fucking rent-boy!!" He laughed out loud at that. "No self-respecting man or women gonna shit on me, let alone give me money for tuggings!"

"Well, you are walking around with no trousers on—"

"I hadn't finished my story! I was getting to that!" he laughed again, raising himself up onto his elbows now. "You young-uns, never any patience."

Presley looked up to heaven, then said, "Maybe we should leave you here then, huh? At this unearthly hour, we've got much better things to be doing than talking to a homeless guy—"

"Alright. Alright. No need to get all feisty. Anyway, this guy TOOK my chicken, then kicked the shite outta me and stole my trousers!"

"You don't usually walk around like that then?" Aaron offered.

"No, I don't!" And he seemed genuinely hurt by it.

"Alright, so what do you want?" Presley asked trying to get to the point of this little pantomime.

The guy raised to his knees now and mumbled, "Just a small donation."

Aaron took his wallet out and looked in the change compartment, and then he saw Presley look over and decided he had better be a bit more generous. He pulled out a twenty-pound note and handed it to the guy. "How's that?"

"It's like Jesus Christ himself - but better! Cheers, Elvis," he shouted with joy and ran off with a funny little skip.

...JUST SOUTH OF HEAVEN/JIM ODY

"What the fuck was all that about?" Aaron said putting his wallet away.

When they got back to the car, they found Elvis snoring like a wild beast in the back seat.

Presley grinned and pointed to Elvis.

"What?" Aaron said.

She opened the backdoor and leant over. With fine dexterity her fingers worked his belt buckle, and slowly and carefully she pulled down his trousers.

"Shit, we've not got time for you to give him a blowjob," Aaron said in a pissy voice.

"I'm not!" she said, bending even further over to remove his shoes too.

"Then what are you doing?"

She emerged holding up a pair of trousers and shoes.

Aaron got it. They got back in the car, and Aaron started it up.

They drove for 100-yards before pulling over. Presley got out and threw the trousers and shoes at the homeless guy.

"Merry Christmas!" she shouted.

"Viva, Las Vegas!" he sung back swinging his hips to them.

***

Travis had clearly seen many better days. It was shocking. His eyes were puffed up, bruised and almost closed from a pounding. He couldn't have been anything other than the loser in a fight. Blood streamed from his nose and mouth, joining together by the time the drops dripped from his chin. His clothes were ripped and pulled to angles that would make the designers cringe.

He was slumped backwards in a corner and barely conscious.

...JUST SOUTH OF HEAVEN/JIM ODY

Dice looked over at him and wondered how long he had left to live. He was no medical expert, but Dice could see he was in a bad way. There was no telling what might be going on internally.

By the time he saw Travis's eyes dart to the opposite corner, it was too late for Dice to react.

***

I've never before wanted to be Sherlock Holmes, nor indeed do I now. This lack of ambition may be the reason why the cogs of my brain took some time to turn full circle. A memory was trying it's very best to tell me something important.

They say smell is the greatest thing to jog and stimulate your memory with a form of association. Of course, this fails to work when you have been told about the smell and not sniffed it yourself. It seems second-hand sniffing is not reliable enough for our brains.

When I was hit by this revelation, I was stripping off my skirt to indulge in a spot of lovemaking. Or rather having sex, as the love was forgotten and replaced by lustful nostalgia.

I was thinking what a fucking annoying smell that vanilla whiff was, when my heart sank. I mean it dropped through the floor. I remembered what had been said at the dinner table regarding the murders.

"...and the bodies all smelt of vanilla..."

I only realised that I'd stopped moving when Martha's worried voice rung out in my ears. "What's wrong, Caper?" she said breathlessly and slightly annoyed.

"I-I can't do this," I stammered looking for my clothes.

"What do you *mean?* This is what *you want*?" she demanded. Her face was very serious. "This is what *I want!*"

"Look, it's not right," I said, thankfully finding my trousers a lot easier than my morals.

...JUST SOUTH OF HEAVEN/JIM ODY

She grabbed my arm. "It doesn't matter as long as we are having fun." Her head dropped down in a familiar act of sadness. "You don't know what I have been through...looking for someone like *you*."

I found my shirt hung on the back of a stool. "What *have* you been through?" I pressed.

"Men think they know what they want, but when it comes down to it they get scared so easily. They turn and run at the slight suggestion of something new. You're all cowards," she gave a dramatic pause. "But I thought you were different. *You were* different. You'd do those things."

Then I heard the bang from upstairs.

"I have to see Travis," I said a little more desperately than I hoped. "No, you can't—" she said, but I wasn't listening. I jogged to the study where I found that Dice was gone, and then with adrenaline pumping, I ran back through to where Martha was.

"He's gone," I said. "He must have already gone upstairs to find sleeping beauty!"

That's when Martha's face twisted up into an evil look of contempt. "You can't go up there," she cackled - but I wasn't listening. Something wasn't right here. I was almost halfway up, taking the stairs two at a time.

She was in hot pursuit.

"You're trespassing!" she shouted in desperation.

"You're kidnapping!" I replied and ran down towards where I heard another crash.

The blood red light that spilled under the door was hardly welcoming, but I bit the bullet and burst through anyway.

Two bodies were wrestling to the death on the floor, and I could just make out Dice underneath. The last time I'd seen him like this he was naked with a girl on top. He didn't look to be having as much fun this time.

...JUST SOUTH OF HEAVEN/JIM ODY

The body on top was not Travis. He was crumpled in a sad state in the corner. A broken body of a man. I'd seen scarecrows look more human than him.

I picked up the first thing that came to my hands. It was some sort of wooden stick - a banister, bat, or a bedpost - and hit the other person over the back of the head with all of my might. It was then that it turned its ugly head towards me. I raised the stick again, but paused too long. I went to swing, but felt a sharp, hard pain to my skull and a flash of white light. Then everything went black.

***

Martha stood in the doorway snarling like a wild beast and holding the metal bar that had just made contact with my head.

Dice had managed to kick himself free and was backing towards the far wall searching for anything that vaguely represented a weapon.

The other guy - who had a face like a baboon's ass - glanced at Martha, as if asking permission to go to town on Dice. She smiled encouragement, and he stumbled forward. He was human, but only just. Deformed, with huge bumps on his misshapen head, you'd be forgiven for feeling a pang of sorrow for him. But he didn't understand life and people. He'd been trained by someone without care. He was angry at the world.

The place was a simple room with not much lying around, however sticking out behind the world's scruffiest sofa was a high heeled boot.

Dice grabbed it as the thing lunged for him, letting out a gasp as he realised there was half a leg still attached to the boot. He gave his gasp some oomph, to make out it was a war cry, and swung the leg around his head like an East German shot putter from yesteryear.

...JUST SOUTH OF HEAVEN/JIM ODY

There was the horrible sound of bone on bone, but the thing still wouldn't go down.

He gave a village idiot grin and like a game lunged again.

***

The van was pretty boring, Chalky had decided. Amy had been asleep now for ten minutes, and Chalky had looked at the playing cards long enough to miss his girlfriend. He also missed his bed.

He looked up at the big house again whilst fumbling with a couple of fluffy handcuffs he'd found in the glove box, and wondered what was taking them so long.

How long does it take to get an antique pocket-watch?

Oh, bollocks to it, he decided. He put the handcuffs in his pocket and jumped out the van.

The full moon was still watching over them, although the sun was now peeking up over the horizon. The wind had died down a touch, although still managed to whip up a few leaves from a nearby tree. "Some of us want some sleep," he mumbled, but there was nobody around to hear.

...JUST SOUTH OF HEAVEN/JIM ODY

Chapter Sixty-Five

The taxi driver had seen many a strange thing in the ten years he had been in this profession, but none stranger than a small guy with knife protruding from his thigh. Even the guy that had taken his pet chicken called Quack-Quack for a walk, now seemed less of a fruitcake. When asked why he hadn't called the chicken Cluck-Cluck, he had replied coolly, "What a stupid fucking name! I can see why you're a cabby, an' not the Prime-minister!"

"What's with your leg?" The taxi-driver asked the guy who stumbled with each step.

"Which one?" Bomb replied winching in pain.

"Well, how many do you have with a knife sticking out of them?"

"Oh, that." Like it was nothing. "It's just a flesh wound."

"Flesh wound or not, you make a mess and it will cost you an extra twenty-five pounds, right?"

Bomb sighed. It had been a long night. "As touching as your concern is, and though I sincerely appreciate it, please forgive me when I say, shut the fuck up and drive!"

"I can see why somebody stabbed you, you fuckin' dick," the taxi driver mumbled. He'd seen it all before. Alcohol and lack of sleep. They all end up fighting or fucking of an evening. In his experience, anyway.

"What was that?" Bomb demanded.

"I said," the taxi driver replied playing for time with a dramatic pause. "I can see somebody stabbed you, should take care of it."

"Hmm," Bomb said feeling in his pockets for the pocket-watch.

But Cutthroat had pick-pocketed it right after Bomb had boasted about it, the thieving bastard.

"Fuck!" He shouted at the top of his lungs.

...JUST SOUTH OF HEAVEN/JIM ODY

"Any more outbursts and you can find another taxi!" Bomb wanted to kill him in a bad way.

***

Dice had hit the crazy man five or six times with the boot, but still the guy held his grip around his throat. Things were getting quite desperate.

Martha was screaming for the guy to get out of the way so as she could hit Dice with the metal bar. The Neanderthal dumb-ass wasn't listening.

It must have been her banshee squeals that brought me back to my senses. When I opened my eyes, I hoped I was still dreaming, but the pounding in my head was much too real and painful.

I managed to get up on all fours without being seen. I was having a problem with my balance, but concentrated on where they were in the room. Without thinking, an act that comes quite naturally to me, I ran at them like a rugby full back.

Martha didn't have time to raise her bloody metal shaft, and I shoulder charged her to the ground like she was a ten-year-old.

Dice was turning a darker shade of purple by the time I kicked the big guy in the head. He turned and swung a large meaty fist in my direction, which I managed to take on my forearm, keeping my sore head as far away from anymore pain as possible.

As Martha made a move for the bar, I slammed a size nine boot on to it. She spun around on the ground and kicked my legs from under me. I fell down hard, but my arm found the metal rod.

The guy looked down at me and chuckled stupidly, and I realised that it was of course her retarded younger brother Benji. The last time I'd seen him, he'd been about thirteen. Short and pudgy. He was now over six foot and although padded, he had tremendous strength. His hair was long and wild, but his eyes stared vacantly through me.

Dice was breathing properly again and was trying to get up, as Benji turned and pushed him back to the ground laughing. He thought it was a game.

I also tried to move and felt a small fist connect with the side of my jaw. I swung a right in her direction and made contact with something hard. Then we were grabbing at each other, and it was almost amusing to think that we could have been this intense downstairs in not too dissimilar poses and making the same sort of grunting noises.

Sex is violent.

So, I'm a little embarrassed to say that whilst Dice was losing to a large built guy with no sense or feeling, I was having problems wrestling with a woman. I didn't even have the excuse of the tight panties cutting off my circulation anymore.

Then Chalky sauntered in and asked one of the world's stupidest questions. "What's going on here then?" he said and I was thinking, *don't just stand there you dope, help us out!*

Dice got in a good kick to the knee which rocked Benji some, then Chalky flew at him and swung the best haymaker I have seen right on the button, and down poor Benji went. Finally, out cold.

I had managed to turn Martha over and was trying to restrain her when she kneed me in the nuts. We were then caught in a strong embrace.

"Caper, what are you doing?" Chalky said. "Are you two fighting or making out?"

"A little help?" I wheezed, my arms burning with lactic acid.

"He's not very good at violence towards women. He usually ends up fucking them!" Dice laughed.

"I'll fucking kill you too," Martha said with a red face. It was good to know she was struggling too.

...JUST SOUTH OF HEAVEN/JIM ODY

I swung out a wild one and kicked her in the stomach, then Dice and Chalky were there grabbing at her arms and legs, trying to restrain her.

Chalky pulled out two pairs of fluffy pink handcuffs. It was a strange magic trick, but I chose not to say anything. I was in no position to take the piss. "I found these in your van," he laughed raising his eyebrows at me. But even smiling hurt my head so I remained poker-faced.

We pulled Martha and Benji together and handcuffed them back-to-back. I had seen this in films. It worked quite well then.

"What now?" Dice said sitting on the beat-up couch - which looked like I felt.

"We call the police," I said. "These people are crazy!"

Dice winked at me, then added, "Just what the fuck were you up to down there?"

I shook my head, "It has been a traumatic experience for us all—" Then I remembered Travis.

"Hey Travis?" I shouted looking over at him. "You alive?"

A low moan followed by a slight movement of his eyes, then he nodded - faintly - but a nod nevertheless.

"Make that an ambulance too," Chalky sighed. He pulled out his mobile phone and dialled the emergency services. "We get the pocket-watch?"

"Dice?" I said.

"Pocket-watch?"

"Small ticking thing. The reason we are here. Why I've not got Scaly Dave."

"Uh, no."

"Shit!" Chalky and I said together.

The search went on.

It was a little after six a.m. when a police car arrived, then less than a minute later the ambulance turned up for Travis.

PC Rogers was a thin man with a small goatee beard cultivated around his mouth with extreme precision. His lips were thin and pursed like he was permanently pissed off with life. He looked like he had a stick up his arse. He wondered just what in the hell was so important on the one time he had done night duty.

"You boys been taking acid tabs, and smoking God knows what?" he said after I told him that a woman had kidnapped a man, then attacked Dice and myself.

As we walked towards the house, I replied, "No sir." I'm always polite to policemen. Must be my guilty conscience.

"Then can you run that past me again - this time you can leave the bullshit out." His lack of smile told us kids had jerked his chain just one too many times, and he could tell if we were talking shit without smelling our arses.

"Just check out the house," I said. "I think everything will become clear."

Just then Chalky came out with an ambulance man and woman carrying a sick looking Travis on a stretcher.

"Jesus!" PC Rogers said, a little too loudly. Travis didn't need to be told that a corpse had more colour than him at that point.

As we got to the staircase another policeman suddenly shouted out, "Roy!"

Then it clicked, as he turned around. "Your name is Roy Rogers?" I sniggered. "Bet you loved in when the press called that heist after you?"

"No time for your wise cracks!" Then to the younger policeman. "What?"

The younger PC sprinted up the few steps and pointed at the paintings.

PC Rogers looked at them. His mouth dropped open wider than Wookey Hole.

"I don't believe this—" he said to no-one in particular.

"What?" I said and looked at Dice who shrugged.

...JUST SOUTH OF HEAVEN/JIM ODY

PC Rogers wiped his brow and said slowly, "Each one of those paintings is of a missing person." He paused. "Apart from the ones already found dead..."

Then I remembered the strong smell of vanilla.

Sex is violent.

The scream was loud and piercing.

Martha had come around.

"And there is the culprit," I said, and Dice then added, "Well fuck me senseless." But I took that to be an expression rather than a request.

PC Roy Rogers called for back-up and after taking all of our names and addresses, he set off to look around the house some more.

We had promised to call into the police station the next day for questioning and to give individual statements.

I was as beat as a blind baboon, though I was sure that I would sleep the sleep of an insomniac.

"We can't speak to Travis about the pocket-watch until tomorrow," Dice said. "We are going to have to keep our heads down and hope that will be good enough."

"You worried?" I asked as Chalky walked over.

"Well, it's not a perfect situation, but nor is incest!" He smiled, but I sensed he was hiding behind humour once again.

Chalky smiled and said, "I just spoke to Amy. She can't believe that she slept through it all!"

"Women, eh?" Dice said.

"Gotta love 'em!" Chalky added.

"Haven't you just," I said, and we walked back to the van ready to go back to our homes for some good honest rest, and if lady luck decided to stop spanking my arse, then maybe I'd get a little shut eye too.

Just one question had remained on my mind: *Where the fuck is that watch?*

...JUST SOUTH OF HEAVEN/JIM ODY

"Hey, boys," the voice of PC Rogers called out. We turned around as he got up to us. "Just thought you might want to know, we found an easel set up with a Polaroid of your friend pinned to the corner. Looks like he was next..." his voice trailed off, as he saw the colour drain from our faces.

"Well blow me," Dice muttered, as the rest of us shook our heads or stared into space. "You were going to have sex with her, Caper."

"Well, I..." I stammered.

"What?!" Amy and Chalky said together. There went my chances with Amy.

"She was an ex-girl-fiend."

"Girl-fiend?" Amy said. She'd not heard my play-on-words before.

"Like a girlfriend, but not as friendly," I said.

"I should say," somebody muttered.

Everything went quiet. The battered face of Travis and the stories of other bodies filled our minds with the macabre.

Only later on did we find out that the rest of the missing males were found dead in the cellar. To hide the smell of their bodies decomposing, they had been doused in - yes, you've guessed it - vanilla.

It was enough to put me off vanilla lattes for life.

...JUST SOUTH OF HEAVEN/JIM ODY

Chapter Sixty-Six

"Well, you boys sure know how to spend a night out!" Chalky said as we pulled up outside his mama's house. He didn't care about the pocket-watch anymore. Having a scrape with death was enough for him to worry more about living to see another day. We had a bond. We'd all go out again on a night of less excitement. And if we ever found that pocket-watch, he'd get a cut. Neither Dice or I were the sort to swindle anyone out of cash.

"You take care now, Chalky-boy," Dice said patting his shoulder.

"Yeah. Good luck with the watch, boys. If you run into any trouble, give me a bell or swing by the club - my uncle knows people who can help."

"Thanks for everything, mate. You still have our word that if we find that watch, you can have a share." I was still shitting my shorts over our lack of an ancient timing device, but once again I was filled with the adventure of it all.

"See ya, Chalky," Amy said, snuggling up to me in the front seat. It had been a long night for us all.

"Take care, Amy."

And off he went. The large bulk of a guy who had really saved our bacon. I knew I would see him again.

"Where are we dropping you off, Amy?" Dice asked after we had stopped waving to Chalky's back.

"You're always trying to get rid of me, aren't you?" She yawned. "Do you have some issues?"

"Look," I said, "there's no reason for you to still be awake at this unearthly hour. Why don't we drop you off, then maybe later you'll give me a ring and we can grab something to eat, huh?"

"You asking her out?" Dice asked amused. I guess he was remembering me dressed as a woman.

...JUST SOUTH OF HEAVEN/JIM ODY

"Shut up and drive," I said feeling embarrassed. I don't know what I was doing. I was happy to be alive. The small hours always loosened my tongue.

She nudged my arm, "So are you?"

"I'm still waiting to take you up on your offer in the club!"

"Give me your number then," she said, and then added, "You can drop me off at the end of the next street. I live just around the corner from there."

"Sure thing," Dice said and turned up the stereo so he could sing along with a punk song.

"I'll see you later then," she smiled and kissed me on the cheek. "See ya, Dice!"

"See ya, Amy," he replied, and I caught him looking at her ass as she got out. I couldn't blame him.

"Bye," I said, and we pulled off.

Then Dice turned to me and said, "How do you do it, man?" And I shook my head with nothing to say. The truth was I'd had more opportunities with women tonight than I'd had in a long time. I put it down to being so worried about a number of things that I didn't have time to be nervous when meeting a beautiful woman.

Tiredness silenced us both.

Hedges blurred around us as we drove down the Cornish lanes. It had been a very long day. We'd done so much, and yet achieved so little.

I glanced at my phone and was met with a video.

It was from Janie, but all I could see was Scaly Dave. I pressed the triangle symbol to play.

Scaly Dave swam slowly around his tank. He looked up at the camera at one point. It wasn't clear whether or not he was sad or had in anyway been harmed. A voiced narrated over the top in a voice they thought might be likened to my fishy friend. "Caper, where are you? Please save me. I want to go home!"

...JUST SOUTH OF HEAVEN/JIM ODY

It ended. I played it again. Then I stared at it for a while before slipping it back into my pocket.

"That's cold, mate," Dice said. All I could do was nod.

I thought back to Dice's comment when we dropped Amy off. He thought I was lucky, but really what did my relationships tell me? One ex was carted off by the police as a suspected serial killer, another had burned my house down, and this one had kidnapped my fish. It was hard to see any sort of luck here at all.

I rubbed my eyes again for what seemed like the hundredth time. We pulled up outside Uncle Fresno's house. All I wanted was sleep and then to go and get Scaly Dave back. Fuck the pocket-watch, and Cutthroat. I just didn't care anymore.

We crept up the porch steps and wandered into the dark hall. It was spooky not knowing the house. My mind was slow.

I saw the movement out the corner of my eye a second before something swung forward and clanged on the back of Dice's head.

The glint of the morning sunlight on metal told me that it wasn't a water pistol that he had aimed at my nuts.

"Where is he?" the gruff cockney accent said through gritted teeth.

I admit I was confused. "Led there on the floor," I said pointing to Dice.

The side of his mouth twitched, and then he said, "Which ball do you least like?" he cocked the hammer and I almost released he contents of my bladder. If there was any blessing, it was that his gun wasn't a semi-automatic, or worse an automatic. This meant that should he miss my balls, he would have to cock the hammer each time, which gave me a valuable second or so, to run like a bitch with a twitch.

I was about to answer, *someone else's*. My stuttering would have taken off the comical glint. Instead, I was barely able to say, "W-who?" I was shuffling from side to side like a crab having a seizure, trying to remain a moving target.

...JUST SOUTH OF HEAVEN/JIM ODY

"Charles Perry. The big black guy."

Shit, I thought, *things are taken a bit of a turn for the worse.*

"What, Chalky? We dropped him off at home."

"Which is?"

"I wasn't driving," I said, thinking that Chalky didn't deserve this arsehole after him. "I was sleeping."

"That's too bad," he said and turned away - then without warning he turned and fired at me.

He was a good shot, but missed my balls by about three inches.

I fell to the ground clutching the area between my upper thigh and my hip. I had felt the impact like someone had fired a ball bearing from a catapult about a foot away, straight at my leg.

"You remember now?" he said, not even saying sorry, which I thought at the time was a bit rude.

"It's coming back," I said through pain. I didn't know the address but gave him a description of the house a few doors down from his.

My opinion on where to put my wallet paid off. A lot of men favoured the back pocket. I'd never understood this. When you sat down it's uncomfortable. Not too mention easy pickings for light-fingered pickpockets. I'd always been a slip-it-in-your-front-pocket kind of a guy. I like to feel it there in front of me.

I keep lots of crap in my wallet - pictures, receipts, cinema ticket stubs from my favourite films, and scraps of paper with telephone numbers scribbled on them. These are all of the things the stopped me from losing as much blood as I could have done. The bullet shot straight through the wallet and into my leg, but thankfully no further than 1cm or so.

He looked at me. Deep into my eyes. He wanted to pull out my soul.

"Caper, eh?" The side of his mouth twitched. "I thought you might be a bit more handsome."

"I hear that a lot," I said trying to be amusing.

...JUST SOUTH OF HEAVEN/JIM ODY

"You think it's funny to fuck another man's wife?"

"I didn't know she was married. She came up to me. Had I known, I would've stayed well clear, believe you me."

He nodded his head. "Really? You think I'm stupid?"

"I didn't comment on your intelligence."

There was no remorse as he raised the gun to my face, and I knew that he was going to shoot me.

I'm thankful that no lights were on, and we could only just see each other.

When I heard the gun go off, I closed my eyes and waited for the pain.

What I didn't see was the guy's arm jerk and his whole body follow suit in reaction.

All I heard was his body thud against the hard-wooden floor. I looked up in surprise. His eyes were wide and a frozen look of horror on his face. A hole the size of an old penny straight had appeared in his forehead.

Thank God, I thought, and looked to see who the sharp shooter was.

And in hobbled a small thin guy with what had looked like a knife sticking out of his thigh.

"Who are you?" I asked. He didn't seem that pleased to see me.

He looked at me like I had just slapped his girlfriend.

"Mind your own fuckin' business. Get up and shut up!"

I looked down at my thigh. "I've been shot," I argued.

He frowned a look with a lack of concern. "*So what?* Am I crying about this knife?" I suppose he had a point - two inches of which was stuck in his thigh.

"Where are we going?" I knew I was pushing it, but I did want to know.

"Where he was going," he pointed to the man led on the floor.

...JUST SOUTH OF HEAVEN/JIM ODY

This was getting pretty fucking weird. "You after Chalky too?"

"Ask one more question and I will either pull this knife out and cut your tongue from your mouth, or I will poke one of your eyes out." *Not much of a choice*, I thought.

The guy bent down and started fumbling around in the dead guy's pockets. *Bloody pickpockets*, I thought. It was a bit much to rob the guy. Then he caught wind of me gawping.

"What ya' starin' at?" he demanded, and I held my hands up in innocence and looked back down the hall to the front door.

As he was searching, I reached down to my leg where the knife was.

Then as quick as lightening, I threw the knife as hard as I could, hoping that it wasn't the handle that hit him.

There was a sickening sound as it sunk into him.

Deep into his other thigh.

"You bastard!" he shouted, and I wondered just where the guns that had been so meticulously cleaned were.

He turned and fired at me, taking a chunk out of the wall a little too close to my head. I rolled out of the way as another shot rang off, and I was beginning to count how many he might have left, when a door banged behind him.

As he turned, I ran quicker than a rabbit from a dog.

The sun could now be seen higher through the open doorway, and somewhere was a beautiful birdsong that sounded out of place.

With each step I felt a jolt of pain, but knew my wallet was damaged a lot more than my leg.

Just where the hell was Uncle Fresno?

Then I saw him. Uncle Fresno stood rigid with a Clint Eastwood sneer.

He wandered out of the shed in a fetching pair of pyjamas, and held a gun and a shovel like it was the most normal thing in

...JUST SOUTH OF HEAVEN/JIM ODY

the world. He looked at ease doing this, even as he tossed over the gun to me.

As the guy stumbled through the door firing off shots like Butch Cassidy and The Sundance Kid in their final scene, I pumped off a couple of my own rounds. I had no idea what I was doing. I'd only ever held a paintball gun and a water pistol, neither of which would've helped me much in this situation.

The pump action had sent me tumbling backwards, but I saw him leave the ground and the crimson spray out like cherry aid. I'd been told that hitting a target from where I stood was extremely hard. I'd got very lucky.

As I began to come to terms with the horror of taking a man's life, I heard an awful twang sound and saw Uncle Fresno swinging the shovel again like it was a driver onto the guy's skull. And I tried to tell myself that I hadn't killed him - but he was still led there never to move again on his own.

Uncle Fresno then looked up at me and shook his head. "I knew I'd have to come to the rescue of you two dumb-asses! I'm surprised you can both wipe your noses and shit in a bowl without my help."

"We are eternally grateful," I said getting up gingerly.

"Huh, full of shit more like! Where's that stupid nephew of mine?"

I nodded towards the hallway.

"He dead?" Uncle Fresno asked, like he was asking whether he was just sleeping. This struck me as being really bizarre. I guess he was from the old school. Where men have no feelings and accepted everything.

"Nah, he might need some smelling salts though?"

"Kick up the ass is all he needs!" Uncle Fresno said, walked purposefully into the house and promptly did just that!

As the morbid scene attracted my gaze once more, I was puzzled to see something glinting in the moonlight. As I got up close, I almost wet myself with joy.

...JUST SOUTH OF HEAVEN/JIM ODY

The illusive antique-watch sat face up in the grass - right time and all.

"Hey, what you got there, partner?" I looked around and saw Dice walking towards me rubbing his backside, and then shaking his head.

"The greatest thing in the world," I said.

Dice gave the goofy look I had got used to seeing just before a quip. "What, a season ticket to the biggest whore house in town?"

"Better."

"Two season tickets?"

"Not even close. Is this here the antique-watch?" I said holding out for him to see.

Then his smiled fell off, "No, it isn't."

"What?" I said and stood still so as not to stand on my heart that had just sunk to Australia.

Then he grinned, the evil bastard. "Yeah, this is it. Or at least it's what they think is antique."

"What do you mean?"

"It's a fake. You can tell by the weight of it."

I felt ill. What if her husband… And then it hit me. Her husband was led out on the floor with a hole in his head. I had a not-so-antique pocket-watch to get Scaly Dave back with, and Janie was free to get away from her husband.

"I bet she knew," Dice then added as we turned back towards the house.

"Knew what?"

"That it was fake. I know she's cute, Caper, but shit, she stole your fish. You're best without her. Give her the fake, take your fish, and get the hell away from her."

I nodded. I was coming to the same conclusion myself.

There seemed to be a lot of crazy women around, and unfortunately, I seemed to attract them like a magnet.

...JUST SOUTH OF HEAVEN/JIM ODY

Dice pulled his knife out and for a minute I was a little worried – I'd only known him again for a day, and who knew whether he was going to attack me too.

"You think I was gonna use this on you?" he commented and burst out laughing.

I shrugged. "Always expect the unexpected," I said.

"Thing was sticking in my side something awful."

Dice and I dragged the guy into the house, where I found that the other guy was missing.

"Where're we taking them?" I asked, and then had to smile as Dice replied, "The back bedroom."

The back bedroom, I thought.

The riddle of the back bedroom will soon be solved, I mused.

As we got to the infamous back bedroom, we saw the other guy already led out on the bed, looking like he'd not had too many worse days than this. Uncle Fresno stood there smoking his pipe.

"What took you so long?" he asked sternly. "You been pullin' each other's peckers?"

"The only reason we keep you alive is 'cause you ain't got shit to leave us!" Dice laughed.

Uncle Fresno grunted and said slowly, "One more wise-ass comment and you'll be spooning with Batman and Robin here."

I reluctantly helped put the guy on the bed with the other dead one, then stood back and tried not to look at them.

The room was tatty and damp, the only light came from a single bulb that didn't stop swaying the whole time we were in there. Shadows danced back and forth like some sort of graveyard shuffle.

"Caper. Pay attention, this is the best bit." Uncle Fresno flipped a switch and the bed started to tilt, and a gap appeared underneath. It wouldn't have surprised me to see a guy in red with a pointy tail leering at us with contempt.

...JUST SOUTH OF HEAVEN/JIM ODY

He then pressed another button, and both the bodies, along with the bedding shot just south of heaven and out of sight.

He smiled and nodded at me, and I almost thought I could hear him saying, *"That could've been you!"* He pressed the first button again, and the bed returned to its original position.

"Always wondered whether it would work," Uncle Fresno said again not cracking his face.

"You do kids' parties?" I asked touching my sore leg again.

Uncle Fresno took a deep breath and said, "I don't know what circus kicked you out and left you on my doorstep, but if I hear another word from you tonight, I think we both know where you are sleeping!" He then winked, which kick started my heart again.

"Let's get some sleep," Dice said, and I thought that was the best thing I'd heard in a long time.

...JUST SOUTH OF HEAVEN/JIM ODY

Chapter Sixty-Seven

It was of no surprise that when I woke up, the morning had magically turned into midday. I looked up at the ceiling and then out at the light pouring in through the window. I didn't know whether to feel lucky or unlucky. The events of the past twenty-four hours had been the sort of things a normal person would never experience in a lifetime.

I pulled back the covers and took a look at my gunshot wound. It stung a little.

Quite frankly, I was disappointed. The skin was white and wet with clear liquid. There was a dark tacky membrane of blood. It was sore but not very impressive. I'm not sure it would be worth a mention should I find myself boasting about wounds.

I grabbed for a towel and wandered out to take a shower. Part of this felt great, but when the soap hit my wound it stung like merry hell.

I put on a blue t-shirt that had the words *Rock-Star* on the front in heavy metal writing, and made my way downstairs.

I was met by my favourite uncle.

"Well, if it isn't the Sundance Kid!" he said with a smirk.

I saw Sian next to him smiling and reading the paper. "I hear you got shot," she said looking up.

"Huh," Uncle Fresno said, "it ain't nothin' but a paper cut!"

I nodded. "Hurts more than a papercut."

Uncle Fresno rolled his eyes. "Really?"

"I was lucky to make it through the night," I said with a grin.

"You want a coffee, soldier?" Uncle Fresno asked, and I couldn't help but wonder whether he was actually warming to me. Perhaps taking a bullet would do that for our relationship.

Then I heard the front door open and close, and in walked Dice. I was surprised because I thought that he was still asleep.

"Hey, Caper," he said.

"How's your head?"

...JUST SOUTH OF HEAVEN/JIM ODY

"It hurts. It feels like I've been hit twice by two separate people."

"Funny that!" I agreed. The truth was he had been lucky too. Being hit on the head can be an extremely dangerous thing. Being hit twice is even worse. Dice could've died or been badly injured.

"Despite what I say," Uncle Fresno started, "I think you boys did okay." He handed me a steaming hot coffee, which I had to smell the strong aroma of before taking a sip. To me, it tasted like a drop of heaven.

Sian then looked up at us clutching her tablet and smiling wide. "You boys even got a quick mention in here. Seems they just had time to put a little footnote in.

Uncle Fresno then clicked his fingers. "Oh, nearly forgot. I had a couple of calls from a couple of TV stations wanting interviews. I said you'd ring them back. Number's on the side."

Well, well, well, I thought. We had almost got up to celebrity status.

"Right, drink up, Caper. We've got to go to the police station and sort out our statements. I've rung Chalky, he's going to meet us down there at one."

"Right, I had better give Amy a ring," I said and grabbed my phone from my pocket, making a quick exit. I noticed that the battery was getting low and made a mental note to charge it when I had a minute.

I carefully tapped in Amy's number, whilst thinking about Scaly Dave and contacting Janie.

"Hello?" a small voice said. I hate meeting someone again the next day. That night before you've built up the relationship, albeit rooted in alcohol or late-night machismo. Come the next day you both wonder whether the other looks back on the evening with regret. You're filled with the feeling they are glad you're not with them. Your insecurities hit a high assuming they're sitting there wondering just what in the hell they were playing at, by wasting their time with you.

"Hi Amy, it's Caper."

"How are you?" It was small talk, but it was nice.

"I'm fine. Well, I was shot, but I'm okay."

"What?!"

"Yeah, those hitmen turned up. They shot me in the leg, but they got my wallet instead. It went straight through and into my leg." I was babbling a bit.

"Jesus! You sure you're alright?"

"Yeah, yeah. Look, d'ya fancy doing something?"

"That's what we'd planned hadn't we," she said, catching me off guard.

I laughed. "Just making sure you still wanted to. You might've come to your senses now."

I heard her giggle, which made me smile. "I've got nothing better to do!"

I explained we were going to the police station, and we could be a while. She insisted on meeting us there, and I was secretly happy with that arrangement.

...JUST SOUTH OF HEAVEN/JIM ODY

Chapter Sixty-Eight

Dexter had snoozed for a few hours in the back of a car clearly the victim of joy riding. The smashed glass was in the front seat. He didn't care though. The large back seats were warm and comfortable and he went straight to sleep.

When he woke up, he got out and started to make his way into town.

He had to find another place to live. He needed food and money, but none of that grew on trees.

It was funny but even when he'd had money, he spent a lot of nights sleeping rough. He'd partied so much that he often got so drunk and wasted he'd sleep wherever his body fell. He'd woken up in all kinds of places. He'd been in a graveyard, a cellar, a supermarket, on a beach, and even in a classroom – although how he'd got there was a complete mystery.

Of course, he'd also had a life of luxury. The huge bed with a mattress that ate him up. He'd relaxed in a jacuzzi he'd had installed in his conservatory. His housekeeper was happy enough to relax in there with him before her shift ended. She was Swedish and spoke little English. This never seemed to be a problem for them.

But, since his monetary demise, it was surprising how easily you could adapt. The body can withstand a great deal. He'd gone days without eating, and suddenly cleanliness was the last of his problems. He even enjoyed taking a shit in public toilets, especially in his local library. They were warm, clean, and made him feel almost normal again.

Dexter remembered the twenty-pound note in his pocket, and was relieved to find it still there. It wouldn't be the first time he'd been robbed whilst catching a little shuteye. Although, as was the usual case you didn't just get robbed, you got beaten up too.

...JUST SOUTH OF HEAVEN/JIM ODY

He wondered just how many bottles of *White Lightening* cider he could buy with his newfound wealth, and pondered on whether he should save some of it - you never knew when a bad day would come upon you. But there were always other days to find wealth. He could easily buy two or three large bottles and still have change for food. Besides, he had a few new songs that he was going to try out and they would bring him a *Greggs* pasty if nothing else.

He walked into the same shop he always did knowing that he would get served here. The Asian guy felt sorry for him. He picked up a couple of two litre bottles of *White Lightening*, and with a sudden skip in his step took them up to the counter.

The Asian guy was not there today. The guy behind the counter was about nineteen, with jet-black hair and a nose ring. He nodded to Dexter, as if they had some sort of bond, but in a way that Dexter didn't mind one bit.

Dexter handed him the twenty, and the guy punched in the amount on the register.

"Shit," the guy said under his breath. "We're all out of change. You got anything smaller?"

"Sure, aside from this fifty and three tenners, I have a whole fistful of cash!"

"I'm going to have to give you a couple of quid in fives."

"Where am I gonna put them, son? Up my ass?" Dexter grinned.

"Ain't there anything else you want?"

Dexter put his filthy fingers on his chin and drummed away through his thick beard. "Hmm. What've you got for two pound?" he then asked.

The guy looked all around the shop looking at shelves of goods. "Let me see," he said, "there's a few things. A crossword book? A magazine? What about a scratch card?"

"It's all of about the same use to me."

...JUST SOUTH OF HEAVEN/JIM ODY

"Food. If you don't mind me saying, you look like you could do with a good meal."

"You got a burger and chips behind the counter?"

"I wish," he grinned.

"Go on then, I'll have a scratch card, I'm feeling lucky. You may as well scratch it off for me too! Save me throwing it away."

"I'm not sure I'm allowed to do that."

"Says who?"

The kid shrugged. "I'm not sure. It sounds like something I wouldn't be allowed to do."

"Really? That sort of attitude will have you working here until you're old and shitting yourself!"

"Okay, fine. I'll do it. What harm can it cause?" He glanced all around anyway. Just in case.

"There you go, Maverick!"

The guy pulled out the card and started to scratch off the grey boxes.

His eyes lit up. "Well, Jesus fucking Christ," he said.

Dexter pointed a finger at him. "Stop fucking with me boy!" He demanded.

The guy looked up, and his chin was almost on the counter.

"You have just won £250,000!"

Everything went black and there was a large bang as Dexter fainted.

When he came around the kid was helping him up. He was also fanning him with the scratch card.

"You won! You actually won, mate!" he was saying over and over again.

It seemed like Dexter's luck had changed again!

...JUST SOUTH OF HEAVEN/JIM ODY

Chapter Sixty-Nine

Upon arriving at the Police station, I was a little disappointed at not receiving a hero's welcome. We'd managed to find, and round up, one of Britain's worst serial killers. We'd put our lives on the line to bring them to justice. Well, I know Dice was quick to point out that I'd had sexual relations with one of them, but that was hardly the point.

I assumed it was like a surprise party. Everyone acting normal and pretending this was just a normal day. I nodded to the Desk Sergeant and went along with the charade of it all being played down. We were all happy they'd managed to keep the press away, although we knew we'd be herded out through the backdoors and into the back of large saloons with blacked out windows later on. Cameras flashing at us, television cameras thrust our way, and news reporters doing their best to catch glimpses of the nation's heroes.

It never played out like that.

The police seemed to think it a little suspicious that an ex-boyfriend was knocking on the door of an ex-girlfriend's house in the small hours, and supposedly unaware she lived there.

Chalky turned up with a bloodshot eye, which I didn't remember seeing him with the night before - later he told us that his mama had given it to him for lying to her. She had swung at him with her open hand, and her thumb had managed to catch him full in his eye.

It wasn't long before we were all marched off to separate rooms and grilled on the facts of why we were there. The agreed plan was that we were searching for Travis, whom had gone AWOL from his bouncer's job that night. Chalky needed to find him because two strange looking dudes were after him. As his vehicle was still at home, he enlisted the help of yours truly and Dice. We had decided to tell the truth about Amy. You know what they say about all good liars - you try to tell as much of the

...JUST SOUTH OF HEAVEN/JIM ODY

truth as possible, so as to sound believable and to not confuse yourself when later questioned again.

I sat there in the small hard chair, which had probably seated the arses of child molesters and bank-robbers, and took long slow deep breaths of oxygen. Had I been a smoker, I might've been chain-smoking with nerves. Interviews in police stations will do that to you. The cold and sparse interior. The stern faces of the police. It all felt wrong.

I had always been able to control my body quite well, and was skilled at being able to quicken or slow down my heart rate when needed. I found that deep slow breaths, along with clearing my head and relaxing my mind, slowed down my heart rate to a 'normal' pace when under pressure.

The next thing was my appearance and my body language. Let's not forget they see liars day in, day out and know what to look for.

You should always look the interrogator in the eyes, but don't hold the gaze too long, this would tell them that you are threatening them and have no respect for them.

Never hide your mouth when you speak, this is a tell-tale sign that subliminally you want to hide or disguise what you are saying.

Don't fidget with your fingers or anything else as these show signs of nerves.

Remain calm at all times and never show your inner feelings; if you are made angry, your speech quickens and you don't have time to think sensible responses.

When speaking there are also ways you should reply.

Try to change the length of pause times from when they finish asking you the question, to when you answer - they will try to look for patterns on how you respond - always keep them guessing.

Elaborate wherever possible - but don't waffle.

...JUST SOUTH OF HEAVEN/JIM ODY

I knew all of this, and still fell apart. I was babbling, praying, and at times almost brought to tears. They were bloody good.

Of course, the room was a lot smaller than I had imagined, and only one policeman questioned me - so there was none of the good cop/bad cop routine I had studied from Hollywood.

The guy smiled at me and helped keep me calm; we flew through the questions with ease, and I was thankful when he said that he was satisfied with my story.

"You dated anyone else you think I should know about?" he asked with a snicker, and I was a flick of a squirrel's tail away from telling him about Trixibelle – and Janie…

I simply smiled and nodded, then replied, "Must be my aftershave, huh?" And he had to smile at that. It was almost insulting he didn't think I was a criminal. I guess coming off as simple can be advantageous sometimes.

The police thanked us for coming and finally congratulated us on capturing the sister and brother killers. I'd still hoped for a press release, or talk of a commendation, or medal, but these were quickly swept under the carpet. I guess they didn't want us to get big-headed.

I couldn't help feeling sorry for Benji. How much of this did he really know was wrong?

I did explain to the police about his mental state, arguing the fact that he wasn't in control of his actions and only did what his sister told him. The police seemed to think that he would go to a psychiatric detention centre and not to prison. He probably would never understand what had happened. They even suggested he might enjoy the place better being around people of the same mentality. Personally, I found this a frightening prospect, even if they were to be medicated.

They also liked to bring up the point that I'd nearly had sex with Martha again that night. We dropped it after that.

And Martha?

...JUST SOUTH OF HEAVEN/JIM ODY

They said that she would never see the light of day.

...JUST SOUTH OF HEAVEN/JIM ODY

Chapter Seventy

"Dave!" I said grinning at him in his large tank. He didn't look particularly pleased to see me. I couldn't blame him. I'd met a woman and got him fish-napped. It was completely understandable that he was giving me the cold shoulder.

"He doesn't look that pleased to see you," Janie said, wiggling in a top that should be worn by a toddler.

"He blames me for getting involved with you," I said, trying not to notice she wasn't wearing a bra.

"D'you wish you'd never met me?" she said stretching out her arms. "Do you regret the night we spent together, Caper?"

I shook my head. "I enjoy it... I mean, I *really* enjoyed it, but it was at a cost. A huge cost. You sort of got what you wanted without any risk."

"I kidnapped your fish."

"Where was the risk in that?"

"He might've eaten me."

"Ha-fucking-ha! The worst he could do is stare you to death."

She took a step closer to me. Before I knew it, she'd flung her arms around me. "Thank you, Caper! Thanks for getting this pocket-watch!"

She pulled away and turned it over in her hands. Her face shone with amazement.

She actually thought it was real and worth a lot of money. I think this said it all.

She then stopped. The smile fell from her face. "I do appreciate this, you know," she said. I didn't believe her.

"I'm sure you do," I replied and went over to Scaly Dave. Carefully I picked up the tank. He didn't like being transported at the best of times. He would never be much of a traveller.

"Hey Caper?" she called to me as I left her large house.

I turned. "Yeah?"

...JUST SOUTH OF HEAVEN/JIM ODY

"Maybe we could go out again, yeah?"

I smiled and looked down at Dave. He didn't say anything, but I could tell he was not a fan of that idea at all.

"I dunno, Janie. I don't think that's a good idea, *do you?*"

"I thought we'd have a future?" she said her voice dropping. She was an actress. They all were. Ex-girl-fiends and ex-lovers knew when to lie and manipulate.

"I think our future is now in the past."

I'd found her pocket-watch and killed her husband, it seemed to me that our brief relationship was already considerably one-sided.

"Bye, Janie."

"Bye, Caper. I'll miss you!" I ignored that. She'd only known me for a number of hours

***

I'd called in to my mum earlier just to let her know I was still alive. She'd scolded me something rotten and blamed my libido for the troubles of the past few days. Maybe she was right. Women would always be my weakness.

The last stop I made took me back to where it had all begun. Well, sort of.

I walked through the doors into the bar. She looked up at me and laughed to herself. Underneath it all I could see that Mo was pleased I hadn't bit the bag and stepped out of the door, as they say.

"Here he is, Billy Bigshot!"

"Hi Mo," I said slightly embarrassed. I made my way to the bar where she was already pouring me a pint.

"Well, you've certainly been having an adventure, haven't you!" She placed the pint down on a beer mat that rocked and winked.

...JUST SOUTH OF HEAVEN/JIM ODY

"It's been a real eye-opener. I've been shot, hit over the head, attacked, threatened, you name it, it's happened."

She nodded. "Got caught up with a few women, is how I heard it."

"There were women," I said trying to be nonchalant. "There were strippers and hard men too. I got shot, did I mention that? But d'you know what?"

"Yes, and go on."

"I think I'm going to enjoy my new job."

"It's hardly work, Caper. It's just like having your weekends all through the week."

"True that," I said and sipped my drink. The old guy was still asleep over at his table. Thankfully he'd changed clothes since the last time I'd seen him.

"I heard your house got burnt down?" she said, as another customer came in. She nodded to him and went to pull his pint.

"Yep. My ex. She took a dim view to me calling it a day with her."

"By that you mean, no longer sleeping with her."

"Yeah, that's about the size of it."

"You stud! Your insurance going to pay out?" she said, placing the pint down for the guy who was staring at her tits the whole time. Mo didn't mind. She found it a perk of the job.

"God knows," I said into my drink. "I'm still waiting to hear."

Another twenty minutes and I was done. Mo walked around the bar and smothered me in a huge hug.

"Just in case I don't see you for a while," she said and pecked me on the cheek.

"You'll see me again."

"On the news, no doubt!"

We laughed, then with a lingering smile I left.

...JUST SOUTH OF HEAVEN/JIM ODY

Two Months Later

I was still awaiting the insurance pay out on my house. I was told I should receive it any day soon. They'd told me this same line for the past three weeks. I wasn't holding my breath.

It was strange that all of this happened in the space of twenty-four hours. Dice and Chalky were both sort of strangers to my life two days ago, but now seemed to be the best friends I'd had since I was swapping bubble gum cards and reading *The Beano*.

Chalky works full time with his uncle at the club, doing this and that. He doesn't tell, and we don't ask. His girlfriend works down the local barbers and gives us all half price haircuts. Our haircuts all look the same no matter what we ask for. But she's really friendly so I don't like to bring it up.

Amy and I have dated a few times; we seemed to be better at flirting with each other than having a relationship. Dice once said to me over drinks, "You take a girl to a strip joint, play a few hands with pornographic playing cards, then leave her in a van. All of this whilst you try and bone your ex. It was never going to be fairytale stuff, *right?*" And I suppose he had a point, it wasn't exactly textbook romance. But life never usually is.

We still remain very good friends and sometimes we drink too much and end up in each other's arms, but it's all good innocent fun.

Uncle Fresno has definitely mellowed to me. He's been teaching me the best way to set traps. For humans.

Scaly Dave was back to his normal chatty self once he had acclimatised to Cornwall.

I heard nothing more than a couple of drunken texts from Janie. In one of them she'd sent me naked pictures. I kept them, just in case.

I had found a small shop for sale in the centre of town, and after showing Dice and Uncle Fresno, we all agreed to buy it.

...JUST SOUTH OF HEAVEN/JIM ODY

Uncle Fresno put up the capital, which I agreed to pay sixty-five percent back to him when the damn insurance cash finally arrived into my bank account. I would live in the flat upstairs, thus why I was paying the larger amount. All proceeds would be split equally in thirds, or percentage wise depending on who bought the goods.

We had contracts drawn up, and I was beginning to think that this might just work out as a career. I felt like an adult finally.

"Hey, Dice," I said as we set up what stock we had. "Look at this brooch I picked up for a fiver." I held up the small jewel like it was a medal I'd won.

"Where the hell d'ya get that piece of crap from?" He smiled. I had a lot to learn when it came to antiques.

"A jumble sale," I confessed.

Dice shook his head. "You'll be lucky to get a quid for that!" But like I said, I was still learning.

"It's worth as much as someone will pay for it," I reminded him. He might've had the knowledge and know how, but I had an eye for things that looked nice, and I was then able to sweet talk people into buying it. The antique knowledge would come. I was an apprentice after all.

The telephone rang for the first time ever, and Dice nodded for me to answer it.

I tentatively picked it up. "Skull & Monkey Antiques?"

"You don't sound too sure, Caper," the female voice said.

"How did you get this number?" I asked politely. I had a horrible feeling that I was destined to have her lurking around corners for the rest of my life.

"The internet. You know, that information highway! You want me to come down and see you?"

"You burnt my house down. Why did you do that?"

"You didn't want me."

...JUST SOUTH OF HEAVEN/JIM ODY

"I didn't want to watch Swindon Town play anymore, but I didn't burn their stadium down!"

"Shame, they might've got a good pay out and built a bigger and better stadium outside of town." She had a point.

"True," I agreed getting side-tracked. "Anyway, that's beside the point."

"You don't want them to have a huge new stadium?" she pushed.

"Yes, of course, I would. I'm talking about you burning my house down. All of my things inside."

"Oh, yeah. Sorry about that. I know you loved that fish too."

"Eh?"

"Finlay Frank, or whatever his name was."

"Scaly Dave."

"Yeah, him."

"Oh he—" I started but stopped.

"He what?"

"He'll be missed," I said letting the words trail off.

"See you, Caper. We'll meet again." She thought she'd murdered my fish. She was a fruitloop.

"That I don't doubt." I put the phone down and turned around to where Dice was sat with a big fat what-the-hell-was-that-all-about look on his face.

"Well?" he said.

I paused then smiled. "Wrong number."

He shook his head, then said, "You'll tell me after a few beers."

And I thought to myself, maybe I will - and maybe I won't.

Just then a guy with a grey ponytail limped in dressed smartly in a tweed suit. He had deep blue eyes and a large gold earring. When he saw the brooch, he smiled as wide as the cat with the cream and said, "I heard you boys had this, how much?"

I nodded to Dice, whose jaw had fallen to the floor. "This brooch," I said, "is a one of a kind. As rare as a sex game in an

...JUST SOUTH OF HEAVEN/JIM ODY

Enid Blyton book and as wonderful as a Thai massage - to you, sir - the cut price, rock bottom, low of the low, almost a steal, a meagre heart breaking forty-pounds."

"Shit, I'd give you that just to shut up!" He laughed and dug into his pockets and pulled out a brand-new alligator-skin wallet.

"This place new?" he asked handing me two crisp twenties.

I kept on my salesman smile and replied, "It sure is, sir."

He then handed me a card. "Anything rare, please be sure to give me a ring. I'm a collector, you see."

I nodded as I looked at the name on the card – Dexter Flynn. His face rang a bell, though I'm not sure where.

"Have a good day," I said. He raised his hand as he left and all three of us were as happy as a pig in the proverbial.

Dice shook his head at the sale. We drank a coffee and looked over the stock and wondered whether we really had enough things that people would want.

***

Outside sat in his car, Randell looked over at the shop. Skull & Monkey. He liked that. But more to the point, he liked what they had there. Not antiques but cash in a safe. A 1975 Cleaverson double lock safe no less.

He knows it's full of cash, because he was there the night Dice got it. Some people were greedy and wanted more. Dice was happy to be part of his team that did over the casino in Redruth, and split. He said he was going to live a life on the straight and narrow now. But they always said that, didn't they?

He smiled and drove off. He'd be in touch soon enough.

***

We had a lot of stock to work though. There was always something that needed to be touched up and restored.

...JUST SOUTH OF HEAVEN/JIM ODY

Then she walked in and we both forgot our names.

"Are you the two guys who helped to catch them killers?" she asked. This was a question that neither Dice nor myself enjoyed answering.

"Who wants to know?" Dice asked taking another sip of his coffee.

She ran her hands through her long blond hair and said, "I'm looking for someone, and I need your help."

Dice scratched his chin clearly thinking this through, and I was lost for words - she was stunning.

"I don't mean to be rude, but what does it say on the sign out there?"

She smiled. "What, *sex is a valid currency in here*?"

I laughed, that had been a small sign Dice had put up for a joke. Sort of.

"No, the large one above the window. The one that could be mistaken for being the name of the shop."

"What, *Skull & Monkey Antiques*?"

"Correct."

"Who's who?" she replied deadpan. I laughed again. She was our fourth customer and was already proving to be the most entertaining.

"It doesn't matter," Dice said. "Point is it says *Antiques*. Not *Lost and Found*, or *Missing Persons Are Us*!"

She paused and seemed to think this one over. "I will pay you of course."

"How much?" I asked instinctively.

"10k," she said like it was small change.

"Come, have a seat," I replied, and both Dice and myself thought that maybe the antiques world could do without us for a while.

"Is that plus expenses?" Dice added.

"Of course, but she can't be harmed."

...JUST SOUTH OF HEAVEN/JIM ODY

We made her a coffee, closed the shop after our successful one sale, and sat down to hear about the missing person.

"So, who are we looking for?" I asked, noticing how she had a small dimple when she spoke.

"My girlfriend TuBee—"

I was puzzled. "What like bride-*to-be*?"

She laughed at that. "No, that's her name. TuBee."

Dice scrunched up his face, like he was chewing the world's most foul tasting sweet. "TuBee? What sort of a name is that?"

"A nickname," she replied. "On account of her wooden leg. You know, TuBee, as in Two-By-Four."

"Uh-huh," I nodded whilst trying to picture this attractive young lady with a wooden legged girl.

"What does she do?" Dice asked.

"That is the problem," she said clearing her throat, then clapping her hands in a dramatic act. "She's an adult entertainment actress."

"A porn star?" We both mused. "With a wooden leg?" She nodded with raised eyebrows. We looked at each other. Then back at her. And then at each other again.

And that is how the story of TuBee - The Porn Star with the wooden leg begins.

But I think I'll save that one for another time.

Acknowledgements

Being an author, is a long and lonely one. There have been a lot of people who have helped me to get where I am today. Too many to mention in but a few paragraphs, but I'll have a go!

A big thank you to Kara and the kids for just being themselves.

A huge thanks to the members of my street team **Jim Ody's Spooky Circus**, who listen to all my crazy ideas and advise me whether they are worth pursuing! Specifically Angela, Simon, Terry, Caitlin, Michelle, Ellie, Diane, Dee, Nicole, Donna. This also applies to my ARC Group, and Promo Group too.

My BETA readers are fantastic, and for this book I depended on the opinions of: Simon Leonard, Angela Guppy, Caitlin Lea Brosseau, Caroline Maston & Theresa Hetherington. It's always a great help to test the waters with you first!

Thanks to all of the members of: **UK Crime Book Club** (especially David and Caroline), **Crime Book Club** (especially Shell and Llainy), **Crime Fiction Addict, Book Connectors**.

A huge and massive thanks to Erin George. Not just because you are a wonderful publisher, but a great friend. You have been a true inspiration, and guide me when I go wayward!

An extended thanks to everyone attached and associated with Crazy Ink including all the Crazy Inklings around the world! This goes to the massive list of pimpers who help promote my book – especially Kimberly Lee. Ham, you are the best!

...JUST SOUTH OF HEAVEN/JIM ODY

A big thank you to my friends and colleagues at Arval UK – a large corporate company (ahem!).

As ever a huge thank you to all the editors working tirelessly to make my meanderings be able to be enjoyed by the masses – Cat you rock! Especially to Shelagh who is also my personal advisor on all the choices I make. I don't always listen, and she doesn't always like what I write, but she sticks around nevertheless!

A great big thank you to Bella James. You've really pushed me to think big, and helped me to not be satisfied with normal. Thanks also to fellow authors Mia Brown, Cheryl Elaine, A.J.Griffiths-Jones, Leigh Russell, Owen Mullen, Malcolm Hollingdrake, Ross Greenwood, Louise Mullins, Maggie James & Kerry Watts, and everyone else who has helped me – there are lot more.

And finally thank you to you, the readers. For reading, for enjoying, and for getting behind me. Without you there would really be no point!

About the Author

Jim has had the misfortune to work in some of the largest corporations in England. This is not something he's proud of. He understands the plight of the faceless-worker lost in a sea of partitions. He's also experienced awkward meetings in glass rooms where others grin and make rude gestures at him in order to put him off. Amusing.

Like Caper, Jim also sent an email around a large company expressing the negativities he experienced. He wasn't marched out, and left of his own accord. Five-years later he was re-employed by them. That doesn't say much about his convictions...

Jim writes dark psychological/thrillers that have endings that you won't see coming, and favours stories packed with wit. This is his fifth book.

Jim has a very strange sense of humour and is often considered a little odd. When not writing he will be found playing the drums, watching football and eating chocolate. He lives with his long-suffering wife and three beautiful children in Swindon, Wiltshire UK.

...JUST SOUTH OF HEAVEN/JIM ODY

He's still not a millionaire, although considers himself to be a professional dreamer.

Follow the author here:

Facebook: www.facebook.com/JimOdyAuthor

Jim Ody's Spooky Circus Street Team:
https://www.facebook.com/groups/1372500609494122/

Email: jim.ody@hotmail.co.uk

Twitter: @Jim_Ody_Author

Instagram: @jimodyauthor

Pintrest: https://www.pinterest.co.uk/jimodyauthor/

Bookbub: https://www.bookbub.com/profile/jim-ody

YouTube:
https://www.youtube.com/channel/UC6IWwZ24CeMH_qtlS2o7TCA

Other books by the Author

Novels:

Lost Connection
The Place That Never Existed
A Cold Retreat
Beneath The Whispers

Contributions to the following Anthologies:

War Paint
Crazy Fools
A.W.O.L. A.I.
The End?
Campfire Tales
Bloody Bonkers
What's Your Superpower?
Vague Book

Made in the USA
Columbia, SC
23 March 2019